ONLY LOVE LASTS

a novel by

Anthony Timiraos

NOTES

Only Love Lasts is a work of fiction.

All of the characters, stories and organizations portrayed in this novel either are products of the author's imagination or are used fictitiously. Some of the events and locations described in the book are also products of the author's imagination or used fictitiously.

Published by Anthony Timiraos Photography, L.L.C.

Permission requests, questions, and/or error notifications relating to this book should be communicated to the author at anthony.timiraos@gmail.com

Website: atimiphoto.com/onlylovelasts.html

ISBN: 979-8-218-27940-0 (Hardcover)
ISBN: 979-8-218-27941-7 (ePub)

Cover photography and design by Anthony Timiraos.

ACKNOWLEDGMENT

Writing my first novel was not the simple undertaking I expected. I would have never completed this project if I didn't have the love, support and encouragement during the past twelve months from my husband and friends.

I'm deeply indebted to them.

Thank you.
(Yes, I have more than three friends.)

DEDICATION

To my husband.

ABOUT THE AUTHOR

Anthony Timiraos was born in Havana, Cuba and currently resides in South Florida with his husband Arthur Crispino who has been by his side for over 53 years. He began his professional career as a Certified Public Accountant in Hartford, Connecticut. Various career advancement moves for both brought them to Boston, New York City and back to Connecticut.

A retirement to South Florida in 2003 was shortened when he accepted the position of Chief Financial Officer for the county's community foundation. After five years, he co-founded, with four other local philanthropists, Our Fund, Inc.. a new community foundation serving LGBTQ+ non-profit organizations providing services in South Florida. He became their first Chief Executive Officer and President in 2011 and retired in 2016 to enjoy writing, travel and photography. Our Fund, Inc. is currently one of the largest LGBTQ+ community foundations in the country.

Only Love Lasts is Mr. Timiraos' first novel. His love for writing, travel, and photography began in his early college years, Today, Anthony has traveled the globe extensively and enjoys capturing portraits of the people he meets and the architecture of places he visits. He is also known for his focus of the male form, which has led to the creation of a captivating body of work displayed in four books.

Books published:
Only Love Lasts – A novel.
It's Who We Are – A photographic tapestry of our diverse planet.
Torsos, Virtues, and Attitudes – A photographic collection of the male torso.
A Time To Look Back – A memoir.
Expose – A collection of classical nude photographs.
Expose More – The continuing collection of classical nude photographs.
Expose Love – A photographic collection of male couples in classical nude poses.
Expose Art – Male nude photography at a virtual art exhibit.

TABLE OF CONTENTS

PART ONE

CHAPTER 1

HOME

A mid-afternoon chill in the breezy southern Connecticut air raced through suburban roads on the last Saturday in March. It was March 26, 2022. King Alfred daffodil blossoms were bursting into the landscape everywhere you looked. The trees began to show their transparent lime-green young leaves. Fruit trees were building strength for their buds, soon to open and add more color to the landscape. You couldn't ignore the birds working on their seasonal nests. All this complimented a vision of a Connecticut spring landscape. A landscape permanently embedded in most residents' minds.

In Old Saybrook, a group of residents from nearby bucolic towns gathered at a local banquet hall owned by a popular catering company. There was a wide range of ages in this group. Most knew each other, and the rest only knew that one person in the room everyone thought they would see. The attire was professional that afternoon. Some folks spoke eloquently, some were seen laughing, and sadly, others cried. Guests were treated to full top-shelf liquors and well-known wines from Napa Valley, California, and Marlborough County in New Zealand. You could hear the clinking sounds of martini glasses anywhere in the room. The caterer's chef constructed an elaborate New England shellfish display, including oysters, shrimp, lobsters, and clams. The aroma from an adjoining table with another chef slicing beef tenderloins was equally enticing. A separate table featured a wide assortment of artisan breads, salads, and sauces.

The guests began their exit at about 5:00 PM. Some lingered in the parking lot for half an hour as the breeze from the mouth of the Connecticut River ruffled many hairstyles. Others drove away. The sun was expected to set at precisely 7:07 PM. Most of the guests planned to be home before dark.

Stephen Porter, a 75-year-old man, returned home alone after attending the social gathering in Old Saybrook. Home to Stephen was a beautifully restored and maintained antique farmhouse on the acclaimed Hamburg Road in Lyme, Connecticut, about 10 miles northeast of Old Saybrook. As in previous spring seasons, he was hypnotized during his drive home by the natural beauty of the new and fresh growth on his neighbors' lawns as he tried to concentrate on his driving along the winding Neck Road toward Hamburg Road. When he reached the beginning of Neck Road, he rolled down all the windows to let the breezes fill the inside of his car with the aroma of freshly cut spring grass. His picturesque views from inside his car were sufficient to offset the hurt and pain that enveloped him in Old Saybrook.

"I don't know why I made all those arrangements." He talked to himself as he turned into his gravel driveway but stopped at the entrance to check his mailbox for useless correspondence. The last time he picked up the mail was over a week ago. He stood by the mailbox, stared at a pile of multiple-sized envelopes and magazines, held them all in his hands, and looked up towards the northern end of his property through the pine trees, rhododendrons, and emerald green arborvitaes growing on both sides of the property line. He turned his head and looked at his house at the end of the driveway.

"I never tire of looking at our house from the end of the driveway. Any time of the year is a beautiful view. Maybe for next spring, I should plant more daffodils around the mailbox." Stephen was obsessed with the look of the house from the street. Whenever he picked up the mail, he looked back, talked to himself, and became convinced he needed to do more work in the front yard.

He turned his head back to the north, stared at his neighbor's driveway, and saw a black Range Rover pull into the Edwards' property and stop in front of their garage doors. Alice, Joe, and their two children, Max and Dana, exited the car and entered their home through the side kitchen door.

"Hey, Mom. I am going to read in my room." Max walked into his bedroom and shut the door behind him for privacy. His door is never locked. The family rules are followed; nobody enters without knocking first. The entire Edwards family also attended the same social gathering in Old Saybrook. They didn't see Stephen picking up his mail when they arrived home.

"*Glad to see they got home safely. Alice must have consumed an entire bottle of the cabernet by herself. I'm surprised she let Max drive home. He was the only guest, besides his sister, Dana, that didn't drink alcohol.*" Stephen continued to talk to himself while looking at the pile of useless junk mail. "*Why do I keep getting this crap in the mail. It's not worth getting out of the car to look inside the mailbox. It's not like the old days. Look at me. I sound like an old man. I guess I'm an old man.*"

He returned to his car, a 2021 Porsche Boxster, and drove inside the three-car garage attached to his house. At the opposite end, inside the garage, there was a 1990 Jaguar Sovereign and, in the middle, a 2019 Honda CR-V. Most of the mail he picked up at the mailbox was deposited inside the trash bins by the garage doors. As he walked into the house through the kitchen door, he removed his coat and hung it next to another coat he recognized. He placed the remaining mail in a large antique ceramic bowl next to his industrial Gaggenau stove and walked to the bar to pour two scotches on the rocks. "Randy, I'm home! I finally picked up the mail. There was nothing important, and most of it never made it inside the house. I'm fixing us a cocktail. I've got lots to tell you about today. I hope you're in the mood to listen. By the way, the caterer gave me a big container with leftovers for dinner tonight. There's enough for several nights, including two Maine lobster tails he packed on ice."

✧✧✧✧✧✧

Dana and Max walked swiftly to their bedrooms as if something important awaited them. Dana's room was on the second floor; Max's bedroom was on the first floor, back of the house, next to the kitchen.

"I'm assuming you both had plenty to eat in Old Saybrook and won't be having dinner tonight," Alice assumes Dana and Max will not come out of their rooms until tomorrow morning. Dana, a 14-year-old blonde and popular Freshman at Lyme High School, grabbed her earphones and mobile phone, selected a pop music playlist she had created, and jumped on the bed to text her friends about her experience today. Max just turned 18, a senior at the same high school. He was tall for his age, with an athletic swimmer's body and thick, wavy, dirty-blonde hair covering half his ears. He removed his dressier clothes, hung them neatly in his closet, and squeezed into his favorite pair of tight-fitting jeans and a t-shirt. He picked up a book he had been reading on his nightstand and checked his emails on his computer. He walked to the beanbag chair before the large picture window and sat ready to read. Facing the backyard, he took in the views before continuing with his book. To the right, in the distance, he saw his next-door neighbor's massive perennial garden beds beginning to show their spring growth.

"I never get tired of this view. Sitting here, admiring the landscape, is important to me. It's great to be home. I don't think I could have stayed another five minutes in Old Saybrook." Max admitted to himself as he stared at the scenery and opened his book where he had left off last night.

Joe and Alice Edwards sat beside each other on the couch in the family room. Each had a glass of their favorite Tuscan wine, which Joe poured for them as soon as they arrived. No words were spoken. Alice looked at Joe with bloodshot eyes. They were both alone in the room and emotionally exhausted. Tears were beginning to run down Alice's cheeks. She cried softly and quietly, holding several tissues in one hand and her glass of wine in the other.

Joe placed his arm around her shoulder. "Everything will be fine, Alice." After a few minutes, He poured more wine and finished the bottle.

"Joe, I should have said something to him. Why did I wait? What should I do now?"

✧ ✧ ✧ ✧ ✧ ✧ ✧

In Middletown, Connecticut, on the western shore of the Connecticut River, 25 to 30 miles north of Old Saybrook, depending on which road you take, Manuel and Maria Sanchez arrived home after attending the same social gathering. They lived on the first floor of a three-family home they purchased five years ago. The Mexican-born couple was met by Josefa, Maria's mother, who lived with them and spent most of her time in the kitchen cooking and baking.

"Buenas tardes mijos. I didn't think you would be coming home this late. I have dinner ready, but we can wait for Enrique to get home. There is no rush, and I am sure Manuel wants to relax a bit before dinner." Josefa was concerned Maria and Manuel were late. She enjoyed caring for the household and ensuring dinner was ready when Manuel wanted to eat.

"Mami, we ate a lot this afternoon and had some drinks. We need to rest. Yes, let's wait until Enrique gets home." Maria offered an excuse to Josefa because they were not hungry.

Enrique, the couple's 19-year-old son, also lived with them. He was not at home and did not attend the social gathering in Old Saybrook because his role today was supervising the family's business, Manny's Landscaping, a retail garden center and landscape maintenance company. Enrique graduated from Middletown High School last year and attended Middlesex Community College part-time while working with his father at the garden center. The retail store and garage for all their equipment were on a heavily trafficked road in Durham, a small town in the southern suburbs of Middletown.

"I'm home! Hi Papi, Mami, and Abuelita. I have the sales numbers and deposit for today with me, Papi. I'll leave it on top of your dresser. Well? How was it? Did everyone behave in Old Saybrook?" Enrique came home in his usual jovial mood, inquiring about the social gathering in Old Saybrook.

"Yes, of course, everyone behaved. It was a lovely reception." Maria did not want to go into the details.

Manuel was sitting in his recliner, reading his newspaper and watching the sports channel on television. "Enrique, thank you for closing up the store today. Did everything go well while I was out?" Enrique's father, Manuel, was 53 years old and suffered from depression. He tried to hide it whenever he was with his family. Maria had encouraged him to seek help. He always refused professional help and claimed he could deal with it alone.

"Yes, Papi. Everything went well. There were no problems today." Manuel always asked the same question when Enrique closed the store. Enrique always politely responded with the same answer.

✧ ✧ ✧ ✧ ✧ ✧ ✧

Louise McCawley's car was constantly backfiring and scaring her neighbors because it sounded like gunfire. She lived with her mother, Mabel, in a two-bedroom apartment over a laundromat business they own on Bank Street in New London, Connecticut, about 30 miles east of Old Saybrook. Louise, an Irish immigrant now a U.S. citizen, was almost 60 years old, living with her 90-year-old mother, also a U.S. citizen. She attended the same social gathering in Old Saybrook and enjoyed a few shots of Irish Whiskey during the first half hour of the reception. Louise was born with a robust pair of lungs and powerful vocal cords. She could whisper on stage at an opera house and drown the full orchestra. When she tried to whisper in a room with 50-60 guests, everyone could hear her. Anyone who knew her loved her.

As guests at the social gathering in Old Saybrook began to leave, Louise drove out of the parking lot and ran through a red light as her car began to backfire. Some of the guests hid behind cars and assumed the noises were gunshots.

"I have to bring this car back to the mechanic on Monday. All it does is fart." Louise was going home to New London. She said a quick prayer for the vehicle to behave, made the sign of the cross and merged into the horrific I-95 traffic from the ramp just before the Connecticut River bridge. She reached New London safely and turned into an alley where she rents a parking spot behind the laundromat. Before she turned the car off, the tailpipe backfired again.

"Oh, fuck! Now I will hear my mother bitch to me about the car. I'm in no mood to listen to her today." Mabel always knew when Louise arrived home, the noises from the car gave away her location. She entered the apartment just in time to hear Mabel's loud words. Mabel could also whisper on stage at an opera house, drown a full orchestra, and Louise's whispers combined.

"That goddamn fucking car always scares the living shit out of me! Louise, what's wrong with you? You are taking your life into your hands whenever you take that fucking piece of shit out on the road. Stop being stubborn and get a new car! One of these days, you are going to kill me. You will be sorry!" Mabel always seemed to enjoy her choice of adjectives.

Louise ignored her but responded in a low voice, but never low enough. Mabel did hear her. "Yeah, yeah, yeah. I heard you before. Leave me alone, old lady. I am not in the mood for your shit today."

Mabel and Louise were known in the neighborhood as having razor-sharp tongues. They argued loud enough so all the neighbors could hear them. Both were comfortable using four-letter words as part of their daily vocabulary and were well-versed with the latest insults in their arguments.

"I'm assuming Lolita and Maritza are closing the laundromat tonight?" Louise yelled at her mother from the living room of their apartment.

"Yes, I went downstairs during lunch to let them eat without customers bothering them." Mabel was always extremely kind to the two ladies who worked for them.

"I feel sorry for any stupid customers who needed help while you were in command." Louise got the last word, as usual.

✿ ✿ ✿ ✿ ✿ ✿ ✿

After pouring two scotches on the rocks, Stephen took out his mobile phone and selected his favorite playlist on his music app account, a selection of operatic music by Verdi and Puccini. He increased the volume controls substantially for the speakers in the family room and adjusted the balances. He heard an aria from one of his favorite operas and began to sing along in Italian as he walked back into the family room.

A wheelchair, a wing chair, and a small side table between the two were strategically placed in the family room in front of the large picture window. The views from the window included the massive perennial gardens in the rear of the house. Stephen sat in the chair and placed the two drinks on the small table to his left. Next to him, he saw Randy Jensen, his husband, in the wheelchair on the other side of the small table. Stephen looked at Randy and turned towards the window to admire the early spring growth in the perennial beds.

"There were many friends there today, Randy," whispered Stephen. He looked at Randy again and saw Randy look back at him, but there was no response. "The Edwards were there, including Max and Dana. Manuel, Maria, and Louise also attended with many friends we hadn't seen in a long time. The food was delicious. Old Saybrook Caterers did an excellent job. I was happy with the outcome. Well, that's not all true.

Let's not go there right now." This one-way conversation continued between the two.

As the Connecticut sky darkened, Stephen flipped a wall switch to turn on the garden lights and floodlights pointing towards the garden. "There, that's better. By the way, I hired Enrique, Manuel's son, to work on the perennial gardens and other jobs around the house for a few hours a week. I don't think we have the time, and Enrique could use the extra money. He is a good kid. He knows us well and is familiar with the house. I trust him with our garden." He turns to look at Randy again. "Enrique is stopping by tomorrow so we can review what the garden needs now and what the regular maintenance should include. You'll get a chance to see him tomorrow." Stephen explained to Randy as he turned again to face the picture window. He did not look at Randy again but felt Randy looking back at him.

Stephen's cocktail was now empty after his second scotch on the rocks. Randy's glass was still full. All the ice in Randy's glass melted. Stephen got up, left the glasses on the table, and pushed the wheelchair to face the television set on the opposite wall. He grabbed the TV remote and selected an old movie he wanted to watch. He began to have flashbacks of his entire day, especially in Old Saybrook. Quietly, he wiped a few tears running down his cheeks.

Alice was still next door in her living room with her husband, Joe, also wiping tears from her eyes at approximately the same time.

Stephen was relieved that the day was almost over, so he reclined on the couch to rest, and shortly after the movie began, he fell asleep.

CHAPTER 2

GARDEN

Stephen and Randy's family room was in the back of the house, facing east towards the perennial garden. The following morning, the early sunlight pierced through the large picture window and lit up Stephen's face, which forced his eyes to open. He was still lying on the couch after falling asleep to a movie he didn't remember turning on the previous night. He also didn't remember how he got to the couch.

"I think I might have done some liver damage last night. I am too old for hangovers!" He confessed to himself just as he saw that the wheelchair beside him was unoccupied. He assumed he had brought Randy to bed or Randy got up on his own after he fell asleep on the couch. Randy had a special hospital bed in the guest bedroom on the first floor.

With much effort, Stephen rose from the couch, fluffed the pillows, turned the television off, turned the outdoor floodlights off, and dragged himself up the stairs to his bathroom on the second floor. He splashed cold water on his face and combed his hair. He looked in the mirror and continued to converse with himself. *"Oh, I look like shit. I must have had one too many scotches last night. I need to sweat out the alcohol from my body. Let's hope I make it down the stairs and not kill myself on the treadmill."* It was time for his usual morning exercises. He found his gym shorts, an old baggy Yale t-shirt, and his favorite sneakers in his walk-in closet. He staggered to the basement, where a section was transformed into an exercise room. He turned on the small television set on the wall to the local news channel and got on his treadmill for his usual 30-minute semi-fast walk. At the end of the 30 minutes, he got on the floor to stretch and lifted light weights for another 30 minutes.

Today, his 60-minute exercise routine felt more like 60 hours, which made him still wonder how much scotch he drank last night. It was now 9:00 AM, and on his way to the kitchen, he focused, again, on the wheelchair facing the television set in the family room. It was still empty. He stood there and stared for a minute without any thoughts. He shook his head as he walked into the kitchen, made a pot of coffee, and returned to the family room to look through the picture window. There, in the perennial beds, Enrique Sanchez was pulling weeds and removing leaves and branches that fell from the oak tree during the winter storms.

He knocked on the window, and when Enrique looked, he waved. He returned to the kitchen and grabbed the non-fat milk from the Sub-Zero refrigerator and two thermal mugs from the cabinet. He poured coffee and a splash of milk for himself and Enrique. Before going outside to the garden, he grabbed his Eddie Bauer fleece vest, put it on over his baggy Yale t-shirt, and sucked in his stomach. He looked at himself in the full-length mirror by the back door and whispered, *"Not bad for 75. No wonder Randy has stayed with me for so many years."* He opened the door and stepped outside to meet Enrique on the patio. The Sunday morning chilled air shocked him as he stepped onto the slate patio.

There he was, the handsome son of Manuel and Maria Sanchez, two hard-working Mexican immigrants who are now proud U.S. citizens. Enrique, born in Middletown, was tall, with dark hair, grey eyes, and thin with complex muscle tones. He wore his signature ripped jeans, tall waterproof boots, and a red plaid wool shirt over a black t-shirt. Enrique had a photogenic look about him. Many mistook him for a professional New York model. That could have been a second career for him.

"Enrique!" Yelled Stephen from the door. "I have coffee for you. You take it with milk and no sugar. Is that correct?"

"Yes, Mr. Porter. Thank you." Enrique responded. "I arrived early and cleaned the beds while you were still asleep."

Stephen thought Enrique might have looked inside through the window and saw him sleeping on the couch with his clothes still on. "Oh no, my good friend. I have been up for some time now. I have been in the gym since 6:00 AM doing my exercises." He now whispered to himself, *"White lies never hurt anyone. If only it were true, I wouldn't need to suck in my bloated stomach filled with scotch."*

"Mr. Porter, I brought a notebook to list your priorities in the garden and work out a schedule." Enrique anxiously informs Stephen.

"That's a good idea, Enrique. I didn't have the time to write my thoughts about what I want to see, so perhaps we can develop something new and exciting in the garden today with your suggestions."

"Let's sketch out the current layout, and we can design the expanded version you wanted me to create on the next page." Enrique tried to move the discussion to create a definitive new layout for the garden. "You have a significantly large variety of plants, most of which can be easily split and used in new areas. We can also consider adding ornamental azaleas and other hearty perennials you don't have, plus a few weeping cherry trees at the entrance to the garden and in the rear. A plum tree towards the rear will add color and height to the landscape. The purple-pinkish blossoms from the plum trees will give you great color in the early spring. Perhaps we can find several items at the junkyard to use as featured sculptures. Please don't laugh. You would be surprised what we can find there that would be terrific in your garden. We must be creative and approach your garden with an open mind!" They both laughed out loud. "Besides, the prices for 'artwork' at the junkyard are always much more reasonable than at an art gallery."

"Excellent thought, Enrique," Stephen responded excitedly. He was confident Enrique would bring a new look to the perennial garden. His ideas could add a different perspective than what he and Randy created. "I trust you will do a great job here, Enrique," Stephen commented in a complimentary tone. "It's time for new 'eyes' to spruce up the garden. It's time for me to let go and give someone talented like yourself a chance for a new expression and creativity in this garden."

Stephen and Enrique continued walking around the beds, pointing to sections that needed significant improvements and expanded spaces. Enrique was fastidious about taking notes and creating drawings throughout the entire tour of the perennial beds.

✧ ✧ ✧ ✧ ✧ ✧ ✧

At the same time, next door at the Edwards' residence, Alice was getting ready to go to her real estate office on Route 1 in Old Lyme. It was Sunday and a beautiful morning for the Open House she had scheduled in Essex. It was a new property she had just signed up to sell this week, and it was already getting many inquiries from potential buyers and other realtors. With a slight hangover from the previous day, Alice gathered the paperwork from her home office on the second floor across from Dana's bedroom. She looked out the window to see Stephen and Enrique walking around Stephen's garden, pointing in various directions while Enrique took notes. She stopped and carefully looked at the two of them. She couldn't hear what they said and assumed Stephen was preparing to spruce up the garden. She speculated that he hired Enrique and his father's company to do the work. Alice didn't know Enrique very well. She knew he was the son of the owner of Manny's Landscaping, a reputable company with many clients in Lyme. She had heard rumors about Enrique's sexuality but never from reliable sources. She ignored them.

Alice finished packing her briefcase and was rushing to her car when she ran into her son, Max, in the kitchen.

"Hey, Mom, I got a call from the marina, and they asked me if I could work today. Someone is out sick. I told them I could but needed to leave by 2:00 PM. That should give me plenty of time to finish my schoolwork. I could always use the extra cash." Max explained to Alice. He was not asking for her approval but wanted her to think he was.

"OK, Max. If you think you have enough time for schoolwork, I approve. Remember that we are going to dinner tonight as a family." Alice wanted to ensure Max didn't have other plans for tonight.

"I will be done before we leave for dinner," Max assured his mother.

He returned to his room and walked into his bathroom to shower. He saw Stephen and Enrique in Stephen's backyard through the bathroom window. Max had seen Enrique working at Stephen's property numerous times but had never met him in person. He recalled a day last September when Enrique began to dig a hole by Stephen's driveway to replace the mailbox. Max was washing his car when he saw Enrique go behind his pickup truck, take off his clothes to his black bikini underwear, and slip into a pair of shorts he found in the back of his pickup truck. He walked back shirtless with only his boots and ripped shorts and continued to dig. Max was stunned by the casualness of Enrique removing his clothes outdoors. He was amazed by the eight-pack ripples on his stomach.

While Max stared at Enrique's abdominal muscles back in September, Alice was by the kitchen window facing the driveway looking at Max, staring at Enrique from behind his car. Enrique knew Max was staring at him, so he positioned himself to give Max the best view.

✿ ✿ ✿ ✿ ✿ ✿ ✿

Later that night, the Edwards family arrived at The Old Lyme Tavern for a Sunday night family dinner. During dinner, Max and Dana talked about school and their friends. Max was less outgoing than Dana and had only a few friends in school. That was mostly by choice. His only extracurricular activity was the swimming team, and he enjoyed working out alone in the school gym after class. Dana was the opposite of Max. She was a freshman at the same high school and was unafraid to talk to anyone. She was very popular, and Max often could hear her giggling and laughing with other friends in the school hallways.

At a time when many of the seniors in his school were beginning to date, Max kept to himself and remained busy between swimming practice, the school gym, his part-time job at the marina, his homework, and his daily reading schedule. Max was an avid reader and spent a couple of hours reading every night before sleeping. He had been averaging about fifteen to twenty books a year. Alice and Joe had always encouraged their kids to read. Dana liked to spend less time reading and more time on her mobile phone texting friends.

As soon as they sat at their table, Alice announced, "I just want you all to know that by the end of the open house I hosted today, I got three excellent offers," Joe was not surprised and very proud of her hard work. Max and Dana congratulated their mother. She then changed the subject and raised a discussion about extended families. She apologized to Max and Dana for not having grandparents, aunts, uncles, and cousins. Alice's grandparents died in Waterbury, Connecticut, before she was born. They had only one child, Linda, Alice's mother. Linda was living with an aunt in Montpelier, Vermont, at the time of the fire. She died when Alice was only five years old. Aunt Eugenia, who became Alice's legal guardian, died while Alice was in college at Wesleyan University in Middletown. This left Alice with no family alive.

Joe's side of the family also lacked extended relatives. Joe owned a real estate development and construction company in Old Lyme. It was originally started by his parents, who died within 12 months of each other shortly after Joe and Alice married. Joe was their only son, worked in the business after college, and eventually inherited it. Over the years since Joe took control, the business expanded significantly with projects throughout Connecticut and southern Rhode Island. Joe and Alice met when Joe hired Alice to market several properties his company had built in southern Connecticut. Alice was well-known in the real estate business throughout the community. Their business relationship turned into a love affair, and they married a year after their initial meeting. Alice did not wish to be the "boss's wife" and "employee" of the company, so she resigned and joined a residential real estate sales company in Old Lyme.

Alice explained to them that after Aunt Eugenia from Vermont died, she found a shoe box of her mother's personal belongings hidden in her closet, including some costume jewelry that was not worth much today, photographs of her mother, Linda, with friends, and letters addressed to her from a high school friend in Waterbury, Connecticut. She told Max and Dana that the letters were gossip notes between two girls and never told them the actual contents. Everything was placed back in the box and stored somewhere in the attic or perhaps on a top shelf of a closet somewhere in the house. She couldn't remember the exact location of the box.

"Someday, we should look at the inside of the box together. I hope I can find it. It's been a while since I have seen it. Maybe we can learn something about my family from the contents." Alice knew the contents of the letters and was unprepared to disclose it to the kids. Joe knew what was written in the letters. He didn't understand why Alice refused to disclose it to Max and Dana. He knew it was her choice to make.

"Dana, you may like some of the jewelry inside the box. After a decade or two, those styles become popular again." Since there was no response from Max or Dana, she thought it best to drop the subject.

✿ ✿ ✿ ✿ ✿ ✿ ✿

On their way home from the restaurant, Alice noticed that the rear spotlights in Stephen's backyard were all turned on.

"Perhaps Stephen is walking around the perennial garden getting ideas on what to do with it this year," Alice commented as she looked through the car window. "I hope he is OK and didn't fall in the garden. I don't want to check on him and let him think we are constantly watching."

Stephen was not outside. Again, he was sitting inside by the picture window with Randy in the wheelchair to his left and two cocktail glasses of scotch on the rocks. Yes, the garden lights and floodlights were turned on again so he and Randy could look outside and discuss the new garden layout Enrique planned to create.

"Randy, did you see Enrique this morning?" Stephen turned to his left and tried to make conversation with Randy. "He arrived earlier than I expected and began clearing out the weeds and debris from the beds. He is a workaholic." There was no response from Randy. "He thinks we should get some artwork at the junkyard and strategically place it in the perennial beds. I thought he was kidding, perhaps making fun of me and the garden. He was deadly serious! I wasn't sure how to respond." Stephen paused, took a gulp of scotch, and continued in a much lower voice. "It's time to let someone else's creativity take over the garden design." He sadly confessed to Randy. "What do you think, Randy? Should I follow his advice?" Stephen saw Randy turn to look at him and shrugged his shoulders—no other response from Randy.

Randy's scotch on the rocks turned into scotch and water again. Stephen's glass was empty. He continued to stare silently toward the garden. The silence lasted for over thirty minutes before Stephen got up and walked up the stairs to his bedroom alone.

CHAPTER 3

1960S

Randy Jensen was born in Waterbury, Connecticut, in 1947. He lived with his parents and two brothers, eight and ten years older, in the Bunker Hill neighborhood, west of the city's center. His father was the Chief Financial Officer for a manufacturing company considered one of the largest employers in the city. His mother was a homemaker.

Randy attended Croft High School and graduated with honors. He was the valedictorian at his graduation in 1965 but was not the most popular student in his class. During the 1960s, public high school students in Waterbury were required to wear dress shirts, ties, and jackets to school. Randy was always the best dressed. He was known for wearing a bow tie to school daily, giving the school bullies more reasons to abuse him. He was called many derogatory names in school, including "faggot", "sissy," "homo," and "mama's boy." Randy had the patience to look the other way and avoid a confrontation he would regret.

Early in 1965, before graduation, Randy was confronted by several of the school's bullies and threatened a beating unless he proved his "manhood" and had sex with Linda Peterson, another senior at Croft High School known to many as the school whore. Linda knew of the bullies' demand and welcomed the challenge to turn Randy into a "man." This was the first time Randy felt afraid for his life and agreed to take Linda on a date to a local drive-in movie theatre in the east end of town, where they both stripped in the back seat of Randy's car and complied with the bullies' expectations. Unfortunately, even though

Randy wore a condom, Linda got pregnant. She would not disclose the father's name to anyone but her girlfriend, Sandra Brooks.

When their family physician gave her and her parents the news, Frank and Vivian Peterson removed Linda from school a few months before graduation and sent her to Montpelier, Vermont, to live with a spinster aunt, Eugenia Peterson, until the baby was born and given away for adoption. The family felt that the embarrassment of having an unwed pregnant teenage daughter was too much to experience in Waterbury's social network.

A few months after Linda left for Vermont, an electrical shortage ignited a fire in the basement of the Peterson's home while Frank and Vivian slept. The fire destroyed the Victorian house in the West End neighborhood while Frank and Vivian slept. They did not survive. At the time of the fire, Linda was six months pregnant and was not allowed by Aunt Eugenia to attend the private funeral. Linda gave birth to an eight-pound, six-ounce girl in January 1966 and named her Alice.

"Aunt Eugenia, I promise to get a job and eventually get my apartment. I don't want to give up Alice for adoption. Please let me keep her and stay with you until I can afford my apartment," She wanted to keep the baby and convinced Aunt Eugenia not to turn it over to a Vermont Catholic orphanage.

☆☆☆☆☆☆☆

During the summer of 1965, before he moved to Cambridge, Massachusetts, to attend Harvard University, Randy had his first sexual experience with another man behind bushes at night in a dark, unlit public park next to the main public library. That same experience was repeated almost nightly during the summer. Sometimes in the same park, other times on visits to Greenwich Village in New York City, which was only a two-hour drive from Waterbury. Randy easily accepted his sexual identity and became sexually active that summer. He was known in the park to be "well-endowed." In September 1965, he began his studies at Harvard. His ultimate goal was to become a lawyer.

Once he moved to Cambridge, Randy felt he had left Waterbury forever and was never in touch with his high school classmates at Croft. Randy was never told Linda was pregnant or that her parents had died in a fire.

✧ ✧ ✧ ✧ ✧ ✧ ✧

Stephen Porter was also born in 1947. He was the only child of Nancy and Burt Porter, who lived in Hull, Massachusetts, in a waterfront home on Channel Street with views of the Boston Harbor. Stephen was known in high school for being very social, overly friendly, and had many more female friends than male friends. He was the school newspaper's editor and chaired the Senior Prom Committee. You could always count on seeing Stephen at almost all school festivities. He graduated in 1965 with honors, and his parents sent him to Boston University near Fenway Park and Kenmore Square in Boston. Since he was an only child, Nancy and Burt could afford the tuition and a small studio apartment near the school. A part-time job at the school's bookstore gave him extra cash to enjoy his weekend activities.

Stephen loved college life. He was known in school as a speed reader with a photographic memory who majored in psychology and could quickly breeze through books, homework assignments, and research papers. His talent gave him the time to socialize and enjoy the party life Boston offered in those days.

During the beginning of his first year at BU, Stephen realized that he was enjoying the company of gay men. He read in the library about homosexuality, and after meeting several more students who had already come out of the closet, he acknowledged his sexual identity as a gay man and was introduced by his new friends to gay life at BU and Boston.

✿ ✿ ✿ ✿ ✿ ✿ ✿

Almost every weekend, some of the gay students at BU and other local Boston area colleges would gather at a private home for cocktails and networking. Born with a "social" personality, Stephen was thrilled to attend these parties and looked forward to them every weekend. It was customary for Stephen to arrive at a party alone and leave with another student. That's where he met Randy Jenson, from Waterbury, Connecticut, a student at Harvard.

A cocktail party on Beacon Street in the Back Bay neighborhood of Boston between Dartmouth and Exeter Streets. It was a cold, windy weekend in late January 1966. The party was in a sixth-floor walk-up apartment with a living room surrounded by bookcases and oak paneling facing Storrow Drive, the Charles River, and Cambridge. The hosts were two Harvard students, friends of Randy, who lived in this one-bedroom apartment. Alan was the son of a prominent architect in Philadelphia, and the other host, Michael, was the son of a well-known politician in Washington, DC, whose last name nobody would disclose.

Randy was in the tiny galley kitchen looking for a glass for his cocktail when Stephen walked in, looked directly into his eyes, and aggressively introduced himself, "Hi, I'm Stephen Porter from BU. What's your name?"

"Randy Jenson from Harvard, nice to meet you." They shook hands, and Stephen kept glaring at Randy's eyes, then shifted his focus to the rest of Randy's body. "I am trying to find a glass somewhere in this kitchen to fix myself a cocktail," Randy confessed in his shy, quiet voice. He is embarrassed to be caught looking inside the kitchen cabinets and uncomfortable with Stephen's eyes fixated on his crotch.

Stephen responded with a witty comment. "Well, that makes two of us. Maybe if we look together for two glasses, we'll have much more success."

Randy smiled back at Stephen and wondered how he would get rid of this aggressive and obnoxious guy. Suddenly, Stephen turned around and faced Randy with two glasses, one in each hand. "So, what's your poison?"

"Scotch on the rocks, please," Randy replied to Stephen as if Stephen was the hired bartender for the party.

"My kind of man. I think I'll have the same." Stephen responded in a dominant voice. "Hold onto these glasses while I find the ice and a new bottle of scotch."

The two walked out of the kitchen with their cocktails into the oak-paneled living room filled with almost thirty handsome and young gay men. They turned towards the large picture window and admired the view outside, an evening winter scene on the Charles River. To their right, they saw, in the distance, the historic Longfellow Bridge, and on their left was the Massachusetts Avenue Bridge. MIT (Massachusetts Institute of Technology) was directly across the other side of the river. They shared personal information about each other.

Stephen was much more aggressive with his questions, and Randy was cautious and calculated in his responses, especially to someone he had just met and acted overly inquisitive. Ironically, both liked what they heard. Randy wondered why he liked Stephen. He was everything he did not like in a man, especially his aggressiveness. Stephen also wondered why he was spending his time with Randy. He needed to be humorous and fully cooperate in the required social exchange a cocktail party in Back Bay demands. Randy needed to be more cooperative with his social requirements. When Stephen was ready to walk away and start a new conversation with someone more outgoing, Randy asked him if he wanted to grab a bite at his favorite Chinese restaurant on Newbury Street. Stephen hesitated for five seconds. Finally, a response. "Yes, let's get the fuck out of here now."

After dinner on Newbury Street, Stephen and Randy walked over to the Bay Village neighborhood. They stopped at the Napoleon Club, a well-known gay piano bar, for drinks and to listen to patrons screeching and belting to tunes played at the piano by a graduate of Emerson College wearing earplugs. You could hear the music of Cole

Porter, Rodgers & Hammerstein, Irving Berlin, and Frank Loesser from the sidewalk. The drinking age in Massachusetts was 21, and Stephen and Randy were almost 20. The bartenders during that time looked the other way as long as their tip jar was filling up.

The extravagantly decorated smokey piano bar was filled with iconic red and gold furnishings, gilt fixtures, and enough stained glass to pass as a house of worship. There, they meet up with several friends who attended the same Beacon Street cocktail party. There was plenty of sexual tension within this group of friends as they sat around in a circle at a table in the bar. Ten men were enjoying each other's company, drinking, and laughing, exchanging stories while trying to decide in their minds whom they would fuck tonight. Perhaps more than one if it was a lucky weekend. None had ever enjoyed a sexual encounter with Randy. He was a virgin to them and a special prize to catch, especially when an occasional soft erection outlined the thickness of Randy's penis in his jeans.

Stephen's large penis also made him popular with this group. He was proud of the bulge in his crotch. Everyone noticed. It wasn't easy to ignore. His jeans were worn and slightly faded at the crotch. He looked around the table of ten men and realized he had sex with everyone except Randy. Stephen felt he needed something new tonight and stayed close to Randy.

After an hour of flirting, drinking, and inhaling smoke from lit cigarettes left on ashtrays and hanging from young men's lips, Stephen asked Randy if he was ready to go. They left the Napoleon Club together, upsetting the other eight men at the table. Outside the smoked-filled piano bar, Stephen invited Randy to his apartment near Kenmore Square for a "smokeless cocktail." Randy hesitated. Stephen grabbed him by the neck, gently kissed his lips, and slowly licked them with his tongue until Randy pulled away. A cab stopped at the bar's front door, and they both jumped inside.

One more cocktail in Stephen's apartment before they slowly began to undress each other on the couch in front of the bed. Lips together, hands touched skin, rolled, and turned over several times. They moved over to the bed and made enough passionate noises to cause the next-door neighbor to bang on the adjoining wall. Randy's mouth was sucking and licking Stephen's left nipple while his right hand was down his pants, searching for his penis to stroke. Stephen had his right hand on Randy's head, pressing on his lips before moving to his nipples. His left hand unbuttoned Randy's pants and pushed them down halfway to below his buttocks to feel the softness of his skin. Randy pulled his head away from Stephen's nipples, looked into his eyes, and began to nibble and lick his left ear and neck while he squeezed Stephen's right nipple. He moved his mouth to Stephen's circumcised penis and began to perform oral sex on Stephen.

When they removed the rest of their clothing, Stephen dragged his tongue over almost every square inch of Randy's body as Randy stretched in bed with his head over the side. He grabbed Randy's hard and thick, uncircumcised penis, pulled the skin back, and inserted it in his mouth almost to the back of his throat, choking for a brief second. He removed it and inserted it again and again. Randy rarely experienced his penis this hard. Stephen slowly moved his tongue to Randy's navel and then over to his stomach and chest. He knelt in bed by the headboard and allowed Randy to penetrate him. A half-hour later, they flipped positions. Randy was now on his back while Stephen entered his body through his anus.

Randy enjoyed having Stephen's penis inside him. It was his first time on the receiving end of anal sex. He took his two hands around Stephen's neck, forced him close to his face, and inserted his tongue inside Stephen's mouth. Stephen seductively sucked his tongue. He then inserted his tongue in Randy's mouth and Randy amorously and slowly licked it.

They continued their erotic lovemaking until it was almost daylight. Before falling asleep, they have orgasms on each other's chest. Randy shot a long stream that reached Stephen's navel and rested on top of the hairs that ran from his penis to his chest. Stephen inserted

Randy's penis in his butt and masturbated. He shot a stream of cum that reached Randy's face. Stephen leaned over to Randy's face and kissed him. They both hugged each other.

This was a seductive erotic encounter neither of them had ever experienced. They trusted each other and let their emotions take them on a sexual joy ride. There was no holding back on Stephen's bed. The room was dark; the only lights came from billboards that reflected from Kenmore Square. Randy and Stephen stood naked in front of the window, looked outside, and enjoyed the cold draft that seeped through the window jamb into the room.

"Well, I never expected this much fun with anyone," Stephen compliments Randy in a strange tone.

"There is a lot about me you don't know. If you want to learn more, we'll need to schedule another date," Randy's reply was meant to encourage another date.

They saw the winter views of Kenmore Square. There was no vehicle traffic, and there were no pedestrians at that hour of the night. They felt alone in the world. Their bodies were soaked with sweat. After a quick shower together, they collapsed in the middle of the bed in a spooning position - lying on their right side, Randy was wrapped by Stephen in a big hug, his arm rested over Randy's waist, and his face relaxed on the back of Randy's neck. They both exhaled together.

✧ ✧ ✧ ✧ ✧ ✧ ✧

That same evening, an eight-pound, six-ounce baby girl was born in Montpelier, Vermont. Her name was Alice Peterson. Her mother, Linda, was taken to the hospital earlier the same day by her Aunt Eugenia after her water broke in the house. Mother, daughter, and aunt survived the day.

CHAPTER 4

1970S

Little Alice Peterson celebrated her fifth birthday on January 25th, 1971. Her mother, Linda, bounced from job to job in Montpelier and refused to enroll in the local community college. She would either quit the job because it did not fit her social calendar or be fired for incompetence. In her last position as a telephone scheduler for a large dental office, she was fired because she insulted a patient on the phone. The customer was demanding a same-day appointment for general cleaning. Linda did not have the patience to deal with the public. The public was also not ready for Linda's attitude.

"She was a bitch on the phone. She told me she was Dr. Cardus' favorite patient and said he would want her to come in anytime she pleased. I didn't know what to do. The doctor was not in the building, so I told her there was a note in her files, which there wasn't, that based on her last x-rays, she needed to go to the emergency room because she had roaches in her vagina" Linda, laughing at the kitchen table, explained to Aunt Eugenia why she was fired.

Aunt Eugenia gave her a stern look. "You need to get another job, Linda. You have a baby to support. Wake up and look at reality around you. Smell the coffee, goddamn it."

She never earned enough money to support her daughter Alice and an apartment, so they lived with Aunt Eugenia, who cared for Alice while Linda worked or was out partying and experimenting with drugs. Her circle of friends in Montpelier was not an impressive group of residents. By the time Alice had her fifth birthday, Linda had been arrested three times, twice for disorderly conduct and once for shoplifting. The Montpelier Police Department knew her well and closely monitored her activities in Montpelier.

"This town sucks! Everyone is a bore. I can't wait to return to Waterbury." Linda complained every day about living in Montpelier.

Aunt Eugenia lived mortgage-free in a modest tiny house in a middle-class neighborhood in Montpelier. Her only source of income was her Social Security check, a small pension from her late husband's maintenance position in City Hall, and a small amount of cash from renting a tiny basement apartment to an unregistered immigrant, Miguel, who worked in the kitchen of a popular local restaurant. Miguel had a good relationship with Aunt Eugenia and enjoyed playing with and teasing Alice. After his shift at the restaurant, he always brought home a large plate of food for Alice and Aunt Eugenia. Linda was rarely home at that time. When she finally arrived home late at night, Aunt Eugenia made sure a plate of leftovers was in the refrigerator for her. Aunt Eugenia and her late husband never had children. She loved taking care of Alice and treated her like her own child.

Linda kept in touch with only one person in Waterbury, her childhood friend, Sandra Brooks. They exchanged correspondence regularly but never physically reunited after Linda moved to Vermont in 1965. Shortly after New Year's Day in January 1971, just before Alice's birthday party, Sandra suggested that Linda contact her old boyfriend, Brian Stone because he had expressed interest in renewing their relationship. Sandra and Linda thought Brian could be the vehicle for Linda's return to Waterbury. After high school graduation, Brian went to work for an auto body shop in Watertown, just north of Waterbury. Linda called Brian at the body shop from the public phone outside a gas station near her house, and they agreed to meet in Montpelier. Brian would drive up on a Saturday morning and stay in a local motel on the outskirts of town until returning to Watertown on a Sunday afternoon. It was about a three-and-a-half-hour drive each way. Whenever Brian was in town, Linda would tell

Aunt Eugenia she would visit friends and walk down the street to the gas station, where Brian was waiting to bring her to his room in the motel.

For Brian, the rendezvous was purely for sex, nothing more. Linda didn't want to believe she was being used as a sex toy, so she ignored the thought that Brian did not love her. Her desire to leave Montpelier was strong, and she still hoped he would be the ticket for her and Alice out of Montpelier and back to Waterbury.

"Brian, when will you let me return to Waterbury with you?" She often suggested to Brian that they move in together in Waterbury.

"Now is not a good time, Linda. Maybe by early summer. I want to be sure I can support you and Alice," He always avoided the discussion. He looked in the opposite direction whenever she mentioned it or immediately changed the subject when Linda spoke of moving in with him. "Oh, let's go hiking this afternoon. A trail behind the motel brings you to the top of the mountain."

Unbeknownst to Linda, Brian was already seeing another woman in Waterbury. She was the auto body shop owner's daughter. They were expected to get engaged in the summer.

During the last week of March 1971, Brian purchased the engagement ring to propose to his girlfriend in Waterbury. He decided to travel one last time to Montpelier that Saturday for sex with Linda before his marriage proposal to another woman. Before returning to Waterbury on Sunday, he planned to break up his relationship with Linda. He arrived in Montpelier after a treacherous drive with light snow and ice falling all morning and met Linda, as usual, outside the gas station on Saturday afternoon. Witnesses who saw Linda enter the pickup truck claimed the two argued loud enough for the gas station attendant inside the building to hear.

Brian and Linda fled at a high rate of speed and drove west towards the motel about 10 minutes away. Brian was doing 55-60 MPH in a 35 MPH zone with snow on the ground. The pickup truck skidded on a large patch of ice and hit a telephone pole head-on. They were not wearing seatbelts. Linda was launched through the windshield from the impact and found dead on a snowbank twenty feet in front of what remained of the mangled pickup truck. Brian was crushed in the driver's seat and died instantly. It took hours for the fire department to extract his body. Alice is now an orphan unless the identity of her father is made public.

In 1972, the week after Alice's 6th birthday, Aunt Eugenia adopted Alice with the help of her pastor and pro-bono legal assistance offered by the State.

✧✧✧✧✧✧✧

Sandra Brooks was shocked when she got the news of the accident. She took Alice's correspondence, pictures, and newspaper articles about her parent's death, placed them in a large envelope, and dropped them in the garbage container next to the kitchen sink. Later that night, she returned to pick up the envelope, brought it back to her bedroom, and shoved it on the top shelf of her closet.

During the mid-1970s, Sandra and her boyfriend, Jack Stone, Brian's older brother, were being encouraged to become members of the "People's Temple," a religious cult founded by Jim Jones. The group was relocating to the new Jonestown compound in Guyana, South America after its founder was accused of financial fraud in California. When some of the group's leaders realized that Sandra and Jack were financially broke, they stopped encouraging their move. In mid-September 1978, unable to raise the money for an airline flight to Guyana, Sandra and Jack placed the move on hold and decided to stay in Waterbury until their finances improved.

Sandra and Jack were part of a motorcycle club in Waterbury. They were known by law enforcement in town for numerous traffic violations and were arrested several times for disorderly conduct. In early November 1978, seven years after the death of Linda and Brian, she and Jack were arrested again—this time for grand theft and kidnapping.

Sandra's mother was the property manager at the 200+ acre estate of a famous Broadway producer and his wife in Washington,

Connecticut, a small town about one hour northwest of Waterbury. Sandra occasionally visited her mother during working hours when the owners were out of town. She became familiar with the house and its contents. On Thursday, November 9, 1978, wearing ski masks, Sandra and her boyfriend, Jack, broke into the house in the middle of the night, tied the owner's hands, and covered their eyes and mouths with duct tape. Jack pushed them to the back of their van and secured their feet together. Sandra ran around the house and filled pillowcases with jewelry and anything valuable. They did not want to hurt the owners and planned on dropping them off in a secluded cornfield about 10 miles from the house.

In less than thirty minutes, the house was turned upside down. Before leaving, Sandra opened the door to a barn at the end of the driveway where the owners had stored many antiques purchased from trips worldwide. A silent alarm notified the police. In less than two minutes, two police vehicles arrived at the property as Sandra and Jack were ready to exit the driveway with the owners tied and blindfolded and a van filled with their valuable possessions. Sandra and her boyfriend were arrested, charged, and imprisoned for ten years.

✿ ✿ ✿ ✿ ✿ ✿ ✿

On November 17th, 1978, shortly after Sandra and Jack were arrested in Washington, Connecticut, Congressman Leo Ryan and several observers and journalists visited Jim Jones's Jonestown compound in Guyana, South America after concerned relatives of the cult's members approached the United States government. Before leaving the compound, the same day of their arrival, Congressman Ryan and everyone traveling with him was killed by a group of Jim Jones' followers. The following day, Jones commanded his followers to drink a poisoned punch. The death toll was over 900 people, including Jones, of which more than 300 were children.

✧ ✧ ✧ ✧ ✧ ✧ ✧

Randy and Stephen experimented with their relationship while in college. They lived separately during the first two years and agreed to have an open relationship. Both took full advantage of the agreement. Stephen, after a long night of studying, enjoyed his walks on the Charles River Esplanade or a park near Fenway to meet other men for sex behind bushes or, if he felt comfortable, invite them to his apartment. It was his reward for the hard work he disciplined himself during the day. He yearned for the innocent cruising, the orchestrated eye contact, the physical touch of another man's skin, and the passionate erotic anonymous sex that ended with a satisfying overflowing release.

Stephen's sex life in college was significantly more active than most of his gay friends in school. He enjoyed hooking up with a man who wanted to experiment with new positions, sex toys, fetishes, inhaling amyl nitrite (poppers) during sex, or just oral sex. He was an assistant professor at BU, and Stephen was one of his steady sexual encounters. They lived in the same building, so it was convenient for the professor to invite Stephen for drinks in exchange for Stephen's help inserting a long dildo in the professor's butt. While he had the dildo inside, the professor performed oral sex on Stephen and shared a small bottle of poppers to enhance their sexual experience. When they were ready to cum, the professor would always swallow Steven's cum while he masturbated and ejaculated on the bed sheets. There was no lovemaking in Stephen's sexual encounters outside his relationship with Randy. Those random erotic events were only to satisfy some of his wild sexual desires and fantasies.

Randy was usually successful in meeting his sexual partners in Cambridge at any time of the day. His favorite locations near his apartment were the Esplanade alongside Memorial Drive, the locker rooms at the gym in Harvard, or just walking around Harvard Square. Randy had his style for meeting other men. There was more conversation with Randy. He had an impressive technique of convincing his prey with words. That was the future lawyer talking. Randy and Stephen had different approaches but ultimately achieved their goals. They enjoyed their freedom and sharing stories about their sexual encounters, especially when the sex got very kinky or they met someone that was into leather or sadomasochism.

One of Randy's late-night encounters alongside Memorial Drive was unusual. A handsome, well-dressed man approached him soon after he stopped and sat on a bench facing the Charles River. He asked Randy to urinate in his mouth behind a large bush. Willing to try anything for the first time, Randy followed him behind the bush, unbuttoned and dropped his jeans, pulled down his underwear, grabbed his semi-hard penis, and urinated on the man's face. The stranger inserted Randy's penis in his mouth and swallowed the rest of the urine while gently rubbing Randy's testicles.

When Randy stopped urinating, the stranger squeezed his testicles with his right hand and inserted them in his mouth. He used his tongue to lick and suck on Randy's penis, a sensation he loved to experience. Randy was handed a small bottle of poppers to inhale. It didn't take long for him to experience an orgasm. The stranger licked and sucked the overly sensitive head dry, stood up, and wiped his face with a handkerchief he had in his coat pocket. They didn't speak to each other after Randy's climax. Both walked away in different directions.

Their friends loved listening to their random sexual encounters as much as they enjoyed sharing. It was common for them to go out on a Saturday night, meet a group at a bar and arrange an orgy with one or several bar patrons. Randy and Stephen were handsome and physically fit, and according to confirmations from their sexual partners, both were extremely well-endowed. All the patrons at Napoleon wanted sex with either or both. Whenever they entered the bar, all eyes focused on Randy and Stephen. Their emotional and physical attraction for each other, combined with their sexual freedom, created a strong bond between them and the opportunity to experience their sexuality while they were still young. They were an inseparable, fun gay couple.

✧ ✧ ✧ ✧ ✧ ✧ ✧

At the start of the new decade, the 70s, Randy and Stephen moved in together to a small one-bedroom apartment two blocks from Harvard Square on Dunster Street in Cambridge. It was an old mansion with plenty of history, turned into tiny apartments convenient for Harvard students. Their apartment was on the main parlor floor with twelve-foot ceilings. It included the original living room and dining room, which was turned into their bedroom, and a section of the original pantry turned into a small galley kitchen. Randy continued attending Harvard and enrolled in their Law School after graduating with a bachelor's degree in business. Stephen commuted to BU across the Charles River for his classes until he graduated. He subsequently enrolled at Harvard to obtain his master's in psychology. Stephen and Randy were excellent students. They studied hard and earned high grades. They also continued socializing with friends, playing hard, and enjoying their sexual encounters between Cambridge and Boston.

Shortly before graduating from Law School in 1972, Randy was offered and accepted a full-time position in a prestigious law firm in Hartford, Connecticut. They moved to Connecticut in the summer of 1972, and Randy passed the bar exam shortly after graduation. Stephen wanted to get his doctorate at Yale in New Haven, Connecticut. He applied and was accepted. He also worked part-time for a non-profit organization providing mental health services for low-income residents in the New Haven area.

Life in Hartford was less social than in their Boston days. Their jobs were very demanding, and Stephen's doctorate studies and commute to New Haven from Hartford absorbed much of his days, including weekends. They lived in Bushnell Place, a high-rise condominium tower in downtown Hartford just east of Bushnell Park in the city's center. Their apartment had striking views of the Capitol building to the west and the Connecticut River to the east. Life in Hartford was partially closeted for apparent reasons. Randy was not "out" at the law firm, and

Stephen kept his personal life private at Yale. Gay life was not as openly accepted in the early 1970s. Randy risked getting fired if the law firm discovered he was gay. They both knew they could be exposed if seen walking into a gay bar. Most of their social life was hosting cocktail and dinner parties at home or accepting invitations to friends' houses.

If they decided to venture out to a gay bar, their trips were limited. They usually included The Warehouse, a lively dance bar inside an abandoned warehouse in an industrial park under the highway on Capital Avenue. The Warehouse was far enough away from the downtown region and located in a low-traffic zone. This iconic dance club was one of the biggest clubs in Connecticut, filled with tremendous sound systems, impressive lighting shows synchronized to the loud pounding disco music that never stopped until closing, a massive bar with friendly muscular bartenders, and staging for performances.

There was a significant diversity of patrons at the Warehouse. Lawyers, doctors, accountants, teachers, college professors, hairdressers, decorators, store clerks, construction workers, priests, television news personalities, college students, and the occasional straight couple, all dressed the same (except for the straight couple), tight jeans with muscle t-shirts or a short sleeve shirt two sizes smaller than it should be. Most patrons wore a handkerchief in their jeans' left or right rear pocket. Your sexual preference was advertised by which side and the color you were letting stick out of the pocket. During the hot summer days, everyone on the dance floor was topless and soaked with sweat as they danced to a sound-blasting light show of the most popular disco songs of the week. For many, it was a place to see and be seen. It was one of the best hangouts in Connecticut to meet gay men. Nobody left The Warehouse alone unless it was by choice.

Whenever Randy and Stephen decided to venture out to The Warehouse, it was not unusual for them to go with one, two, or three other guys for a group sexual encounter in someone's home after the bar closed. An invitation to an after-hour naked pool party was customary during the hot summer nights. Those pool parties usually turned into a pool orgy.

At the opposite end of "bar scenes" was Chez Est, commonly called the "wrinkle room" because most patrons were older gay men. The bar was in the same location for years until it was forced to move in the late 1970s. It was well known as a dingy, dark, extremely conservative, smokey piano bar near the downtown district. Younger men seen at the Chez Est were most likely hustlers. The good ones were expensive to hire, and the amateurs were either inexpensive or gratis. Many of Chez Est's patrons had the financial resources, so paying for a sexual encounter was not an issue. Most of the hustlers made a good living there at night. For some, it was considered a part-time job for the extra cash on hand. Chez Est was an excellent hangout alternative if you liked older men and needed extra money or you didn't want the pounding music and flashing light experience of The Warehouse.

✿✿✿✿✿✿✿

In 1978, gay men in the United States and Sweden and heterosexuals in Tanzania and Haiti began showing signs of what is called HIV/AIDS today. In 1980, there were thirty-one deaths related to HIV/AIDS in the U.S. Rumors began to surface about an uncurable "gay disease" killing gay men. Casual unprotected sex within the gay community came to a halt.

CHAPTER 5

1980S

Almost nine and a half years after her mother's untimely death, Alice enrolled at Montpelier High School in September 1980 after graduating from her local elementary public school. The new high school was built on the western perimeter of Montpelier on the opposite side of the Winooski River. Aunt Eugenia didn't like to get up early in the morning and drive Alice to school. Her health was beginning to deteriorate due to her chain-smoking habit, so most mornings, she stayed in bed until 10:00 or 11:00 AM. Bus service to the school was several blocks away.

On a typical school day, Alice was up by 6:00 AM. She managed to do some of the housework in the morning, including laundry and prepared her school lunch and something for Aunt Eugenia to eat during the day. At 7:00 AM, she walked several blocks to hop on a bus that would take her directly to Montpelier High. If snow was expected during the night, she was up earlier than usual and shoveled a narrow walk to the street and sidewalk before she got ready for school. She liked getting out of the house and enjoyed the social interaction on the bus with her friends. Alice participated in numerous school activities, learned to be independent, and desperately dreamed of leaving Montpelier after graduation.

Due to Aunt Eugenia's poor health, Alice did most of the chores around the house. On her way home from school, Aunt Eugenia would give her money to stop and pick up groceries at the neighborhood supermarket. She picked up just enough groceries to walk home with books in her backpack and the grocery bags in her hands. Aunt Eugenia rarely left the house. Her car just sat there most of the time.

Not surprisingly to anyone including Aunt Eugenia, Alice graduated from Montpelier High School in 1984 with high honors. She was the Valedictorian at the graduation ceremonies and received a full 4-year scholarship at Wesleyan University in Middletown, Connecticut. Her Valedictorian speech was a memorable statement to her classmates and teachers. Her favorite lines were the "calls for action" remarks.

> *"...Move on and take on whatever challenges come next in our lives.... we each have the potential to inspire others, including our future children, by being true to our values and committing ourselves to worthy goals....*
>
> *.... When this ceremony ends, let's not just pursue success and recognition. Make kindness, generosity, and respect towards our increasingly diverse planet your priority."*

She saved her handwritten speech in a book she always admired, Profiles in Courage by John F. Kennedy.

Aunt Eugenia bought Alice a used 1980 Honda Civic as a graduation present so she would have transportation at Wesleyan. She also wanted to ensure Alice returned to Montpelier for periodic visits. Miguel, Aunt Eugenia's tenant in the basement apartment, was an auto mechanic in Mexico before crossing the border to the U.S. He examined the entire car and checked the engine thoroughly before Aunt Eugenia purchased it from another family in the neighborhood.

It was a hot summer of 1984 in Vermont. The cool Canadian breezes that usually blow through the green-covered mountains were insufficient to offset the burning rays from the sun. Aunt Eugenia's home didn't have air conditioning, so the heat in the house, especially the second-floor bedrooms, was intolerable. Two old oscillating electric fans provided some air circulation.

By mid-August 1984, it was time to start packing the Honda Civic for her ride to Wesleyan University, about three and a half hours from Montpelier. The excitement of leaving Montpelier was overwhelming for Alice, and the look on her face all summer confirmed her desperate desire to go and start a new life. She was grateful to Aunt Eugenia who taught her to be self-sufficient. Her experiences in Montpelier would help her adapt to her new surroundings in Middletown and settle quickly. The dream of leaving Montpelier had finally arrived. She was still sad about leaving Aunt Eugenia alone in Montpelier but knew the school was close enough for home visits. Aunt Eugenia took credit for Alice's independence and had always encouraged her to leave Montpelier and experience the world.

It was a sad and, at the same time, joyous goodbye for Alice on Monday morning, August 13, 1984. The car's trunk was filled with her luggage, the gas tank was full, and her backpack was full of school entrance paperwork. A New England Road map was placed on the dashboard near the driver's side. A school directory and a bird's eye drawing of the campus with her dorm building circled in red ink were on the front passenger seat. Aunt Eugenia came outside with a small bag of cookies for the road trip. She had baked them the night before when she finally realized and accepted that her "Little Alice" was not so "little" anymore and was leaving for a better life and education. Miguel stood at the end of the driveway to wave goodbye. Alice looked inside the car to confirm that everything she needed was there. She closed the passenger side car door and returned to the kitchen door where Aunt Eugenia was standing, wiping tears from her eyes with a dishtowel that was looped around the stretched elastic waistband of her skirt.

"I'm very proud of you, Alice. I am going to miss you terribly. I knew this day would come. I didn't expect it would arrive this quickly. It seems like only yesterday you entered my life. I was there the day you were born. I am here when you are leaving the nest. I am forever grateful you kept me in good company all these years. Please take care of yourself and visit often." Aunt Eugenia was fighting back the tears as she held Alice's hands.

Alice hugged her and whispered, "Please don't cry. This is an exciting day for both of us and the saddest day. You made me who I am today. I will never forget you and will always be grateful. You should be proud." Alice was choked up also as tears began to run down her cheeks. Before she got inside her car, she looked over at her bedroom window on the second floor and recalled the many nights she spent looking outside, frightened, wondering what her future would be like. She got in her car, didn't look back, and drove away.

☼ ☼ ☼ ☼ ☼ ☼ ☼

It was April 12, 1986, five years after opening day. Louise McCawley was at Windows on the World on the 106th floor of the World Trade Center, looking towards the Empire State Building and the other skyscrapers in midtown Manhattan. She was there for a job interview as the Front of House (FOH) Scheduler. Recommended by a friend who managed the Banquet Sales department, she was still determining if she had the qualifications to do the job. Insecure, nervous, and afraid to meet the Director of Human Resources, who kept her waiting, she continued to stare out the window. It was a spectacularly clear spring day in New York City. The views were unlimited and went as far as the southwestern Connecticut coast to the right and northern New Jersey to the left. Windows on the World was a classy restaurant catering to refined customers. She was an Irish immigrant with what she would call an informal vocabulary.

"What the fuck am I doing here? I don't have the qualifications for this job. I'm going to make a fool out of myself. I don't think I fit in here. I should run for the elevator before they start laughing at me." She was talking to herself, looking out towards the north. Afraid she didn't fit in, she was still fixated on the views and suddenly convinced herself that her potential should be as unlimited as the views outside. She knew she should "fake it" and demonstrate confidence in front of the HR Director. Otherwise, she might as well turn around and go home.

She was still nervous and felt her hands shaking. The door next to her opened, and Mr. Tom Landon, a handsome young man in his early 30s dressed casually, greeted her and shook her hand. She was immediately relaxed. The FOH Manager, Mr. Stephen O'Reilly, was inside the HR Director's office. The interview with Landon and O'Reilly went better than she expected. They made her feel very comfortable. The job was offered to her, and at the end of the formal interview process, they asked if she had any questions. She looked out the window again and asked, "Is everyone that works here Irish?" Landon and O'Reilly looked at each other and laughed. She wondered why they laughed; her question was not meant to be funny.

"No, not everyone, Louise. We have about every possible nationality working here, as you can imagine. Perhaps that's why the restaurant is called Windows on the World." Mr. Landon replied to her only question. On her way home, she was excited to tell her mother, Mabel, about her new job, but then she thought perhaps she was the only one who had applied for the position.

It took Louise a couple of weeks to feel comfortable in her new job. The scheduling process was computerized. It was her first time in front of a computer. She always wondered why they gave her the job since she had no restaurant or computer experience. She knew the keyboard because she learned to type on a manual typewriter in Ireland. The FOH Manager worked closely with her during the first two weeks. She was initially overwhelmed but eventually took over the job independently. Because of her position, she had to interact with everyone on the FOH staff. That was the best part of the job for her. Everyone loved her. She was down-to-earth, honest, and had a great sense of humor. FOH employees who suddenly had scheduling issues would come to her, and she worked miracles to resolve conflicts quickly. Mr. O'Reilly never worried about being short-staffed during a shift. Louise knew her job well, but more importantly, she knew how to please management.

✿✿✿✿✿✿✿

Alice excelled at Wesleyan and was heavily involved in school activities and social programs. She lived in the dorm during her first two years and subsequently rented a small apartment in Middletown with two other roommates.

While living in Middletown, Alice visited Aunt Eugenia during the holidays and school breaks. Aunt Eugenia's health deteriorated from heavy smoking, but she always told Alice there was nothing physically wrong with her. On Saturday, February 7, 1987, Alice got an early morning call from Miguel telling her that Aunt Eugenia had died during her sleep. Alice was shocked and could not speak. She was an orphan again. Her roommates were in the room when Alice took the call and consoled her the rest of the day while she planned to return to Montpelier to deal with the cremation and estate arrangements.

Aunt Eugenia did not want anyone to fuss over her after she died. Her wishes for burial were simple. She wanted to be cremated, and her ashes spread on a windy day from the top of Hubbard Tower in nearby Hubbard Park. It was always windy on top of Hubbard Tower, so as soon as Alice received the ashes from the crematory, she drove over to Hubbard Park with Miguel, climbed to the top of the tower, and released the contents, which were carefully wrapped in a plastic bag and placed inside a cardboard box. The New England cold winter breeze created a cloud of dust that floated over the park as far as the eye could see. In less than a minute, the dust disappeared and was absorbed into the bright white winter snow covering the park.

✧ ✧ ✧ ✧ ✧ ✧ ✧

Aunt Eugenia never had children. Her only relative was Alice. In her will, Aunt Eugenia left her small estate to Alice, including the modest two-bedroom house. While Alice gathered some of Aunt Eugenia's items at home to donate to charity, she found a shoebox on the top shelf in Aunt Eugenia's bedroom closet. The box was labeled "Linda's Personal Items – give to Alice" on the outside. Inside, Alice found the Croft High School Yearbook of 1965, costume jewelry, photos of her mother Linda alone and with friends from high school, several pictures of a girl with the name "Sandra" written in the back, newspaper clippings of the tragic house fire in Waterbury where her grandparents, Frank and Vivian died while sleeping, and correspondence from someone in Waterbury by the name of Sandra Brooks. She connected this name with the girl in the pictures. All the envelopes are addressed to Linda from Sandra, at least two dozen - all were opened.

The letters were folded, stuffed back in the original envelopes, and wrapped into one bundle with a small ribbon. Alice carefully unwrapped the bundle and began to open each letter. She started to read Sandra's letters in chronological order. Halfway through the second letter, Alice's eyes opened as she covered her mouth with her hands. "Oh, my god!" she yelled in the room, all alone, loud enough for Miguel to hear her and rush into Aunt Eugenia's bedroom.

"What's wrong, Alice? What did you find?"

"Oh, nothing important. There is a box here that has my name on it. It seems like it was just some personal belongings of my mother. It's just junk jewelry, old photos, and some memorabilia." Alice was physically shaken by one specific comment in several of Sandra's letters. She returned all the letters to the appropriate envelopes, wrapped the bundle with the same ribbon, and placed the shoebox inside the trunk of her car. By this time, Alice's hands were shaking, and tears began to roll from her face. Miguel noticed Alice was crying outside and walked over to console her. Alice kept the contents of those letters to herself.

✧✧✧✧✧✧

Miguel filed for legal residency and was granted a green card before Aunt Eugenia died. He was promoted to head chef at the restaurant the same year he got his green card and married his girlfriend of five years. Expecting their first child, Miguel wanted to buy the house from Alice, so he arranged for a mortgage at a local bank and purchased the property in the early summer of 1987. Alice drove to Montpelier to legally transfer the property to Miguel and his wife. After signing the paperwork, she stood outside her 1980 Honda Civic in the parking lot of her attorney's office, looked towards the center of town, and said a final goodbye to Montpelier. Miguel approached her with his wife and thanked her for selling the house to him at a price that he could afford and the bank was willing to finance. It was at least twenty percent below market value. Many memories were left behind – some of them she took with her. The shoebox she had found in Aunt Eugenia's closet, with her name on the outside, was still inside the trunk of her car.

✧✧✧✧✧✧

Alice majored in Economics and graduated with a bachelor's degree from Wesleyan in June 1988. She was offered numerous positions in New York City, working for well-known financial institutions. She turned them all down. She wanted independence in her job, so she got her real estate broker's license in Connecticut, moved to a small apartment in Old Saybrook, Connecticut, over a garage attached to a private home, and joined a real estate sales company covering southeast Connecticut. After six months, she had already sold three houses, and two more were waiting for the title to transfer. She knew what was required to be successful in this field, honesty, good instinct, patience, and continued personal contact with the community. That strategy gave her a steady flow of new listings and clients wanting to purchase homes in the area. She quickly became the top sales agent in her office. Before the end of the decade, she bought her own home, a small antique house on North Main Street in Essex, Connecticut, a few blocks from the Connecticut River.

She was successful, attractive, intelligent, aggressive, and very social within the community, but she had little time to date men. Most single men her age were afraid to ask her out on a date. She looked and acted like a high-powered female CEO for a Fortune 500 company. That scared many eligible bachelors away. It was not her intention. She only wanted to be successful in life, financially secure, and remain independent.

Alice made numerous investments by purchasing acres of land in Lyme and Old Lyme, Connecticut. She entered into partnerships with contractors who subdivided the lots and built homes. She marketed the properties and sold them individually for a significant profit, earning the nickname "Golden Girl" within the industry. She never lost a dime on any of her real estate deals. Alice Peterson knew what to buy, where to buy it, what to build on the lot, and how to sell it.

✧✧✧✧✧✧✧

Louise arrived at work at 7:00 AM, five days a week, and left by 6:00 PM. She loved her job, and the FOH staff always respected her for her no-nonsense, street-smart attitude. She was not afraid to reprimand staff when they were late for work or the company received a customer complaint.

"Why are you late today? Too much drinking last night?" was her famous comment when staff tried to sneak in late without being noticed. *"Get the fuck in there and do an extra good job today."* She was Mama Louise to many long-term staffers. Every morning, she stopped in the kitchen to get her cup of coffee, walked over to the empty dining room ready for lunch service, and sat by the window to admire the view, meditate, and mentally plan her day. She often thought about her past and plans for her future as she stared into the skyline of Midtown Manhattan. These views inspired her to excel despite having no formal college education.

She took over the management of the entire FOH area even though her supervisor, Mr. O'Rielly, the FOH manager, was still her direct supervisor. She was dedicated and a hard worker and the staff always respected her.

On Wednesday, April 12, 1989, her third anniversary at Windows on the World, Mr. O'Rielly gave her a well-deserved raise and promoted her to a new position, Assistant FOH Manager. She was surprised and personally thrilled.

"This old broad from Ireland knows her stuff. Don't fuck with me, Chef. I have brand-new balls. I am the new Assistant FOH Manager." She jokingly told the Executive Chef the morning after her promotion as she poured her coffee in the kitchen and walked towards her favorite window in the dining room.

✿ ✿ ✿ ✿ ✿ ✿

On June 12, 1987, Sandra Brooks was released early for good behavior. Her ex-boyfriend, Jack Stone, served his complete sentence and was released in March 1989. Near the end of their time in prison, they were both infected with the HIV/AIDS virus after sharing needles with other inmates. They never reunited.

By the end of the decade, the number of known HIV/AIDS-related deaths in the United States was over 50,000.

CHAPTER 6

1990S

A new year and decade finally arrived. On Monday, January 22, 1990, five to six inches of snow were on the ground in Hartford by 6:00 PM. Randy walked home from work, about five blocks. As he entered the elegant lobby of his condominium building, he stared through the contemporary large floor-to-ceiling windows that framed the park and the State Capitol building. The Capitol was built in the late 1870s and described by its architect, Richard M. Upjohn, as "modern secular Gothic." The contrast between the "modern contemporary" building he called "home" and the "modern secular Gothic" style of the Capitol building always astonished him. He admired and respected the age differences. Both were considered "modern" in their day.

Through the window, he saw a flat white carpet of snow covering the road, grass, bushes, and trees evenly. In the distance, the State Capitol had the same blanket of snow covering its rooftops and central tower dome. The snow must have been the same in the 1870s. The lit streetlamps provided soft winter shadows on the pure white snow that blanketed the park and the driveway leading up to the front steps of the Capitol. Later today, the plow trucks will push the snow carpets away from the roads, and a sand-hurling machine will disperse sand from the back of the trucks, ruining the purity of the white snow and turning the streets into an ugly light brown mudpack. Unfortunately, that was needed to keep road traffic safe. Randy turned to the concierge, picked up the mail, and went up the elevator to the condo where Stephen was home from work earlier than usual because of the snowfall.

"Honey, I'm home!" Randy yelled comedically to Stephen and dropped the mail on the dining room table.

"I am in the kitchen prepping dinner. Make us a cocktail, and I'll be in shortly. Let's sit by the windows and enjoy the park views before the plows and sand trucks destroy it." Stephen expressed similar thoughts about the snowplows.

Randy looked outside through the windows in the living room and saw the same view he witnessed downstairs, fifteen stories higher. His eyes now returned to the dining room table. Focused on the mail, he stopped and examined a large, thick envelope addressed to him with no return address, which was comingled with a pile of magazines and unwanted promotional circulars that usually get deposited directly into the trash bin. He carefully opened the thick envelope and found the following note with old letters and other documents.

January 15, 1990
Randy Jensen
Bushnell Place
Hartford, CT

Dear Randy,
It has taken me several months to find you. Once I did, it took me another two months to decide if I should write this letter, the reason will be obvious to you. My name is Sandra Brooks, and I was Linda Peterson's best friend at Croft High School in Waterbury. The three of us graduated the same year, 1965. Unfortunately, Linda did not attend the graduation ceremony. Not sure you will remember Linda. To refresh your memory, you took her on a date to a drive-in movie a couple of months before the end of our senior year at Croft. I recall that some of the school bullies forced the date on you. That's another story, the bullies are not the reason for writing to you.

About a month after your date with Linda, she became ill, so her parents took her to their family doctor. Linda and her parents learned that she was pregnant. Her parents were ashamed and embarrassed. They did not want Linda to live in Waterbury during her pregnancy. They feared all the neighbors would criticize and look down on the family once they realized she was not married and expecting a child. Linda would not tell anyone who got her pregnant, so they sent her to live with an aunt in Montpelier, Vermont. The plan was to place the child up for adoption immediately after birth. Before the baby was born, Linda's parents, Frank and Vivian, had an unfortunate accident and perished in a fire at their home. In January 1966, Linda had a baby girl and named her Alice. She did not return to Waterbury since no family lived there. She wanted to stay with her aunt in Vermont until she got a job and earned enough to support an apartment and her daughter. She convinced Aunt Eugenia to let her keep the baby and not give her to the Catholic orphanage for adoption.

Linda would never disclose the name of the father to anyone but me. She was determined to raise the child alone. She ended up staying with her aunt after the baby was born because she could not find a steady job to support an apartment and the baby. Unfortunately, around the end of March 1971, Linda died in a car accident. Her aunt cared for little Alice, who was six years old at the time of the accident, and legally adopted her the following year.

Linda and I kept in touch with each other after she left Waterbury. I usually got a letter from her at least once every other month. I always responded to her, and she kept writing back to me. I am enclosing all the letters I received from her. As you can read in them, she loved her daughter very much but admitted she was not much of a "mother" and let her aunt raise the child most of the time. In her second letter, she responded to me after I asked her who the baby's father was. She named you as the father and claimed to be 100% certain. She had me promise that I would never contact you or tell anyone. I kept that promise for years. Today, I feel that I must break my promise.

I am writing to you at my kitchen table, knowing that my current illness will take this secret to my grave unless I share these letters. I don't know what happened to Aunt Eugenia in Vermont or little Alice. If Alice were still alive today, she is not little anymore. She must be around 24 years old.

Perhaps you may want to find and reach out to Alice, or if you decide to honor Linda's request for secrecy, that is OK also. It's up to you. I don't think it will take long for anyone to do some investigating and locate Alice.

Wishing you nothing but the best,
Sandra Brooks

Sandra died of an HIV/AIDS-related illness the week after Randy received her letter. Randy could not respond to Sandra because she did not provide a return address. The address in the envelopes she included had been cut out with a razor blade, and the postmark in the large envelope indicated Phoenix, Arizona. Randy couldn't believe what he just read. He reread Sandra's letter and focused on the words, "She named you as the father...."

✿ ✿ ✿ ✿ ✿ ✿ ✿

The start of a new decade and year differed for the Sanchez family in Guadalajara, Mexico. Manuel Sanchez was in his early 20s with big plans for the future and a desire to succeed, become financially independent, and live in the safe suburbs of Guadalajara with his family. He managed a variety store selling everything from hardware supplies to clothing but always thought of owning his store in the future. His wife Maria, 19 years old, had the same goals for the family. She was a nurse's assistant for a local health clinic during the day and went to school in the evening to become a nurse. They lived in a modest, average three-bedroom house with a center courtyard owned by Maria's mother, Josefa, in a middle-class neighborhood on Calle Rayón near the corner of Calle Vidrio. Their living arrangements with Maria's mother allowed them to save a significant portion of their salaries for their future. Josefa was a widow and stayed home to take care of household chores and Manuel and Maria's newborn baby girl, Julia. She received a small pension and had saved all the life insurance proceeds when her husband died of a stroke about three years ago.

It was a partly cloudy morning in Guadalajara with a cool temperature of 50° F on January 22, 1990, the same day Stephen received the large envelope from Sandra Brooks. Maria woke up at 6:15 AM and went downstairs for coffee already brewed by her mother, who was up at 5:00 AM. Manuel was already downstairs in the kitchen reading the morning newspaper.

"Good morning." She grabbed her coffee and returned upstairs to shower and dress for work. Before leaving, she picked up Julia, who had just awakened, and brought her to the kitchen for Josefa to feed her breakfast. "Goodbye, my sweetie," Maria kissed Julia goodbye. She turned towards Josefa, "Goodbye, Mami. I have school tonight, so I will not be back until after 8:00 PM." Maria headed towards the front door and looked at the clock to confirm her timing for the bus. It is now 7:00 AM.

Manuel stood by the front door, holding her backpack. "Goodbye, Maria, be careful out there. It is a strange world!" Manuel expressed his concern for her safety after reading about all the crime in their neighborhood.

They both laughed at Manuel's comment, and she began her walk as always, about four blocks, to hop on a local bus that took her to her job at the health clinic. She removed her headphones from her backpack, placed them on her head, and turned on her small transistor radio to a local popular music station. The volume was as high as possible to drown out street noises and horny men who spent their time whistling and sneering at women who passed them.

Before she reached the bus stop, she heard, through her headphones, someone yell, and then a woman screamed, followed by multiple gunshots coming from a house next to her on the same side of the street. The sounds were loud enough to drown out the music coming out of her radio. She stopped and hid behind a parked car for protection.

"What's going on? I am staying behind this car," Maria said to herself as she removed her headphones and stuffed them in her backpack.

"Let's go! Quick! Get out of here and jump in the truck. Make sure nobody is watching us. If you see any witnesses, don't think twice. Shoot them." Maria heard someone yelling from inside the house. Three men ran outside, rushed through the gate at the property entrance, stopped, looked up and down the street to confirm nobody saw them, and got inside a muddy black pickup truck waiting for them. The truck raced to the corner and disappeared when it turned left.

Maria saw their faces, close enough to describe them, and made a mental note of the license plate number of the pick-up truck. The three men and the vehicle driver did not see Maria hiding behind the parked car that protected her. Her medical training at the clinic forced her to rush through the door of the house without thinking if there was any danger inside. She found a family of five on the floor, executed with multiple bullet holes in the back of their heads and chests, including a young boy who could not have been older than six. There was blood splattered all over the inside of the house. She stood in shock for about 30 seconds, picked up the phone in the kitchen to call the police, ran outside, and vomited on the sidewalk. Her work at the clinic exposed her to some unpleasant bloody scenes, but never like what she had just witnessed. This picture would be engraved in her memory forever.

A police car was already stopping in front of the house while she was vomiting. In less than three minutes, a dozen police cars and emergency vehicles surrounded the property and blocked the street. Maria was taken to the police station to describe what happened and who she saw leaving the house.

Before the end of the day, the pick-up truck was found 15 miles outside of Guadalajara. The owner had reported the vehicle stolen that morning. A security camera recorded the robbery, providing photographic evidence of the murderers. The following day, Maria's description of the three men and driver was printed in the local newspapers. Her name, the only witness to the crime, was kept confidential in the press to avoid retaliation.

1990s   53

Maria's description and the video were instrumental. All four were arrested within a week and charged with murder. They were known to be part of a drug cartel that had established networks to sell drugs in the city and surrounding towns. Maria was asked to identify the three plus the driver in a lineup at the station and testify in court when the case went to trial. Since she was the only witness to the murder of five family members, and there was no other proof that the men committed the crime except for the video of the men stealing the get-away truck, her presence at the trial was significant for the prosecution.

The local cartel had connections at the police station and successfully got her name and contact information. That's when the local drug lord put a price on her head.

✧✧✧✧✧✧✧

Randy sat at the head of the table in the dining room and immediately called Stephen to share Sandra's note and Linda's letters.

"Stephen! You will not believe what I got in the mail today." Randy yelled to Stephen, who was still preparing dinner in the kitchen.

"Randy, if it is another piece of junk mail from the auto dealer we promised never to buy from again, please tear the postcard and throw it in the garbage. Don't bother showing it to me."

"No, Stephen. This is serious. I think I am a father!"

"I hate to tell you, Randy, but I would predict that is almost impossible. I don't recall having experienced any morning sickness or cramps." Stephen responded to Randy with a giggle.

"You are right, Stephen, 'almost impossible' but not 'totally impossible,'" assured Randy as he walked into the kitchen to be with Stephen. "Do you remember me telling you about the girl I was forced to take on a date to a drive-in movie to demonstrate my 'manhood' during my senior year in high school?" Stephen and Randy came out of the kitchen and into the dining room with serious looks on their faces.

"Yes, of course. How could I forget? You grossed me out!" Stephen had a confused look on his face.

"If I had refused, those idiot school bullies would beat me up."

"What does that have to do with what you got in today's mail?"

"Take a look and read for yourself." Randy handed Stephen the letter from Sandra and all the correspondence from Linda. Stephen's mouth was wide open after reading the first couple of letters, and both eyes bulged in their sockets.

"Randy, dinner will have to wait. This is more important." Stephen was stunned after reading a few of the letters.

They continued reading and analyzing the contents of Linda's letters to Sandra. They wished the corresponding responses from Sandra were included so they could learn more about both Sandra and Linda. Randy was shocked to know he was the father of a baby girl who was no longer a baby.

"Stephen, we need to hire a private investigator to help us locate Alice."

"Are you sure you want to meet her? You have no obligation, Randy."

"I want to know if she is alive and well. I don't think I want her to know I am her father. I don't know. I know I can't ignore these letters. I can't turn around and walk away", Randy explained in a desperate tone. "It doesn't seem fair for Alice. Knowing the identity of her father after all these years may be more damaging to her. Maybe not. Maybe just staying away is the answer. I still want to know if she is OK. We can decide if it's best to contact her or stay away after discovering more about her."

Randy and Stephen were both perplexed as to what should be their next step. They both agreed to keep this new surprise to themselves and hire a private investigator to find Alice. They decided to wait and make decisions about contacting Alice once they got more information from the PI. Randy only wanted to know now if she was alive and where she lived. He was unsure if he ever wanted to introduce himself to her as her father. He felt that if Alice had known about him, she would have tried to find and connect with him by now.

The following day, Randy and Stephen hire Dale Stratford, a private investigator from Hartford Randy's law firm had previously engaged. They gave him copies of the letter from Sandra and the correspondence from Linda. Dale assured them that if Alice were still alive, it would not be challenging to assemble her history and find where she was living, assuming she was still residing in the United States. Randy also asked for any information about Linda and Alice's past. Detective Stratford left their apartment satisfied and with a broad, happy smile. He knew he had just landed a good-paying, simple job.

✿ ✿ ✿ ✿ ✿ ✿

The drug lord had no choice but to prevent Maria from testifying, even if he had to murder her entire family. If there were no witnesses to identify the four drug runners to the crime, the judge would have to release them immediately.

News of the contract for Maria's head reached the detective in charge of the case. He contacted Maria and Manuel and ordered 24-hour surveillance at her home. The family was devastated. It was dangerous for anyone to leave the house. Manuel realized that even after the trial, Maria and the entire family were still in danger. Contracts like this usually had only one expiration date –the day the contract terms were executed. They could not believe it was time for the whole family to consider leaving Guadalajara and, perhaps, Mexico.

Their dreams were shattered. Her decision to offer a description of the murderers was morally the right thing to do, but a personal mistake that could not be reversed. Maria and Manuel had no choice but to leave the country. If they stayed and Maria testified in court, the local cartel would find an opportunity to hunt and execute the entire family like animals. Perhaps the cartel would not even wait for the trial. It was in their interest to eliminate Maria. The sooner, the better. The family's escape plans had to include Josefa. Manuel was also concerned for her safety.

Manuel and his mother-in-law, Josefa, had small savings accounts at a local bank. On Thursday, February 1st, 1990, late in the afternoon, just before the banks closed, Manuel and Josefa went to the bank with a police escort, closed both accounts and withdrew all their savings in cash. The following day, at about 1:00 AM, to avoid being noticed by the police officer in front guarding their home, Manuel and Maria, with their one-year-old daughter, Julia, and Maria's mother, Josefa, climbed over the rear cinderblock wall in their small backyard to a neighbor's property. They rushed through and hid inside their neighbor's car parked outside the front door.

Their neighbor drove them to San Luis Potosi, about five hours away, and left them at the Catedral Metropolitana, the local cathedral. They met Father Arturo Mendoza, who had a reputation for providing a safe space for Mexicans hunted by the drug cartel. Father Arturo ushered them to a secret windowless room in the church's basement and gave them food and water. They arranged with Father Arturo to hire a local parishioner willing to take the risk and drive them from San Luis Potosi to a friend's home in Nuevo Leon in the middle of the night. It would be a 6-hour drive, perhaps longer, if they had to use the back roads.

By noon on the same day, news of their escape began circulating in the police station. It only took one hour for the drug lord to learn of their escape and issued an increased reward for the murder of any Sanchez Family members, including one-year-old Julia. Anyone who provided refuge to them or helped them reach the border would also be killed. News of the bounty reached other drug lords at the Mexican/U.S. border. The local drug lord in San Luis Potosi came to see Father Arturo a few hours after the Sanchez family was escorted to the church's basement. He warned Father Arturo that he would be included in the contract if they found the Sanchez Family near Catedral Metropolitana.

At 11:00 PM, Father Arturo opened the basement door, and the family rushed into a small van waiting outside. All the rear seats were removed, and a pile of dark-colored blankets were neatly folded by the back door. Manolo, the driver, instructed them to get inside quickly, lay on the floor, and cover themselves with the blankets until they reached their friend's home in Nuevo Leon.

They arrived at their friend's home early in the morning and quickly hired Emilio Tedano, a local "coyote" with experience taking immigrants across the border into Texas. Payment to the drivers and Emilio came from the cash they withdrew before they left Guadalajara. That cash was beginning to dwindle.

Manuel's cousins lived in San Antonio, Texas. As soon as they crossed the border, they would try to reach Zapata, Texas, where his cousin would meet them and bring them home to San Antonio. Crossing the border meant finding a safe location to cross the Rio Grande. Emilio, the coyote, had experience and four paddleboards buried near the river's shore. The paddleboards were needed to get across the river. The difficulty was getting to Zapata on foot without being noticed by the U.S. border patrol. The second most challenging part of the trip was crossing the river in the middle of the night and lying flat on your stomach using your hands to paddle slowly across the river. Standing on the paddleboards or creating any wake would get them noticed and arrested.

"This is not going to be an easy crossing," explained Emilio after seeing Josefa and Julia. "I will have someone drive us as close to the paddleboards as possible. Reaching the river's shore on foot will still take two long nights. We cannot travel during daylight. We will find a place to hide and rest during the day."

Maria was concerned for Julia, who was only one year old, and Josefa, who was overweight and the oldest in the group. "My mother must stop more often and rest at night. I don't think she can walk all night. Julia is still very young and will have to stop more often."

"We must move quickly, or else we will be caught," Emilio emphasized again. "Rest periods will have to be kept at a minimum. I have a backpack in my car that is big enough for Julia to fit inside. It has two holes in the bottom for her legs and is wide open on top for her arms and head. She will fit in there comfortably. Manuel will have to carry Julia. You, Josefa, and I will carry a minimum food and water supply in the other three backpacks."

"What happens if we get injured or can't walk anymore unless we rest longer?" Josefa asked Emilio in a concerned voice.

"We will have to leave that person behind." Emilio's response was bold. "When we rest during the daytime, we must stay hidden in the forest under a layer of tree branches to avoid being seen. Once we cross the river, traveling in the dark may take another two days to reach a safe location. You can carry just enough food and water to last four or five days. Health bars are nutritional, filling, and lightweight in your backpacks. Be sure to bring enough of them. We are not going on a picnic, so don't bring forks, plates, or glasses. We will eat with our hands.

Manuel looked at Maria and Josefa. "It's going to be difficult with the baby. We risk everything if she makes a sound when the border patrols get near us. We'll have to control her; otherwise, our efforts will be wasted if caught."

The following day, just before sundown, Emilio is at the front door with an old SUV being driven by his brother, Benedicto. The Sanchez family and Emilio entered the old rusty automobile with heavily tinted windows. Benedicto drove to the highway toward the Rio Grande. About two hours later, they exited the highway. The van reached a dirt road and Benedicto turned off the headlights. A half-hour later, the SUV stopped. Emilio ordered the family to exit quickly with the supplies, and the van made a U-turn and raced back to the main road in the dark. It is almost 9:00 PM.

"Follow me—a single line. No talking. Listen and touch my shoulder if you hear anyone's voice. Do not make a sound." Ordered Emilio in a serious and militant tone.

The Coyote was at the head of the line. Behind him was Maria, followed by Josefa, and at the end of the line was Manuel carrying Julia on his back. The path was rough and uneven. It was 3:00 AM when Emilio made them stop for their second fifteen-minute rest. They still had about two more hours before the sun peeked through the horizon. That meant two more hours of walking in the dark. Seeing the ground was difficult because flashlights could not be turned on. Josefa had already twisted her ankle several times. Julia was sneezing and coughing more than usual. Manuel took her from the altered backpack and carried her in his arms.

A small splinter of daylight could be seen on the horizon through the lightly forested woods. Emilio stopped and selected a rest spot about 100 feet from the trail. They all gathered tree branches and created a small circular site where everyone could rest and be hidden from view by the foliage.

They heard voices. Another Coyote was walking on the trail with about a dozen crossers trying to reach the border. Emilio told everyone to stay behind the brush. He took out a gun from his backpack for protection. Maria was shocked to see a weapon next to her. The group passed, and they were safe.

As soon as the sun set, the Sanchez family, led by Emilio, continued its path to the river. At 1:00 AM, Julia began to cry. Manuel took her out of the backpack and felt she had a slight fever. He gave her as much water as she wanted and continued walking. Julia was now asleep and quiet inside the backpack.

It was almost 5:00 AM, and they reached the buried paddleboards and the shores of the Rio Grande. Manuel took Julia out of the backpack and noticed she was lethargic and not breathing. "Oh, my God. NO, NO, NO!" Manuel yelled out in an angry tone.

Emilio ran over to Manuel and realized Julia was not breathing. "Give her to me. I know what to do." He put her on the ground and began CPR. Maria was confused. She ran over to them and wanted to interfere. Manuel held her back. Even though she had medical training, Maria was not prepared to provide CPR to her daughter. Emilio seemed to know exactly what he needed to do to save Julia.

"Maria, I don't know what happened. She felt like she had a small fever a few hours ago. I gave her water, and she seemed fine before I put her back inside the backpack. I wrapped her in her blanket to ensure she was warm and comfortable." Manuel explained to Maria and Josefa.

Emilio continued CPR for almost 30 minutes as the family sat there watching, tears running down their cheeks and into the dry leaves resting on the ground. He stopped. "I am sorry, she is not responding." He covered his face with dirty hands and sobbed.

✧✧✧✧✧✧✧

Two small hand shovels inside the backpacks were to be used to dig out the paddleboards. They now had a second purpose, to dig a tiny grave for Julia. Manuel and Emilio picked a spot away from the trail and began to dig as the sun rose over the hills on the other side of the river. Maria and Josefa covered Julia's little body with her favorite blanket. The two women are holding each other, unable to stop crying. Maria has Julia's body on her chest. They walked over to the grave. Emilio and Manuel took Julia's body away from Maria, placed her slowly inside the grave, and covered her with dirt. Emilio raked the surface, leaving no markings for border patrol to notice. A morning none of them will ever forget. A burial site Maria, Manuel, and Josefa will, most likely, never be able to visit.

✧✧✧✧✧✧✧

On April 6th, 1990, there was a call for Randy at his law firm. Randy's secretary, Carol, interrupted his meeting with an associate.

"Mr. Jensen, there is someone for you on line two named Dale Stratford. He will not tell me the purpose of his call and demands to speak to you. Should I tell him you are in a meeting?"

"No, Carol. Transfer the call to me. Thank you," replied Randy. "Jim, I need to pick up this call. Let's continue this discussion later. Please close the door behind you.

As soon as the door closed, Randy picked up the phone. "Hi, Dale."

"Sorry to bother you at work, Randy. I have a preliminary report for you. I can stop by your apartment tonight, go over it together, and determine our next step, if there is one," suggested Dale.

"Yes, let's plan for 7:00 PM. Stephen should be home by that time," replied Randy.

✧✧✧✧✧✧✧

The same day Julia was buried, they crossed the Rio Grande at sundown in darkness and continued their journey on the Texas/USA side, through similar rough terrain. Josefa's ankle was swollen and wrapped in fabric ripped from the bottom of Manuel's t-shirt. They continued traveling at night, in darkness, resting during daylight under the brush. They finally reached Zapata, Texas, at 2:00 AM on the second night after crossing the river. Emilio brought them to a safe house to wait for Manuel's cousin from San Antonio, about three hours away, who would take them back to his house. It was time to say goodbye to Emilio.

"I am so sorry for your loss. I will never forget this journey." Tears were running down Emilio's face. His voice was quivering and challenging to understand. "I had a young daughter who died in my arms less than a year ago. She was very ill with cancer. I couldn't do anything to stop her suffering. Julia reminded me of how much I loved my daughter." Emilio wiped the tears away from his face with his jacket sleeve and left a streak of dirt across his face. "Hope you have a safe and successful journey to your final destination, wherever it ends." He hugged Josefa, Maria, and Manuel, turned towards the gate at the property entrance, and returned to Mexico.

There were about a dozen other immigrants in the safe house. There weren't enough chairs or beds for everyone. Manuel and Josefa found stale bread and coffee in the kitchen area. They sat on the floor in the corner of a room and stretched out with their eyes shut to wait for Manuel's cousin. In their minds, they revisited their experience during the past several days. Maria couldn't sleep and sat on the floor by the large picture window in the rear of the house. She stared outside and waited for the sunrise, which was beginning to show just over the cinderblock wall surrounding the property, protecting and hiding them from the outside world. She stared at the small, newly planted vegetable garden on this side of the wall to provide the food and nourishment needed for future immigrants crossing the border. The sunlight began to beam through the window and blanketed Maria with warmth. She was now blinded by the light piercing through the windowpanes. She did not move – she closed her eyes for a few seconds, then opened them again to stare at the garden. A small garden was expected to feed the heavy flow of hungry immigrants passing through this property.

Manuel got up, walked over to Maria, sat on the floor beside her, held her hands to his face, and they both quietly shed tears thinking about Julia. It is the start of another day without Julia, the beginning of their new life. It was time to start planning their own garden.

✿ ✿ ✿ ✿ ✿ ✿ ✿

Randy left his office at 6:30 PM and walked home. As he approached Bushnell Park, the odors from the exhaust of city buses turned into a refreshing early spring scent from the park. The tulips planted in the urns outside the entrance of his building have just blossomed. He always stopped to see the view from the lobby windows towards the Capitol building. It has changed overnight from a pure white snow theme to a lime green spring theme. Randy opens the door to his apartment, and Dale is already in the living room, sitting on one of the two club chairs facing the couch. On the coffee table, there are three copies of the report. Stephen is at the bar making drinks for everyone.

"Hi Randy, glad we were able to meet." Dale greeted Randy as Stephen delivered the drinks and sat beside Randy on the couch. "I just finished this preliminary report based on our discussions back in January. Before I do more research, I thought it was best to get updated so you can decide how you want me to proceed." Dale was nervous and anxious to report back to Randy. He was unsure how to begin. He stumbled in his speech pattern.

"Listen, Dale. Let me stop you for one second. Maybe we should first read your report, and then you can embellish more, and we can be more direct with our questions." Randy suggested when he saw that Dale stuttered and was unsure how to begin the meeting.

It didn't take long for Randy and Stephen to read the report. It started with Linda (Alice's mother) at Croft High School in Waterbury and ended with Alice, a single woman in her early 20s living in Essex, Connecticut. It also included newspaper clippings of real estate advertisements with a headshot of Alice. Clippings of Linda's parent's death in Waterbury, the automobile accident in Montpelier, Vermont, and a copy of the adoption papers when Aunt Eugenia adopted Alice.

"WOW! She is beautiful," commented Stephen while looking at the real estate ads.

"She has her father's genes," Randy replied with a quirky smile. Stephen and Dale laughed. "Why are you both laughing? It is true!"

After a few more minutes of re-reading sections of Dale's report, Stephen opened the conversation. "So, where do we go from here?"

"If you want to reach out to Alice," Dale suggested, "you have her address, home, and work phones. It should be easy to contact her. I can do that and plan for father and daughter to meet...."

"No." Randy interrupted Dale. "I have not decided if I should honor her mother's request for privacy or reach out to her. I need more time. Frankly, I was not expecting you to find her this easily, and to know that she is only a few miles away from us makes our decision more difficult."

"I fully understand, Randy," Dale held back. "You and Stephen should review and discuss this together. Call me if you have any questions. When you decide on the direction, I am happy to help you if you need me."

Dale got up from the chair and walked to the front door with Stephen and Randy behind him.

"Thank you, Dale, great job. We will keep you posted on our decision," Stephen told Dale as he closed the door.

Randy was overwhelmed and unable to gather his thoughts.

"Stephen, I think we need another drink before dinner." He walked back to the living room and stood in front of the window facing the State Capitol and the spring landscape of Bushnell Park, waiting for Stephen to bring their second cocktail.

"Randy, there is no reason to make any decisions tonight," suggested Stephen from the bar, "We can discuss it as much as you want but don't feel you have to decide the next step right away. Let it sit in your mind for as long as you need." Stephen returned to the living room to console Randy, who seemed frightened and had a scared look on his face. "Let's sit by the window and enjoy the view before dinner. We have nothing to worry about. This report shows that Alice is successful in her real estate business. She is beautiful. I don't know what her mother Linda looked like, but Alice has your look. Whatever you decide will be the right decision." Stephen was now trying to change the subject to get Randy's mind away from this issue temporarily. "How was work today?"

✧ ✧ ✧ ✧ ✧ ✧ ✧

Alice developed an excellent reputation within the southern Connecticut's real estate industry. In May 1996, Joe Edwards, an executive with Edwards Real Estate Development, became acquainted with Alice's standing in the business. He contacted her for an interview and offered her a position with the company to develop and manage a sales and marketing department for his company. Joe was the founder's son and was taking on more responsibilities in the company. The real estate market was booming in Connecticut, and Joe felt the company needed an aggressive sales force to market and sell properties they were developing.

Alice was very successful with Edwards R.E. Development, perhaps too successful. She fell in love and married Joe in the summer of 1998, two years after the job interview. In September 1998, Alice left the company and started her own real estate sales office in Old Lyme.

Just before they were married, Alice sat down with Joe and showed him her mother's shoebox and all the letters. "Since we are going to be married, and we should not keep any secrets between us, I think it is best that you read these letters. After you are done, let's discuss it, and tell me your thoughts."

"WOW!" Joe was visually stunned by its content. "I don't know what to say or ask."

"There is nothing to say or ask," Alice replied. "I have not tried to reach out to Randy Jensen. I don't even know where he lives or if he is still alive."

"Aren't you curious? Do you think he knows he has a daughter somewhere out there?" Inquired Joe.

"Yes, I am curious. Who wouldn't be curious after reading these letters? I don't know why my mother kept his name a secret from everyone, including me. I should follow her wishes. If he knew he had a daughter, I would assume he would try to find me and reach out."

"Alice, whatever your mother's reason was back in 1965 is irrelevant today. When we have children, they may want to know their grandfather, even if he is dead. You have no other relatives; I would like to meet him if he is still alive. I can't imagine he would not be interested in having a relationship with you!" Joe is trying to convince her to find her father and reach out to him. "What's the worst that can happen? You don't have to see him again if you don't like him. If you like him, you and our future family can develop a relationship with him. There is no downside to finding your father." Joe knows that the decision is up to Alice. He would respect whatever she decides to do.

"I hear you, Joe. Perhaps someday." Alice placed the letters back inside the shoebox and returned the box to the upper shelf of her closet.

Joe knew this was a sensitive topic for Alice and was unsure if he should continue to bring it up after their marriage.

✧ ✧ ✧ ✧ ✧ ✧ ✧

The Sanchez family stayed in San Antonio for only a few weeks. Maria's cousin, Pablo, lived with his wife and teenage son in Middletown, Connecticut. He offered to help relocate the Sanchez family to Middletown with some assistance from their local Catholic parish. He assured them that job opportunities were better in Connecticut, far from the Mexico/U.S. border. Manuel liked being as far away as possible from the drug cartel in Mexico.

Manuel, Maria, and Josefa agreed to relocate to Middletown. Manuel purchased a used car, and on April 7, 1990, the following day Randy and Stephen received the report from the PI, they left San Antonio on a new journey to Middletown, Connecticut. Once settled, they hired an attorney to help them apply for permanent residency in the United States.

Every day, Julia appeared in their minds. Maria grieved the loss of her first and only child every night before sleeping. Josefa was heartbroken to see Maria's look on her face whenever Julia's name came up during conversations. Manuel always felt responsible for Julia's death and carried a picture of her in his wallet. Years after Julia's death, Manuel continued to have nightmares.

CHAPTER 7

2OOO PLUS 1

Louise McCawley lived in a rent-controlled apartment with her mother, Mabel, on the Lower East Side of Manhattan and continued to work nearby at Windows on the World in the north tower of the World Trade Center. Management liked Louise because she was loyal, dependable, hardworking, honest, and dedicated. Unfortunately, she had a sharp tongue, a heavy Irish accent, and an endless vocabulary of four-letter words she used freely as adjectives. She was a *"no-nonsense, no-bullshit woman"* and not afraid to tell anyone to "fuck-off". Management appreciated her hard work, so any jobs assigned to her could not have direct contact with customers.

Mabel was a seamstress in Ireland. She married an American citizen in the early 1970s and moved to New York with Louise, a daughter from her previous marriage. After her second divorce in 1978, Mabel stayed home and worked on most of the alterations for a high-end men's clothing store in lower Manhattan. Working as a seamstress kept her busy for several hours daily, including weekends. The earnings were sufficient to cover rent, household, and most personal expenses (including her weekly Irish whiskey pint and cigarettes). Louise and Mabel lived very frugal lives in New York City. Mabel's divorce settlements were deposited in savings accounts, and whatever was left over at the end of the month from Louise's paychecks at Windows on the World was also deposited to their savings account.

Louise and Mabel considered leaving the hustle and bustle of Manhattan if they could replace their New York City incomes in the suburbs. She found a "For Sale" ad in the New York Times for a large laundromat in New London, Connecticut. It was further than she wanted, but she still called the number to learn more about the business. After a half hour on the phone, she arranged to meet the business broker in New London on September 11, 2001. That meant she had to arrange a day off from work and get an early train to Connecticut.

It was 6:00 AM on September 11, 2001, "Mom, I am leaving. Not sure what time I will be back from New London. I will call you before I get back on the train home," and Louise was out the door headed for the subway to take her to Penn Station and board an Amtrak train to New London. It was the 6:49 AM train going to Boston with several stops, including New London. She sat by the window and admired the change in scenery. It began with the dark tunnels of Penn Station and midtown Manhattan to the greener open spaces of the Connecticut coast. The train arrived in New London at 8:20 AM, and she was met by the broker, who took her to his office to review the business details before a physical site visit. They walked inside the office just before 9:00 AM and found everyone staring at the lobby's television set. The local news station showed video clips of a plane crashing into the north tower of the World Trade Center.

"Oh, my God! What the hell is going on? That's where I work. I would have been there today if I hadn't come to Connecticut. My friends and co-workers are there now. How the fuck are they going to get out?" Louise held her hands on her face and began to sob. "Oh, my God! This can't be happening. Who is the mother fucker responsible for this?"

A few minutes after nine, while she watched a news reporter interview a person who witnessed the crash, Louise saw another plane crashing into the south tower behind the reporter. She screams, "Oh my God, not again! I need to get home right away. My mother is home alone in lower Manhattan." By 10:30 AM, both towers had collapsed. She tried to call Mabel, but the phone lines were down. She was desperate, restless, and physically shaken at the broker's office. She contacted a friend in the East Village and asked her to walk to her apartment and ensure Mabel was safe. All train service to and from Manhattan ceased.

Louise cannot return home until service is restored. Mabel was safe and alone in the apartment.

It took a few days for Louise to get home to Mabel. She stayed in a local hotel in New London near the laundromat and spent the time investigating and researching the laundromat business. She sat at a bus stop bench across the street and watched all the activity going in and out of the laundromat. Those few days in New London gave her time to grieve the loss of her co-workers who died in the North Tower and consider the business venture. She was anxious for a departure from Manhattan. The attack on the World Trade Center and the eventual collapse of both towers convinced her it was time to leave New York. It would take little to persuade her mother, Mabel.

The space the laundromat occupied was leased from an investor/landlord who owned the adjoining retail storefront and four apartments on the second floor above both businesses. Before returning to Manhattan, she arranged to meet him the following Saturday morning at her hotel lobby.

"Hi, you must be Louise. My name is Randy Jenson. I own the real estate where the laundromat you are considering purchasing is located."

"Oh, Hi, Mr. Jenson. I'm Louise McCawley."

After the brief meeting at the hotel, they walked over to the property, and Randy showed Louise a two-bedroom apartment above the laundromat available for rent. "This is the perfect setup for my mother and me. The laundromat has sufficient space to set up a small tailor shop where Mom can continue her alterations business, and we can live upstairs in the apartment." The owner of the business was asking for a fair price. The rent for the apartment was less than her rent control apartment in Manhattan. It seemed like an easy decision to make.

Louise finally returned home to the Lower East Side. The streets were empty and had a new distinct odor of burnt rubber everywhere you turned. The buildings and the neighborhood had different personalities from what she remembered before her trip to New London. She was finally at home, but no longer did it feel like home. She walked inside the apartment and immediately reviewed the business details and her strategy with Mabel. It was easy to convince her. Both were excited to enter this new venture, but more importantly, they were thrilled to leave New York. Louise made a low offer for the business, and after some minor negotiations, a counteroffer was accepted. She contacted Randy, who agreed to a standard five-year lease for the laundromat space and the apartment above.

On Thanksgiving day of 2001, Louise visited the remains of the World Trade Center tragedy. She prayed at the corner of Greenwich Street and Vesey Street, walked over to Saint Peter's Roman Catholic Church on Church and Barclay Streets, and left a dozen roses at the altar in memory of her co-workers. She cried all the way back to her apartment.

On December 1st, 2001, Louise and Mabel closed the door of their rent control apartment on the Lower East Side and left for Connecticut in a 1998 Toyota Corolla Louise purchased in New London.

"We are ready to leave this dump, Mom. I thought I would never see the day! Let's pray we're making a wise decision." Louise got inside her car and drove away. A small moving truck with their belongings, including Mabel's sewing equipment and supplies, followed them to New London.

✿✿✿✿✿✿✿

Randy and Stephen started investing in commercial real estate in coastal towns between New Haven and Stonington, Connecticut. On January 1st, 2002, they hired a real estate managing firm, AJR Investment Management, to oversee the properties and collect the rent so they could remove themselves from some of the responsibilities of owning commercial property. The firm was managed by one of the three owners, Ross Thomas.

The collapse of the World Trade Center towers in New York City forced many to re-evaluate their priorities, including Randy and Stephen. For many years, they considered owning a second home to escape Hartford on weekends. They usually rented in different parts of New England during the summer months, including the New Hampshire and Vermont mountains, Ogunquit (Maine), Provincetown (Massachusetts), and the Connecticut coast. Their favorite location and most accessible commute from Hartford was the southeastern coast of Connecticut.

In early March 2002, Stephen contacted Ross at AJR Investment Management for a residential real estate agent recommendation. He gave them the contact information for Alice Edwards, part owner of AJR Investment Management, with her husband, Joe.

Stephen contacted Alice and gave her the parameters of what they wanted to purchase. By the end of the week, Alice called Stephen, and they agreed to meet on Saturday morning at her office in Old Lyme.

While waiting to see Alice in her office, Randy grabbed Stephen by his elbow and dragged him to the rear of the reception room to show him an advertisement display hung on the wall. "Stephen, do you know who this woman is? Alice Edwards is Alice Peterson!"

Stephen is puzzled. "Who the fuck is Alice Peterson?"

"My daughter! Don't you remember Dale's report? Edwards must be her married name. I didn't know she got married. Why would I know? I haven't been following her. Please take a close look at her photograph. It's the same photograph in the real estate ad Dale Stratford brought to our house several years ago. I still have it at home."

"Oh! FUCK! Are you sure?" Stephen responded in a desperate, low voice, so the receptionist did not hear him.

"Positive."

"I think you're right, Randy. I didn't put two and two together when I spoke with her on the phone. What are we going to do? We can't leave now. She knows we're here."

"Play dumb. Don't introduce me by my last name. Introduce me as Randolph." Randy, fearing exposing himself inadvertently as Alice's father, began to sweat in the lobby as they waited for Alice.

"Hi, Stephen. Sorry for the delay. Great to meet you in person." Alice entered the waiting room with a huge smile and a friendly voice.

"Hi Alice, this is my partner, Rand...olf." He almost used 'Randy.'

"Pleasure to meet you, Randolph. Before we head out to look at properties, I thought I would show you, in our conference room, the various listings we will see today." Alice began her sales pitch for each property they were going to visit. She didn't connect Randolph with Randy Jensen. Stephen had difficulties referring to Randy as Randolph. His last name was left out of the conversation with Alice.

Alice drove them to see properties in Old Lyme, Chester, Essex, and Old Saybrook. The last stop was a property in Lyme, close to Alice's office just north of Old Lyme. "I waited to show you this property because it has everything you wanted, four beds, three and a half baths, an attached 3-car garage, large windows for sunlight, privacy, a new kitchen, and many other great features you did not have on your list," Alice explained as they walked in through the front door. "By the way, the barn at the north end of the property has a large guest room with a galley kitchen and a full bathroom. You can use it as a guest room, office, or art studio. The large window facing the back yard has a great view of the property."

Randy and Stephen felt they had found their weekend home. It fits their needs, and the price was in their range. They were almost ready to make an offer, but Alice made a comment that forced them to reconsider. "Oh, just for full disclosure, I represent the current owners and live next door with my husband, Joe. We have been here since we got married in 1998. We both love the neighborhood. Our property line is about midway through the woods on the other side of the barn. You can barely see our house. We are quiet and promise to be good neighbors if you decide this home is for you."

Alice drove them back to her office, where Randy and Stephen left their car. "Thank you, Alice, the best house was the last one you showed us. Let us think about it, and we will contact you soon." Stephen nervously explained to Alice.

"Yes, if you like it and want to make an offer, please do so as soon as possible. There have been many showings on this property recently, and I would hate to see you lose it." Alice warned them with the typical realtor comment when a client hesitates to make an offer.

They shook hands. Randy and Stephen walked to their car and drove away before either of them said one word. "Well, that was a close call. Her last comment about the danger of losing it if we don't make an offer is a typical standard realtor's warning." Stephen explains to Randy.

"Yes, it is a standard warning, but it's true. We can't assume nobody is interested in the property," replied Randy. After a few minutes of silence, enjoying the Connecticut country views from the front seat of Stephen's car, Randy revisits the discussion about the house. "Stephen, I think you are on the same page as me. I want that house. I don't care that she lives next door. They live far enough from the house, and perhaps having her next door may be ideal if I tell her I am her father someday."

"That day will be awkward! Don't worry, Randy. We'll call her when we get to Harford and make an offer," Stephen assures Randy.

✧ ✧ ✧ ✧ ✧ ✧ ✧

They arrived home, and as soon as they got settled, Stephen picked up the phone and called Alice to make an offer on the house.

"This is great, Stephen. You will love your weekends in Lyme. I need some information to complete the offer. Will you and Randolph hold title to the property jointly?" Alice inquires.

"Yes"

"I don't have Randolph's last name."

Stephen hesitates and stumbles on the phone. "Yes, of course. His last name is Jensen."

"Jensen. J-E-N-S-E-N. Jensen?" Alice wrote it down and looked at the name carefully. She said to herself. *"Why is this name familiar?"*

"Yes, that is correct. The home address for Randolph is the same as mine."

"Got it. You must send me a check for ten percent of the offer amount. I will call the current owners with your verbal offer and see where we go." Alice told Stephen as she looked at Randolph's name again and again. She still wondered why it sounded familiar. She continued writing the offer and forgot about the name 'Jensen.'

✧✧✧✧✧✧✧

Manuel Sanchez always considered himself an entrepreneur. He dreamed of owning his own business, and now, after escaping the drug cartel in Mexico, he felt he should pursue his dream. When he arrived in Middletown, he worked for a landscaping company owned by a neighbor. Two years after settling in Middletown, he purchased the lawn maintenance equipment from his neighbor and the client list. He leased an abandoned gas station outside Middletown with an empty oversized garage to store the equipment. He invested in new, efficient commercial lawnmowers, hired a new crew to work with him, and slowly built a successful business. He turned the abandoned gas station and the adjacent space into a retail garden center.

After five years, the garden center business was booming, his client list for grounds maintenance tripled, and he expanded his retail operations to a large tent in the rear parking lot.

✧✧✧✧✧✧✧

It was the middle of June 2002 when Randy and Stephen received the title to their weekend home. They took a week off from work to spend time in Lyme and get settled. Their three-acre property would need someone to maintain the landscape. During that first week, Randy was driving down Hamburg Rd and saw a pick-up truck with a trailer parked on the road. The trailer had a sign that read "Manny's Landscape and Maintenance." He took down the telephone number and called the company when he got home. Randy agreed to meet with Manuel Sanchez, the business owner, the following day.

When Manuel arrived, Randy toured the property with him, and Manuel quickly gave him an estimate to maintain the lawn. Randy accepted. The two acted like they had been best friends since birth. Randy offered Manuel all the lawn mowing equipment in the barn for free if he had one of his workers empty and clean the barn. The equipment was left in the barn by the previous owner. Manuel called the supervisor assigned to this area, and the barn was emptied by the end of the day.

Twelve years after arriving in the United States, Manuel was still experiencing nightmares from their border crossing. He can't forget the morning he noticed Julia was not breathing. Whenever he couldn't sleep at night, he would sit in a chair by the window and stare at the outside world for hours. Maria tried to encourage him to seek help, but he always refused.

His new business occupied most of his time and kept his mind from thinking about Julia. Maria finished her nursing studies, became a registered nurse, and got a job at Middlesex Hospital in Middletown. Josefa maintains the household and bakes desserts she sells to a well-known local Mexican restaurant. She also managed the rental portion of the three-family home Manuel and Maria purchased several years ago. Josefa developed the art of collecting rent from the tenants. She was efficient and rugged. She trained the two apartment dwellers to pay their rent by noon on the first of the month. Otherwise, she was at their doorstep knocking on the door.

Manuel and Maria tried very hard to have another child. They placed enormous pressure on themselves but were unsuccessful for many years. They considered fertility drugs, but Manuel didn't want chemicals to be part of the process. Maria had a medical background and was willing to try, but she respected Manuel's decision. They continued trying until their dream came true on April 10th, 2003. Maria gave birth to a healthy seven-pound, eight-ounce baby boy. They named him Enrique after Manuel's late father. Finally, Maria and Manuel were both filled with love.

✿ ✿ ✿ ✿ ✿ ✿ ✿

The day after purchasing their new weekend home, Randy and Stephen considered hiring an interior designer to help them furnish the house. Alice, who had wondered where she had seen Randy's last name, gave them contact information for three local designers to interview. They met with all three and hired Josh Brickell, whose recent renovation projects matched Randy and Stephen's taste. Josh spent time with them during the summer, picking furniture and paint colors for the interior. The last furniture delivery arrived for the guest rooms just before Thanksgiving weekend. The house, including the guest suite in the barn, was declared fully furnished and decorated.

Since their weekend home was ready to show off to friends, it was time to invite some of them from Hartford for Thanksgiving. Randy and Stephen invited two couples from Hartford and Josh, the interior designer, and his partner, Jose, for Thanksgiving dinner. That weekend's snowfall kept the Hartford friends there all weekend. They enjoyed the fireplace with earlier-than-normal happy-hour cocktails and plenty of turkey leftovers. The winter views from the large windows in the family room kept everyone engaged with nature.

The New York Times was delivered and spread all over the floor. Some guests picked up books from the bookshelves in the library adjacent to the family room and read; others watched videos rented at the video store before the storm. It was a continuous snowfall. The blanket of snow provided a magical winter scene to stare at, reflect on the past, and plan for the future. There was plenty of food, alcohol, conversations, and laughs—no reason to venture out on the road.

✧ ✧ ✧ ✧ ✧ ✧ ✧

On March 4th, 2004, after trying for several years, Alice and Joe finally became parents. Alice delivered a boy, and they named him Maxwell, after Joe's father.

Alice spent several weeks at home after the birth of their first child. Shortly after Max was born, she hired a nanny, set up a small home office, and eventually returned to work selling real estate. Her work hours were flexible enough to give her time to spend with her newborn baby boy.

Three years later, another baby. This time it's a girl, Dana. Max was only three years old, and now another newborn was in the Edwards household. Alice insisted on a full-time nanny until they were old enough to attend school. If Alice and Joe had an event to attend on a night the nanny was off work, Stephen and Randy, their next-door neighbors, volunteered to babysit for them.

PART TWO

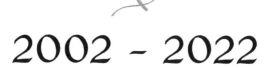

CHAPTER 8

2002 – 2022

The collapse of the World Trade Center towers was a horrible shock and a wake-up call. Everyone was concerned for their safety and the future of the country. The event forced many, including Stephen and Randy, to concentrate more on their investment strategies and retirement plans. Stephen and Randy wanted to be financially comfortable and retire to their home in Lyme when they reached 65. They decided to shift a significant portion of their investments toward commercial real estate in southeastern Connecticut. AJR Property Management was already successfully managing a few buildings they already owned, so any new property they purchased was assigned to Ross at AJR. They achieved their personal investment goals and sold half of their real estate holdings. In 2012, shortly after their 65th birthday and eleven years after the terrorist attack on the WTC, they both retired from their full-time jobs, sold their condominium in Hartford, and moved to their home in Lyme full-time.

Between 2002 and 2022, twenty years, there were many changes in their lives. Randy's two brothers died from heart ailments. His father died from a sudden stroke, and his mother died from breast cancer two years after his father's death. Randy did not have a close relationship with his two older brothers. Nieces and nephews were also distant. During the same time, Stephen's parents were diagnosed with cancer. He didn't have siblings, so he felt responsible for their care. They still lived alone in the same house Stephen grew up in, so Stephen was concerned about their well-being and made weekly overnight trips to visit them in Hull, Massachusetts. Depending on the traffic, it would take him three to five hours each way. Eventually, he convinced them to move into an assisted living facility close to their hometown, where they would get 24-hour care if needed and remain close to their roots and friends. They both died in 2015, within six months of each other.

In 2019, Randy suffered a mild stroke during a Fourth of July barbeque with friends in their backyard. Stephen immediately got him to the hospital, and he underwent a quadruple bypass. Movement on his left side was partially impaired after the stroke. He was released from the hospital and spent two weeks in a rehab center before returning home. On good days, Randy could get around the house without any help. On other days, he required assistance with a walker or a wheelchair. Stephen's health was excellent for his age. After his annual checkups, he was proud to hang the doctor's report on the refrigerator door.

✧ ✧ ✧ ✧ ✧ ✧ ✧

Louise and Mabel were still running the laundromat and tailor shop in New London. Four years after they purchased the business, they hired two women to help them manage the operation and help Mabel in the tailor shop since she was getting close to 90 years old and could not be left alone in the laundromat. Now that Louise had more free time, she wanted to expand her income sources and began a house cleaning business. She also wanted to get out more and have other contacts besides the laundromat and her mother. In less than a year, she obtained several housecleaning assignments that kept her busy 4-6 hours a day, five days a week.

When Randy and Stephen retired in 2012, they hired Louise to clean their house twice a week for four hours each time. Louise became very close to Randy and Stephen, and they were always there for each other. When Randy had difficulties getting around the house due to the stroke, Louise was there to help him. She became the "sister" Randy and Stephen never had. They treated each other like family.

✿✿✿✿✿✿✿

After Alice showed Joe her mother's shoebox and the letters from Sandra, she hid the box in her closet and refused to think about the contents. When she met Randy and Stephen, she had not connected Randolph or Randy Jensen to the 'Randy Jensen' in Sandra's letter to her mother. She assumed that if her father were still alive, he would try to find her and reach out if he was interested in connecting. It was not a priority for her. She considered Joe, Max, and Dana her priority. Joe would not pressure her to find out if her father was still alive. He thought of the letters often but never discussed the issue with Alice because he knew how Alice would respond.

During a rainy mid-afternoon on the last Saturday in January 2020, the roof at the Edwards' home developed a small leak, and water got inside the attic and into Alice's closet. The roof was repaired the following day, but the closet had to be emptied because the walls needed new plaster and fresh paint after the leak. Alice's clothing was moved to either Joe's closet or a clothing rack Alice purchased at the hardware store next to her office. Other items in boxes were stacked in the corner of the bedroom until the closet repairs were completed and painted.

When the closet was emptied, Alice looked at the boxes. *"Oh, my God, there is that shoebox with my mother's belongings. I have not seen that in 20 years."* Alice found her mother's shoebox partially damaged from the water leakage. She opened it and looked through the costume jewelry, newspaper articles, and the bundle of letters from her mother's girlfriend. Most of it was soaked but not wholly damaged. *"I remember the day I opened this shoebox at Aunt Eugenia's bedroom in Vermont."* She continued to talk to herself as she opened the letters again to dry them on a towel she placed on the floor. She began to reread some of the letters.

"I can't believe what I'm reading! Oh no, this can't be true. I never made the connection. How stupid am I?" She runs downstairs to find Joe.

"Joe, you have to come upstairs quickly." She was trying not to show urgency to avoid Max and Dana's interest. When they arrived at their bedroom, Alice closed the door behind her. "Look at this letter. Look at the name Sandra refers to as my father."

"WOW! Are you sure it's the same person I'm thinking about? Why didn't we make this connection sooner? I remember reading this letter before we got married, but I also didn't make the connection when you introduced me to Randy and Stephen."

"Yes, I'm certain it's the same person. Randy never mentioned where he went to high school. He would always say that it was an experience he did not want to recall. Here is their yearbook. This is Randy's graduation picture. He still looks the same!" Alice is pacing back and forth in their bedroom.

"What are you going to do now?" Joe looked at Alice and tried to calm her down.

"I don't know. I need to think about this. Maybe nothing. Please help me out, Joe. What should I do?" Alice continued to be emotional and desperately searching for options.

"Now is not the time to make that decision. Let the letters dry on the towel, and let's go downstairs. It's time for our Sunday cocktails. Max and Dana plan to watch a football game in the family room in a few minutes. You and I will sit outside wearing our parkas and holding a cocktail to discuss it further. By then, you will be calmer and more rational." Joe calms her down as he always does.

They sat outside on their terrace and ate the jalapeño stuffed olives from the bottom of their empty martini glasses. Alice looked at Joe and said, "I'm not going to do anything, Joe. Let's wait and see what happens. I don't think Randy knows I'm his daughter. Let's wait. I imagine he would have said something to me if he knew I was his daughter. Maybe not. What do you think, Joe? Should I approach him? How do I do that? All I have is questions and no answers. It sounds like I'm thoroughly confused. Maybe it's the martini."

"I think it's the jalapeño inside the olives causing you to be irrational." Joe laughs as he bites down on his second stuffed olive. "You don't have to do anything, Alice. Wait. Time is on your side.

✧ ✧ ✧ ✧ ✧ ✧ ✧

It was an early evening in April 2022. The skies were clear and beginning to darken. The full moon exposed itself early through the trunks of the tall pine trees and partially lit the leafy ground cover on a wooded path that became the shortcut to and from the Edwards' home. The aroma of pine needles was all around the path. The breeze from the north made the branches sway as it chilled the air and created a more aromatic scent. The trail was carved between the two properties through the pine trees, rhododendrons, and arborvitaes planted within twenty-five feet of the property line. It was created by years of footsteps from the two households going to and from each other's homes. After sunset, the darkness made it difficult to see the uneven ground where large boulders and tree roots, hidden under the leaves, became a hazard for walking in the dark. The full moon that night was insufficient lighting to make the shortcut safe without a flashlight. There was also an occasional bear sighting. Confronting a bear in the path was not something anyone desired.

Stephen was returning home after having dinner with Alice and Joe at their home. Max, their 18-year-old son, was at work at Chester Marina. He arrived home just as Stephen was ready to leave. Dana, their 15-year-old daughter, was attending a school rally. On his way home, Stephen took the same shortcut through the small path between the two properties. Randy always reminded Stephen to bring a flashlight and his mobile phone whenever they visited the Edwards in the evening. Stephen didn't hear him this time before leaving the house and forgot to carry his mobile phone and flashlight. He had difficulties getting through the rough terrain – afraid to fall, hurt himself, and unable to call for help.

"I don't want to hear Randy bitch if I fall and get hurt. Who the hell is going to hear me scream while I'm on the ground struggling? I may have to spend the night here if I fall," Stephen was frustrated and talked to himself as he got near the end of the path.

He finally arrived home safely without injuries. He walked over to the family room and saw Randy sitting in his wheelchair facing the rear window towards the garden. "Randy, I'm home! You didn't remind me to bring the flashlight and mobile phone. I almost fell halfway through the goddamn pathway. It's very dark without a flashlight, even with a full moon. Actually, I was more concerned about confronting a bear than falling." Stephen is getting ready to sit next to Randy.

"Randy, let me turn the floodlight on so you can see the work Enrique started in the perennial beds." Stephen reaches for the outdoor light switch and turns it on. "There, that's better." Stephen did not hear any response from Randy. He walked over to the bar and poured two scotches on the rocks. He placed them both on the small table with two coasters between the wheelchair and a wing chair.

"Dinner with Alice and Joe was wonderful. They missed you very much. Max and Dana were not at home, so it was just the three of us. It was a quiet dinner; you would have enjoyed their company. They are both excellent cooks." Stephen was searching to make small talk with Randy. "The perennial beds are all cleaned up, Randy. Enrique split many overgrown perennials and moved them to the new sections he had created. We are scheduled for a delivery of ornamental dogwood and cherry trees tomorrow, including two plum trees." Stephen continued to update Randy on what was happening in the garden. He saw Randy look outside, then turn and look at him. Randy had no comment, only a brief smile on the right side of his face.

"Randy, I know this will be difficult for you, but we need to talk about it now that we are both in our 70s. Unfortunately, we will not live forever, and I don't want us to take any secrets to our graves." Stephen started a discussion he knew would be difficult for Randy to engage. "It's time to tell Alice you're her father. Whenever I see Alice, I feel uncomfortable knowing about your relationship with her and not being upfront and disclosing it." Stephen saw Randy staring at the perennial beds outside. "I can take the lead on this discussion with Alice. I think she would be pleased and proud to be your daughter. Just think of the response from Max and Dana. They will know their grandfathers during their lifetime." There was still no response from Randy. Stephen felt awkward and continued to stare, with Randy, at the perennial beds with an empty glass of scotch. Randy's glass was still full. Most of his ice had melted again by this time.

The mysterious silence in the room continued for at least a half hour. Without saying a word, Stephen got out of the chair and made himself another drink. It is almost 11:00 PM. He left the full glass at the bar and went to bed. Before leaving the room, he looked at the wheelchair, noticed Randy was not there, and assumed he had gone to bed alone.

✿ ✿ ✿ ✿ ✿ ✿ ✿

The following morning, the alarm clock awakened Stephen. He rolled out of bed and dragged himself to the bathroom for a splash of water on his face and hair. As usual, he walked to his closet and found his gym clothes and sneakers on a shelf. He approached the family room and saw the empty wheelchair by the window, a glass filled to the top next to it, and another full glass on the bar. *"Oh, Randy must still be in bed,"* he commented to himself.

Carefully going down the basement stairs to his home gym, he turned on the television set to watch the local news while he still tried to focus his sleepy eyes. He looked at the treadmill for a few seconds and reluctantly began his thirty-minute fast walk, followed by another thirty minutes of stretching and weight training. He realized he was getting bored with his exercise routine and considered hiring a personal trainer to help him revise his daily workout program. *"Where will I find someone that will come here at 7:00 AM? Maybe an online trainer. I won't have to give him coffee. Maybe I can find one on the internet?"* Stephen was happy to have a small research project during his morning coffee.

When he finished his daily workout routine, he returned upstairs and turned on the coffee pot to brew an entire pot. *"It's early April and warm enough to enjoy the fresh spring air,"* he went outside, talking to himself and humming some of his favorite operatic arias. He wiped down the small table and chairs on the patio by the kitchen door and left his tablet and an empty coffee mug on the table. Back inside, still humming arias, he grabbed a thermos, filled it with coffee, and returned outside with a small container of skim milk. He was having difficulties connecting to the Wi-Fi network on the patio, so he quickly gave up on his research for an online personal trainer. As he finished his first cup of coffee, Max walked around the corner of the garage and met Stephen on the back patio.

"Hi, Mr. Porter." Max is surprised to see Stephen sitting outside. He was expecting him inside the house where the temperature was warmer. Max visited Stephen because his father encouraged him to stop by periodically and ask if he could do anything for him around the house. Sometimes, all Stephen wanted was a short conversation with another adult.

"Oh, Hi, Max. Please call me Stephen from now on."

"Oh, OK. Sorry," Max replied in a surprised tone. He always referred to Stephen and Randy as Mr. Porter and Mr. Jensen. "I wasn't sure you were awake, but I wanted to stop by and let you know that I have some free time on weekends until school is out. If there is anything I can do to help you around the house, I hope you will call on me. I'm happy to help you in any way I can." Stephen was surprised by Max's generous offer.

"Thank you very much, Max. That is very nice of you. I appreciate it very much. Would you like to sit with me and share this large thermos of coffee?"

"That would be great, Mr.... I mean, Stephen,"

"Please, do me a favor and go inside the kitchen. There are several coffee mugs in the cabinet above the coffee maker. Please bring two with you. Enrique will be here shortly. There is more skim milk in the refrigerator if you think what is here will not be enough for you and Enrique. You might as well bring the skim milk out."

Max's eyes opened up when Stephen mentioned Enrique's name. *"Enrique is on his way? Perhaps I will finally meet him,"* Max told himself while he searched for coffee mugs in the kitchen cabinet.

Max walked back outside with two mugs and a container of skim milk and sat with Stephen. They sat together and were silent for a few seconds, admiring the spring air and cool temperature. "Looks like you're planning to expand the perennial beds, Stephen. I can see them from my bedroom window. They are looking great."

"Yes, Enrique is helping me this year. He is very talented and creative. Have you ever met Enrique?" Stephen looked at Max. He expected Max to say 'yes.'

"No, I don't think I have ever met him. Is that the guy who fixed your mailbox last year?" Max knew Enrique by name only. He wanted Stephen to think he didn't know him. Max was confident Enrique was the same person he had seen working on Stephen's property several times.

'Yes, that's the same person. He is a wonderful, strong, and hardworking guy."

"Yes, he looks like a hard worker." Max was concerned that his words would make Stephen think he was a voyeur. "I have seen him around your property, occasionally, when I'm mowing our lawn. It's great to have someone like Enrique helping you in the garden."

"So, tell me, Max, what's going on with your life these days? We never get a chance to sit and talk as neighbors. Do you remember when you were younger? Randy and I would occasionally babysit you and Dana when your parents had to attend an event on the days your nanny was off. Times have changed. Look at you today. You're grown up and no longer a child." Stephen wants to make Max comfortable and talk about himself.

"Yes, I remember you and Randy at our house trying to play with us and exhaust us so we would get tired and go to bed." Max chuckles as he recollects those evenings with Randy and Stephen.

"Oh, yes, I remember also. We would also get tired and fall asleep on the couch until your parents arrived," Stephen confessed to Max.

"Now that I'm older, life is different. I'm very busy with schoolwork, swimming practice, the gym in school, and my wish list of books to read. I'm amazed I still find time to surf on the internet, watch some television or sit, look out the window, and do nothing but meditate." Max was embarrassed to disclose to Stephen the meditation portion of his activities.

" Sitting and looking out of the window is a healthy exercise. As I get older, I tend to do a lot of it. When I stare out the window, I like to reflect on the past, my wonderful life with Randy, the mistakes I made in life, but more importantly, think about how lucky I am to be alive and here." Stephen became sentimental and looked over to the garden beds.

"How did you and Randy meet?" Max did not realize he would get a long-winded history of their life in Boston at Harvard and Boston Universities. Halfway through Stephen's story, Enrique walks around the garage and sees Stephen and Max.

"Oh, hi, Enrique. Did you ever meet my neighbor Max?" Stephen was excited to make this introduction.

"No, I haven't." Enrique quickly responded to Stephen. He now turns towards Max and looks into his eyes. "Hi, Max. I have seen you occasionally, mowing your lawn or washing your car when I work here for Mr. Porter."

"Sit and have a cup of coffee, Enrique. You and Max should get to know each other more." Stephen was beginning to sound like a matchmaker. "Max, you should see some of Enrique's art. A selection of his work is displayed at a gallery in Chester."

"I work at Chester Marina after school a few days a week. I would love to stop by and see it someday."

"Maybe we can stop after work for pizza across the street from the gallery and then walk over to tour the gallery." Enrique just found an excuse to spend time with Max alone.

Enrique and Max exchanged contact information and agreed to meet later this week after work. Stephen has a smile on his face and is pleased that he introduced new friends.

✧ ✧ ✧ ✧ ✧ ✧ ✧

Louise raced up Hamburg Road and turned into Stephen's driveway without slowing down. Now, she is leaving behind a trail of dust from the gravel in the driveway and suddenly stops next to Enrique's pickup truck. Today is her day to clean the house. Her car is parked on the side of the garage, where Stephen, Max, and Enrique can see her dented front fender. As she exits her vehicle, she waves at the three of them. "Good morning, gentlemen!" Her morning greeting was louder than the voice of a square dance caller at the Iowa State Fair. Loud enough for the neighbors to hear her. Louise walked into the house and began her usual routine. The first thing she sees is the wheelchair in the family room. She stopped, looked at it briefly, and brought it to the garage.

Still outside having coffee, Stephen excuses himself. "Well, guys, I must go inside and shower. Enrique, why don't you show Max the birdhouses you put up last summer? They are all occupied."

"Yes, of course. Oh, by the way, Mr. Porter, I have the trees you ordered in the back of the pick-up truck," Enrique informs Stephen.

"Enrique, please call me Stephen," he corrected Enrique the same way he corrected Max. "Maybe you can ask Max to give you a hand unloading the trees. I'm too old to help you."

"I'm happy to help you, Enrique, but first, let's go and look at the birdhouses; I'm curious about what you have done with them." Max offered to help without Enrique asking.

Stephen walked into the garage through the patio door. He was going to take the garbage pails to the street and suddenly realized it was a different date than the scheduled date for garbage pickup. He didn't understand his confusion. Before he entered the house, he saw Randy's wheelchair at the opposite end, next to the Jaguar. He shook his head and continued inside the house.

"Goddam, Louise must have moved the wheelchair again," Stephen whispered to himself but left it there.

Enrique and Max walked over to the back of the perennial gardens to examine about a dozen birdhouses Enrique had nailed on tall posts. You can hear the birds chirping, flying in and out of each tiny house, and bringing back food for the ones that have just hatched or straw to create new nests.

"Max, did you know the newborns leave the nest eight to twelve days after hatching? Most of them stay at least ten days before flying off.... When you buy or build a birdhouse, the wood must be untreated, with holes on the sides for ventilation and a few on the bottom for drainage. You must also provide protection to keep out raccoons, snakes, and other predators. Birds are attracted to birdhouses because they need shelter and protection.... The number of eggs a bird can lay ranges from one up to fifteen or sixteen.... You can identify the bird by looking at the egg's size and color." Enrique lectured Max as they walked around the birdhouses. Max was impressed by his knowledge and passion for the outdoors.

Max quickly realized that Enrique had done his homework on bird nests. He continued his "Show & Tell" lecture and dragged Max into the woods behind Stephen's property. It is a 120-acre lot donated by one of Stephen's neighbors to the Lyme Land Conservation Trust a few years ago.

"Max, have you ever walked around this property? It's a wonderful nature preserve. The wildlife is awesome. I've learned so much sitting under a tree and studying the wildlife around me. You should try it." Enrique pointed to the trees and showed Max where other birds had created nests. They continued walking about 250 feet deep into the nature preserve. They were both surrounded by nothing but trees. Total privacy, no houses in sight, no street noises, nobody could see them. All they could hear was the sound of their shoes crushing leaves that fell from the trees last Fall. They also listened to the distant noises created by the wildlife. They stop to look at a large nest high on a tree. "It must be a hawk's nest." Enrique pointed out to Max as he got closer behind him.

Max was admiring the hawk and its nest, while Enrique was admiring Max's body. He stood behind him and stared at Max from his toes to his buttocks to his neck and hair. He got close enough to smell Max's wavy blonde hair partially hidden under his baseball cap. Max did not notice. Enrique touched Max's shoulder and told him he had to get back and unload the truck. He had other deliveries scheduled for the morning.

They both returned to Enrique's truck, unloaded the new trees, and agreed to meet sometime this week for pizza and a tour of the art gallery in Chester.

"It was nice to meet you finally, Max. I enjoyed our walk together and look forward to seeing you again later this week. Thank you for helping me unload the trees," Enrique told Max from the cab of his pickup truck with a broad smile showcasing his ivory-white teeth.

"Yes, same here, Enrique." Max noticed Enrique's smile again. *"Why would he say 'finally'?"* He asked himself several times as Enrique's pickup truck left Stephen's driveway.

Alice was leaving her house, walking towards her car. She saw Max standing still in Stephen's driveway, staring at Enrique's truck driving away. She questioned whether Enrique's friendship was good for Max, they were both very different, and perhaps Enrique's influence may change Max's goals for college and law school. She didn't want to judge and restrict Max's friendships but was concerned that friends with different goals and perspectives could revise Max's plans.

Alice met Enrique and his father, Manual, at a mutual client's home a year ago. She knew their business had an excellent reputation in the county but felt that Enrique was quiet, acted strangely, and was not friendly. Alice didn't understand his behavior.

Dana was in her room on the second floor, texting her girlfriend. She looked out the window and saw Max and Enrique unloading the pickup truck. She also saw her mother looking at Max while he stared at Enrique's truck turning onto Hamburg Road. Dana has two friends in school who identify as gay. Since the beginning of the school year, she had suspected that Max might be gay but would not discuss her suspicion with anyone.

Dana and Alice could not hear Max and Enrique's conversation.

CHAPTER 9

EXPECTATIONS

Enrique was scheduled to deliver about a dozen shrubs, two dozen assorted perennials, and six cherry trees to Chester Marina a few days after meeting with Max at Stephen's backyard. He remembered Max saying he worked there after school and was determined to find him after all the plants were unloaded. Enrique walked around the marina on his own. He didn't see Max, so he ventured to the main dock. Max was at the end trying to install new navigational equipment in a 60-foot motor yacht. He saw Enrique walking towards him, yelled out to him, and waved.

"What are you doing here? How did you get past the security gate?" Max questioned Enrique in a friendly tone.

"I asked the dockmaster if you were working today. He just pointed in this direction and let me inside." Enrique was happy and excited that he had found Max. "I just delivered a truck full of plants for the front garden renovation here at the marina and remembered you said you worked here after school, so I thought I would stop by and say hello and see if you want to join me for pizza tomorrow, Saturday night. We could go to the gallery afterward for the tour I had promised you of my artwork hanging there now." Enrique submissively explained to Max.

"Yes, that would be great." Max looked at his calendar on his mobile phone and scheduled 'Dinner w/ Enrique.' Enrique smiled and showed those gleaming white teeth to Max. "I get out of here at 6:00 PM tomorrow. Should I meet you at the restaurant around 6:15 PM? Does that work for you?

"I have a few deliveries scheduled for Chester on Saturday, so I will do those at the end of the day and then meet you there at that time." Enrique was ecstatic to arrange some private time with Max. He didn't want Max to notice his excitement.

"Hey, have you ever been inside one of these large yachts?

"No, they are a bit out of my price range." Enrique was shy about admitting it.

"Well then, take your shoes off, and welcome aboard. I'll give you a quick tour while my boss does some errands in town." Max reached out to grab Enrique's hand and help him come on board. He noticed Enrique's strong arms and his long fingers. "I'm trying to install new navigational equipment for a customer, but I'm having difficulties understanding the installation instructions. I need a few minutes away from it, so I'm glad you're here. Let me take you down and show you the interior space." Max led the way down a few narrow steps and showed Enrique the interior salon with a galley, sitting, and dining areas. "Oh, the berths and head are down this hallway – that's a marine term for beds and bathroom. Follow me," Max purposely stood against the doorway to the primary berth and motioned for Enrique to enter the room. "It's a bit snug down here. You're thin. You can squeeze in." Enrique placed his left hand on Max's waist; Max had his left hand on Enrique's right shoulder as he squeezed between the doorway and Max's body. He got through, but not without slowly rubbing Max's torso. Both faces came close enough to feel each other's breath.

"WOW! This is beautiful, Max. It's a small space, but it looks very efficient. I could sleep here very easily."

"Yes, I could also," Max replied in a low voice.

"I would love to be financially successful to afford a yacht like this one. I would live in it all year round!" Enrique was excited to see the inside of a large yacht.

"You would have to take it down south for the winter; otherwise, you will freeze your ass off – unless you have someone to keep you warm." Max smiled at his comment. Enrique looked at him, and they both laughed.

"Yes, I know what you mean. I get it. Perhaps the money is better spent on other things. I'm sure the maintenance costs for this yacht are outrageous." Enrique realized that his dream of owning a yacht this large might be overreaching. "Maybe I'll concentrate on a house and a new car first." They both laughed.

"You don't want to know the maintenance cost of operating this yacht, Enrique. You'll get depressed. Let's get back upstairs before we get caught snooping around." Max was behind Enrique. His back came close to Max's face as they climbed up a few steps from the cabin. Max stared at his bubble butt. It was evident that Enrique worked out a lot at a gym. His buttocks were as round as a beachball. He knew the workout routine needed to achieve that look.

After spending a few more minutes talking on the dock, Enrique left after confirming their dinner date and gallery tour tomorrow night.

✿ ✿ ✿ ✿ ✿ ✿

After he visited with Max, Enrique finished his deliveries and drove to the garden center as his father requested. Manuel had an appointment in Madison and didn't want to leave the employees in the retail shop unsupervised. Enrique knows that his father never liked leaving the retail shop unless a family member was there to supervise the employees and ensure there was no inventory theft. When Enrique arrived at the garden center, Manuel left for his Madison appointment.

The garden center business was growing every year. During the spring months, the traffic in the retail store was always chaotic. After a cold and snowy winter season, everyone was eager to plant and work on improving their gardens. It was now getting close to 5:00 PM. Only a handful of customers stood by the register, waiting to pay for their purchases. The rest of the center was empty. Enrique began to lock up and helped the last customers load their cars.

He arrived home with a big smile because he felt he had experienced a productive day seeing Max in the afternoon. He was also anxious to meet him for dinner tomorrow night. Maria greeted him in the kitchen. She noticed his jubilant mood.

"Enrique, what did you do today to make you so happy?" Maria noticed Enrique's cheerful mood.

"Nothing special, Mami. It was just a great day. Everything happened as planned," Enrique replied to his mother. His trip to Chester Marina was successful when he finally found Max and arranged to meet for pizza and a tour of his artwork tomorrow. He did leave out the details of his meeting with Max and the date with him tomorrow night when his mother wanted to know more about his day.

"What did you have planned? I hope it wasn't something deceitful."

"No, Mami, I didn't rob a bank today." Enrique laughed.

Abuela Josefa intersected the conversation between Maria and Enrique. "Enrique, go in the bathroom and clean up before your father gets home. I'm serving dinner as soon as he arrives," Josefa liked to control the timing for everyone to sit together at the dinner table. That's what Manuel insisted.

Maria just got home before Enrique. She was exhausted because she worked an extra half-shift at the hospital every day this week. As soon as she arrived home, she looked inside each pot and oven to see what her mother had prepared. Manuel was expected to arrive soon from Madison.

Enrique showered quickly, put on a pair of cotton sweatpants and a T-shirt, and went to his small bedroom in the rear of their first-floor apartment. He looked in his closet to choose what to wear for his dinner date with Max. Unable to find his black jeans, he returned to the kitchen and asked his grandmother. "Abuela, did you wash my black jeans recently?"

"Si, mi amor. They are in the dryer. They should be dry by now."

"Gracias, Abuelita." Enrique runs down to the basement and brings his black jeans and everything else in the dryer to the apartment.

He selected his favorite tight-fitting short-sleeved white shirt, folded the shirt and jeans neatly, and placed them inside his gym bag with a clean towel and toiletries. Since he was not driving home tomorrow evening after completing the last delivery, he would have to shower and change from his work clothes to his "date-with-Max" clothes at a recently joined gym in Chester. Coincidentally, Max was doing the same after he got home from work.

Manuel arrived home from his trip to Madison. He asked Enrique for the closing sales figures and the cash deposit he always takes to the bank in the mornings on his way to the garden center. Enrique knew the process well and was prepared with all the numbers. They indicated a sharp increase in sales from the previous year. Manuel hoped that this year, the retail side of the business would significantly improve over last year.

It was time for dinner. Manuel always felt dinner with the family was an important event at night and insisted that everyone ate at the same time unless it was a school night for Enrique or other important events that would prevent them from being together at home. Tonight, Manuel started a conversation explaining why he made a trip to Madison.

"I went to see the landlord that owns the land and building at the garden center. He plans to sell it. I knew this day would come, but I never knew when. I hoped he would hold on to it for a couple more years until we got more established and creditworthy for a mortgage. He wants to sell it to me at a reasonable price, but I need to find a bank or private investor to give me a mortgage. The bank that holds the mortgage for this house and all the cash accounts for the business has refused. They claimed that we are over-leveraged. They are idiots. They don't know what they are talking about. I wouldn't need their mortgage if I had the personal equity they require. That seems to be always the same excuse for these ultra-conservative banks. They are unwilling to take any risk, but they will charge you more than market rate interest, depending on how dark your skin looks to them." Maria, Josefa, and Enrique could see that Manuel was distraught. He continued criticizing the banking industry throughout most of the dinner. "Perhaps if I were born here in this country or did not look like a Mexican, it would be easier for me to get a mortgage."

Manuel hoped Enrique would carefully listen to his words and learn the difficulties of running a business. He believed business was affected mainly by outside sources, almost always beyond the business owner's interest and control.

"The landlord has a couple of interested buyers who plan to tear down the building and build a small shopping center with about a dozen retail stores and commercial offices on the second floor. He prefers to sell the property to us but can't wait forever. He plans to move to Florida and wants to liquidate his real estate portfolio for his retirement. I have to act fast and find a bank to give me a mortgage. If I can't find a mortgage, we will have to move if we can find a suitable location or close the business." It was difficult for Manuel to say, 'Close the business.' "I'm going to continue searching for a lender. I can't imagine a local bank would not be interested."

"Papi, I don't know what to do to help you find a mortgage, but if there is anything I can do, you should tell me. We should be working together." Enrique felt helpless and didn't know how to help his father.

"I will take care of the problem. There is no reason for everyone to worry about it. You can help, Enrique, by ensuring our sales numbers steadily increase, and our expenses are controlled." Manuel changed the conversation since he had Enrique's attention. He was now focused on the importance of family and continuing their tradition. Manuel had been telling Enrique to settle down, start dating seriously, and find a wife who would give him children. He wanted to retire someday and give Enrique the garden center and landscape business. It was upsetting for Enrique every time his father raised the subject. This time, he mentioned his friend Roberto and his daughter Myra. She was the same age as Enrique and attended the same community college.

"Roberto tells me that Myra keeps asking about you. Have you called her? She is brilliant. Someday, when you own the business, she or someone like her can help you run it."

"Papi, don't try to fix me up with Myra. She is very nice, but I don't want to date her. I'm not ready to get married. You always bring this up, and my response is the same. I want to study and earn enough money to have my apartment. I need to be able to support myself before considering supporting anyone else. Besides, I'm nineteen years old. I will be twenty soon and old enough to make my own decisions." Enrique was upset by his father's constant pressure to get married and raise a family. He was also concerned about obtaining a mortgage so the business could continue in its current location.

"You can't live by yourself the rest of your life. You need to get married and raise a family." Manuel was persistent. He didn't want to end the discussion. Maria and Josefa sat quietly at the table and did not participate.

Enrique finished his dinner, picked up the dishes, and placed them in the dishwasher. He was upset by the dinner conversation and angry at his father. Manuel continued his lecture on raising a family while Enrique excused himself to finish his homework. He went to his room and closed the door behind him.

✿✿✿✿✿✿✿

Max obtained permission from his boss to leave work half an hour earlier than his scheduled time. He had his backpack in the car with his jeans, a tight-fitting t-shirt, a towel, shower gel, and hair product. He drove to the gym he joined when he started working at Chester Marina and walked into the men's locker room, where he undressed, got his towel and shower gel, and entered the open shower room. It was quiet at the gym. A late Saturday afternoon, about two hours before closing. There was one other person in the shower room. Max walks over to a showerhead across from the person already showering and facing the wall. He turned the shower knob to full strength and faced the other person. He looked up, and his jaw dropped when he saw Enrique standing in front of him, about eight feet away, completely naked, under a spray of steamy hot water.

"Oh," Enrique was speechless to see Max naked, "I didn't know you were a member here." Enrique began to lather his upper body.

"Yes, I joined a few months ago. I usually use the gym at school, but sometimes I like coming here after work. It's close to the marina." Max was embarrassed to look at Enrique's naked body, so he turned to look over his head or to the left towards the entrance.

"You have a great body, Max. It's obvious you work out a lot." Enrique stared at Max's penis and buttocks when Max was not looking at him. "Now that I know you're a member here, maybe we can work out together. I could use some help."

"I don't think you need my help, Enrique. You look great." Max was flustered to tell Enrique he looked great but needed to return the compliment. "I'm on the swimming team at school. The practice sessions are usually two hours. My entire body is sore when I get out of the water. Swimming is a great workout. It tones many muscles that a standard gym workout usually does not affect. I stay away from the gym the day after swimming practice. My poor body needs a rest. You should consider swimming as part of your routine."

While Enrique and Max lathered their mostly hairless bodies, they continued with casual conversation. Since no one else was in the shower room, Enrique pumped more gel from his bottle, grabbed his uncircumcised penis, pushed the skin back, and lathered the head. His penis got hard, so he looked toward Max to see if he was looking back at him. Max did notice but pretended he was not looking and faced the entrance to the shower room. From the corner of his eye, he noticed that Enrique had turned his body with his back facing him, giving him time to look at his butt. Enrique took more shower gel in his hand and inserted it between his butt cheeks. He quickly turned around and found Max staring at him with a semi-hard penis. Enrique's penis was now fully erect, throbbing, and covered in soap suds. He pumped more gel on his hand and spread it again on his penis and scrotum.

Max sensed a competition between them, so he lathered his penis, rubbed the head with more gel, and squeezed his testicles while he looked at Enrique. Max's penis was now fully erect and throbbing also. If he continued stroking it, he would have an orgasm in the shower room. He was flustered by how quickly his penis grew and hardened. He felt out of control and faced the wall, turned the shower knob to the 'cold' position, and tried not to look or think about Enrique. After a minute under cold water, his penis subsided but remained long and semi-hard. Enrique is still lathering his penis while looking at Max's back. He continued talking and hoped Max would face him so he could get a better look at his entire body. Max rinsed off, turned around, and faced Enrique as he dragged his ten fingers through his hair and casually flexed his biceps and six-pack to impress Enrique. Max left the shower room with a smile on his face to dry off and get dressed.

He faced his locker while slipping on his tight-fitting designer boxer briefs. Enrique walked in with only a towel wrapped around his neck. Max could hear his penis slap his thighs at each step he took toward his locker.

"Those are great boxer briefs, Max. Are they comfortable?"

"Yes, very much."

"I usually wear low-rise bikini briefs. I find them to be the most comfortable for me. I guess everyone has different comfort levels," Enrique replied, staring at Max's front bulge on his pure white, tight-fitting boxer briefs where the head of his penis was clearly outlined.

"I change over to a jockstrap when wearing gym shorts." Max continued the underwear conversation with Enrique.

"Yes, I do too. Here you go," Enrique threw a G-string jock strap from his gym bag to Max. "This is the style I like to wear under my gym shorts."

Max didn't know what to do with Enrique's jockstrap. It looked like something a male stripper would wear at a strip club. The snap on the side made it easy and quick to remove from your body and throw to the crowd of screaming women or, perhaps, men. He held it up, examined it, and threw it back at him.

"Oh, don't be frightened. The jockstrap was clean," Enrique assures Max.

"I wasn't frightened. I didn't plan on catching a flying jockstrap." They both laughed, got dressed, and left the gym.

"Max, why don't you leave your car here and we can go together in my pickup? There is limited parking in the center of town, and your car should be safe here in this shopping center." Enrique found a way to have Max ride with him to the restaurant. He knew the plan would give him more time to spend with Max.

"Yes, that's a good idea. Let me throw my backpack in the trunk of my car." He walked to his car and dropped off his backpack while Enrique got in his pickup and drove to meet Max at his vehicle.

"WOW! This pickup truck is great. Did you just run it through the car wash?" Max was impressed by the cleanliness of the truck. "I didn't notice your truck when we met at Stephen's house the other day."

"I usually clean it a few times a week. The garden and landscape business can be muddy at times. I wanted to be sure it was clean for tonight.

"Well, I'm impressed. Glad we went in your pickup. My car is not as clean as this." Max confessed in an apologetic tone.

At the restaurant, they both sat outside at a private table. They each took turns talking about themselves and their families. Max was saddened to learn about Enrique's family's troubles in Mexico and why they left their country. Enrique was emotional when he talked about a sister he had never met, who died during their escape to the United States. Max opened up about his family. His mother never knew her father and how her mother died in Vermont. He explained to Enrique that he had no cousins, aunts, or uncles and had never met his grandparents. They both shared their future goals. Max wanted to go to Harvard and eventually become a lawyer. Enrique wasn't sure because his finances were limited. He wanted an apartment, college, and, hopefully, to own a business. He told Max that he felt obligated to work with his father. He was not convinced he wanted to inherit the business. He would never disclose this to his father. It would crush him.

"Let's move on and go to the gallery before they close," Enrique suggested as the waiter dropped the bill on the table. They both split the check.

"So, how long have you been painting?" Max inquired as they crossed the street towards the gallery.

"Practically all my life, but professionally since my junior year in high school. I was enjoying my art class in high school, and my art teacher took a special interest in me." Enrique stopped for a moment to think about what he was saying. "That's another story for another day." He pauses again to think about what he just told Max. He didn't want to explain his comment any further. He was frightened that his relationship with his high school art teacher would come out during their chat. "I paint in the basement of my house. It's not the perfect setup, but I have the space and privacy I like and need. Living at home with both parents and a grandmother is not easy. My bedroom is so small that two people would not fit inside."

"Hi, Margaret. This is Max, a friend of mine. I wanted to show him your gallery and my work. Did anything sell since I was here last week?"

"Glad you're here, Enrique. I just got off the phone with a customer interested in one of your paintings. If they purchase it, that is the second painting I sold for you this week!" The gallery owner, Margaret, was excited to share the news with Enrique.

"That's terrific. WOW! Let me know if you need me to speak with them. I'm happy to meet them at the gallery when they are here." Enrique was very accommodating. He knew what had to be done to sell a painting.

They walked over to the back of the gallery where Enrique's paintings were hung. "Max, everything on this wall, all six paintings, are mine. I wonder which two are, hopefully, sold." Max admired the paintings while Enrique gave him a brief interpretation of each. He was impressed by his impressionist style. He liked the way Enrique used his brushstrokes to show an impression of form and unblended color with a noticeable emphasis on the location of the light.

"Enrique, this may be a dumb question, but how did you develop your style?"

"Oh, it's not a dumb question. Sometimes I ask myself the same. I guess after a few years of painting different subjects, admiring most of the old masters' works I find on the internet, practicing on canvasses or anything that will accept my paint, and paying attention not just to the critics but to my soul, I have come to develop my style. It's fair to say that I have *'evolved'* over the years. That's very cliché to say, but it is true. I look at some of my work from last year or two years ago and see a significant difference in my style. I love the work of impressionist artists. I try to emulate their brush stroke. I enjoy painting with bright colors and tend to do many landscape scenes. I also enjoy painting the human figure. Finding models who will pose for me in my basement is difficult. I don't have the financial resources to pay for professional models, so I do a lot of my work from photographs I find online. Perhaps I can convince you to model for me. I want to experiment with painting nudes. How about it? Want to pose?"

"Oh, I don't know about posing nude," Max responded sheepishly.

"I'm beginning to sound like I'm eighty years old. I'm nineteen. How old are you, Max?"

"I just turned eighteen a couple of months ago. I'll be nineteen next year."

"Max, we're both young and full of dreams." Enrique looked out the window towards the sculpture garden behind the gallery. Max follows his eyes to the exact location, a beautiful full-body bronze sculpture of a naked man sitting on a bench in the middle of the garden. "That piece must be new," Enrique commented as he stared at the sculpture and the garden. "I've never seen it here before. It's beautiful. I would love to meet the artist. Every time I come here and look through this window towards the courtyard, I see a different view. Sometimes, nothing changes, but what I see is different."

They both examine the nude sculpture in silence. Max decides to break the stillness. "I'm impressed by how much you do. You work with your father at the garden center, study part-time at the community college, create art, and in your spare time, you go to the gym. You must get up very early in the morning."

"Yes, I have to get up early. Otherwise, I couldn't accomplish all the things I wanted in life. I also like to meditate, relax, and sit by myself, staring out my window at home or from the bed of my pickup truck. I enjoy staring at the landscape. It responds to me and often guides me. I know it sounds corny, but it is important to me. It re-energizes my batteries." Enrique was a bit embarrassed that he had exposed himself this deeply. He felt comfortable with Max and shared private moments he never discussed with anyone, including his family. "I'm embarrassed to tell you so much about my personal life, Max. I hope I'm not boring you this quickly."

"Don't be embarrassed. We are getting to know each other. Today, we've seen more of each other physically than originally planned." Max chuckled at his comment. Enrique looked at him and smiled gently.

Max tells Enrique about his meditation routine. "Yes, I enjoy meditating also. I have a beanbag chair in my room in front of a large picture window. Before I start with my homework or a book I'm reading, I sit there and look outside for at least twenty minutes. I get many questions answered by staring at the landscape. Every time I look, I get different views. It's a routine that's important to me."

There was silence for a few seconds, and suddenly Enrique looked at Max. "Let's get in my pickup truck. There's a place nearby I want you to see." They leave the gallery, run to Enrique's pickup, and drive away.

"A dirt road nearby will bring us to the shore of the Connecticut River. I usually come here with my lunch while working in this area." The road came to an end. They both got out and walked fifty feet to the banks of the Connecticut River and sat on a vast boulder partially submerged in the water.

"The view is terrific from here." Max was impressed Enrique found this great location. "It's also very private. Are we allowed to be here? Who owns this property?"

"The town of Chester owns it. Not too many people know about this place. Sometimes, residents will be parked here enjoying a meal on the shore during lunch hour or in the early evening. I like coming at this hour. I'm always alone, and nobody is around to bother me while I meditate." Enrique stares at Max's eyes and Max does the same. He placed his arms around Max's shoulder and brought his head closer. He kissed him gently on the lips. Max did not pull back. Enrique stopped, looked into Max's eyes, and kissed him again briefly. He used his hands to caress Max's face and kissed him more passionately for the third time. This time, he tenderly licked Max's lips with his tongue.

Max gently grabbed Enrique's hands and slowly made him stop. "I think we should get back to my car. It is getting late, and I have to get up early in the morning."

"Oh, OK." Enrique was embarrassed that he had forced himself on Max. They both got inside the pickup truck to return to Max's car. "I hope you don't think I'm a creep. I kissed you because I like you and hope we can get together again."

"I enjoyed spending time with you tonight. Thank you for the tour of your artwork." Max was looking at Enrique as he was driving.

They were getting close to Max's car, and both felt awkward. When they reached Max's car at the gym's parking lot, Enrique turned toward Max, "Will I get to see you again?" Enrique was afraid he pushed himself too hard and too quickly.

"Yes, I hope we do," Max placed his hands on Enrique's knee and brushed his hands up his groin. Enrique could feel the warmth and comfort of Max's hand on his penis through his black jeans. Before leaving, Max leaned over to kiss Enrique with the same affection and passion Enrique gave him at the shore of the Connecticut River. Max left the pickup truck, got in his car, and drove away. Enrique drove out of the parking lot behind Max, smiling and overwhelmed by how well their evening had ended.

✿ ✿ ✿ ✿ ✿ ✿

Max arrived home after his date with Enrique to find Dana in the family room, watching a video. She looked at Max and asked him about his date.

"What makes you think I was on a date? You're so nosey. Why don't you stick to your own business? I don't act like a detective behind your back, so stay away from mine." Max lectures Dana with a smile on his face.

"Well, my dear brother. Take a good look at yourself in the mirror. You're wearing your favorite 'slutty' outfit, your hair has too much gel, and you never come in at this hour with a big smile. I can smell your cologne all the way here. I smell two different colognes. You got too close to your date or decided to wear two different brands." Dana delivered her assessment of Max's look without losing a beat. "So, did you get lucky tonight, Max? It certainly looks like you did."

"Oh, God. Please guide me. What should I do with my dear sister? She needs to get a life." Max was surprised at how obvious he looked to Dana. "If you spent less time being the detective, perhaps you would have been out today on a date instead of at home watching stupid movies." Max goes into the living room to say goodnight to Joe and Alice. They are enjoying a Saturday night glass of wine and the verbal exchange between Max and Dana.

"Mom and Dad, does she belong to this family? I think she was adopted. Where did she come from?" Max jokingly questions if Dana is part of the family.

"I love you too, Max." Dana had the last word.

Max walked over to his room and closed the door behind him. He sat on his beanbag chair in the dark, looking out to the backyard wearing only his tight boxer briefs. He pulled them down, exposed his penis, and stroked it until he had an orgasm on his chest and stomach. He thought of Enrique in the showers at the gym while rubbing his cum all over his chest and squeezing the last drop from the head of his penis.

✧ ✧ ✧ ✧ ✧ ✧ ✧

Enrique had a bit longer ride home. It started to rain just as he got home. Abuelita Josefa was still awake watching her Spanish novelas on television. Manuel and Maria were in their bedroom.

"Mijo, you missed dinner. I left a plate of food for you in the oven. Are you hungry?" Josefa was concerned that Enrique did not get a meal tonight.

"Gracias, Abuela, I ate out with a friend tonight. I'm full.

"Nobody told me you were not going to be here for dinner tonight. I wish I had known. Anyways, the food will be good for tomorrow." Josefa was very close with Enrique. Losing her only grandchild, Julia, over twenty years ago was a brutal blow to her. She knows his father struggled with depression and didn't want Enrique to follow him.

Enrique walked into his tiny bedroom, closed the door, turned the lights off, and looked out the window to see the reflection of the street traffic shining on the wet pavement. He undressed, sat on the edge of his bed facing the window, leaned back, and masturbated while he thought of Max and his vision of Max in the showers at the gym. He climaxed on his thigh and pinched his nipples with his left hand.

Just before midnight, Enrique sent Max a text message.

ENRIQUE: Hey, I had a great time tonight.
MAX: Yes. Me too. Thanks for the gallery tour.
MAX: BTW, Do you smell like you're wearing two colognes?
ENRIQUE: ????????
MAX: Never mind, I'll explain another time. Good night.
ENRIQUE: Good night. Let's plan to get together again soon.
MAX: Yes. I would like that very much.

CHAPTER 10

PREPARATION

The Edwards family enjoyed dinner at home the night after Max's date with Enrique. Joe and Alice expressed concern about Stephen's ability to maintain the house. "Max, you should stop by and visit with Stephen periodically," Joe knows that Max and Stephen get along well. "Ask him if he needs help with anything around the house or if you can pick up something at the shopping center. We should be good neighbors and look out for each other."

"Yes, Dad. I've stopped several times. I'll knock on his door tomorrow before I go to school and ask if he needs anything I can pick up when I return in the afternoon after swimming practice. He's usually up early in the morning."

"Max, we didn't get a chance to talk last night when you got home. Where did you go?" Alice was anxious to ask Max but did not want to be overly inquisitive. "You got home late."

"Nowhere special. I met a friend after work, and we went for pizza." Max didn't want his family to know he had dinner with Enrique. "I left you a note that I wasn't coming home for dinner. Did you get it?"

"Yes, I did. Thank you, Max."

"He must have had a serious date because he was dressed very nicely when he got home. He wasn't wearing his work clothes, so he must have changed somewhere." Dana is still curious about Max's date last night. She continued teasing him, hoping he would disclose something new she didn't know.

"Dana, why are you so preoccupied with everyone's whereabouts? You need to change your outlook." Max responded to Dana after her comment, hoping the conversation about his date would end.

"Dana, if Max wants to tell us more, he will. Mind your own business. You're not the house detective." Joe lectured Dana.

"Oh, I know everything that is going on in this household. Nothing escapes me – watch out!" Dana was making fun of Max and her father's comment.

"Well, bravo for you, Mrs. Columbo!" Max was now making fun of Dana by associating her with the wife of the television detective she watches constantly. "You will be a lonely old woman if you continue spying on others. Nobody will ever ask you out, and you will spend the rest of your life watching old detective movies."

✧✧✧✧✧✧✧

On his way to school the following Monday, Max stopped at Stephen's home and knocked on the front door. There was no response. He walked around the house towards the backyard. Before he got to the patio, he heard someone talking. He sees Stephen standing next to a wheelchair having a conversation with himself. Max backed away so Stephen couldn't see him and called out his name. "Stephen! Are you in the backyard?" He let Stephen see him entering the patio. "I knocked on your front door, but there was no answer. I thought you would be back here with your coffee."

"Oh, Hi, Max. Good morning. Sorry, I was out here enjoying the early spring stages of the garden and didn't hear your knock. Do you want some coffee?"

"Thank you, but I'll pass. I have to get to school. I stopped by to ask if you need anything from the shopping center. I can pick it up for you on my way back from swimming practice this afternoon."

"That's very kind of you, but I'm OK. I need to get out of the house more often. Louise is coming to clean today, so I'll go out for a stroll when she is here."

"OK. You have my phone number, so don't hesitate to call or text me if you need anything." Max noticed that there were two mugs of coffee on the patio table. One was empty, and the other was next to the wheelchair and full. He turned around, returned to his car, and left for school. He couldn't get the thought of the empty wheelchair and a full mug of coffee next to it out of his mind.

Stephen waited to hear Max's car pull out of the driveway. He turned towards Randy and the perennial beds. "Randy, if you're too cold on the patio, we can go inside. I just wanted you to see the garden from the patio." He pushed the wheelchair inside the house through the kitchen door and parked it in the family room, facing the picture window and the garden. "Your chair is by the window, Randy, whenever you're ready to sit and relax. Let me know if you need anything. Louise is coming today to clean. I need to leave the house for a while and do some errands. You'll be safe with Louise. She won't bother you."

✿ ✿ ✿ ✿ ✿ ✿ ✿

Stephen heard Louise's car as soon as she turned into the driveway. He was in the bedroom getting dressed for a shopping center trip.

"Mr. Stephen, it's me, Louise. I'm here." The sound of her voice ricocheted all over the house.

"Hi, Louise. I'm in the bedroom, getting ready to go out for a few hours. There's coffee in the thermos for you. I'll be out in a few minutes.

"No rush. I'll have some coffee before I get started." Louise poured herself a cup of coffee, walked to the family room, and saw the wheelchair by the window. "Why does he keep dragging this damn wheelchair out of the garage?" She asked herself as she dragged it out of the family room again and moved it to the garage. She was back in the kitchen drinking her coffee when Stephen walked in.

"Good morning! Perhaps I'll join you for another cup before I leave." Stephen always enjoyed people stopping in for visits. Louise was the exception. He liked leaving the house when Louise was there because she talked too loud and too much, distracting her from her job. Today, Stephen was in the mood to converse with anyone, even Louise.

"You had company out on the patio this morning?" Louise asked in a questioning tone.

"Why do you ask?" Stephen now feels Louise is being nosey.

"I picked up two mugs of coffee, and one was still full."

"Oh, yes. Max stopped by before going to school."

Louise wonders why Max would stop for coffee and never touch it.

✩ ✩ ✩ ✩ ✩ ✩ ✩

Max arrived at school confused after his brief encounter with Stephen. He saw his best friend, Ashley, in front of her locker. Ashley has known Max since first grade at Lyme Elementary School. They had always been best friends but never romantically involved. There was a strong bond between them that nobody understood. When Ashley's parents got divorced during her first year in high school, Max was there to help her and listen to her. She was an only child, and Max filled the role of her brother. When Max questioned his sexuality at the end of his sophomore year, he approached Ashley and came out to her. She was there to listen to and love him as if he was her brother. Max did not want to come out publicly. She was his best friend, and he knew she would keep the secret until he was ready. Whenever someone asked her out on a date, she would get Max's approval before agreeing to go out. She trusted Max and his opinion. Their relationship was built on respect, friendship, love, and trust.

Ashley was a beautiful girl. The boys were not attracted to her during her first two years in high school. She was intelligent and friendly, her hair was tied in a ponytail, and her school outfits were conservative, neat, and perfectly ironed. Her glasses were always on her face. At the beginning of her Junior year, Ashley transformed into a woman. She was still intelligent and friendly, but now she was popular and confident about her style. She removed her eyeglasses and wore contact lenses.

Her wardrobe style became more contemporary and less conservative. She loosened the ponytail, became popular among her classmates, and participated more in school functions. All the boys wanted to date Ashley. Only a few got that chance. Many of their classmates could not understand the relationship Ashley and Max shared during their school days. They both seemed like they belonged together in life. Everyone knew they were just best friends.

"Ashley, we need to talk soon."

"Oh, don't you say 'good morning' first? Where are your manners?" Ashley jokingly criticized his greeting.

"Sorry. Good morning. I meant to text you earlier, but I had an errand to do before driving to school and didn't have time." Max sounded anxious to spend time with Ashley alone. "Can we have lunch alone in the cafeteria?"

"That's almost impossible, Max. When our friends see us alone, they want to know our business and flop themselves next to us. Are you working at the marina after school?"

"Yes, but I have about a half hour of free time before I clock in. Let's meet in the parking lot after school. I can give you a ride home before driving to work," Max was trying to be accommodating.

"I'm working today, so maybe you can drop me off at the shopping center." Ashley works part-time as a receptionist at a doctor's office three days a week.

As soon as Ashley walked away from Max, two bullies from the football team passed close to Max and whispered 'faggot' to him. Max was stunned and ignored their comment. This was not the first time someone called him a 'faggot'. He knew it would not be the last.

✿ ✿ ✿ ✿ ✿ ✿ ✿

As soon as his last class was over, Max raced to his car and waited for Ashley to show up. Ashley was right behind him. She opened the front passenger door and got inside Max's car. "So, what's going on?

Why were you so desperate to talk to me? Did you do something wrong? You look like you did. You have that guilty look," Ashley is teasing Max. She knows him very well.

"Oh, stop it. I do not." Max thinks she is kidding. "I had a date Saturday night."

"Holy shit!" You didn't warn me! You do have a guilty look on your face. You must have got lucky that night. Did you have sex? Do I know him? Was he hung?" Ashley is very bold and open with Max. He is the same with her.

"Oh, that's all you think about, tramp! No, I didn't have sex with him. I could have, but I pushed back. I was afraid. Don't ask why! I'm still trying to find out."

Max went into detail about his entire evening with Enrique. They arrived at the doctor's office, and when Ashley got out of Max's car, she looked at him with a smile. "Max, I'm very happy for you. Don't look so guilty about Saturday night. You deserve it. I hope you get together with Enrique again. He sounds like a wonderful guy. You know that I can't give you my one hundred percent approval until you introduce me to him."

"Ha, Ha. Yes, I think we'll have another date together. I'm sure you will get a chance to meet him. Have a good afternoon at work. Love you!

Love you too, Max," Ashley waved to him as Max drove away and headed toward the marina.

Max was so excited to tell Ashley about his night with Enrique that he forgot to ask her to be his date at the Senior Prom. When he reached the parking lot at the Marina, Max sent her a text.

> MAX: "Excited to tell you about last night. I forgot to ask you an important question. Will you go to the Senior Prom with me?

> ASHLEY: "Yes, I was waiting for you to ask me. When I left you today, I thought you would ask Enrique instead of me. Perhaps Lyme is not ready for same-sex dates to the prom."

✿ ✿ ✿ ✿ ✿ ✿ ✿

It was getting close to the end of April in southern Connecticut. The cherry tree blossoms had already fallen from the trees. The dogwood's flowers were now beginning to burst open. The tulips were close to blossoming, and that fresh New England air, filtered through the spring showers of April, lingered everywhere you go. Max was happy to be going to the Prom with Ashley. He considered asking Stephen to lend him his Jaguar but was afraid to approach the subject with him.

The same day Ashley agreed to be Max's date for the prom, Max built up enough confidence and went to see Stephen. "Stephen, I hope you don't mind if I ask you for a favor. I don't want you to feel pressured to say 'yes.' I agree with your decision if you don't think it is a good idea."

"What is it, Max? Just ask me. It can't be a bad idea if the favor comes from you." Stephen wondered why Max would ask him for a favor.

"My Senior Prom is in a couple of weeks. I'm taking my best friend, Ashley. I have known her since first grade." Max was a bit nervous to ask Stephen and concerned that Stephen would say 'no' or that he would feel obligated to say yes but didn't want to lend Max the car. "I would like to borrow your Jaguar to take her to the prom that evening. I will return it after I drop her off at night." Max was even more nervous now and overly concerned about Stephen's response.

"That is a great idea, Max. Your friend will be pleased. Yes, of course. You can borrow the Jag for that special evening. There are a couple of conditions. No alcohol, you must return it with a full gas tank, and before your prom date, you have to wash it and apply a coat of paste wax." Stephen was thrilled that Max would use the Jaguar for a special occasion. It had not moved outside the garage for several months.

"Your conditions are extremely fair, Stephen. I'll plan to wash and wax it the week before the prom. Thank you! I can't wait to tell Ashley. Perhaps I will surprise her and show up at her house with the Jag." Max was smiling, relieved, and grateful.

"That's a better idea. I would offer to be your chauffeur if you didn't have your driver's license. Maybe not. All your school friends would laugh!"

✧ ✧ ✧ ✧ ✧ ✧ ✧

Max gathered all the supplies to wash and wax Stephen's Jaguar the week before the Senior Prom. He walked through the path to meet Stephen and get the keys. "Max, before you start washing and waxing the car, let's start it up and take it out for a spin. It has been a while since the car has been out. Let's hope the battery is not dead. You drive, and I will ride with you." The Jag started quickly, and Max drove it out of the garage so Stephen could open the door. "While we are out, let's stop for gas, and if we have time, let's have lunch at the diner." Stephen was just as excited as Max to take the Jag out for a drive through town. The jet-black car with tan leather interior was in perfect condition. All the windows were down as they drove through the town center towards the gas station. Everyone on the sidewalks noticed the unmistakable elegant style of the 1990 Jaguar. Stephen was sitting in the front passenger seat feeling very proud and showing off the young, handsome driver chauffeuring him through town.

At the gas station, Max got out and reached into his pocket to pay for the gas. Stephen stopped him and gave him his credit card. "Max, don't be silly, it's my car. Fill her up." After filling the tank, they drove across Main Street and parked in the diner's parking lot. It was now time for lunch.

"Who did you say you were taking to the prom? Your girlfriend, I suppose." Stephen didn't want to be too inquisitive but wanted to converse with Max.

"Well, it's complicated. She is not my 'romantic' girlfriend. She is a very close friend I have known since first grade in grammar school."

"There is nothing complicated about that, Max. Times have changed since my prom days. I attended my prom with a date. Life is different today. I would take Randy to the prom if Randy and I were your age today. Nobody would dare blink an eye." Stephen stopped to think about what he had just said. "Well, maybe some of the parents would object. Who cares? They aren't important. They don't matter." During the past decade, Stephen became more confident about discussing his relationship with Randy with anyone. "Max, there is a famous quote from Dr. Seuss that I love to recite. I'm sure your parents read it to you when you were young. 'Be who you are and say what you feel because those who mind don't matter and those who matter don't mind.'"

"I love that quote. It's simple, and it says a lot. Being gay today was not what it was twenty or thirty years ago. Unfortunately, there's still much homophobia in today's world. Even here in Lyme." Max looked out the diner window towards the street. He saw cars traveling in both directions, people walking about, going in and out of the businesses across the street. Stephen noticed a change in Max's tone and facial expression. He looked confused.

"Max, I'm at an age that I don't give a fuck what people think of me. I wish many younger LGBTQ+ community members felt as confident as I do. I suspect too many are living in the closet." Stephen looked around the restaurant and lowered his voice. "I only wish I had the network and strength to help them feel comfortable about their sexuality and live the life they are born to live. I'm saddened when I see someone hiding 'who they are' only because they fear what others will say or do." Stephen paused again and wondered if he had said too much. "Max, I'm an old man with many years of experience. I know a gay person when I see one. Nothing hurts me more when I see someone hiding their sexuality. It's not healthy." Stephen realized he was taking over the conversation. He thought perhaps the topic was not something Max wanted to discuss because Max's expression had changed from the time they were in the Jaguar. The food arrived at the table, which served as a point to change the conversation.

After finishing their lunch, the waitress brought the check to the table. Max tried to pay again, but Stephen beat him. He gave the waitress his credit card and asked for a container to take the other half of his sandwich home.

"Thank you, Stephen. I wanted to treat you for lunch since you let me use the Jag for the prom."

"It's my pleasure. I'm glad the Jag is getting some good use and a fresh coat of paste wax. We should get back so you can do your work."

They drove back to Stephen's driveway, car windows down and Stephen feeling very elegant and proud again. Pulling into the driveway, they noticed Enrique's pickup was next to the barn. "Oh look, Enrique is here."

"Yes, I was expecting him. He was going to do some work in the garden, and I wanted to talk to him about painting the inside of the studio."

Stephen exited the car and started walking directly to the backyard to find Enrique. Max picked up the bucket he left by the side of the garage, dishwashing liquid he uses for soap, several towels, and a large boat brush, and began to rinse the car with the garden hose.

"Look who is here." Stephen stopped when he saw Enrique walk around the corner of the garage. "You guys talk for a few minutes; I must go inside and make a quick phone call."

"Hi, Enrique. You didn't tell me you were going to be here today." Max wonders why Enrique didn't tell him he planned to be at Stephen's house even after Max told him yesterday that he would be washing the Jaguar in Stephen's driveway.

"There was a change of plans. I had a cancellation this morning, and Stephen wanted to talk to me about painting the studio and moving some plants in the garden. You must be happy that Stephen is letting you take the Jaguar to your Senior Prom." Enrique admired how well the Jag had been preserved.

"Yes. He's very generous. I hope Ashley is surprised when she sees me drive up with the Jaguar. I'm not going to tell her until I pick her up."

"She is going to be surprised when she sees you driving it. Hopefully, she won't think you stole it. If I were driving it, everyone would think I stole it." Enrique sadly admitted that a person of Mexican heritage would not likely be driving a Jaguar.

"I wouldn't think that of you."

"Thank you, Max, and I would have said 'YES' if you had asked me to the Senior Prom.

Max was embarrassed and believed Enrique was serious. "I would love to take you, Enrique, but you know how difficult that night would be for us."

"Yes, I know. I understand. I was only kidding." Enrique was happy that Max considered it.

Max continued spraying the Jaguar with the garden hose by the side of the garage. He set it down on the driveway and brushed the vehicle with water and dishwashing liquid he poured into the bucket. He accidentally got some soapy water on Enrique's t-shirt, who was standing too close to the Jaguar.

"Hey, watch what you're doing, Mr. Max." Enrique grabbed the hose, pointed it at Max, and jokingly sprayed his t-shirt.

"Oh, you also had some soap on your t-shirt, so I rinsed it off before it caused any damage." Enrique offered an excuse for soaking Max's t-shirt. Their nipples and abs are now exposed through the wet t-shirts.

"Very funny, Enrique." Max wrestled the hose away from Enrique and sprayed his upper body with more water.

"You're in trouble, Mr. Max." They were running in circles around the Jag. Max had the garden hose. Enrique grabbed the bucket with water and dishwashing soap and poured it over Max's head. Max sprayed Enrique's crotch and buttocks as he tried to run away from Max's reach. They laughed and yelled at each other, which made Stephen come outside to see what was happening. Dana was already looking out of her bedroom window, watching the playful scene between the two.

"You're both acting like 10-year-olds! Look at you, soaked and full of soap. Take your clothes off inside the studio, and I will pick them up and throw them in the dryer. You can wear the robes I keep in the closet for guests." Their childlike behavior amused Stephen. "Thank God I don't have kids."

Max and Enrique broke out laughing at Stephen's comment. "Max, I think I have an extra pair of shorts for you in my gym bag. I'll run to the truck and meet you in the studio." Enrique ran to his pickup truck while Max went to the studio, removed all his clothes, and grabbed a towel from the bathroom to dry himself. He was standing naked in the middle of the studio when Enrique walked in with two pairs of shorts in his hand.

"I wish I didn't have any shorts in the truck. We would stay naked the rest of the afternoon."

"Give me one of those shorts before Stephen walks in on us," Max was worried Stephen would walk in and find them both naked.

"Not until I kiss you." Enrique is teasing Max.

"Not now, Enrique. Behave yourself." Max got close to Enrique and tried to grab one of the shorts from his left hand. Enrique grabbed Max's penis in his right hand, rubbed the head, and gently kissed his lips. Max allowed Enrique a few seconds until he realized he was getting an erection. He pulled away and gave him the towel to dry himself. Enrique undressed as Max quickly slipped on the shorts he borrowed from Enrique. His erection created a noticeable bulge.

Stephen walked in to pick up the wet clothing while Max quickly turned to face the back wall so Stephen wouldn't see his erection bulging on his shorts. Enrique, still naked and exposing his hard penis, was still trying to slip on his shorts, "Let me have your wet clothes now so I can throw them in the dryer. They will be dry in a half hour." Stephen noticed a flustered look on their faces when he entered the studio without knocking.

"I will be outside washing and waxing the Jag." Max left the studio with only his sneakers and Enrique's shorts. His erection was still causing a noticeable bulge.

✧ ✧ ✧ ✧ ✧ ✧ ✧

The studio attached to the barn needed a new coat of paint. Stephen wanted to approach Enrique about painting the interior. "Enrique, I want to have the inside of the studio painted soon. The condition of the walls is embarrassing for any overnight guests to see. The last time we had it painted was shortly after we moved in 2002. Are you available? I will give you a key; you can work on this project in your free time." Enrique was wearing shorts with no underwear. He was still showing a noticeable erection. Stephen ignored it and pretended he didn't see it. He did wonder why they were both showing erections under their shorts. "I'd like to have all the painting completed by the beginning of the summer. I'll pick up the supplies you need at the hardware store, including plastic covers to protect the furniture. Does the timing work for you?"

"Yes, Stephen, no problem. I can squeeze this in on weekends and perhaps at night during the week when I'm not in school." Enrique was anxious about the extra cash.

"Great! Here is an extra key to the door. I will pick up all the paint and supplies you need tomorrow. Let me show you what needs to be done in the perennial garden." Stephen and Enrique walked out of the studio. Enrique locked the door and thought about spending time at night with Max alone in the studio.

✧ ✧ ✧ ✧ ✧ ✧ ✧

At the same time Enrique worked on the perennial beds in the back of the property, he was daydreaming about Max, who was waxing the Jaguar in front of the garage. He remembered their date and how Max delicately rubbed his right thigh and pressed on his groin with his warm hands. He recalled how Max kissed him at the end of their first date, the tenderness of Max's lips when they touched his lips, and how Max nibbled on his lower lip while gently caressing his face between his warm palms. He still felt Max's tongue licking his upper lip. Enrique had never felt this romantic with anyone else. Whenever he thought about their brief time in the pickup truck, he got an erection challenging to control.

Max was polishing the Jaguar and simultaneously experienced flashbacks of his date with Enrique. Seeing him naked in the studio returned memories of their time in the gym showers. He enjoyed Enrique's romantic response to his kiss at the end of their date and wanted to see more of him. He wanted to experience making love to him, holding him, smelling him, and licking his warm and smooth body. He wants to satisfy Enrique and experience a joint climax. He was also anxious for Enrique to taste his body. It's not about having sex for Max but about romance, experiencing affection, and feeling each other's touch.

✿ ✿ ✿ ✿ ✿ ✿ ✿

The Jag was clean and shiny. Max drove it inside the garage and walked inside the kitchen to bring Stephen the keys. Stephen did not hear him. Max saw Stephen sitting on a chair by the rear window with the wheelchair beside him. Stephen was talking to someone. There wasn't anyone else in the room so he walked to the laundry room, picked up his dry clothes in the dryer and changed back into his clothes. He took Enrique's clothes out of the dryer, folded them on the counter in the laundry room, and left them there with the shorts Enrique lent him.

"Maybe Stephen is on his mobile phone and wearing earphones." Max thought to himself. He left the keys on the kitchen counter with a note and walked to the rear garden to say goodbye to Enrique. He told Enrique that Stephen must have been on the phone and, when he left, to remind him that the Jaguar keys were on the kitchen counter. Enrique looked into Max's eyes and grabbed his elbow to show him a private corner of the garden on the other side of the oak tree. When they reached the tree, Enrique passionately kissed Max.

Dana was looking at Enrique from her bedroom window. She saw Max was approached by Enrique and escorted to the far end of the garden, where she couldn't see them anymore. *"Oh, shit. Where are they going? I can't see them anymore. I should go outside and see if I can figure out what those two are planning to do,"* Dana told herself disappointedly. She ran outside to her backyard for a better view. She didn't want to get too close and walk through Stephen's perennial garden. She could not find them. After a few minutes, she returned home and found Max sitting in the family room with Joe.

"Where the hell did you go flying to, Dana?" Joe saw Dana hastily leave the house towards the backyard.

"Nowhere special. I thought I saw a bear from my room upstairs."

"So, you ran outside to encourage the bear to eat your brains? What's wrong with you?" Max responded to Dana's excuse for rushing out to the backyard, but he suspected the real reason was to spy on him and Enrique.

Unbeknownst to Enrique and Max, from his chair in the family room, Stephen could see their sudden romantic and "not-so" discreet act of love on the other side of the oak tree. Stephen smiled as he witnessed their passionate kiss. He looked at Randy sitting next to him. "Isn't that sweet, Randy? Reminds me of us."

CHAPTER 11

LESSONS

It was a quiet late Wednesday afternoon in April. Max was home alone doing his homework after spending a couple of hours swimming in the school's Olympic-sized pool. He heard a knock on the front door, looked out the living room window and saw a black limousine parked in the circular driveway by the front door. He opened the door. A handsome and tall, well-dressed man in his early 50s wearing a dark gray suit, a perfectly starched white shirt, and a solid black tie carrying a small brown box, approximately one foot cubed, stood facing Max. "Hi, sorry to bother you. I have a scheduled delivery for Mr. Stephen Porter, your next-door neighbor, but it seems he is not home. Would you accept the package for him? I'll leave a note in his mailbox to let him know the package was delivered here."

"Yes, I'll take it. He must be on the back patio and didn't hear the doorbell. I'll bring it to him later today. Thank you." After Max agreed to accept the package, he looked at the older and handsome, well-dressed man and thought to himself, *"What would it be like to jump in bed with someone that hot and twenty or thirty years older than me? This guy is very sexy. Enrique would enjoy a threesome with him."* Max took the box, they both exchanged a flirtatious smile and he returned to his room to finish his homework. The box had no return address, only a large label with Stephen's name and address printed in black ink.

An hour later, Max picked up the box and carried it through the path to Stephen's home. He assumed Stephen was on the patio, so he walked towards the back and found Stephen sitting next to the wheelchair, asleep. He backed up a few yards on the side of the garage and called his name. "Hey, Stephen!" He gave Stephen a few seconds to realize he was approaching the patio.

"Hi, is that you, Max?" Stephen woke up and quickly covered the glass of wine next to the wheelchair with a cloth napkin that was wrapped around a plate of cheese he had fixed for himself and Randy.

"Someone tried to deliver this box to you, but you didn't answer the door. The man came to our house and asked if I would accept it. I said, 'Yes.' I hope I did the right thing. After the man left, I wondered if you didn't answer the door because you didn't want the package."

"Thank you, Max." Stephen quietly stared at the box for a few seconds. Max assumed Stephen knew its contents. He placed his left hand on top of the box and rubbed it gently. "Well, let me take this inside. Wait here for a minute." Stephen tried to grab the box with one hand. It's heavier than he anticipated. Max asked if he needed help, but Stephen didn't respond. He placed his glass of wine on the table, grabbed it again with both hands, walked into the house through the kitchen door, and placed it on a shelf in the pantry. He stared at the box again and waited a minute before returning outside.

"Max, can I interest you in a glass of wine."

"No, thanks. I'm fine. I need to get back home and finish my homework. No one is at home and I left the back door open."

"Well, sit and talk to me for a few minutes. I think you told me you were taking a friend to your Senior Prom, is that right?" Trying to change the subject, Stephen asked Max about his prom date as he walked from the outside kitchen door towards the table on the patio.

Max was sitting between an empty patio chair and an empty wheelchair. He was observing the glass of wine covered by a cloth napkin and wondered why the glass was hidden under the napkin. *"Someone else out here with Stephen?"* He thought to himself. "Yes, I've known her since first grade. She's my best friend."

"Well, that's terrific. You're going to have a great time with all your friends." Stephen noticed Max looking at the wheelchair and the wine under the napkin. "Do you have many friends in school? Don't they come to your house and hang out?" Stephen tried controlling the conversation to avoid discussing the box Max had just delivered or the wheelchair and the wine.

"Yes, I guess I do have many friends. I know almost everyone in my senior class." Max was wondering where this conversation was going.

"Let me tell you something. It's a lesson you should never forget," Stephen sat on the chair next to Max, leaned close to him, and looked directly at him with his eyebrows raised. "If you have one friend, you are fortunate. If you have two friends, it's a miracle. If you tell anyone you have more than three friends, you're a liar."

✿ ✿ ✿ ✿ ✿ ✿

On Wednesday morning, a local landscape designer purchased three truckloads of trees and bushes from Enrique for a new residential construction site on the Connecticut River in Old Lyme. It was the largest individual sale the garden center had ever experienced. The landscape designer, Joel Richmond, was a young, handsome, 40-year-old gay man who kept staring at Enrique and insisted that the first truckload be delivered by the end of the day. Enrique had to load the truck and planned to deliver the trees by himself.

"Joel, my delivery staff is out on the road and won't return today. I can make the first delivery myself but need help unloading."

"No problem, Enrique. I will help you. I can be there at 5:00 PM." Joel was anxious to get delivery because he had scheduled a crew to plant the following day.

Enrique arrived at the construction site at exactly 5:00 PM with the garden center's biggest truck full of trees. He saw Joel coming out of the enormous contemporary house wearing boots, a pair of tight-fitting jeans, and an unbuttoned plaid shirt exposing his chiseled hairy chest. After the truck was emptied, Enrique went to the cab and retrieved a

<small>ONLY LOVE LASTS</small>

clipboard with paperwork for Joel to sign. "Enrique, I'll meet you inside the house. Do you want a bottle of water?"

"Yes, thank you, Joel. I'll be there shortly. I need your signature on the invoice." When Enrique entered the kitchen area, Joel stood there looking at his landscape plans, exposing his muscled upper body with his shirt off.

"Do you want to see my landscape plans for this house?"

"Yes."

Joel stands next to Enrique and explains to him where the trees are being planted. He got closer and closer to Enrique, and Enrique turned to face him and kissed him. They both engaged in lustful sex on top of the kitchen island.

After their climax, they got dressed and headed out the front door. "I think you have two more truckloads of merchandise to deliver here." Joel was anxious to see Enrique again. "Perhaps tomorrow at 5:00 PM again?"

"Yes, why not. I'll be back." Enrique thought it was a great, impromptu sexual experience. The same scene was repeated on Thursday and Friday.

✧✧✧✧✧✧✧

Max's eyes opened wide after Stephen's 'three or more friends' comment. He didn't know how to respond to Stephen. There was an uncomfortable silence on the patio as Max processed what he heard. Stephen realized that he might have frightened Max. He sat back in the chair and looked towards the garden. He then turned his head toward the old oak tree.

"You're right, Stephen. I only have one true friend. It's Ashley. I'm lucky to have her as a friend." Max realized what Stephen was trying to teach him. "Thank you. You just made me realize something I never considered."

"Oh, I'm sorry, Max. I didn't mean to be so authoritative and opinionated. I hope I didn't scare you. I have much knowledge to spread out for others to benefit. That's what happens when you get to be my age, you become opinionated." Stephen laughed as he continued offering excuses for his aggressive statement. "I can't help myself. People can accept what I have to say for what it's worth or ignore it. It comes from an eccentric old queen who has experienced life as many would never dream." His voice was returning to an angry tone. "If people don't like what I say, they can all go and fuck themselves. That's my attitude, and I'm sticking to it." Stephen winks at Max.

"I Agree," Max responded by laughing.

"You want to know something? My parents taught me to be a good person. I always followed their advice. One important lesson I learned during high school was that other parents didn't necessarily teach their children the same important life stories I was taught." Stephen was recollecting his early teenage years with a painful look. "Unfortunately, many parents believe that education begins when their children enter the school building and ends when they leave in the afternoon. That's where the conflicts start. I needed to learn what to do when confronted with someone who only hated me because they thought I was different. I didn't think I was different. I was taught to be a model citizen, and I behaved like one. Many of those kids in school are taught to hate people like me. Hate is not passed down in your genes. It is taught." Stephen's voice volume increased, and his tone became angry. He forgot why he was responding to Max in this manner. Max continued to listen politely.

"My parents would tell me, 'Stephen, don't pay any attention to them. They're not your friends.' Ignoring the punches in my stomach, the name-calling, and the practical jokes in front of other classmates was difficult to ignore. Eventually, they got tired of abusing me. I think they realized I was stronger than they expected. My problem didn't go away. They just transferred their hate to someone else. Today, I listen to politicians on television, and I say to myself, '*Who taught those assholes to hate.*' It's obvious how they learned it." Stephen continued rambling on with his tirade.

"Yes, I know what you're saying. I have seen kids in school experience the same." Max held back and did not want to confess to Stephen that he experienced high school bullying during his first two years. "Did you know that suicide is the third leading cause of teenage death?

"Those numbers don't surprise me, Max. Unfortunately, many parents still see bullying as 'just part of being a kid,' they don't realize that their thinking is a lack of understanding that leads to many negative effects for victims, including suicide," Stephen added to Max's research.

"I believe life experiences make a person who they are. I find myself learning about life every day of the week. Everything I see, everywhere I go, and everyone I speak to contributes something for me to consider." Max didn't want to hold back his feelings. "My experiences, good or bad, usually make me stronger and more confident. Sometimes, I look back four or five years ago and see how much I have changed. I know it is a change for the better. A day doesn't go by without my parents teaching me what is right and wrong. They have taught me what love is and what hate can cause. I still have bad days. I suppose I should plan on having bad days occasionally." Max was surprised he opened his thoughts to Stephen. "There are times I feel like a sponge trying to absorb everything around me and letting go of what could be harmful to me or others."

"That's what makes us who we are, Max. We are willing to learn about life from our own experiences. Many people I've met don't have a clue; they were never taught to live." Stephen stopped to consider what he just told Max. He looked again at the giant oak tree behind the perennial garden. "That old oak tree has experienced a lot over the years. It has brought Randy and I much pleasure in our lives. We have taken good care of it. We feed it every year and trim the rotten branches every spring. In return, it has given us years of its beauty to enjoy. I'm still learning about life. The lessons never stop, Max. There are experiences I have had recently that I don't like. I'm dealing with them in my old age. Something is going on in my life right now that wants to make me stronger. The older I get, the harder it becomes to accept change. You'll understand what I'm telling you as you get older because you'll have the same experiences."

"I understand what you're telling me, Stephen." You could hear the spring breezes blowing through the new leaves on the old oak tree. Max and Stephen look in that direction at the same time. "I think that tree is listening to us and wants to contribute to our conversation. Perhaps it's holding back secrets it wants to disclose." Stephen remembered the time he saw Max and Enrique kiss behind the tree.

"Well, if that tree starts talking, you and I are running inside the house." Max blurted out a humorous comment to lighten up the conversation. He remembered he had a secret about that tree. He also recalled that kiss with Enrique behind the tree a few days ago. He was confident nobody saw them.

"Let's not wait for the tree to start a conversation with us. Let's go inside. I want to show you something." Stephen led the way.

✿ ✿ ✿ ✿ ✿ ✿ ✿

Dana was dropped off at her house by a girlfriend's mother. She noticed Max's car in the driveway, but nobody was home and the back door was wide open. She stopped briefly and thought, *"Max must be inside Stephen's house. I don't see him on the patio."*

Alice came home early and also noticed Max's car outside but Max was not home. "Dana, have you seen Max?"

"No, no one was home when I came in about half an hour ago. He must be at Stephen's house. The back door was left open. I'm surprised a bear didn't walk in for a visit."

"Why is he spending so much time with Stephen? Should I be concerned?" Alice thought to herself. She saw Max's door to his room was open and could see, from the hallway, his desk light was on, and schoolbooks opened. *"No, I'm not going to snoop around his room."* She walks away and goes upstairs to her bedroom.

✿✿✿✿✿✿✿

Stephen directed Max towards the living room by the baby grand piano, which displayed several silver frames with photographs. "Look at this photo. It was taken in 1966 at a gay cocktail party in Boston's Back Bay neighborhood. This is Randy standing next to me. That was the party where Randy and I met for the first time."

"WOW! That's terrific. It's great to have a photo of the first time you met."

"Yes, it's special for us. Our friend took the photograph and gave it to us as a present when we celebrated our 25th anniversary. We didn't know the photo existed."

Stephen looked at the other frames. "Here is a photo of Randy when he graduated from Law School at Harvard. You must be excited about attending Harvard in September."

"Yes, I can't wait. I'm staying in the dorm for my first semester, but I plan to rent a small studio apartment near the school."

"Randy studied very hard. His grades reflected his hard work. He was very generous and volunteered to tutor many students who needed help graduating. We still hear from some of them today. They were very grateful Randy was there when they needed him. That was his style. He always gave back whenever possible." Stephen looked at Randy's photo and rubbed the glass with the back of his palm.

Max pointed to one picture of Stephen and Randy that was professionally posed. "Oh, Stephen, this one is sexy. When was this photo taken?"

"A photographer we know took that for our fortieth anniversary. He wanted us to be completely nude. Randy refused. He negotiated nude from the waist up, so the photographer brought out those two small black bikini bathing suits. I was certain Randy would have issues stuffing his 'junk' inside that tiny bikini and walk out without having our picture taken. Much to my surprise, he stripped naked in front of the photographer and slipped on that tiny, stretched bikini. We had a great time during the photo shoot. I was pleasantly surprised by how good we looked for our age. We would look much hotter if the photo were taken twenty years earlier!" Stephen was reminiscing about his younger days with Randy. "Many memories on top of this piano. I wish I could set back the calendar." Stephen's moods kept swinging from sadness to joy.

"These photos are wonderful." Max enjoyed listening to Stephen talk about the photos. "They tell a story about your life with Randy. You should write your memoir – 'My Life with Randy.' There's a lot of love in these photos, and your story should be exposed to demonstrate to anyone struggling with their sexuality that healthy and loving gay relationships exist."

"I considered writing our story when we retired and moved here from Hartford. Randy was against the idea. He didn't want our personal lives opened to the general public. I understood his concern." Stephen paused for a few seconds. "I have no regrets about my life with Randy. In our younger days, we used to go to the bars in Boston and pick up a guy for a threesome or orgy with two or three other guys. We were a wild couple. When I lived alone, I would go out late at night and have sex with strangers three to five times a week in the park. I can't recall how many guys I fucked behind bushes. Randy was the same when he lived alone in Cambridge. It was a time to experiment with our sexual desires. Those were the days before HIV/AIDS. When we moved to Hartford and started our careers, our threesomes and group sex parties were rare and extremely limited." Stephen was not holding anything back. Max was surprised Stephen was disclosing so much about their sexual encounters. He didn't want to interrupt Stephen. He let him continue. Max knew Stephen needed someone to listen. There was a silent moment when Stephen stopped to gather his thoughts.

Max wanted to let Stephen know he was listening and cared about the subject. "I was born after the peak of the HIV/AIDS crisis, but I have read a lot about it and feel like I lived it. The personal stories that people have documented touched me. Listening to you talk about those you knew who lost their lives is a history lesson many people I know need to have."

"Max, I've learned many valuable lessons in life. Educating people that need it most can be frustrating. You can bring the camels to a watering spot but can't force them to drink it. There are many thirsty camels out there who are too stupid to drink the water. That should not stop you from bringing them to the watering spot, even if they refuse to drink."

"I get it. You're right." Max replied to Stephen in a somber tone. There is silence in the room. Stephen is rearranging the framed photographs on the piano.

"Every time Louise polishes this piano, the photos are not returned in the manner she found them. I always have to fix them after she leaves."

Max looks at his watch and tries to find an excuse to go home. "I need to get back home. I left the house without writing a note to my parents so they don't worry about me."

"Oh my God, look at the time. Sorry I kept you here listening to my boring lectures." Stephen apologized for keeping Max.

"I'm grateful for our conversation today. It was not boring. I have learned a lot about you and a lot about myself. Thank you. I thought I would drop off a box, and instead, I got a master's degree on 'Lessons in Life' by Stephen Porter." Max walked over to the kitchen door, and before leaving, he turned around and hugged Stephen. Stephen was caught by surprise. He put his arms around Max and whispered to him. "Thank you, my friend."

✿ ✿ ✿ ✿ ✿ ✿ ✿

"Randy, I hope Max learned something today. I don't think I scared him when I told him about our sexual encounters during our younger days," Stephen whispered after Max left. "I felt he wanted to tell me something about his relationship with Enrique. Maybe next time we meet. You know I would never force it out of him.

CHAPTER 12

NEWS

It was a dark, windy, rainy New England Monday morning in late April. You could feel the cold and dampness creeping in through the outside walls. The Senior Prom was in less than a week, and graduation was only six weeks away. Max was up and out of bed at his usual time. He stumbled over to the window, naked with an erection, rubbing his sleepy eyes to examine the morning landscape and weather – cloudy, wet, and soggy. Before he showered, he sat on his beanbag chair and masturbated with mental images of Enrique naked.

After he showered, he dressed appropriately for heavy wind and rain and sat at the kitchen counter with Joe and Alice to discuss Harvard and his move to Boston in August. He realized he was running late for school, yelled out for Dana to hurry down the stairs, and ran to his car with her. When they left the driveway and turned onto Hamburg Road, he saw Louise's car turning into Stephen's driveway. They waved to each other.

He was the last student to arrive at his first class. The teacher handed him a note from the principal's office asking him to see Dr. Donahue, the Principal, after his swimming practice. It was rare when someone was called to the principal's office for doing something good, so he spent the rest of his day in school trying to remember what he did wrong. At 2:00 PM sharp, he exited the locker room adjacent to the indoor pool and walked to Dr. Donahue's office with a nervous and concerned look. His hair was still wet after he showered in the school gym to rinse the chemicals used to chlorinate the water in the pool. His backpack, with wet spots from his Speedo and towel, was hanging from his shoulder.

"Oh, there you are, Max. Please have a seat." Dr. Donahue noticed Max was most likely wondering what he had done wrong and tried to make him comfortable. "When students get a note to see me, they immediately think they did something wrong. Well, you did nothing wrong, Max. Don't be nervous. I have great news for you. It's that time of the year when our school counselors and I meet to discuss logistics for the graduation ceremony. Max, I have known you since your first day as a freshman at Lyme High School. I'm proud to inform you that based on your grades, feedback from your teachers, and school activities, the school counselors and I unanimously agreed that Max Edwards will be the 2022 Class Valedictorian at the graduation exercises in June."

Max was caught by surprise and wasn't sure how to react. Dr. Donahue was waiting for a response. After a few seconds of awkward silence, he focused on Dr. Donahue's comment and spoke. "I'm honored, Dr. Donahue. Not sure I know what it means. What are my responsibilities? Are you sure I'm qualified?" Max was still unsure how to react to the news or the questions he should be asking.

"Being the class Valedictorian is a huge honor. It is a recognition of your hard work and your leadership. Max, you've set an excellent example for your classmates and have raised the bar for others to follow. At the graduation exercises, your job will be to give the Valedictorian address to your classmates, dignitaries, and guests. I can help you write the speech if you need help, but I know that the best speeches come from the speaker's heart. It should be your personal 'farewell' address for your classmates to remember and celebrate what everyone has accomplished, give inspiration for the future, and build excitement for everything that will come after graduation." Max was listening intensively to Dr. Donahue and felt an immense amount of pressure to deliver on expectations.

"This is a letter from me nominating you as the Valedictorian. Bring it home and show it to your parents. Have them call me here tomorrow if they have any questions or concerns. We are confident you will deliver a terrific address and make your classmates, family, and friends proud of you." Dr. Donahue stood up from his desk chair and reached across his desk to shake Max's hand. "Congratulations, Max. I'm proud of you, and I'm certain your family will be proud when you show them this letter."

Max walked out of Dr. Donahue's office, stunned by the news and unsure he could deliver what was expected. He knew he had never disappointed his family, making this new assignment more challenging. He reached out for his phone and texted Ashley.

> MAX: Hey, I just got out of Donahue's office.
> ASHLEY: What the fuck did you do wrong?
> MAX: No, it's what I did right. I'm the class Valedictorian at graduation.
> ASHLEY: I was expecting it. CONGRATULATIONS! Very proud of you!
> MAX: The pressure is overwhelming. TY XXOO

✧ ✧ ✧ ✧ ✧ ✧ ✧

That same morning, Max was dressing for school, Louise was getting ready for her drive, in the pouring rain, to Stephen's home in Lyme.

"I'm leaving now Mom. Lolita and Maritza are downstairs already, so you have no reason to go down and supervise the laundromat. The weather outside sucks, so stay in the apartment until I return." Louise yells to Mabel, who is watching the local weather reports on their television with the volume turned up because Mabel has difficulties with her hearing and will not wear a hearing aid.

"Yeah, yeah, yeah. I heard you. Leave me alone. I'll do whatever I want to do." Mabel didn't hear Louise because it was the same comment every morning before Louise left the apartment for her house cleaning work. Louise didn't hear Mabel either for the same reason.

Around lunchtime, Lolita ran to the apartment to ask Mabel if she would come down and watch the laundromat while she ran out to pick up lunch. Maritza had left to do a personal errand. Against Louise's wishes, Mabel agreed. She grabbed her cane, walked down the stairs, and sat in a swivel chair in the office, from which she had views of the front and rear entrance doors.

Two other customers were doing their laundry when a man with a sluggish walk wearing a stained sweatshirt and ripped jeans entered the laundromat, looked around, and walked directly to the office. He saw Mabel sitting in the swivel chair with her cane on the table beside her. He pulls out a gun from his sweatshirt pocket, points it at Mable, and demands that she place all the money, including coins from the change machine, inside a pillowcase he pulled out of his back pocket.

"What the fuck is wrong with you? This is a laundromat. The little money we have is in coins. There isn't enough in this place to make shooting an old lady like me worth your time. You're a fucking moron, you stupid son of a bitch." Mabel got up from her chair slowly, grabbed her cane, and with all her strength, swiftly smacked the man on the left side of his face with the bottom of her cane, knocking out three teeth that flew across the room, covered in blood. The strange-looking man was shocked to be assaulted by a 90-plus-year-old lady with a cane. He let out a loud, painful screech.

The two customers in the store ran out the front door to call for help. The man dropped the gun on the floor and raised his hand to cover his mouth. She tried to hit him again, but he ran out of the laundromat with blood dripping out of his mouth. "Come back here, you mother fucker. I'm not done with you yet." She started to go after him but could not run, and before she reached the front door, Mabel stopped and looked out of the laundromat window to see the man with a bloody face running up the street. She suddenly felt she was in trouble and collapsed on the floor.

When the police arrived, they found Mabel face down on the floor, a trail of blood stains from the office out the front door, a toy gun, and three teeth on the floor covered in blood. The police officers tried to revive Mabel until the ambulance arrived. They were not successful. It was later determined that she died from a heart attack. Security cameras recorded the event clearly, including Mable telling the man he was a 'fucking moron' and 'a stupid son of a bitch.' The man with the three missing teeth was apprehended before the end of the day.

Louise was cleaning Stephen's home when the police officer who found Mabel called her on her mobile phone. She raced home to find her mother dead on the floor of the Laundromat, covered by a blanket. She stood quietly in front of Mabel's body for several minutes before crying softly, thinking of their years together and the care she provided her.

Mabel died of a heart attack caused by her attempt to chase the man who threatened to steal her money with a toy gun. Her last words were, "Come back here, you mother fucker. I'm not done with you yet." Her last sight was looking through the laundromat window at the man she hit with her cane, running with blood on his face.

✧ ✧ ✧ ✧ ✧ ✧

Enrique was at the garden center all day. Customer traffic was slow because of the heavy winds and rain, which lasted most of the day. He spent most of his time in the back office refining a social media campaign he developed last month targeting business accounts. At closing time, he reset the registers, recorded the sales activity for the day, and prepared the bank deposit. Manuel expected to see the sales numbers and cash deposit when he arrived home. Sales and deposits for the day were not impressive, and he knew his father would be upset by today's business.

Manuel was not at the garden center because he had two separate appointments with bankers he thought might be interested in providing a mortgage to purchase the real estate occupied by the garden center. Time is running out, and he is concerned the landlord will sell the property to a developer interested in tearing down the current structure to build a shopping center and office complex.

The first banker meeting ended with this statement by the banker:

> "Mr. Sanchez, we have carefully reviewed your personal financial statements. Unfortunately, we are unable to provide you with a mortgage. Because of your home mortgage, you are leveraged to the maximum amount we prefer with a transaction of this nature. I'm afraid you don't have enough equity over and above what we believe should be the value of the business, real estate, and personal assets to make us feel comfortable."

The second banker meeting was similar.

> "Mr. Sanchez, thank you for considering our bank for your mortgage. My colleagues and I have reviewed all your numbers very carefully, but unfortunately, you don't have the personal net worth we require to make this type of loan. Even though we would have a lien on the business and real estate, we don't believe it is sufficient for us to be comfortable lending you the money. Perhaps a more aggressive financial institution will be better for this type of transaction."

Manuel arrived home depressed and disappointed with the business world he was forced to engage and negotiate. "Maria, these bankers are not telling me why they are not providing me with a mortgage. If my last name was not Latino sounding and I didn't look like a Mexican, they would all be running after me, wanting my business. I told them I would not need their stinking mortgage if I had the assets and personal net worth they required to make this transaction."

Enrique overheard the conversation Manuel had with Maria. He was frustrated and lost because his father had not included him in the negotiations with financial institutions. He felt he had much to offer in these discussions and could prepare a better presentation for the banks to consider. Enrique expressed his feelings during dinner that night about participating in the business.

"Papi, I wish you would let me help you find a mortgage so we can buy the property. If a banker sees that your son is invested in the future of the business, you might have a better advantage. Give me a chance. I know we can prepare cash flows that show we can pay back the mortgage without difficulties."

"There is nothing you can do, Enrique. Bankers only care that you have enough personal assets they can easily acquire if you default. If you are of Mexican heritage, they want twice as much in secured assets." Manuel felt strongly that financial institutions were discriminating against him.

Maria agreed with Enrique but was careful how she suggested that Enrique participate. "Manuel, I think it would be a good experience for Enrique to go with you to these meetings. It can't hurt, and perhaps it might help to show bankers that there is a younger generation you are grooming at the garden center to help you expand the business. Enrique can present how he upgraded the inventory controls and implemented all the technology he has worked on during the past year. He can also discuss his social media strategy, which has helped bring new business clients."

"Maria, I don't think it would be helpful. Bankers don't care about those things. All they want is more deposits in their bank and fewer loans going out, especially to American citizens with Mexican blood." Manuel looked at Josefa and wondered if she agreed with her daughter. Josefa had no expression and remained neutral by staying silent during dinner. Maria knew Josefa was on her side.

"Papi, you can't do everything at the garden center by yourself. If you want the business to grow, you must delegate some of your responsibilities and seek help when needed. I spent most of today working on my social media campaign targeting new business accounts. I wish you will let me show you what I have done this past month. It has generated several new business accounts, including Chester Marina. I'm targeting real estate developers and construction companies, large and small. It's working – I can show you the results over the past month." Enrique was disappointed because he felt his time was wasted if his father didn't support projects he implemented independently.

"So, you spent all day in the back room while our employees and customers walked out with merchandise they didn't pay for. You are not doing what I asked you to do. I would rather have you on the floor protecting our inventory than work on a stupid social media campaign that will not get us a mortgage from a bank."

Enrique, showing frustration, knew arguing with his father about the business was a waste of time. Maria was agitated about the conversation. She changed the subject and spoke about her day at the hospital.

✧ ✧ ✧ ✧ ✧ ✧ ✧

After he met with Dr. Donahue, Max rushed home and sat on his beanbag chair to look out the window and reflect on what Dr. Donahue told him. The heavy rains had temporarily stopped, and he reread the letter from the Principal.

Mr. Maxwell Edwards
Hamburg Rd
Lyme, CT 06371

Dear Max,
You have demonstrated impressive academic and personal achievements at Lyme High School during the past four years. Your school counselors and I have seen you grow and become an example for future generations of students to aspire to. The faculty has unanimously expressed the same appreciation for your hard work.

Your dedication and the inspiration you have given your classmates have not gone unnoticed. We are thrilled to inform you that we have selected you as the class Valedictorian at the Graduation ceremonies of 2022.

Our sincere congratulations to you and your family. We hope you will always remember your days here at Lyme High School.

Best wishes for continued success,

Dr. Ted Donahue, Principal
Lyme High School

He takes a photograph of the letter with his mobile phone and attaches it to a text for Enrique.

> MAX: Hey, look at this letter.
> ENRIQUE: That is terrific, Max. Congratulations. You deserve it.
> MAX: Thank you. I was speechless when the principal told me.
> ENRIQUE: Now you have to write a "killer" speech.
> MAX: Yeah, the pressure is on.
> ENRIQUE: How about pizza some night this week?
> MAX: Yes, I'm working at the Marina on Thursday. How about after work?
> ENRIQUE: Let's meet at the gym. We can work out together, shower, and go for pizza.
> MAX: Perfect. See you at the gym around 6:00 PM.

It took Max a few hours to realize the importance of being selected as valedictorian. After his text to Enrique, he was doubly thrilled - the honor bestowed on him in school and his second date with Enrique on Thursday. He took his letter from Dr. Donahue and posted it on the refrigerator door for his family to see when they arrived.

Alice was the first to come home from work and knocked on Max's door after she saw the letter on the refrigerator door. "Max, why didn't you call me at the office? Congratulations! Wait until your father sees this letter. He is so proud of you, Max. I can't wait to show him." Max opens his bedroom door, and Alice hugs him. "I'm very proud of you. Your father will have this letter framed and hung in the family room."

Dana was dropped off by her friend's mother and walked into the kitchen with earphones, listening to her favorite tunes. She heard Alice and Max's excitement outside his room and decided to investigate. "What's going on here? What's all the noise for?"

"Read this letter, Dana." Alice proudly held the letter for Dana and would not release it.

"This is great news, Max. My big brother is going to be a star in school. WOW! I'm the sister of a celebrity. Congratulations. I can't wait to tell my friends. I think I'll start now. I don't want anyone to beat me to the news." Dana ran upstairs and began calling all her school friends on her list.

"You want the world to know something? Just tell Dana. She knows how to distribute news quickly." Max laughed along with Alice.

✧ ✧ ✧ ✧ ✧ ✧

Stephen arrived home after lunch with a friend in Essex and an afternoon shopping at the outlet stores in nearby Clinton. The heavy rains made it very difficult for him to drive. He noticed Louise had left and did not finish cleaning the house. The vacuum cleaner was left in the living room, cleaning supplies were left on the kitchen counter, and the laundry was still inside the washer. He tried to reach Louise on her mobile phone, but the call went directly to voice mail. He was concerned something serious had happened for Louise to leave suddenly without finishing her work. He put the cleaning supplies and vacuum away and turned the television on to see the local news. There was Louise on the television screen being interviewed by a reporter, discussing the robbery attempt at the laundromat and her mother's death from a heart attack caused by the robbery. Stephen was shocked, walked over to the bar, and poured himself a scotch on the rocks. "Oh, Randy. Look what happened to Louise and Mabel. I don't know what to say. I need to reach Louise."

✿ ✿ ✿ ✿ ✿ ✿ ✿

After Enrique helped Josefa with the dishes, he went to his room and searched the internet for "How to prepare a presentation for business financing." He was determined to help his father obtain a mortgage. He bookmarked a few sample presentations and considered getting his hands on the business accounting records. The company's bookkeeper had been warned not to give any information to anyone, including family, without his father's approval.

He shifted his thoughts to Max and planned how they could sneak inside Stephen's studio for a few hours together and alone. Thursday night after pizza could be a perfect time, but he was unsure he could convince Max. Enrique yearned to touch Max's skin and was anxious to embrace him in bed. He dreamt of making love to him several times and masturbated every night, thinking of him and his smooth and silky body.

✿ ✿ ✿ ✿ ✿ ✿ ✿

Stephen was still distraught because he was unable to connect with Louise. He called Alice to tell her about the incident at the laundromat in New London and asked her for permission to ask Max if he would drive him to New London. The start of rush hour and bad weather on I-95 were not ideal conditions for Stephen to drive. Max agreed and left immediately.

As they approached the laundromat, they both saw police vehicles blocking a section of the street. Max finally found a parking space and parked Stephen's Porsche almost two blocks from the laundromat. They walked inside and found Louise sitting in the small office in the swivel chair, surrounded by police officers obtaining evidence of the attempted robbery. Louise raised her head and saw Stephen and Max. She ran to them in tears and embraced both.

"My life and dreams have changed today, Mr. Stephen." Louise was unable to explain to Stephen and Max what had happened. "Thank you both for coming to see me. I need friends to be with me."

"We are here for you, Louise." Max tries to console Louise. He was saddened to see her, a strong woman weakened by the loss of her mother and the attempted robbery. The dark clouds outside and the brightly lit interior helped create a mirror reflection on the windows facing the street. Max saw himself standing next to Stephen and Louise. It was a view he never forgot.

CHAPTER 13

RESEARCH

Max needed to start working on his outline for the valedictorian speech he was expected to deliver in a few weeks at his graduation. Today, he had already experienced a busy day at school, followed by swimming practice, work at Chester Marina, and ending at home with a delicious but heavy meat ravioli dinner. If he had his choice, he would have grabbed a book to read and lay in bed for the rest of the night. Instead, after dinner, he walked over to his desk, grabbed his computer, and sat on his beanbag chair in front of the window. He opened his word processing program and began a new document.

He raised his eyes above the computer screen, looked outside, and saw a blurry landscape in his backyard. He didn't try to focus his views, but instead, he attempted to recall his personal experiences at school during the past four years: two years of bullying and abuse by some of his classmates, followed by two years of the COVID-19 crisis.

He looked at the blurry landscape for inspiration and remembered the advice he was given by his parents and people he respected. He let his mind wander while his fingers typed his notes with whatever flashed before him.

✧ ✧ ✧ ✧ ✧ ✧ ✧

"Hey, Mom, I started to write an outline with thoughts about what to include in my speech on Graduation Day. What would you want your speech to highlight if you were the Valedictorian?"

"I don't think I have ever told you, Max, but I was the class Valedictorian when I graduated high school in Montpelier, Vermont," Alice confessed to Max.

"I never knew, Mom. Why didn't you tell us?"

"My life in Montpelier was not the same as here with you, Dana, and your father. It's a long story that someday you will hear. Right now, you must concentrate on your speech. Go to the bookcase and find the book 'Profiles in Courage' by President John F. Kennedy; you will find a copy of my speech in an envelope neatly folded inside the book. My suggestion to you would be to read the book and my speech before you begin writing your speech. You will get plenty of inspiration from both to get you started. You will recognize similar life lessons you have been taught since birth."

"Yes, I know exactly where to find the book. Thank you, Mom."

As Max walked away from Alice towards the bookcase, she gave him one more suggestion. "Oh, don't forget when you are writing your address, be honest with yourself. Write from your heart. Show the audience who you are. Give your classmates directions for the future. You will never go wrong if you show confidence, believe in yourself, and believe what you tell them."

Max stopped, turned around, and looked at his mother to absorb what she had just told him. In his mind, he repeated two critical comments she made and asked himself an important question, *"...be honest with yourself...tell the audience who you are. Does she know?"*

He picked up the book his mother suggested. Inside, he found Alice's handwritten speech to her graduating class in 1984 neatly folded inside an envelope labeled '1984 Valedictorian Address – Montpelier High School.'

Joe was sitting in the family room watching the national news when Max picked up "Profiles in Courage'" from the bookcase. He asked his father the same question, "Hey, Dad, I started working on my outline for the Valedictorian address, and I would love to pick your brain for a minute."

"Yes, of course, Max. How can I help?"

"If you were the Valedictorian, what would you want your speech to highlight?"

"I'm assuming you spoke with your mother about her speech. I see you have the book where the speech is filed. We have a unique filing system in this house."

"Yes, I plan to read the speech and the book, but I also want your feedback. What would your speech be like." Max sits beside his father on the couch and anxiously waits for his feedback.

"My speech would be nothing like yours, Max. It doesn't matter what my speech would be like. Right now, it is all about you. You must personalize your speech and don't worry about what I would say. Make it yours, and only yours. Search inside your soul for answers. You are not a kid anymore. You are a man whose personal experiences have helped you become the wonderful person you are today. Don't be afraid to tell the audience something they may not want to hear. Give them direction and remember one important factor when standing in front of your classmates and guests, never forget that you're in control of the moment. Show that you are in charge while you are at the podium. Become the leader they want to see," Joe stopped briefly and looked at Max. He saw himself the day he graduated high school. "If you follow what is in your heart, you will be the highlight of the graduation ceremony. Max, make them remember you for a long time."

"That's great advice, Dad. Thank you. I promise to make you and Mom proud."

Max returned to his room after getting feedback from his parents. He read his mother's speech and then started to read "Profiles in Courage." Before falling asleep, he opened his computer and added more notes.

✿ ✿ ✿ ✿ ✿ ✿

Enrique was closing the garden center alone on Thursday because his father was in New Haven at a meeting with a new bank that had expressed interest in providing a mortgage for purchasing the garden center's real estate. He drove on back roads he knew very well and got to the gym in Chester in record time, twenty minutes.

Max left the marina and only had a five-minute drive to the gym. They both arrived at the same time. "That was perfect timing," Enrique greeted Max outside with a welcoming smile.

Max smiled back, "It didn't take me long to get here. Do you want to work out together on legs, chest, or arms?"

Enrique scanned Max's body and suggested, "Let's do a simple upper-body workout. It's our first time working out together, and I prefer to take it slow and see how we work together."

"Sounds like a plan to me. I swam in the school's pool this afternoon, and my entire body is still sore."

"Maybe you will let me massage your stiff body later tonight after dinner." Enrique smiled at Max again and raised his eyebrows at the mention of "massage." Max smiled but did not respond.

Inside the locker room, they picked side-by-side lockers and stripped naked to put on their jockstraps, gym shorts, and tank tops. "Oh, there is that famous flying jockstrap." Max made fun of Enrique's jockstrap and recalled the last time they were in the gym's locker room.

"OK, I'm ready for our workout. Let's see how strong you are, Mr. Max," Enrique responded by making fun of Max.

They spent just over an hour lifting weights and talking. They were both open and honest with each other and shared their personal experiences over the past week. Max told Enrique about Mabel's death and the attempted robbery. Enrique was honest about his disappointment with his father on how he runs the garden center and his unwillingness to include him in his discussions with potential bank lenders.

After finishing their workout, they were back in the locker room. They stripped naked, grabbed their towels and toiletries, and walked to the showers. It was almost closing time at the gym. They were the only members in the locker room and showers. Max took the opportunity to be more aggressive this time, showing off his body and teasing Enrique by flexing his biceps, holding his breath to emphasize his stomach muscles, and slapping the head of his erect penis on his left palm. Enrique was not going to be held back. He leaned against the tile wall under the spray of water from the shower head, soaped his chest, squeezed his left nipple, and began to masturbate with his right hand facing Max. They laughed out loud and ceased playing with themselves when they heard someone enter the locker room. It was time to rinse with cold water, get dressed, and go for pizza.

There was a chill in the early evening air in Chester. They both decided to brave the temperature, sit outside where there was more privacy, and share a large Margarita Pizza.

"Max, we've been teasing each other sexually over the past several weeks, and it has been fun. Every time we get together, I learn more and more about you. I like you very much, but we always go home without plans or suggestions to take our sexual likes and desires to the next step. I have dreams of having fun in bed with you, but we never get to experience each other sexually. I don't want to be overly aggressive, but I know making love is what I want to do with you, and I don't think I can wait much longer." Enrique felt awkward but knew he needed to take this conversation to the next level. "I want to know if you have the same feelings for me as I do for you. What I'm trying to say is.... I want to make love to you in a bed, not in the back of my pickup truck or the showers at the gym. If you don't feel the same, I need to know now."

"Enrique, nothing would please me more than to rub my skin against yours. I would love to take you, hold you, and lick your body until you cum. I can't believe I'm saying that, but that is how I feel, and I don't care if you think I'm a pig. I don't think your parents would let you invite me to your bedroom so we can enjoy a night of passion, and I'm sure my parents would also have issues with the same invitation to my bedroom."

"I have a solution." Enrique pulled a key on a silver keyring from his pocket and showed it to Max, "This is the key to the studio at Stephen's property. We could sneak inside late at night, and nobody would see us. I can pull into the driveway with my headlights off and park on the far side of the barn. Stephen will not hear or see my pickup truck. All you have to do is sneak out of your house without your parents knowing you are gone. Maybe climb out of your bedroom window. We would be safe in the studio and could spend two or three hours together."

Max liked the plan, but at the same time, he didn't want to sneak out of the house and deceive his parents. "I would love to do it. What if we get caught?

"Anyone who walks in on us deserves to see what they find. We are not having a wild sex party with drugs and alcohol. It's just the two of us making love. I'm sure we'll be safe." In a low voice, Enrique looked into Max's eyes and continued. "I was hoping we could try it tonight. What do you think?"

"Are you crazy? I don't know if I can. I would have to go home and hope my parents go to bed by 10:00 PM. That is their usual time, but sometimes they watch television in their room and talk until 11:00 or 12:00 PM."

"Max, we are not breaking the law if we are caught. Stephen would never have us arrested for entering the studio at night. If we told him we wanted to make love there tonight, he would most likely send us a dozen roses." Enrique wanted to convince Max but didn't want to pressure him. "I'm confident if we came out to Stephen and asked to use the studio so we can be alone, he would give us his blessing.

Max didn't need much convincing, "OK, let's do it. I need some excitement in my life."

"I have to stop and fill up the pickup with gas. I will meet you inside the studio at 10:00 PM. The door will be unlocked, don't bother knocking. Let's text each other if there is any change in plans."

✿ ✿ ✿ ✿ ✿ ✿ ✿

Just before he reached Stephen's driveway, Enrique turned off his headlights and slowly drove to the opposite end of the barn, where the pickup truck could not be seen from Stephen's windows. He walked over to the studio's door in the back of the barn facing the perennial gardens, unlocked it, and entered. Enrique was in the process of painting the inside of the studio, so most of the furniture was pushed to one side of the room. Large plastic drop cloths were covering the curtains to protect them from paint splatters. He removed the plastic covers temporarily and closed the curtains to prevent light inside the studio from reflecting out. He pushed the mattress to the middle of the floor, lit a small candle to have a minimal amount of light, and placed it on an end table near the entrance door. Enrique removed all his clothes and stretched out on the couch with his legs spread, rubbing his penis with his right hand and squeezing his testicles with his left hand.

It was precisely 10:00 PM when Max walked inside the studio to find Enrique sitting on the couch with his legs spread open, playing with his hard erection, waiting for Max to arrive and undress.

"I've waited a long time for you to fuck me," Enrique whispers as Max closes and locks the door behind him.

"I'm ready for the massage you promised, Enrique," Max jokingly replies to Enrique's horny comment. They both laughed. Enrique got up from the couch and helped Max remove his clothes while kissing him on the neck, chest, and nipples. Max stretched out on the mattress, face down, and Enrique massaged his arms, legs, and back. He moved closer up his thighs to Max's butt and used his lips and tongue to give Max a sensation he had never experienced.

Their night of passionate lovemaking continued non-stop. At one point, Enrique slipped on a condom, spread lubricant on his penis, and slowly penetrated Max. It was a painful first-time experience for Max, but after Enrique's long penis was entirely inside, Max relaxed, allowing Enrique to continue thrusting in and out. Enrique's penis became rock-hard inside Max. He pulled out, gave Max a condom, and laid on his back, anxious for Max to fuck him. After rolling the condom on his penis, Max squeezed lubricant on it and inserted it inside Enrique while he played with Enrique's skin covering the head of his uncircumcised penis. Enrique wrapped his legs around Max's shoulders and guided Max's penis inside him. It seemed to get longer and harder as he pushed inside Enrique. He pulled out and entered again. He continued with the same motion for several minutes. Afraid of having an orgasm too soon, Max removed his penis from inside Enrique and began to nibble on his ears as he moved toward his nipples.

Just before midnight, they both took turns having orgasms on each other's chests. They licked each other dry, kissed, and rested for several minutes, feeling each other's bodies and holding each other tight while sharing stories about their past.

Soon after, they both left the studio. Max quietly crawls out through his bedroom window, and Enrique drives away in the darkness, undetected by anyone.

When Max got inside his bedroom, he removed all his clothes, sat on his beanbag chair facing the backyard, and masturbated thinking of Enrique's body and the sensations he experienced with anal sex. He shot his cum all over his chest again as far as his lips while squeezing his testicles, pretending Enrique had them in his mouth. Enrique arrived home and masturbated on his knees, thinking of Max as he shoved his middle finger inside his rectum. He also has an orgasm for the second time tonight.

Max heard his mobile phone buzz. It's a text from Enrique.

> ENRIQUE: You're a very sexy guy. I couldn't get enough. I just jerked off thinking of you.
> MAX: I did the same!. A big load. I wish you were here.
> ENRIQUE: Next time. I hope we do this again very soon. Good night.
> MAX: Good night. Let's chat sometime tomorrow.

✧ ✧ ✧ ✧ ✧ ✧ ✧

Louise had difficulties coordinating a traditional Irish wake for her mother at a local New London funeral home. During the four-hour "open casket" visitation period, she wanted a local Irish band to play traditional Irish folk music, a caterer to provide food, and a bartender to serve Irish beers, whiskeys, and other hard liquors. The funeral home would not allow it. They claimed the noise would upset the families in other rooms. The liquor could not be allowed because of insurance and liability issues. "What the fuck? Why even call it a wake if you can't drink and have fun," Louise told the funeral director. She compromised her expectations and agreed to host a normal *"visitation"* period at the funeral home, followed by drinks and a DJ at the laundromat, which will be closed for business during the traditional Irish wake.

It was Friday afternoon, and Max agreed to drive Stephen to the wake after he got out of school. They arrived at the funeral home to find Louise socializing among the small crowd of friends who came to pay their respects. Louise was throwing a party and would not let any of the guests mourn the passing of her mother, Mabel. "Mother would prefer people drinking and partying at her funeral. She didn't want anyone to cry at her wake. I'm just following orders, that's all."

The visitation period ended at 6:00 PM, and everyone walked over to the laundromat for the remainder of the Irish wake. There was a sign on the door of the laundromat – "Happy Third Birthday, Mabel." The non-Irish guests were confused. Someone in the group explained that in Irish tradition, the day someone dies is their "third birthday." The first birthday is their actual birth, the second is their baptism, and the third is when they enter the Kingdom of Heaven. The DJ turned up the volume and played traditional Irish folk songs. Louise began to dance by herself with a pint of Irish beer and encouraged the other guests to do the same. There was a large spread of food in the rear of the laundromat for everyone to help themselves. Guests brought some of the food, and the caterer brought the rest, including the desserts.

Friends who had never been to an Irish wake were in shock. Those who had experienced Irish wakes were thrilled to party with Louise. Max and Stephen were shocked, but that did not stop them from partying with Louise and the fun guests. Since Max was his designated driver, Stephen felt comfortable drinking a few shots of Irish whiskey with his Guinness Stout. Max wished his family, and Enrique was with him to experience this unusual style of honoring a loved one who had passed.

It was time for a toast, so Louise borrowed the microphone from the DJ and whistled very loud to get the guest's attention.

"I loved my mother very much. She made me who I am today, and I will be forever grateful for her love and guidance. Friends would say we fought a lot and called each other many unsightly names. That is true. But we still loved each other very much, and I will never forget her. I know many of you will never forget Mabel, and I thank you all from the bottom of my big Irish heart for coming today to be with me as I move on to a new chapter in my life. So, Mabel, if you are listening to me, please listen carefully because I'm only going to say this once," Everyone in the room laughed as Louise asked them to raise their glasses. "May your glass be ever full. May the roof over your head be always strong. And may you be in heaven half an hour before the devil knows you're dead. We love you, Mom. Rest in peace."

CHAPTER 14

PROM

The morning after Mabel's wake, Stephen stumbled out of bed with his hands on his head, trying to rub away a terrible hangover. The three healthy shots of Irish whiskey, complimented by three Guinness beers, pushed him over his limit. As he was getting out of bed, Max was already outside rinsing the powdery dirt that had collected on the surface of the Jaguar after he washed and waxed it last week. He insisted that the car be spotless for tonight's Senior Prom.

Wearing his gray silk robe, Stephen tried to focus as he walked to the kitchen, searching for a remedy for his pounding head. Before he looked for something to alleviate his headache, he opened the kitchen door to the garage and yelled, "Good morning, Max. Do you want coffee?"

"Yes, that would be great, thank you. I'll be in soon," Max responded, looking at his watch to confirm he was on schedule to finish all his errands before picking up Ashley in the early evening.

This year's Senior Prom was held at a local banquet facility in Haddam, about a twenty-minute drive from Max's home. The banquet hall was selected by the prom committee, chaired by Ashley. The committee selected the facility because it was chic, had great food, and had impressive views of the Connecticut River from the large windows in the back of the room. It also had a romantic outdoor patio by the water that could be seen from inside.

Still struggling with his hangover, Stephen set up the coffee maker, reached for coffee cups in the cabinet, and grabbed the skim milk in the refrigerator. He tried to recall his time at the laundromat yesterday, but most of it was blurry.

"Good morning, Randy. You won't believe the wake for Mabel yesterday. I don't remember most of the night, but it was a fun party with food, drinks, friendly people, and loud Irish folk music. I think she had a DJ, or maybe there was a live band. I don't recall. Yes, Randy, that was the wake. You would have walked out the back door. Max and I stayed for a while. I wanted to leave earlier but didn't want to piss off Louise, and you know how she gets." He didn't want Randy to notice he had a terrible hangover, but based on his staggering, it would be obvious to anyone.

He walked inside the pantry, reached for an old can of tomato juice, opened it, and poured it into a pint glass with several ice cubes, a few drops of hot sauce he kept in the refrigerator, and a few slices of lemon. He glanced at the glass briefly and guzzled its content. When he finished his Virgin Bloody Mary cocktail, he saw the box Max had brought him last week. He knew what was inside the box but refused to do anything with it.

Max finished rinsing and drying the Jaguar. He entered the kitchen and heard Stephen conversing with someone again. He didn't know it was coming from inside the pantry until Stephen came out. "Oh, there you are," Max was surprised to see Stephen looking like he had slept out in the woods all night. "I heard someone talking. I didn't realize it was you. Is the coffee ready?"

"Yes, let's go sit outside. I need fresh air. I'll pour and bring it out." Stephen hoped to feel better after guzzling his virgin cocktail. He still needed to inhale some fresh garden air on his back patio. "The car looks great, Max. I would love to be your chauffeur tonight. I have the perfect black suit, a chauffeur hat, and tall black boots. It was part of a Halloween costume I wore many years ago. I was supposed to look hot and kinky. I looked more like an old Nazi general. Am I repeating myself? Did I tell you about my costume already? Unfortunately, if I drove you to your prom, your classmates would think I was your chaperone. I only want to take a photo of you and your friend Ashley in front of the Jaguar. I hope you plan to stop with Ashley at home before heading to the prom."

"Yes, my mother warned me already. If I didn't bring Ashley to the house, she would drive to the banquet hall and drag us outside."

"I hope you realize how important your prom will be. You will always remember this day. Enjoy it while you are young," Stephen began to get sentimental with Max, "Life always seems to rush by quickly." He paused and looked out into the perennial gardens.

Max changed the subject. "I don't know if Enrique told you, but we met at the Chester Gym the other night and worked out together. After we were done, we went for pizza. He is a great guy. We had a good time together." Max wasn't sure it was a good idea to tell Stephen about meeting Enrique on Thursday night.

"No, I haven't seen Enrique. He is coming over on Sunday to continue painting the studio. Glad to hear you are both getting along. Enrique is a wonderful young man. Not sure what I would do without him." Stephen began to realize that Max and Enrique were seeing each other privately. He was confident that the kiss he witnessed behind the old oak tree a couple of weeks ago was not a one-time show of affection.

"He is a hard worker." Max was cautious to say anything about his meetings with Enrique. He didn't want Stephen to figure out they had been romantically involved. "I can't believe how much he does during the week. I hope his parents appreciate his enthusiasm."

"Yes, he has a lot on his agenda." Stephen looks at Max and tries to get more out of him. "That reminds me, I was in the studio on Friday, and it seemed like he was there this week. I don't recall seeing his truck in the driveway. Did he tell you he was here?" Max's face blushed. He couldn't recall if Enrique moved the furniture back to where he found it on Friday night. "No, he didn't mention it. Maybe he stopped in while you were out." Stephen didn't respond.

Max drove to Old Saybrook to pick up Ashley's corsage, a boutonniere for his tuxedo, and the tuxedo he rented. He found a parking spot outside the florist shop and tried to enter the store, but the door was locked. The florist doesn't open for another thirty minutes, about the same time most stores in the area open for business. Jason, the owner, sees Max trying to open the door, goes to the door, and lets him inside. He locked the door after Max entered.

"Hey, Max. You're a bit early, but come in anyway. I'm working on your flowers now. You can come in the back room and watch."

"Oh, sorry. I didn't realize the time."

"Why don't you drag that stool over here and watch me create magic with flowers," Jason, a young, handsome gay man in his early 30s, was enamored with Max when he came to the shop and placed the order last week. Max's wet gym shorts from washing the Jaguar emphasized the bulge on his crotch and outlined the head of his penis. "Did you spill water on yourself?"

"On, no. I was washing the car I'm taking tonight to the prom." Max realized that the gym shorts' fabric was light, and when wet, you could almost see through to the skin if you weren't wearing underwear, making it easy for Jason to see and enjoy the view. He shoved his right hand inside his shorts and rearranged his crotch while Jason stood there and watched.

"I would have done that for you," Jason commented flirtatiously and with a smile on his face.

"You didn't react fast enough. Perhaps your loss," Max senses Jason was interested in seeing more of his penis. The shop had not opened yet, and there were no customers inside. Max pulled down his gym shorts to expose half of his penis. Jason noticed what Max had done and looked directly at him. He pulled Max's shorts down to his knees, grabbed his penis with two hands, and performed oral sex on Max. The sensation was overwhelming for Max. Jason dragged his tongue down to Max's testicles and continued to lick while Max held Jason's head and dragged it up and down his scrotum. He ejaculates all over Jason's face in less than ten minutes.

"We could do this every Saturday if you are in the mood," Jason commented after licking all the remaining cum off Max's penis. Max used his fingers to wipe his cum off Jason's face. They both kissed and Jason licked Max's fingers. He felt guilty that he had let Jason perform oral sex on him, but he still took Jason's personal phone number when it was offered. Jason finished the corsage and prepared a white gardenia boutonniere for Max's tux. "Hope to see you again, Max. Please don't be shy about calling me. Perhaps next time I'll let you fuck me."

"Yes, it sounds like fun. I will. Thank you, Jason." Max paid for Ashley's flowers. His boutonniere was on the house.

He walked over to the tuxedo rental store and tried on the tux he reserved, a white dinner jacket with white satin lapels and black slacks with a black satin stripe on both sides. A heavily starched pleated shirt with imitation pearl studs, a black cummerbund, and a matching bow tie. The tuxedo fit him like a glove. Everyone at the shop, including customers, walked over to Max in front of the three-way mirror to admire the 1930s "Hollywood" style tux he selected to wear at the prom.

He raced to the Marina, where he was scheduled to work until 4:00 PM, giving him enough time to rush home, shower, dress, and pick up Ashley at 6:00 PM sharp. On his way to work, he got a call from Enrique and answered on the car's speakerphone.

"Hey, handsome. I want to let you know that I'm your "backup" if Ashley gets sick and cannot attend the prom." Enrique was joking, but in his heart, he was serious.

"That would be fun. I can see people's faces when we walk in together, holding hands. I think Ashley would even let you wear her dress."

"You are making fun of me, Mr. Max. It's not fair."

"No, I'm not. I would be proud to take you with me under different circumstances. I don't think you will fit in Ashley's dress, so we would have to get you a tux like mine. By the way, there is a rumor around school that two gay guys are bringing male dates to the prom, and one girl is bringing her girlfriend. I hope everyone welcomes them the same.

Enrique was somewhat envious of Ashley and wished he was going with Max. "Well, I just called you to wish you a great evening and let Ashley know that if she changes her mind about going, make sure she calls me."

"You are very generous, Enrique. I will tell her but don't wait around for her call." Max changed into his work clothes in the locker room at the marina. He thought about his sexual experience with Jason at the florist shop and compared it to previous anonymous sexual encounters.

✧ ✧ ✧ ✧ ✧ ✧ ✧

After leaving the marina at 4:00 PM, he hurried home, showered, dressed in his Hollywood tux, applied hair product, facial moisturizer, a touch of bronzer on his cheeks, and two quick spays of designer cologne. He found the aviator sunglasses he purchased at the local drugstore and walked out of his room looking like a confident movie star who had just won an Academy Award. Joe and Alice were shocked to see him. He looked like he had aged ten years. Their child looked like a man, a young and handsome man.

"Oh, Max. I almost didn't recognize you. You are going to be the talk of the prom tonight. I hope Ashley picked out a beautiful dress for tonight. Otherwise, nobody will notice her with you standing by her side." Alice was proud of her handsome son.

"Mom, don't tell her that when she comes over. She will be hurt."

"My lips are sealed. I would never dream of telling her or anyone else but you. Don't tell Dana what I just said because it will get back to Ashley before you even get to her house!" Max, Joe, and Alice laughed together in agreement.

"I heard my name. What's going on downstairs?" Dana opened the door to her room and yelled downstairs.

"Dana, come down and see how handsome your brother looks for his prom." Joe encourages Dana to join the rest of the family.

"WOW! Is that my brother under those clothes? Holy shit, Max. You better hope Ashley has a killer outfit, otherwise, she might as well stay in the car all night. Wait a second. The Jaguar is too nice of a car if she picked out a typical Kelly-green bridesmaid dress. If she did, she might want to bring her own car."

"Stop it, Dana. I'm going to pick her up and bring her here. Please don't say anything about her dress if you disapprove."

"Don't worry, big brother. I know my place," Dana replies with a smirk.

"That's what I worry about, Dana. You never know your place." Max gives Dana a serious look. "Oh, I forgot to tell you. Stephen wants to come over when I return with Ashley to take pictures of us in front of the Jaguar. I told him it was OK and would call him when I returned with her."

"Yes. That would be very nice. He is generous to let you use his car." Joe kept looking at Max and recalled his Senior Prom many years ago. "Where did the time go? It seems like my prom was just yesterday. I never looked as good as you do, Max," Joe was beginning to recall his last days in high school and his first year at Harvard. He was always a good student at Harvard and a friend to everyone in his dorm. He felt it was his time to pass the baton to his son.

✿✿✿✿✿✿✿

Max arrived at Ashley's small, modest home in Old Lyme, approximately two blocks from the Long Island Sound shore. Ashley lived with her mother, Abbie. Her father left them for a younger woman about three years ago and is now living in Las Vegas. The weekend after Max invited her to the prom, Ashley and her mother took the train to New York City to find the perfect dress in vintage thrift stores around SOHO, East/West Village, Chelsea, and Hell's Kitchen neighborhoods.

"Hi, Max. Oh, my God! You look wonderful in that tux. Wait until you see Ashley's dress. The flowers you picked out are terrific. She is going to love them." Abbie was very excited for Ashley. "I was thinking about your parents the other day. We have not seen each other for at least two or three years. How are they? They are going to miss you when you move to Harvard. I'm glad Ashley is going to UCONN. Maybe I'll see her on weekends." Abbie hoped to see Ashley every weekend but knew that once Ashley settled in her dorm, her weekend trips home would only be on holidays.

Ashley came down the stairs while Abbie and Max were still chatting in the foyer. Max saw her and almost didn't recognize her. She wore a black satin gown with white trim and white opera gloves. Her hairdresser fixed her long hair and makeup to resemble a sophisticated princess going to a ball. She wore a dozen fake pearl necklaces of different sizes around her neck and carried a small clutch covered in imitation pearls. Her outfit looked like it was custom-made just for her.

"WOW, Ashley, nobody will recognize you. Where did you find that dress? You look very elegant."

"It's a long story. Mom found it at a thrift store in the East Village. It was stained and two sizes too big for me. We bought it and took it to a seamstress someone had recommended in New London."

"Wait a second, was her name Mabel?"

"Yes. How do you know her?"

"It's a long story. Her daughter Louise is Stephen's housekeeper. You know she died last week after an attempted robbery at the laundromat. She suffered a heart attack.

"I picked up my dress the day before the robbery last week. Mom and I were shocked when we saw the news."

"I drove Stephen to New London the night she died. And again, to the Irish wake."

"Mabel was amazing. She took the dress apart and rebuilt it to my size. She gave me these gloves and told me to go out and buy fake pearls for the accent. She was so excited about this dress that she cried when I tried it. She told me I would have men throw themselves at me when I walked into the room. She was hilarious." Ashley remembered her experience with Mabel.

"Yes, and her mouth was as filthy as the sewer." Abbie couldn't get used to Mabel's choice of four-letter words. "She did an amazing job with the gown. She also worked her Irish magic and got rid of all the stains. I don't know how she did it."

"Ashley, you look extremely elegant and stylish." Max admires her looks. "Wait until you see the car we are traveling to the prom."

"WOW! How did you get this car? Where did you get it?"

"It belongs to Stephen, our neighbor. I asked him to borrow it and he was thrilled to lend it to me for the night."

"Ashley, you should feel very confident about your look. Talk to everyone and show them your big, beautiful smile. Make them all remember you." Abbie was very proud of Ashley.

Ashley and Max got inside the Jaguar and drove to Max's home. Before arriving, he called Stephen to let him know they were on their way. Stephen grabbed his camera and walked through the path to Max's home. At the same time, the elegant black Jaguar turns into the driveway. Joe and Alice open their front door to greet Max and Ashley.

"Hi, Stephen. Wait until you see Max. He looks like a Hollywood star. You are not going to recognize him." Alice was excited to see Max and Ashley together. When Ashley exited the car, Alice, Joe, Stephen, and Dana could not believe how beautiful she looked. A fairy tale elegance never seen at a Lyme High School Prom. They both posed for pictures before driving away to the party.

Stephen returned home with his digital camera and uploaded the files to his computer. "Look, Randy. Max and his date are standing in front of our Jaguar. I will have this picture blown up and placed on the piano. We should be very proud of our grandson. I wish they knew how proud we are of them."

✿ ✿ ✿ ✿ ✿ ✿ ✿

At the same time Max and Ashley were having their photos taken in front of the Jaguar, Joel, the landscape architect, called Enrique at the garden center and invited him to his house for a swim in the pool. Enrique was in the process of closing the garden center and decided to stop by Joel's home in Essex. When he arrived, Joel's husband opened the door.

"Oh, I didn't know Joel was married," Enrique commented when Paul opened the door and introduced himself as Joel's husband.

"Welcome, Enrique. Joel told me all about you. He is in the pool." Paul escorted Enrique through the house and out through the back patio doors to the pool deck.

"Hi Enrique," Joel came out of the pool naked, grabbed his terrycloth robe, and poured cocktails for the three. They sat by the patio table facing the hot tub and talked for almost an hour.

"I didn't stop at home to grab my Speedo. I hope you don't mind if I jump in naked in the hot tub." After the first cocktail, Enrique began to tease Joel and Paul.

"Not at all. We are right behind you," Paul removed all his clothes and all three were in the hot tub, where they talked, touched, and felt each other's bodies for almost one hour. They dried themselves with beach towels Joel had left on the lounge chair and walked into the house to the bedroom. Enrique spent the next hour fucking Joel and Paul, as they requested, until all three climaxed on Joel's hairy chest.

✿ ✿ ✿ ✿ ✿ ✿ ✿

When Max and Ashley walked inside the banquet hall, heads turned in their direction. Together, they displayed a sense of style seen in the 1930s Hollywood parties. Dancing continued through dinner. Everyone was enjoying themselves. Max noticed that three same-sex couples were attending. That made him feel good about himself, and he wondered if it was time to come out to his family.

The two well-known bullies on the football team also attended the prom but were drunk with their girlfriends before they arrived. They had a bottle of tequila in their car and kept going outside for shots. One of them walked by Max and whispered, "I thought you would be here with your faggot boyfriend from Mexico. I saw you both having a romantic dinner in Chester." Max didn't respond and walked away.

"What the fuck did he tell you, Max? Look at him. He is so drunk he can't even walk a straight line." Ashley was concerned the bullies would ruin the evening.

"Nothing important. Don't worry; they don't even know where they are." Max didn't want Ashley to be concerned.

Ten minutes later, the second bully walked over to Max," Hey Max, someone just scratched your pretty Jaguar outside. You better go out and look." Ashley was in the ladies' room, so Max stepped outside to ensure Stephen's car was not damaged. A false alarm. He realized it was a way for the bullies to get him alone and outside. It was the wrong time for the bullies to take advantage of Max. He was not going to let them abuse him tonight. When they approached him in the dark parking lot, one of them tried to trip him and drag him into a wet and muddied spot. Max swung his fist with all his strength and hit one of them in the nose. When the other bully got closer, Max kicked him in the groin, forcing the bully to drop to his knees. Before he got up, Max pushed his upper body into the mud. He hurried back to the banquet hall, saw the banquet manager by the front door, and warned him there were two drunk guys in the parking lot trying to damage cars.

The manager called the police just as the two bullies returned to the banquet hall. One had a severe bloody nose dripping on his all-white tuxedo. The other strolled into the men's room with his hands on his abdomen and his tuxedo covered in mud.

"Hey, Ashley, I think it is time for us to leave," Max stops Ashley as she exits the ladies' room. They saw the bullies walking toward the men's room.

"Yes, let's go. Those two have blood all over them. My friend Julie invited us to her house for a small party. There will only be ten couples, and none will have blood on their face." Ashley was happy to leave and avoid arguments with the bullies.

"Perfect, let's go before they come out of the men's room." Max was relieved that Ashley was ready to leave. As they were walking towards the exit, two Haddam police officers were entering the banquet hall. "Thank you for coming officers." Max greeted the two officers. "The two you need to question are in the men's room with blood and mud on their tuxedos." Ashley and Max got inside the Jaguar and drove to Julie's home for a more intimate late-night party.

A half-hour after they arrived at Julie's home, two other guests joined the party and shared their experience watching the two bullies and their girlfriends trying to leave the parking lot under the influence of alcohol. The two officers stopped them, backup officers arrived at the banquet hall, and a quick search of their car revealed an opened bottle of Tequila and other drugs. All four were taken to the police station. Max smiled as soon as he learned the outcome. He never told anyone he was the cause of the bloody nose and the muddy tuxedo.

CHAPTER 15

STUDIO

Sunday afternoon, the day after the Senior Prom. Max sat in his room, facing his computer screen, trying to write his Valedictorian speech. It had been several hours, and all he had on the screen were his welcoming and acknowledgment remarks. He got up from his chair, stretched out in bed, stared at the ceiling, and searched his mind for content. Nothing. He walked into the kitchen and grabbed an apple to eat in his room. Nothing. He looked through the window towards the thick woods in the rear of the property for answers. Nothing. Still looking for inspiration through the window, he stared at the cloudless Connecticut blue sky. He saw nothing. He recalled the advice he got from his parents and Stephen; nothing seemed to help him get started. He read and re-read notes he had been making for several weeks. Nothing. The only phrase in his mind was, 'Be yourself,' be yourself,' be yourself.' That phrase kept ringing all afternoon. He doesn't know what it means.

"*Am I too young and inexperienced to help guide my classmates to a successful future after graduation? What am I doing? I should not have agreed to take on this responsibility.*" Still looking out the window, "*I know my speech is out there somewhere, but I don't see it. Maybe I'm looking in the wrong direction. Maybe it's not meant to be out there at all.*" He realized he was not focused on writing the speech. He looked at his watch. It was 4:00 PM. Still, all he had on the screen for over three hours were his welcome and acknowledgment comments. He picked up his mobile phone to send a text.

MAX: Hey, how about tonight at 10 PM?
ENRIQUE: Yes, working all day until closing at 5 PM.
ENRIQUE: In the studio?
MAX: Yes.
ENRIQUE: See you there.

✧ ✧ ✧ ✧ ✧ ✧

As in the past, at 10:00 PM, Max quietly crawled out of his room through the window and walked through the path towards Stephen's studio. He saw Enrique's pickup truck turning into the driveway with headlights off. Enrique parked in the usual obscured space next to the barn and entered the studio quietly with his key. Max was sixty seconds behind him. When they met inside, no words were spoken. Curtains were drawn closed with no lights, and the same candle was lit as they passionately removed each other's clothes while kissing, hugging, and rubbing their bodies together. They relaxed on the mattress with no urgency to leave. They knew each other's most sensitive parts of their bodies and used that knowledge to reach maximum pleasure and release. When they stopped, they stayed close together, quiet, and ignored the time. They were both still naked, still hard. Enrique's back was leaning against the wall. Max's head was resting on Enrique's lap.

"Sex with you is a different experience than the few encounters I have had with other men." Max surprised Enrique with this comparison. "I feel very comfortable and satisfied when we are naked in bed. I'm open and trust you with anything that turns you on and makes you feel good. I never thought that getting fucked would please me but watching you while you fuck me turns me on, especially when you climax while you are inside me."

"So, how many encounters have you experienced with other men?"

"Oh, I had a feeling you would ask. Not many."

"When was your last?" Enrique turned Max's face towards his.

"I let the florist perform oral sex on me the day I went there to pick up Ashley's flowers. It wasn't planned. It just happened. Well, you know, we're not in a committed relationship. We're young and should be experimenting with our sexual desires. I wouldn't mind having a threesome with you and Jason. He's very handsome. How about you, Enrique? When was the last time someone fucked you or sucked your dick?"

"I made a last-minute late delivery the other day to a construction site. The landscape architect helped me unload the truck. We were alone in the property. He let me fuck him on the kitchen counter. He was very hot." Enrique was honest with Max about his sexual experiences. "He called me yesterday afternoon at the garden center and invited me to his house to swim in the pool. I didn't know he was married to another man. I ended up fucking both of them in their bedroom. They are both very handsome men. I wish you were there with me. We should plan a sexual encounter with them."

"Yes, if you think they were hot, count me in. How about your first experience?"

"My first one was my high school art teacher. He invited me to his home when I was a Junior in high school. He wanted to show me his art studio. That's not all he showed me. I was only sixteen, and he knew it. He kissed me, and when I kissed him back, he took all my clothes off and buried his face in my crotch. He wanted to fuck me all the time. That was my first experience as a 'bottom'. The relationship continued for several months. I started to see other guys, and he probably found other students willing to get fucked all the time." Enrique was not embarrassed about disclosing his first gay sex experience. "When was your first time, Max?"

"I drove down this dirt road in East Haddam near the river because I had heard it was a nature preserve great for hiking. When I reached the end, only one other car was parked in the parking area. I got out of my car and proceeded to walk the trails. After a quarter of a mile, I see this handsome guy sitting on a huge boulder with his shirt open. He started a conversation with me, and before I knew it, he unzipped my pants and pulled my dick out. I didn't stop him. He sucked my dick until I came all over his face. I never went back there. He wanted to see me again, but I was afraid and threw out his phone number." This was the first time Max had ever told this story.

"You know something, Max? You're right. We should have an open relationship now. We're young and should be experimenting as long as we are safe and don't hurt each other or anyone else."

"I'm open to it. I wouldn't object. Depends on the identity of the other participants." Max's interest perked up. "Maybe we should share details about our sexual encounters with others right after it happens. That will turn us on."

"Good to know. I would enjoy that with you. I hope neither gets jealous and storms out of the room in the middle of an orgy."

"I think we are at a point in our relationship that if it becomes an issue, we would talk about it and not react with unnecessary drama," Max assured Enrique.

"I agree." Enrique stopped rubbing Max's temples and thought about his relationship with Max. He stared at the curtain blocking the window and asked himself, *"Will we ever become more than just fuck-buddies? What do I do or say to Max if I want more? He leaves for Harvard in mid-August. What should I do or say before he leaves? Should I let him go with no response on my part? I'm afraid of losing him. I don't want our relationship to end."*

"How is your Valedictorian speech coming? Enrique changed the subject immediately. "Graduation is just around the corner. You should be finished with it or close."

"It's funny you ask." Max delayed his response to Enrique. The look on his face and his attitude changed dramatically. "I have been trying to work on my speech, and I don't seem to be able to get my thoughts organized besides the basic introduction remarks," Max confessed to Enrique in a frustrated voice. "I'm stuck and can't seem to go anywhere.

I keep looking at my notes," Max paused for ten seconds. "They don't seem to help me. I don't know what to do next."

"Sounds to me like you are fighting with yourself. What's holding you back? It's not like you. Let yourself go," Enrique placed his hands on Max's forehead and rubbed his temples again. "You need to approach this project differently than others you have mastered. When you sit in front of your computer, feel free to write down anything that comes to your head. You can edit afterward. When I need to be creative with my paintings and feel frozen and unable to move forward, I take off all my clothes and paint naked. It makes me feel free. You should try it. Lock yourself in the room, remove all your clothes, and start writing. It truly works for me."

"That's very funny, Enrique. If I sit naked in front of my computer, I may start surfing the internet for porn."

"Nonsense, you have a strong determination to succeed. You will get through this process. I'll help you."

"Nothing will ever be written if you come in my room and get naked with me." They both laughed. "I don't know. Maybe I'm getting too much advice and not leaving room for my own input. The common suggestion I seem to get is to *'be yourself, Max.'* I'm having difficulties with that advice. I don't know why. Am I too young and inexperienced? What's holding me back? How can I guide my classmates to their next chapter in life when I'm not out in front banging the drum myself?"

"I think you just answered your question. You're not being honest about yourself to your classmates and your family. Secrets always hold me back. Maybe it's time for you to expose yourself, come out publicly," Enrique realized that he must be careful what he tells Max. He didn't want Max to feel pressured and leave the room without feeling better about his speech. "If your classmates disapprove, who cares? It's your life. You were born gay. You don't need their approval or anyone else's approval. Your family is very contemporary. I'm confident they will understand it is not a choice. They will still support you and love you, Max. You will never go wrong by being honest to yourself and honest to the people you love." Max looked confused. Enrique felt he had to slow the conversation down. "Maybe we won't have to hide here anymore."

Enrique stopped and thought about his situation at home. "You are very fortunate to have an understanding family. My mother would be fine with me being gay, but my father would struggle. I have considered coming out to them, but something is holding me back. Maybe I'm just afraid of my father's reaction, especially now with the pressure of getting a mortgage to buy the land the business occupies." Enrique paused again. He considered his life with Max ten or twenty years from now. He had never considered a long-term relationship with anyone, but their mood tonight and conversation made Enrique think more about a life together with Max.

"Max, have you ever considered what it would be like for us ten years from now?" Enrique focused on Max's eyes as Max turned his head quickly to look at Enrique and wondered if he meant what it would be like for them, together, ten years from now or as individuals.

"My education is critical to me. I want to graduate from Harvard and attend law school four years from now. That is my priority right now. Ten years from today? Who knows? Maybe I will be at a law firm or have my own law office. Do you know where you want to be ten years from now?"

Enrique was disappointed that Max did not consider their relationship in the future. He didn't want to discuss a long-term relationship at this time. "I think my future is already carved out for me by my parents. If we can obtain a mortgage, my parents expect me to take over the business within the next ten years so my father can retire. I still want to continue painting. Hopefully, it will pay for some of the bills." Sadness hovered over Enrique and Max as they considered their very different economic futures. Enrique was hoping to hear Max say something about their relationship. Max didn't understand the question, and Enrique wondered if Max chose not to respond about their relationship in ten years on purpose.

"Max, there is a pad and pencil in the desk drawer. Go get it and write down what comes out of my mouth, whether you like it or not." Max is confused but still gets up from the mattress and reaches for the pad and pencil in the desk drawer.

"OK, I'm ready. Don't go too fast. I'm not a stenographer."

Enrique began to yell out suggestions for Max to consider in his speech. He was going fast and didn't want to stop.

"Slow down. I can't write that fast!" Max was overwhelmed by Enrique's suggestions. He liked most of them and wanted to ensure he wrote them all on the pad.

"Talk about the sacrifices everyone had to make during the COVID–19 pandemic. Acknowledge anyone, student or teacher, who died during that time or came close to dying. What did you learn from the pandemic? Tell them why you are a better person from the experience. It is likely that your classmates learned the same and are stronger today because of the experience. You have to bring it out of them. Make them feel good about themselves. They are just as scared about their future as you are."

"What makes you think I'm scared of my future?

"You are. I can see it in your eyes. If you were not scared, your speech would have been finished by now. Please don't kid yourself, Max; I was scared when I graduated last year. I got over it quickly. You will also."

"I don't want this speech to be all about me." Max stops writing.

"It's not just about you. It's about the entire class. Most likely, your school experiences and feelings now are similar to those of your classmates. If you show them how those experiences help you become a better man, they will take that and say the same about themselves. You need to make them feel good without telling them directly that they are 'wonderful.' Let them find out that the past four years of their lives molded them into adulthood. It's not just about you, Max. You are giving them instructions on how to feel good about themselves and the past four years, whether they had good or bad experiences. The past four years developed them into the person they are, you are."

"I get it. I like where you are going with it." Max got up from the mattress and opened the curtain just enough to peek into the garden. "We need to take a five-minute break, Enrique. This is a lot for me to process all at once." Stephen's outdoor lights were still on. As he stared out into the rear perimeter of the property, he realized that he had the opportunity to be a leader and give his classmates the same confidence he needed to succeed in the future. As he looked out into the woods, he saw a candlelight reflection on the windowpane of Enrique, naked on the mattress, hard, and staring at him. "Why are you staring at me?"

"I'm not allowed to stare? I like what I see in front of me. Not just the body but, equally, the soul. I have tasted every square inch of your body and seen the love you share with others and me. There is nothing I don't like. " Enrique wanted to open up the conversation about their relationship but realized Max was stressed about his speech. Bringing up the future of their relationship would have only created greater stress levels.

"You are very sweet, Enrique. There is a huge difference between looking out into the garden from this viewpoint and my bedroom window. I see a lot more I could not see before." Max's eyes were focused directly out the window. "There is a lot more open space from this view. Room for creativity. Space to grow. Thank you, Enrique. You've given me what I needed to understand my notes and the feedback I got from you and others." He realized that Enrique just lit a fire under him. He needed to take that torch and make it his own. He now has more material for his speech than he needed.

"Enrique, I need to inspire my classmates to do the right thing in life without sounding like a sermon from their parents." Max walked away from the window towards the mattress, where Enrique diligently wrote notes for Max to consider. He takes the pencil and pads away from Enrique, pushes him to the middle of the mattress, and gets on top to start their lovemaking again. The second time tonight was even more passionate and rougher.

✿ ✿ ✿ ✿ ✿ ✿

Stephen was in the family room looking towards the perennial garden, ready to turn in for the night. The rear floodlights were still on. He saw two empty glasses on the patio table and Randy sitting in the wheelchair outside. He walked over to the kitchen to go out and bring Randy and the glasses into the house. As he approached Randy, he looked at the studio picture window and noticed the curtain drawn with only a small opening in the middle where a faint light inside reflected on the windowpanes. He thinks to himself, *"I wonder if Enrique was here painting and left a light on? Maybe Enrique is still in the studio? Alone or with someone else?"*

He brought the glasses to the kitchen and Randy with his wheelchair to Randy's bedroom. He decided to walk over to the studio to turn off the light. Before he reached the studio's door, he saw Enrique's truck parked on the far end of the barn, where it could not be seen from Stephen's home. He returned to the house and sat on his front porch in the dark, where he could see who came in or out of the studio.

✿ ✿ ✿ ✿ ✿ ✿

After having their second orgasm the same night, Enrique and Max cuddle together on the mattress, kissing, licking, and nibbling each other. Enrique's mind traveled to mid-August when Max was expected to leave for Harvard. Max is biting his nipples while Enrique asks himself, *"Will I still see him when he leaves for Harvard? How can we have a relationship after he leaves? Does he want to see me after he leaves? Could he fall in love with another Harvard student? Maybe I'm not smart enough for him."*

ONLY LOVE LASTS

"You're very quiet. What's going through your mind?" Max realized that he was sucking on Enrique's nipples, and there was no response from Enrique. Max was still hard and noticed that Enrique had turned soft quickly.

"Oh, I'm sorry. My mind just went nowhere. I was enjoying the moment with you sucking on my tits." Enrique hesitates but whispers a request. "I don't want it to stop."

"Why would I stop? It seems like I'm enjoying this more than you."

"Max, you have no idea how much I enjoy your lips on my skin. I'm a lucky guy."

"So am I, Enrique, so am I" Max continued to nibble and suck on Enrique's nipples. He slowly moved towards his stomach and licked his navel. Enrique held Max's head and pushed his hair away from his face to see Max's eyes.

"You have beautiful eyes. I can see your heart through them. I like what I see."

Max raises Enrique's hips and buries his face on Enrique's crotch. The sensation was overwhelming for Enrique. He masturbated and had his third orgasm of the night shortly after Max penetrated him again. Max climaxes inside Enrique again.

✧ ✧ ✧ ✧ ✧ ✧ ✧

"What time is it?" Max is looking for his watch.

"You don't want to know."

"Oh! I can't believe it's almost 2:00 AM. I have school tomorrow. I'll be a mess.

"Not if you think about me and our time here tonight." Enrique grabbed Max and kissed him before they left. "I have a day off from the garden center tomorrow and plan to return here to finish painting this room for Stephen. I will most likely see you sometime after you get home from school.

✧ ✧ ✧ ✧ ✧ ✧

Stephen was still sitting on his front porch in the dark. He heard Enrique's truck ignition and saw Max walking through the path towards his bedroom window in the back of his house. Enrique drove out with headlights off. Stephen's mystery was solved.

CHAPTER 16

SPEECH

"Max, if you don't get up soon, you're going to be late for school," Alice was concerned she hadn't heard Max in his room getting ready for school.

"I'm up, Mom. I'll be ready quickly." Max finally was out of bed, but after spending the day yesterday trying to write his speech and several hours at night with Enrique until 2:00 AM, he felt a massive hangover. As soon as he got out of the shower, his phone buzzed with an incoming text:

> ENRIQUE: On my way to paint at Stephen's studio.
> ENRIQUE: See you when you get out of school.
> MAX: Yes.
> ENRIQUE: Nice time last night.
> ENRIQUE: I enjoyed spending time with you.
> MAX: Same here. I got to run. Very late.

Dana jumped in Max's car with him, and they raced out of their driveway for their 4-minute drive to school. Because they were late, the closest parking space was at the far end of the lot. They both raced into the building. Dana stopped at her locker across from Max's locker and looked over at Max to notice he was fiddling with the combination lock and could not get it opened. Suddenly, Ashley stopped to help him.

"Max, you look like you haven't slept all night. What happened? She quickly opened the lock for him.

Dana interrupted their conversation, "I told him the same in the car. I thought he was going to slap me. You better stand back, Ashley."

"Good morning. Thanks for the compliments, ladies. I must look like shit today.

"Sorry, but you usually look neat, your clothes ironed, and your hair combed nicely. None of that is in front of me this morning. Let's talk over lunch. I'm also late for class today."

"I should have stayed home today!" Max was frustrated and embarrassed that he couldn't open his locker and needed help from Ashley. His hands were still shaking due to lack of sleep.

"It's not too late to get back in the car. We can go to the beach! I'll follow you. I always follow my big brother." Dana was not kidding, and Max knew it.

"Go to class, Dana. No beach for you today."

✿ ✿ ✿ ✿ ✿ ✿

Max needed help to concentrate in school. He was tired from lack of sleep, and his mind was focused on his conversation with Enrique from the previous night. He sat in each class and wrote drafts of his speech in his notebook. His mental radar was not picking up class lectures until his English literature class. There was an in-depth discussion of the poet Walt Whitman, and his English teacher, Mr. King, noticed Max wasn't participating in class and was focused on something else in his notebook.

"Max, tell us why you think Walt Whitman wrote *O Captain, My Captain?*" Mr. King was trying to bring Max back into the class discussion and away from whatever he was writing in his notebook. He thought embarrassing him was the best way.

Max was caught by surprise. He only heard part of Mr. King's question and assumed Mr. King wanted to know the poem's origins. He paused briefly to gather his thoughts and pushed his speech papers under his books. "He wrote it in response to the assassination of President Lincoln."

"I'm certain you have read and studied the poem, Max. Tell me what you believe is the irony in the poem?" Mr. King was still trying to trap Max.

Max didn't hesitate. "The narrator calls out for the captain to celebrate a war victory. The captain doesn't answer because he died on his ship before returning home. The irony is that he managed to protect his ship during the war and return it home safely, but it cost him his life, and he could not enjoy the important victory celebrations."

Mr. King continued with Max. "What is the lesson we all should learn from this poem?"

"There are consequences for everything we do in life." Max was surprised by his answer. "I mean that our actions always return to us with a reaction. Whatever we do in life, there is always a response. Victory in the war fields comes with a price. Walt Whitman relates President Lincoln to the Captain of the ship. The United States is represented by the ship. President Lincoln guided us through the horrors of the Civil War and ended slavery. Our country's two major historical events caused the President to lose his life. He didn't live long enough to see the benefits of what he accomplished. Walt Whitman is also telling us to enjoy life now because there may not be a tomorrow."

"Thank you, Max. Does anyone want to add anything to Max's comment?" Mr. King looked around the room for responses. There was complete silence. He looked at Max. Max smiled back at him.

✿✿✿✿✿✿

Max walked into the school cafeteria, where Ashley was waiting for him. "What did you do yesterday that made you late for school today?" Ashley and Max sat together in their usual corner. Ashley was trying to understand why Max looked messy this morning. "You must have cleaned up in the men's room after I criticized your looks this morning. There is some improvement, but you still look like shit."

"Don't blame me. I was out and didn't get home until after 2:00 AM."

"Where did you go?"

"I worked, unsuccessfully, on my speech most of the day, so I gave up and met Enrique in Stephen's studio last night."

"Oh, that explains a lot."

"Well, it wasn't all sex. He helped me focus on my speech and gave suggestions that made me look at my speech from a different angle. I couldn't get my mind away from the speech after I got home last night and today during classes. I wasn't paying attention in class and wrote four or five pages of draft content based on our discussion last night. Unfortunately, I got caught during English Lit class, and Mr. King tried to embarrass me. I outsmarted him. He became the Captain, and I was the Ship."

"What the hell do you mean?"

"Never mind, it's a long story." Max thought about his responses during his English Literature class and smiled again.

✧ ✧ ✧ ✧ ✧ ✧ ✧

As soon as swimming practice was over, Max raced home, and as Enrique suggested, he locked the door to his room, took off all his clothes, and sat naked in front of his computer to transfer the handwritten notes he took during class to his computer. He added more content to his notes, edited, added more, and edited more. The basic layout of his speech was almost complete when his mobile phone buzzed with an incoming text.

> ENRIQUE: Hey r u home?
> MAX: Yes, I'm working on my speech.
> ENRIQUE: I'm in the studio. I need help moving
> furniture. I don't want to ask Stephen, and I don't want
> to drag and scratch the hardwood floors.

MAX: Be there soon. Can I come naked?
ENRIQUE: ????? Yes.
ENRIQUE: Want to look like a pervert to your
neighbors?
MAX: ha, ha, ha.

Max arrived in the studio, and shortly after, Stephen walked in while they moved the furniture back to its original locations before Enrique started painting. "Gentlemen, thank you for your hard work. The studio looks wonderful with a fresh coat of paint. I like this color much better. It brings the outdoors inside. I like to see the drapes open all day, and maybe I should remove them. Oh, I can decide later."

"Glad you like it, Stephen. It does bring a lot more natural light inside the room." Enrique is a bit nervous about Stephen's comment and wonders if he knows he has been meeting Max in the studio for the past several weeks. "You may want to leave the drapes just in case you or your guests want privacy."

"That's a good suggestion, Enrique. What do you think, Max?"

"Oh, I agree with Enrique; some people like to walk around naked and not be seen by the outside world."

"Well, maybe you are right. If they like to walk around the house naked, they most likely like to be seen naked by the outside world. I know the type. I was one of them until my body got old and flabby. Now, you and Enrique would likely not care who sees you naked unless you hide for other reasons."

There was silence in the room. Max felt an awkward warmth on his face. His eyes connected with Enrique's eyes. A quirky smile comes out of Enrique. "Well, I have to run into town. Thanks again for helping Enrique with the furniture, Max." As Stephen reached the door to exit, he turned around very dramatically and looked at both, "Oh, by the way, you should change the sheets on the bed weekly. Just replace them when you leave at night with the backup in the linen closet outside the bathroom. You can leave the dirty sheets by the kitchen door inside the garage. Louise will wash them and return them to the linen closet. It's not healthy to lay on dirty sheets." Stephen dramatically opened the door and left the room with one final comment, "Ta -Ta!" Max and Enrique's jaws were wide open. They didn't know what to say.

"He knows!" Max is in shock as he whispers to Enrique.

"No, shit, he knows. If he were upset with us, he would have told us."

"I felt like he invited us to return as often as we wanted. I need to think about this a bit more. What if he tells my parents?" Max was nervous he would be outed before he outs himself to his family.

"Stephen would never do that. He would encourage us to tell our parents, but he would never tell our parents he caught us fucking in his studio." Enrique was confident that Stephen would keep this secret.

"Maybe we should approach him and tell him we are sorry and will not do it again."

"Nonsense, we will be back, perhaps tonight. Stephen prefers to be ignorant about our sexual encounters. If anyone asks him, he would not be lying if he said, 'I don't know anything about Max and Enrique's relationship.'"

"Perhaps you're right. Maybe we should stay away from the studio for a few days."

"Nonsense again, Max. I have a class at the Community College tonight. After class, I will meet you here at 10:00 PM as usual."

"Text me when you leave class to ensure I can leave without being noticed."

"Oh, Max, my Max. You can be a baby, but you are my baby." Enrique grabs Max's butt and kisses him. Max was surprised Enrique referred to him as 'my Max.'

✿ ✿ ✿ ✿ ✿ ✿ ✿

Max returned home after helping Enrique move the furniture in the studio back where it belonged. He walked into his room and continued where he had left, typing and editing his speech in the nude.

A few hours later, Joe knocks on Max's door, "Hey Max, take a short break and join us for dinner. I have steaks on the grill, and we are all eating outside. It's perfect weather to eat outside on the patio."

Max quickly puts on his gym shorts and opens the door to his room, "Thanks, Dad; I could use a break. Let me wash up, and I will be out in a couple of minutes." Now that his mind was away from the speech, Max began to think about what Stephen had said in the studio, *'Oh, by the way, you should change the sheets on the bed weekly. Just replace them when you leave at night....'* Max looked at himself in the bathroom mirror and asked himself, *"Did he mean it? Does he know for sure, or was he trying to trick us?"*

"Max, dinner is ready. Come outside," Alice yelled to Max, who was still looking in the mirror, thinking about Stephen's comment.

"You were up late last night. Were you working on your speech? I woke up a little after 2:00 AM and thought I heard noises outside. It must have been a bear. Then I heard you walking around in your room at that hour."

"Oh, yes, I got up in the middle of the night to work on my speech." He knew it was not a true statement. He sensed that Joe and Alice also knew.

✧ ✧ ✧ ✧ ✧ ✧

Alice, Joe, Dana, and Max sat around the outdoor patio table after dinner and talked for over an hour after eating. Before 10:00 PM, Dana was in her room with her earphones, listening to her music and texting friends. Alice and Joe were watching television in their bedroom. Max was getting ready to meet Enrique. He crawled out his window carefully so as not to make any noise and slowly walked over to the path and alongside the barn to get to the studio door.

Just as Max was closing his bedroom window after crawling out, Alice forgot a client's folder in the kitchen that she needed to review for a meeting tomorrow morning and walked down the stairs to retrieve it. When she found the folder on the counter, she noticed, through the kitchen window in the distance, an image of a man, who looked like Max, walking towards the door to Stephen's studio. Immediately to the right, she recognized Enrique's truck parked by the studio door behind rhododendron bushes that had been recently trimmed. She ran upstairs to tell Joe, but he was already asleep. She can't see the studio from her bedroom window, so she finds her sneakers, shorts, and a T-shirt and goes outside.

Stephen felt Enrique and Max would return tonight, so he sat outside on his front porch in the dark. He saw Enrique's truck with the headlight off, turning in his driveway and parking on the other side of the barn. At the same time, he saw Max walking through the path towards the studio door. He smiled, finished his scotch on the rocks, and decided to go to bed and let the boys have fun. When he got up from the chair, he saw Alice beginning her walk on the path after Max had already entered the studio. He quickly walked over to the side of the barn behind Enrique's truck to stop her from going further.

"What are you doing here?" Alice is shocked to see Stephen approaching her.

"That is my question, and this is my property. I should be asking you," Stephen responds in a whisper.

"My son is in there with someone I don't know I should trust."

"So, what will you do, walk in on them? What do you expect you will see?"

"He is my son, and I have the right to know what he is doing there."

"Yes, you do. But finding this way is not good for you or your son. I suspected the same but never asked nor tried to barge in on them. It's not my business. He is over eighteen and has the right to make his own decisions. Alice, you can do whatever you want. He is your son. I will not stop you. If he were my son, I would wait patiently until he told me himself, and then, I would love him just the same. So, if you want to barge in on them, go right ahead. If you want to follow my advice, go back home and don't wait up for him to interrogate him. Just act like you expected nothing and saw nothing. Talk to Joe. I think he will agree with me."

Stephen sensed Alice was distraught. He grabbed her hands, held them close to his chest, and then placed his arms around her shoulders to comfort her.

"Thank you, Stephen. I'm not sure I agree with you right now, but I know I will be glad I listened to you tomorrow morning. I love my son whether he is straight, gay, bi, trans, or any other alphabet letter. You are right. I don't want to find out by walking in on him unexpectedly."

"Go home, don't make any noise going up the path. Talk to Joe, and if you and Joe want to get together for a quick chat, I'm happy to give you the time. I consider you and your family my family.

Alice returned home and found Joe still sleeping with the television on. She grabbed her notebook computer and searched the internet for 'finding out your son is gay.' "

Stephen returned home, walked over to the family room, and saw Randy sitting in the wheelchair. He walked over to the bar and prepared two scotches on the rocks. "Randy, you will never believe my discussion with your daughter. How do I begin to tell you the story?"

✿ ✿ ✿ ✿ ✿ ✿ ✿

Enrique and Max were making love in the studio while Alice and Stephen debated on the other side of the barn. Before leaving, they stripped the bed, and Enrique brought the dirty sheets over to the kitchen door inside the garage. Max crawled back into his bedroom through the unlocked window. He heard his mobile phone buzz when he got in bed. It was an incoming text message.

> ENRIQUE: Oh, Max, my Max. Good night.
> MAX: No texting while driving. GN.

CHAPTER 17

OUT

Max couldn't sleep thinking about the speech and the suggestions Enrique, his parents, and Stephen gave him. All he kept hearing was, 'be yourself, be yourself, be yourself,' He asked himself, *"How can I be myself when I'm not being honest about who I am? Am I a fraud if I decide to hide behind my sexuality? What happens when I move to Harvard? Should I be out of the closet in Cambridge and closeted in Lyme? What if my parents find out before I tell them myself?"* He finally fell asleep with all these questions on his mind. At 5:00 AM, he leaped out of bed, sat in front of his computer, and continued to type and edit his speech.

✿ ✿ ✿ ✿ ✿ ✿

Alice had difficulties sleeping, too. About the same time Max got out of bed, Alice shook Joe's shoulder. "Joe, wake up. We need to have a conversation."

"Oh, Alice, can it wait until I have my coffee?" Joe was barely awake.

"No, this is extremely important. It's about our son, Max."

"Are you sure this can't wait? It can't be serious. Max never does anything wrong."

"No, he hasn't done anything wrong, but you need to know what's going on in his life." Alice was determined to share her experience with Joe before coffee. She explained to Joe everything she witnessed and her meeting with Stephen outside of Stephen's barn.

"I'm not surprised, Alice. I suspected that he might be gay."

"What do you mean you *'suspected he might be gay'*? You never told me." Alice was disappointed Joe never shared his suspicion.

"I agree with Stephen. We should not confront him. Let him come out to us on his own. We trust Max. I'm sure he is safe and not doing any drugs. We should be grateful we have a son like Max. I trust him one hundred percent, and if we approached him about last night or asked him if he was gay, it would crush him. Let him come out to us on his own. Please don't do anything to make him feel you know what he is doing with Enrique. He is over eighteen and has the right to make his own decisions. We are here if he asks us for guidance, but other than that, we accept him, love him, support him, and give him our blessings."

"Oh, Joe. How could you be so calm at a time like this?" Alice was not hearing what she wanted Joe to say.

"That's' because I suspected that he was gay. I think you also did, but you blocked those thoughts out of your mind. You can't tell me you are surprised by what you saw last night or, I should say, what you didn't see, thanks to Stephen. I can't imagine what would happen if you had walked into the room."

"I can't imagine it either. I should thank Stephen personally. This is still very upsetting to me. It's not because I don't want him to be gay. I love my son and will love him no matter what he is. I'm afraid for his future. Being gay is so much more accepted these days than when we were growing up, but he is still part of a minority that is still being discriminated against. There are politicians out there that if it were their choice, Max would be sent to a deserted island with all the other gays in this country. I don't want my family to be labeled a second-class citizen by anyone. I know I can't change him. I don't want to change him. At the same time, I don't know how to protect him. I'm his mother... we are his parents, and we have an obligation to protect him."

"Max doesn't need protection from us. First, he is over eighteen, so we are not obligated to protect him. He would be the first to tell us if he needed us, and when he does reach out, we will be right behind him to support and protect him. Meanwhile, please don't get into his business unless he asks us. Alice, it would be best to keep telling yourself that Max is an adult and will manage independently. If he needs help from us, he knows he can come to us. You love our children just as much as I do. Trust me on this one. Do nothing. When you see him downstairs, act the same as you did yesterday. Let him come to us when he is ready to come out. Don't force him out of the closet. You will regret it. Let him control this experience."

"Yes, Joe, I know you're right. It's not easy to sit here and do nothing when you don't know if he is hurting inside."

"Alice, trust me, if he is having sex with Enrique, he is not hurting inside. He is having a good time." Joe smiles. "Enrique is a very handsome guy with a great body. I have a feeling that he will come out to us soon. Be patient, don't push him. When he does, we must assure him that nothing will change in this household. He must know that we still love him and support him."

✧ ✧ ✧ ✧ ✧ ✧ ✧

Max completed the first draft of his speech and jumped in the shower to get ready for school. He knew there was still much editing, but he was happy with his planned message. When he got out of the shower, he reached for his mobile phone before going for a towel.

> MAX: Hey, still asleep?
> ENRIQUE: No, on my way out the door. Going to the garden center early. I have many deliveries to make in the afternoon.
> ENRIQUE: What's up?
> MAX: I'm coming out to my parents tonight.
> ENRIQUE: OMG!!!!!!!!!!
> ENRIQUE: What made you decide now?

ONLY LOVE LASTS

MAX: You.
ENRIQUE: What did I do?
MAX: You made me realize I needed to be honest with myself, my family, and my classmates. I'm going to take this one step at a time.
ENRIQUE: I'm proud of you, very proud of my Max. A bit jealous, also.
MAX: I'll call you after I meet with them tonight.

"Good morning, Max. You're running late for school again?" Alice saw Max rushing out to his car.

"Yes, sorry, I can't stay for coffee. I got up at 5:00 AM to work on my speech and didn't realize how fast time passed."

"Be careful driving. Don't speed. You have time."

"Thanks. Dana is already in the car waiting for me."

After swimming practice, Max goes home and sits on his beanbag chair facing the window. He stares at the trees outside his backyard, where the afternoon spring breezes are blowing the white blossoms from the Japanese Dogwood on the lime-green lawn. He can see some birdhouses in Stephen's property hosting cardinals, chickadees, blue jays, sparrows, and robins. New families of birds are on their way. He compared the changes in his landscape view to the continuous changes in his life.

Max was thinking about his "coming out" talk with his parents. He planned to get them both together on the patio before dinner. How and what he tells them will have to come from the heart. He was unable to write notes about what he would say to them. He cannot rehearse that speech. He knows he has to feel confident about himself.

When he left his bedroom, Joe was preparing salmon and spring vegetables in the kitchen. "Hey Max, we have salmon for dinner tonight grilled on cedar shakes left over from the new roof we installed last year."

"Sounds like a great dinner. Is Mom home yet?"

Alice came down the stairs and got three glasses of wine. "Let's sit outside and share this bottle of wine before dinner. Max, I'm assuming you will join us. Dana is out with friends tonight planning their summer parties."

"Yes, that would be great. It's just what I need."

"Oh, why is that? Joe asked.

"I wanted to speak with you about something important to me." Max felt nervous. His hands began to tremble a bit.

"Well, it's' the perfect time to chat tonight. Let's sit outside." Alice wondered if this would be Max's coming out speech. The three of them sat around the table on the patio. There was silence. Joe looked at Max, and Alice looked at Joe.

"We are all ears, Max. Tell us what's on your mind." Joe encouraged Max to relax in hopes that he would get comfortable, stop being nervous, and open up about what he wanted to tell them.

Max felt he was on stage now, and there was no turning back. " You both taught me a lot about life. I was sitting in my room this afternoon, looking out the window, searching for words to say to you today. I was lost. All I heard was 'Be yourself,' a lesson you both taught me for as long as I can remember. You also taught me to be honest with my family, friends, and, most importantly, myself. I know how much you appreciate it when you can be a part of my life. You like knowing about my accomplishments and also my disappointments. I can see the look on your faces when I came home from school with high grades. I also appreciated your support when things I did upset you. I'm grateful for the life lessons you both continue to teach me." Max paused for a few seconds to gather his thoughts. He saw Alice's eyes beginning to water.

"I have struggled with my…" Max pauses again to catch his breath. His eyes began to tear up. "… with my identity for three or four years. Who am I? What does Max want out of life? What does he want to be? What makes Max happy? These were just a few questions I asked myself almost daily. As I was getting older, I began to realize that, sexually, I liked boys more than girls. I tried to block that thought from my mind, but it kept returning. I tried being intimate with girls, which did not work for me, so I tried it with boys. Finally, I felt comfortable and sexually satisfied. I feel awkward discussing my sex life with my parents, but I think it is important that you know about my experiences and why I have accepted my sexuality as a gay man. It's not a choice. It's who I am. I've learned that from my own experiences. For the first time in my life, I know Max Edwards. I'm proud to be Max Edwards, the gay son of Joe and Alice Edwards." He paused again for a few seconds. "I hope you understand and still love me as much as you did before we sat out here tonight."

"Max," Joe clears his throat and wipes a tear running out of his eye. "I think I speak on behalf of your mother also. We are incredibly proud of you. Coming out to parents is not an easy task. I hope this experience was not made more difficult for you by us. We loved you before tonight and even more now. As you can see, we are happy for you and slightly emotional." Joe and Alice laughed as they both wiped tears from their faces.

"We are extremely proud of you, Max. I'm happy that you have accepted your sexuality and are not fighting to be someone you are not." Alice reached over to Max and held his hand.

"I still believe I hit the jackpot when I was born. I'm proud to have parents like you." Max also sheds a few tears.

"We have a good reason to celebrate and finish this wine. Maybe we need to open another bottle." Joe tries to turn the evening into a festive night. "Oh, let's not forget Dana. I think you should speak with her when she gets home. Tell her whether you want it broadcasted to the world or just information for her. She is her own Public Relations company. It's amazing how quickly news gets around with her."

"Yes, I thought about her talent. I will tell her to keep it to herself until graduation." Max clarified his intent.

"Max, are you seeing anyone special or dating anyone you want us to know." Alice was careful about how she would ask Max if he had a current boyfriend.

"Yes, I have been seeing Enrique. I think you know him. He works occasionally at Stephen's home. His family owns a garden center in Durham. We have only been dating for about two months. I like him. We are not in a serious relationship, and he knows I'm leaving for Cambridge in August. I suppose we will see less of each other. His parents don't know he is gay. He feels his father will have difficulty accepting it, so he doesn't want to approach them yet.

✿ ✿ ✿ ✿ ✿ ✿

Enrique was making his last delivery for the day in Middletown. He drove home, showered, and went to the basement to continue painting a portrait he had started a few weeks ago, an impressionist-styled oil painting of a nude male reclining on a mattress. Josefa was home getting dinner ready. Maria arrived home from work just as Enrique was going downstairs to the basement.

"How was work today, Mami?"

"Very busy. My legs hurt from standing up all day. Where is your father?"

"My last delivery was nearby, so I didn't return to the garden center. I told Papi I would go home after my last delivery and work on my painting. You should sit, rest, and put your feet up before we eat. Papi had an appointment with a banker in New Haven, so he was going there after he closed the garden center."

"I guess he will be late tonight. I'll call you when dinner is ready."

"Let me know if you need anything, Mami. I will come up and sit with you." Enrique was concerned that his mother was working too hard at the hospital.

Shortly after he got his paints ready, he heard his father's car outside on the driveway. Manuel hastily parked his car, got out, and slammed the door shut. He opened their apartment door, and Enrique immediately knew something was wrong.

"Where is Enrique?" Manuel shouted from the kitchen door as he entered the apartment.

"He is downstairs painting," Josefa replied.

"Enrique! Get up here right away!" Manuel yelled as his face turned red.

"What's wrong, Manuel?" Maria walked into the kitchen and saw the rage on Manuel's face.

"You will find out as soon as Enrique gets his ass up here."

"I need to check on something in my room," Josefa whispered to Maria.

"What's wrong, Papi? Why are you so upset?" Enrique saw the look on his father's face and knew this was serious.

"I met with a banker in New Haven today to get an update on my application for a mortgage. Besides turning us down, he tells me that his son Jaxton used to date my son Enrique. So, I looked at him and told him he was mistaken. My son is straight and only dates women. Then he tells me that he also thought his son was straight until he caught you and his son naked in bed one night," Manuel stopped for a few seconds and looked at Enrique for a response. Enrique looked out the kitchen window to gather his thoughts and what he would say to his father. "Well, Enrique. I assume you will tell me he was lying to me."

"No, Papi. I cannot lie to you, Mami, or Abuelita. It is true. I dated Jaxton for several weeks until his father barged into his room one night. I left and never saw him again."

"Are you telling me this was a one-time incident you never repeated with another man?"

"No. That would be a lie. I'm gay. I often wanted to tell you both but feared how you would react. I didn't want you to be angry at me with all the pressure trying to keep the garden center at the same location. Yes, I'm gay. That should not change anything. I was born this way. It's not something I chose to be. You must understand...."

Manuel interrupted Enrique. "I don't care what you want to be anymore. I want you out of my house before dinner, and I don't want you in the garden center either. I will not have a son who will be called a 'maricon' everywhere he goes. Go pack your bags and get out." Manuel stormed into his bedroom and slammed the door. Maria followed him.

"Manuel, you can't do that to your only son. Being gay is not a choice. Please don't do this. Don't do something you will regret. We lost our only daughter when she was just a baby. I don't want to lose my only son. Please, Manuel, don't throw him out of the house and out of your life. Talk to him," Maria was trying to make Manuel change his mind.

Enrique went to his room, grabbed his backpack, and stuffed it with as many clothes as possible. He picked up his mobile phone and keys to the pickup truck. On his way out the door, Maria tried to stop him. "Enrique, please don't leave. He didn't mean what he said. Where will you go? Please stay. I will talk with him."

"Mami, it's no use. You know he won't change his mind. I'll find a place to stay tonight. Tomorrow, I'll start looking for a job. Don't worry about me. When I find an apartment, I'll return to get the rest of my things." Enrique saw his mother's tears running down her face. "Don't cry, Mami. Maybe this is the best for all of us."

CHAPTER 18

HOME

MAX: Where are you? I tried calling you. No answer.
I Left a VM.

Max tried to connect with Enrique via text and voice message to let him know all went well at his coming-out meeting with his parents. There was no response. After dinner, Max started to help clean the dishes when his mobile phone buzzed with an incoming text.

ENRIQUE: Call me as soon as you get a chance.

Max was anxious to speak with Enrique. He sensed something was wrong if Enrique wanted to talk on the phone. "Hey, I tried calling, but there was no answer. I was worried. What's going on?"

"You won't believe what happened," Enrique's voice was shaky on the phone. He had the speaker phone turned on in his truck. There was a lot of street noise in the background, which made it difficult for Max to hear.

"Where are you? You don't sound like you are home," Max was still concerned.

"Someone outed me to my father today. He came home furious and confronted me with the facts he was told. I didn't deny them. He reacted just as I suspected. He threw me out of the house and told me not to come to the garden center. I packed some clothes, and I'm trying to find a cheap motel I can stay in tonight until I can find a new job and apartment."

"I can't believe he threw you out of the house. Enrique, you are not staying in a roach-infested motel. Come here, and you can sleep here tonight. My parents know all about you and our relationship. They will be fine with you here tonight." Joe overheard the conversation Max was having with Enrique.

"What's going on, Max? What's happening with Enrique?" Joe asked while Max tried to understand Enrique with all the loud background noise on the phone.

"Someone outed him to his father. His father threw him out of the house. He has no place to go. I told him he could stay in my room and sleep on the futon couch. He is embarrassed and doesn't want to come over."

"Give me the phone. Let me talk to him."

"Enrique, this is Joe, Max's father. Max told me what happened to you today. You are welcome to come and stay here tonight. I insist. There is no reason for you to go to a motel. Max has a space for you in his room. Please spend the night here with us. We can help you find a more permanent place later."

"Thank you, Mr. Edwards. I'm having problems finding a motel room at this hour. I don't want to bother Max, you, or your wife with my problems."

"Nonsense. I'm handing the phone back to Max. See you in a bit."

"Enrique, don't waste time driving around trying to find a motel at this hour. Stay here, and we can figure this out calmly." Max and Joe convinced Enrique to stay overnight.

✿ ✿ ✿ ✿ ✿ ✿ ✿

"You just threw your only son out of the house like he was trash. He is my son, too; this is our home, not just yours. How could you do this without talking to me first?" Maria is still distraught and angry at Manuel. Josefa is in her room with the door closed, listening to all the arguments.

"I know what I'm doing, Maria. I cannot have him living here or involved with the garden center," Manuel was confident his actions were warranted.

"You don't know what is going on out there in the world. You will regret this day for the rest of your life. Your depression will ruin you and our marriage if you don't seek medical help. I will not tolerate your behavior anymore unless you see a doctor this week. You think about it and tell me your decision tomorrow when you come home from work after spending the entire day at the garden center without your son." Maria leaves their bedroom and goes to sleep in Enrique's room.

✧ ✧ ✧ ✧ ✧ ✧ ✧

After Max and Joe convinced Enrique to stay at the house, Alice needed to make a private phone call and went upstairs to her home office to use her phone. "Hi Stephen, this is Alice. Sorry to bother you at this late hour."

"Oh, hi Alice, no, no bother. I was watching television. Let's say the TV is on, and I was gazing out the back window. There is rarely anything worth watching on TV."

"Yes, I know exactly what you mean. There are two reasons for my call. First, I wanted to thank you for stopping me last night. You were right. I spoke with Joe this morning, and he agreed with you, also." Alice was anxious to tell him about tonight's events. "Second, there is an interesting turn of events tonight. I wanted Max to tell you himself, but something else came up, which I thought you should know now. Max came out to us before dinner tonight. He was nervous. We assured him that we still love him and support him. Nothing has changed. Unfortunately, Enrique was outed to his father this afternoon, and when his father came home from work, he threw Enrique out of the house."

"What? I can't believe Manuel threw him out. I knew he was suffering from depression, but I never expected him to throw their only son out of the house. Where is Enrique now?" Stephen was shocked and concerned for Enrique.

"Max, with our approval, offered to let him sleep here tonight until he finds his own place. That's why I'm calling you. He's on his way to our home as we speak. I know you own several commercial and residential properties that AJR Investment Managers oversee. Perhaps you can call them tomorrow and find out if they have a small studio available for rent."

"I'll get on it first thing in the morning. I'm sure we can find something for Enrique."

"Thank you, Stephen."

"My pleasure. I like Enrique very much and want to do whatever is needed to make him feel he has a support system to get him through this difficult time. You can count on me, Alice."

"Yes, I'm sure he will appreciate your help. Oh, and by the way, we never had this conversation."

"What conversation?" Stephen knows how important it is for Max to come out on his own.

"I'm glad you understand. I want Max and Enrique to come out to you on their own. I'll encourage them to come and see you in the morning. Max is off from school."

"Great. I'll have coffee ready and a box of tissues on the table for my tears.

"Stephen, I feel close enough to tell you that you are an old dramatic queen."

".... and I'm proud to be one!" They both laughed before saying goodnight.

✧ ✧ ✧ ✧ ✧ ✧ ✧

Dana was dropped off at home by her friend's mother. When she entered the house and saw Joe, Alice, and Max sitting quietly in the living room, she knew something was wrong.

"What's going on? You never sit in this room unless someone died. Who died?"

"Dana, I can't believe you said that." Max laughs. "Nobody died."

"So why are you all sitting here looking very suspicious? Did I do something wrong?" Dana wondered if she had done something wrong.

"No, Dana. Nothing is wrong. It's a night for celebration and a night to help out a friend who needs it. Max, you want to update Dana?" Joe smiled and assured Dana she was not in any trouble.

"Mom, Dad, and I talked earlier tonight. I told them I was gay."

"Oh, I knew that. Tell me something I don't know. Oh, and don't tell me you are dating Enrique because I know about that also." Dana suspected it, but she was uncertain.

"I knew that would be her response. She knows everything before it even happens! Dana, I would like it if you kept it to yourself until graduation. It is important for me, and I hope you can keep your mouth shut for a few more days." Max was serious about his request, and Dana agreed to keep it to herself as long as she was allowed to tell her school friends after graduation.

"Yes, you can tell anyone after the ceremony is over. By the way, someone outed Enrique to his father earlier today. When his father got home, he threw Enrique out of the house. Enrique will be staying with us until he finds his own place. It's important to me that you treat him like a welcome guest. He needs our support. He has nobody else to turn to."

"Oh, my God. I can't believe any parent would throw their child out for being gay. What's wrong with this world? Don't worry, Max, I will treat him just like I treat my only brother at home."

"That's what concerns me." Max knew that Dana was only looking for laughs.

"I'll be in my room if you need me for anything," Dana turned and went to her room when Max saw headlights from the driveway shining through the windows into the living room wall.

"Enrique is here," he opened the front door and went outside to meet him. Enrique parked his truck on the side of the garage, grabbed his backpack, and walked towards Max. They met face-to-face and immediately embraced. Alice and Joe could hear Enrique from inside the house, crying uncontrollably. Max held his head against his shoulder. "I'm here for you, Enrique."

Alice and Joe looked out their living room window and saw their son consoling a man needing love and support. She grabbed Joe's hand and whispered to him. "I'm very proud of our son."

✿ ✿ ✿ ✿ ✿ ✿ ✿

Alice prepared a plate of salmon and vegetables left over from dinner for Enrique. "I'm sure you haven't eaten anything, Enrique. A delicious salmon fillet with vegetables from tonight's dinner is on the kitchen counter for you. Max, be sure that Enrique doesn't go to sleep hungry. I have a busy day at work tomorrow, as does Joe, so we are going to our bedroom."

"Thank you, Mr. & Mrs. Edwards. I'm grateful for your hospitality."

"You are welcome, Enrique. Tomorrow is another day. We are happy to help you in your time of need." Joe assured Enrique that he was welcomed into their home.

"Oh, I suggest you both see Stephen tomorrow morning. Update him on what's happened. Perhaps he has an apartment for Enrique. You know our real estate investment management company oversees several properties he owns, and there might be an excellent deal for you." Alice wants to encourage them to see Stephen early in the morning but doesn't want Max to know she has already brought Stephen up to date on Max's coming out and Enrique's homelessness.

"Good night, Mom."

"Thank you again for everything you have done, Mr. & Mrs. Edwards."

"It was our pleasure, Enrique. Tomorrow will be a better day. Max, shut all the lights and lock the doors when you go to bed."

"Yes, Dad. You know I always do." Max replied as he always does when Joe gives him the exact instructions almost every night. Alice and Joe went upstairs and closed the door to their room.

Enrique looks at Max. "I can't thank you and your parents enough. I didn't know what I was going to do. I thought of parking somewhere and sleeping inside the pickup truck."

"I would never let you do that."

"I hope Stephen has a small apartment for me. I have money saved in the bank, which should be enough for a security deposit and a few months' rent until I get a job. Maybe I can sell a few more of my paintings. I'll call the gallery in the morning and maybe lower the prices. I can try to find a few other galleries that will represent my work. Maybe one in New Haven and the other in Stonington or Newport."

"We'll deal with that tomorrow. Now you need to eat, and maybe we can watch a movie if you want."

"I have a lot on my mind, Max. I think I would rather sit around and talk to you."

"I'm here for you, Enrique. We can talk the whole night if that makes you feel better."

It was almost midnight when Max and Enrique decided to go to sleep. Max grabbed the bed sheets and a pillow from the linen closet in the hallway.

"I hope you don't mind, Max, but I usually sleep naked."

"Why would I mind? I sleep naked also."

They walked into Max's room, and Max stretched out the sheets on the futon while Enrique undressed and searched inside his backpack for his toothbrush. Max undressed and brushed his teeth by the bathroom sink beside Enrique, both naked. They kissed and crawled under the covers in each of their beds. A few minutes later, Enrique got out of the futon and crawled under the covers with Max. He whispered, "I need someone to hold me tonight."

✧✧✧✧✧✧

Manuel couldn't sleep. He was awake most of the night, standing by the window looking out the street. There was nothing to see. He was convinced that throwing Enrique out of the house would make him realize his mistake, return home, and begin dating women. At the same time, he doubted Enrique's return. He didn't understand why he questioned himself. He continued to stare out the window, searching for answers. He couldn't find any. It was 5:30 AM when he entered his closet and dressed for work. Josefa was still in her room. Maria was up most of the night in Enrique's room and finally fell asleep around 3:00 AM on his bed.

Manuel arrived at the garden center earlier than usual and planned his day without Enrique there to help him. Through the small window in his office, he looked at the trees, bushes, perennials, annuals, and garden equipment for sale. He asked himself, *"What have I caused?"*

✧✧✧✧✧✧

It was just before 6:00 AM. "Wake up, Enrique. It's time for a run. Let's go," Enrique reluctantly got out of bed grabbed a pair of running shorts from his backpack, a T-shirt, socks, and running shoes. Max was already up and waiting for him by the kitchen door. When he came out of the bedroom, Max teased him, "It's a short three-mile run with a few hills to tighten and perk up your bubble butt." Max was practically pushing Enrique out the door.

They both returned soaked with sweat a little over a half hour later. "You shower first. I left a towel and washcloth on your bed. There is liquid soap and shampoo in the shower."

"Thanks, Max. I'll be quick."

Max poured himself a cup of coffee as Joe walked into the kitchen for the same. "How did you guys sleep last night?"

"Fine. We were up until just past midnight. Enrique wanted to talk."

"That's healthy after all he experienced."

"I suppose. I just listened to him. He seems to feel better this morning. I forced him out for a three-mile run."

"You're brutal."

"Enrique walks into the kitchen. "Good morning, Mr. Edwards."

"Good morning, Enrique. Hope you slept well last night."

"Yes, I did, thank you. The only problem is that I must have bored Max all night talking. He got even this morning by forcing me on a three-mile run with hills."

"I don't feel guilty. He needed the exercise. I'm going to shower," Max leaves the room, and Enrique finds himself alone with Joe.

"I wish we had met formally under different circumstances. I have seen you and your wife occasionally while working in the garden at Stephen's, but we have never been officially introduced. I hope I'm not giving you a bad impression of me."

"Not at all. We know it's a difficult time for you, and we want to support you. If Max thinks you are a great guy, Alice and I think the same."

"That's very kind of you, Mr. Edwards. I plan to find an apartment quickly. I have some money saved, which should be sufficient for a security deposit and a few months' rent until I get a job."

"I don't think you'll have a problem finding an affordable apartment. Alice was going to check on the MLS rental listings, and I will ask around in the office. Be sure to see Stephen today, I know he owns several small apartments, and maybe one is available." Joe wanted to encourage Enrique to find an apartment but didn't want him to think he was being pushed out the door. "

Joe goes back upstairs with his coffee and a second mug for Alice. Enrique finds himself alone in the kitchen. He refilled his coffee mug, opened the back door, and walked to the table on the patio. He set his mug on the table and continued walking to the edge of the slate floor to absorb the views. He whispered to himself, *"This is what I want out of life. A home and a loving family."*

✿✿✿✿✿✿✿

Max and Enrique visited with Stephen and updated him on yesterday's events. "Well, gentlemen, you could have knocked me over with a feather. I never expected you were both gay. I'm happy for you both but sorry that coming out for Enrique was not a pleasant experience. This is a lot of news for me to absorb early in the morning."

"I don't know, Stephen. Something tells me my mother and you had conversations before Enrique and I came to see you." Max smiles. "There are three mugs, a thermos full of coffee, skim milk, napkins, and three teaspoons on your patio table before we arrived. Were you expecting someone else?

"I was sworn to secrecy. Don't drag it out of me because I'll never tell." Stephen smiles back.

"Stephen, I suppose Mrs. Edwards also told you I was looking for a small apartment. She suggested I speak with you because she knows you own several small units around southeastern Connecticut. I have money saved and can afford to give you a security down payment and several months' rent in advance."

"Yes, I own several small condo units in Chester and Old Saybrook that I rent out. I'll have to ask the management company I hired if anything is available now or soon." Stephen stopped for a few seconds and offered an alternative he had considered last night. "Let's discuss another option for you. Would you consider living in the studio you just painted in exchange for ten hours a week of work around the property? You won't have to put up any security deposit or advance rent. The studio is furnished so you don't have to buy any furniture. You will have access to cable TV, internet, air conditioning, and all utilities, and you can use the washer and dryer in the house."

"Enrique, that sounds like your best and only option right now." Max looked at Enrique and encouraged him to accept Stephen's proposal.

"Stephen, are you sure you will be comfortable with me living on your property? You have your privacy right now, and if I move into the studio, some of that privacy will be lost."

"Enrique, I'm at an age where I need someone to help maintain this house. Here is an example: I need to hire a painter to paint the outside of the house. I don't expect you to do it, but you can help me select and supervise the workers. I don't have the strength to manage this project myself." Stephen was hoping Enrique would agree to the arrangements.

"I would be crazy not to accept your offer, Stephen. When can I move in?"

✧ ✧ ✧ ✧ ✧ ✧

It was closing time at the garden center. The registers were reconciled, and the staff prepared the sales reports. Manuel was in his office after spending a difficult evening last night. He sat behind his desk and pulled a blank sheet of paper from the printer next to his computer. He takes his pen and writes a note.

As soon as all the employees left the property, Manuel locked the doors and returned to his desk. He opened the right bottom drawer and retrieved a small box. He turned to the bottom left drawer and found the gun he had purchased to protect himself and the store from being robbed. He took one bullet from the small box, loaded the gun, inserted the barrel in his mouth, pointed towards the top of his head, and released the trigger. Manuel died instantly.

The note he wrote was found on top of his desk.

> *Maria, Enrique, and Josefa*
> *Please forgive me.*
> *I'm sorry.*
> *I love you.*
>
> *Manuel*

PART THREE

CHAPTER 19

GRADUATION

Enrique returned to Middletown to gather the rest of his clothes, personal belongings, paintings he had completed, and others that he considered work-in-progress. There was no one home. He had planned to return in the evening to ensure Manuel and Maria were home. Even Josefa, who rarely left the house, was not at home. *"Mami and Papi should be here by now, and Josefa never leaves. What's going on? "* He sensed something was not normal but continued to gather his personal belongings. When he finished loading his pickup truck, he got a call from Maria, who was informed of Manuel's death by the Durham Police and had just arrived at the garden center with Josefa. He rushed to the garden center. It was one of the most difficult days in his life. Enrique stayed with Maria and Josefa for a few days, but after the private funeral service, he moved to the studio on Stephen's property with Maria's blessing.

The garden center needed Enrique. Maria encouraged him to go back and take over the management of the business. His primary goal was to obtain a mortgage and buy the property so they didn't have to move to another location or close the business. He called the landlord to inform him of his father's death and negotiated another thirty days to find a mortgage before the landlord agreed to sell to a developer interested in the property.

Enrique got financial information from the bookkeeper and prepared projections demonstrating that the garden center could afford a $900,000 mortgage. The business had just over $400,000 in reserves, which could be used as a down payment without depleting the company's working capital. The purchase price for the land and building was $1,300,000.

Max helped Enrique with the report to show prospective lenders. He suggested that Enrique get feedback from Stephen and his parents. Stephen was first. After examining the information for a good hour, he told Enrique that he would be willing to be the mortgagor, assuming his accountant and attorney could verify the financial disclosures in his report.

"I don't know why a bank would refuse Manuel. I assume the numbers in your financial history are accurate, and the projections seem conservative for the next five years. I am willing to make this investment. I know you and your mother, Enrique. I trust you will make a huge success of the garden center. I'll call my attorney, who handles my properties' closings, and ask him to review this document and write a mortgage agreement. He will likely need additional information to confirm your projections, so I will ask him to contact you directly."

"I can't believe what I'm hearing. Stephen, I didn't show you these projections because I wanted you to lend me the money." Enrique was shocked and speechless. "I don't know what to say. I never expected you to take the role of the bank. My father would not give any of the garden center's financial statements to prospective lenders. He would always tell me that it wasn't their business how much the garden center made. He expected they would rely on his salary, which was all he would disclose." Enrique knew the banks needed more information before committing to a large mortgage.

"Enrique, you and Max did a good professional job compiling this report. If the past financial information in this report agrees with the financials your C.P.A. prepared, I consider this a very safe investment." Stephen knew that the interest rate on his loan would be better than what he was currently getting from his bank. "I also believe the selling price of $1.3 million is below current market value. You are getting an excellent deal, and the garden center can continue to flourish in its current location."

"Yes, it will continue to flourish. I know I have a big job to do there, and it's going to be twice as hard without my father to help me. I know the business very well. I know it can be a huge success." Enrique was confident his father would approve of him taking over the management of the garden center.

✿ ✿ ✿ ✿ ✿ ✿ ✿

Max spent the days before graduation locked up in his room, helping Enrique with his financial projections and writing, editing, and rehearsing his speech in front of his full-length mirror. He knew graduation day was important for him and his classmates and wanted to ensure that his speech would be remembered.

Enrique moved into Stephen's studio and planned to use the barn as his painting studio. He arrives at the garden center at 7:00 AM every morning and doesn't return until 8:00 or 9:00 PM. He promoted two long-term employees as managers who will share responsibilities for opening and closing the store and supervising the lawn and landscaping teams on the road. The new promotions would allow him to schedule some free time.

Graduation day finally arrived. Max had his speech on his tablet and a printed copy inside his graduation cap just in case his tablet failed. He rehearsed his speech so many times that it was almost entirely memorized. It was a Thursday, and the ceremony was to start at 2:00 PM with the procession of graduates coming from the school gym to the athletic field in the rear of the campus. Enrique took the afternoon off from work and drove Stephen to the ceremony in Stephen's Jaguar. Alice, Joe, and Dana went together in Alice's Range Rover.

It was a beautiful early summer day in southern Connecticut. The breezes felt like sitting in front of an air conditioner. The bright sun was just warm enough to make those cool breezes enjoyable. Most of the audience and graduates wore fashionable sunglasses, making the athletic field look like a Hollywood scene. Once the audience members were seated, the school band began to play the traditional Graduation March song. The music and the beginning of the procession brought out many emotions between the graduates and the excited audience. It started with the flag carriers carrying the Stars and Stripes, the State of Connecticut flag, and the Lyme High School flag, followed by the dignitaries who would be seated on the temporary stage. You could sense the excitement in the audience and an even more vital energy with the graduates. Some of the dignitaries' traditional speeches were the same given every year at every graduation they were invited to speak. When it was time to hand out diplomas, every student got a chance to walk across the entire stage, one by one, to the applause of their classmates, family, and friends attending.

The afternoon was moving quickly for Max. He looked at the program and realized it was his turn to speak. Principal Donahue introduced Max with a very personal, hugely complimentary introduction. Max stood up and heard Joe, Alice, Dana, Enrique, and Stephen's loud applause, whistles, and cheers in the middle of the warm ovation from his classmates and school officials. He reached the podium, looked at the crowd, smiled, and took a deep breath to relax. It was his time to take control of the moment.

> *"Board of Selectmen, Principal Donahue, faculty members, administrators, family, and friends. Today, my fellow graduates and I are thankful for your efforts in making this day a reality. Unfortunately, some teachers, administrators, and students are not here physically, but they are here with us spiritually. It is important to recognize them today because they are also part of our success. They are also the reason we are all here..."*

Max named all the teachers, administrators, and fellow students who died during the past four years, primarily due to the COVID-19 pandemic. After every name he mentioned, there was applause from the graduates.

> *"...we are all thankful for many of the same reasons,*
> *primarily the excellent education our dedicated*
> *administration and teachers provided us..."*

Max noticed his hands were shaking. He ignored it and continued.

> *"...our education doesn't just start on this campus in*
> *the morning and end when we walk out the door in the*
> *afternoon. Many family members and friends were part of*
> *our education during the past four years. They are all part*
> *of our lives. They significantly affected our growth during*
> *the past four years and will continue to affect us in the*
> *future. Reach out to them. Let them know how grateful*
> *you are..."*

Max looked at the crowd of graduates and saw Ashley sitting on the third row. He quickly recalled the impact he had on her when her father left the family and filed for divorce.

He continued with his speech. You could have heard a pin drop on the grass by this time. Everyone was listening.

> *"... It's our turn now. It is our turn to guide the next*
> *generation of graduates. It is our turn to pass down what*
> *we receive. It's our turn to make sure nobody is denied*
> *access to the same quality of education we received here*
> *and in our daily lives. It's our turn to tutor someone who*
> *needs one-on-one help. It is our turn to demonstrate*
> *to others what is right from wrong, what prevents our*
> *society's growth, and what causes them fear. It's our turn*
> *to be involved in our communities. It's our turn to take*
> *on leadership roles and continue to make this world a*

better place to live. It's our turn to ensure that books are available in the library without prejudice...."

He paused when the audience stood and applauded his last comment. His eyes focused past his classmates and saw a smile and a look of proudness coming from Alice and Joe. He smiled back at them and continued with his speech.

"...we are the generation of change. If we want to help make our planet a better place to live, we must agree to follow the advice of Mahatma Gandhi: "Be the change you wish to see in the world." Commit yourself this summer to take on Mr. Gandhi's challenge. Decide on a specific project to help create the change you want. Don't just sit there and complain about the world surrounding you. Please do something about it. Work on it yourself or join a group with a mission that matches your objective. Only you can change the world with your actions. Your complaints do nothing...."

Max received another standing applause from the crowd and paused to see his classmates' faces. He remembered many of them from first-year orientation four years ago. He saw how everyone has transformed into adulthood.

"...we stand here today looking into our future and looking back at our past to understand how we got here today, how we learned from our success, and how we learned from our disappointments. I stand here in front of you, remembering first-year orientation. We began high school as children and today, we are adults looking to our future. Our future begins here today. We have completed four years of education that will help us leap into that future we all dream of experiencing. What we do with what we learn here will determine our success.

*Some of us will attend college, and others will enter the
workforce. Each of us will travel in different directions.
We will all have challenges ahead of us. What I learned
about those challenges is to meet them straight on with
your head held high and your heart wide open. Don't be
afraid of those challenges. They are part of our continued
education after we march out of this field.....*"

Max received another applause which forced him to pause his
speech. He recalled getting bullied in his first year and how he handled
it. He met the bullies straight on, his head held high and heart wide open.

*"...imagine if everyone graduating here today lived up to
their potential during the next four years. Imagine how
amazing that would be and the impact you'd have on the
lives of many fellow world citizens...."*

Max knew he was getting near the end of his speech and wondered
if he should eliminate his last paragraph or deliver it as planned. The
audience applauded his previous remarks, and all he heard inside his
head was, "Be the change you wish to see in this world."

*"...we should fight discriminatory practices like bigotry,
inequity, injustice, homophobia, and many others.
They seem to be prevalent these days as our world
becomes smaller. Discrimination in our communities
and throughout this planet should never be tolerated. It
will only reverse our economic and social growth. Many
citizens are forced to move from one corner of this planet
to another for a better life. When they make this sacrifice,
they will tell you they did it because they want their
children to have what they could not experience, freedom
and liberty for all. Help them acclimate to their new
home. They will contribute to our growth, not take away
from it...."*

Max and Enrique looked at each other. Enrique was smiling back.

> *"...unfortunately, when they reach their new home, many are subjected to discriminatory acts by their neighbors and politicians elected to speak on their behalf and protect them. 'Be the change you wish to see in this world.' Know your neighbor. Learn about their culture, their religion, and their goals in life. Make it your goal and commitment in life that you will teach your children, our next generation, the beauty and comfort of love and the harm that hatred causes. Love and hatred are two words that are not born in us. We are taught to love by the love we get from family and friends. We are taught to hate when we witness the hatred and discrimination that is sadly supported by many. If you allow hatred to enter your lives and decide to look in the other direction because you claim it doesn't affect you, you are just as guilty of hatred. Imagine the change we could implement if everyone here today worked on improving equality for all, not just a select few, but all...."*

Afraid of going over his allotted time on the podium, Max considered going straight to his ending paragraph or the next one he had prepared. He decided it was his time on the podium and didn't care if he exceeded the allotted time. He took control of the moment and delivered what he had initially planned.

> *"...we have all experienced difficult moments in our personal lives and interactions here at Lyme High School. Sometimes, those interactions here in school turned personal and hurtful. I was the victim of personal verbal and sometimes physical attacks by various class members. You know who you are. You forced me to question my existence in this world. I dealt with it by keeping my*

head up high and never wavered. I refused to let you
destroy me. I knew that, in time, I would understand
who I was. Today, I, Max Edward, stand before you, my
family, classmates, friends, educators, and those who
bullied me. I stand here to say that I am a proud gay
man. I am not broken. I did not choose my sexuality. As
a (non-practicing) Christian, I am what God intended
me to be. I am loved by a wonderful family and a small
group of friends. I am the proud gay son of Alice and Joe
Edwards...."

Max was not expecting the ovation he heard after his last remarks.
All of his classmates stood up and cheered. The ovation did not stop.
It seemed to get louder. Finally, Max encouraged his classmates to sit
down.

"...as you leave here today, remember that you might
never cross paths with some of your classmates again, or
maybe we will be lifelong friends with somebody here.
Either way, I'm certain that we want to wish every single
one of our classmates success and happiness in every
endeavor we choose to pursue. I look forward to the
day I may be working with some of you. I am confident
that we have much to offer to the world as a generation,
and I am excited for the next chapter of our lives. I am
also extremely proud to have been selected as your
Valedictorian today.
Let's move on and do great things!
Thank you."

By this time, Max had the audience wrapped around his little
finger. They gave him a third standing ovation. Max was puzzled by
the overwhelmingly positive response during his speech and the loud
cheers at the end. He looked at the crowd and saw Ashley standing

on her fold-up chair, cheering. He saw his parents and Dana cheering. Enrique and Stephen were on their feet, waving the white tissues they got from Alice. It was a moment Max would never forget. He walked away from the podium, relieved, confident, and proud. He turned around before leaving the stage and shook hands with all the dignitaries. As he stepped down and returned to his seat, he realized he created the moment he intended, a memorable graduation speech.

The first line from the next speaker in the program was... "I learned something valuable today, never follow Max Edwards when asked to speak in front of a group. He is a hard act to follow."

Sections of Max's speech, including his coming out paragraph, appeared in the local paper the following day. His speech was the only one from the graduation ceremony quoted in the news.

✧✧✧✧✧✧✧

It was almost 4:00 PM when the graduates marched back inside the gymnasium building. Alice invited Stephen, Enrique, Ashley, and her mother, Abbie, back to their house for celebratory drinks, hors d'oeuvres, and barbeque chicken on their back patio.

"Max, your speech was excellent. You were the best speaker on the stage. Your coming-out statement at the end was perfect. I loved how you talked about being bullied and dealing with the issue. It was very personal and an effective way to tell your story. Alice, you and Joe must be very proud of Max." Abbie complemented Max when they arrived at the Edwards' home.

Enrique wanted to get close to Max, hug him, and congratulate him. He felt awkward and didn't know how Max would react in front of family and guests.

"Thank you, Abbie. I wasn't sure I was going to expose my coming-out statement. I decided at the last minute to include it."

"Well, I think including it provided a good education to the audience." Alice wanted to be sure everyone knew Max's family supported him.

"When do you leave for Harvard, Max?" Abbie inquired.

"I decided to leave my car here in Lyme. Mom will drive me there on August 15th so I can get settled in the dorm before classes begin. When I visit, I can take AMTRAK from Boston's South Station to the Old Saybrook train station."

Enrique's ears perked up. He realized that he had less than two months before Max left. There were many questions he wanted to ask Max before they separated. He knew he had a short time to get the answers.

"Thank you for inviting me, Mr. & Mrs. Edwards. I have to leave because I need to go back to the garden center and catch up on my paperwork," Enrique knew it was late and still had paperwork to finish at the garden center.

"I'll walk you to your truck, Enrique."

"Thank you, Max." Enrique opened to Max as they approached the truck, "I should return to the studio around 9:00 PM tonight if you want to meet me there. I am still trying to get organized in my new home. Maybe you can help me tonight, or we can sit around and watch a movie."

"Yes, sounds like a good idea. Text me when you get home." Max agreed to meet him as they walked to Enrique's pickup truck.

Enrique knew he had to say something to Max about the future of their relationship. "Max, it has been difficult for me during the past two weeks. I haven't had the opportunity to sit with you and talk to you about us, together or maybe not. I want you to think about it first. I didn't want to bring the subject up until we both took the time to think this out. I hope you understand, but we should know where this relationship is going when you leave for Harvard. I don't want either of us to get hurt."

"I understand, Enrique. I am leaving town soon, and it is only fair that we talk about this before I leave."

"Thank you, Max." Enrique didn't get a clue from Max about his intentions to continue their relationship while he was living in Cambridge. He was afraid the relationship might end on August 15th.

"I'll see you later tonight." Max looked into Enrique's eyes and kissed him quickly on the lips.

As Enrique drove away, he licked his lips and tasted the distinct flavor of Max's saliva. That beautiful June sky at the graduation ceremonies turned into dark stormy clouds waiting for the right moment to drop buckets of rain. As Enrique drove north to the garden center, the dark clouds followed him. The heavy rains began as soon as he entered the garden center.

CHAPTER 20

APPROVAL

Heavy rains forced the graduation BBQ at Joe and Alice's home to be moved inside. Ashley and her mother, Abbie, left the Edwards home around 7:00 PM. A few minutes later, Stephen, who had brought his umbrella, walked through the path in the rain to his house. He took a shortcut through the garage and brought Randy's wheelchair from the storage area to the picture window in the family room. He turned around after making two scotches and water and saw Randy sitting in the wheelchair, looking out into the garden as the heavy rains soaked the garden beds.

"Rainstorms like this provide nourishment to the roots deep into the soil," Stephen turned the outside flood lights on for a better view. "Randy, did you notice what a great job Enrique has done with the garden beds this year? I'm very proud of him. I wonder what will happen to these beds. What will the 'next generation' do with them?" He stood by the window, recalling Max's speech while waiting for a response from Randy. After a few minutes, he turned around to ensure Randy was still with him. "I suppose there is some truth to the phrase nothing lasts forever. I strongly believe that only love lasts. It lasts past our lifetime. We don't own anything, Randy. We are just leaseholders of the life we see around us. Soon, all this will belong to someone else, and another generation will be in charge after they are gone." He looked at the garden beds and shook his head. "Oh, what's the use? Why do I care?" Stephen began to feel old, alone, and worthless after spending the day at a high school graduation in the middle of young men and women ready to take over the world.

Bright headlights coming from the driveway quickly shone inside the family room. "Oh, it's Enrique returning from the garden center—another late night." Stephen was pleased to have someone else living within the property. "I feel more comfortable having Enrique live in the studio. I hope he's happy there." He looked out the front window and saw Enrique running to the studio in the rain. "He needs an umbrella. I'll have to bring one to the studio tomorrow. I'll leave it outside by his front door." He looked over at Randy for his approval. "No, Randy, I'm not mothering him. The poor boy works day and night, seven days a week. He needs help occasionally. I'm here with nothing else to do. The least I can do is give him an umbrella. That's not mothering him. I'm certain he will appreciate the thought. At the same time, it makes me feel good that I can help him."

✿✿✿✿✿✿

Enrique walked into the studio, soaked from the heavy rains. He removed all his clothes, hung them in the shower, grabbed a towel to dry himself, and put on a pair of gym shorts before reaching for his phone to send a text.

> ENRIQUE: Hey, I just got home.
> ENRIQUE: Do you want to come over?
> MAX: I'll be there shortly.

Enrique questioned whether he should bring up a discussion about the future of their relationship. It was an inspiring day for Max, and he feared the conversation would be a downer after a successful day. He decided not to mention it tonight and see if Max brings it up. A few minutes after responding to Enrique, Max ran in the heavy rains from his house down the path to the studio door Enrique had left unlocked. He was soaked by the time he got inside.

"Wait there, don't drip water all over my apartment. I'll get you a towel."

"Should I take my clothes off?" Max, willing and able, gave Enrique a smile and an eye wink.

"Why not? You will later tonight anyways," Enrique replies sarcastically.

"Hilarious, Enrique." Max dried himself, and Enrique gave him a pair of gym shorts to wear in the apartment.

"Here, these shorts will fit you. Put them on; otherwise, I'll have to remove my shorts to make you comfortable."

"This was the first time I visited you without having to crawl out of my bedroom window in secrecy. I told my mother I was coming over to see you." Max was relieved he didn't have to sneak out of the house.

"How did she respond?"

"She told me not to get wet." Max was surprised by his mother's short response.

"That's great, Max. I suppose you can stay all night."

"You might get tired of me and want some other visitors."

"I don't need anyone else as long as you are here close to me." Enrique's reply to Max was calculated. He wondered how Max would reply.

Max looked at Enrique, grabbed the back of his neck, and pulled him closer to his lips so he could kiss him.

"Thank you, Max. I needed that kiss. It's been a rough couple of weeks. Your speech today made me realize how lucky I am to have you here and to have your family and Stephen's support. I don't know what I would have done without their generosity," Enrique teared. Max hugged him.

"I feel that when life gets ugly, only we have the power to change it. You don't give yourself enough credit, Enrique. Everything you are experiencing now will only make you stronger. The garden center will be extremely successful because of you."

"I hope you're right. I'm glad you are here tonight. I need you close to me." There was a deafening silence in the room. Enrique was waiting to hear more from Max. He wanted Max to start the conversation about the future of their relationship. Max only looked out the window as if searching for his next line. He noticed the floodlights were turned on. After a long minute, Enrique broke the silence, "How about if we watch an old movie on television?"

✧ ✧ ✧ ✧ ✧ ✧ ✧

"You'll have to agree with me, Randy, that it has been a crazy couple of weeks. It started with the horrible news of Manuel taking his life. I felt very sorry for Maria, Enrique, and Josefa. Enrique took control of the situation, and it seems like the garden center will survive with a little help from me. I plan to use the money from the insurance company to give Enrique a mortgage on the property. We don't need the money. Our current investments provide sufficient cash to live comfortably in this house. I felt good that I was able to help Enrique." Stephen continued to stare at the garden beds being inundated with rain. After a few minutes of silence, he began another topic, "I wish you could have come to Max's graduation. You would have been just as proud as I was of our grandson. Max's speech was among the best graduation speeches I have ever heard. The applause he got at the end lasted a long, long time."

Stephen continued to look outside as he described the graduation ceremony in detail to Randy. He wanted to change the subject again but was worried about Randy's response to the subject he wanted to discuss. The room was silent again until Stephen got out of his chair, looked at Randy, and began with his new topic.

"Randy, I know what you will say, but I'm bringing this up again. I don't care if you disagree with me." Stephen was feeling confident but afraid of the discussion. He started to stutter a bit but immediately took control. "Randy, it's' time to expose ourselves to Alice and her family. I don't know how many years I have left in this world, and I don't want to be cremated with any secrets in me. I have supported your position on this topic all our lives, but it is time now to be realistic. I can't find any good reason why we shouldn't tell Alice she is your daughter! No reason at all! They already act like family to us. Why don't we just come out and tell her? I know you wanted to follow Linda's request for secrecy and privacy, but Linda is long gone, and there is no harm to anyone if we disclose your relationship with Alice. Frankly, I think Alice would be thrilled to know. Can you see the look on Max and Dana when they find out?" Stephen did not hear any response. "Randy, I feel very strongly about this. You need to look at the situation from my point of view, and you will have no reason to disagree with me."

Stephen walked over to the small table beside the wheelchair and placed his cocktail glass on top. As his hand moved away, he bumped into the glass and spilled his drink on the side of the wheelchair and the floor. That side of the wheelchair had a leather pocket, and when he wiped the outside of the leather pocket, he found a small envelope with several photographs inside. All the photos were of Alice in high school and later in life after giving birth to Dana and Max. Stephen stopped, sat on the floor, and examined the photos.

After another long silence, Stephen got up from the floor and looked at Randy. "I don't know how you got these photos, but this is the sign I wanted to get from you. We will invite Joe and Alice on Sunday for brunch, and I will explain. How did you get these photos? It's not important now. Thank you, Randy."

✿ ✿ ✿ ✿ ✿ ✿ ✿

Enrique and Max sat on the couch next to each other, watching an old 1930s movie. They laughed at the movie stars' campiness and overly dramatic classic performances. They both rolled and laughed on the couch, making fun of the dialogue and imitating the characters. Max picked up quickly and changed his facial expression to look like

ONLY LOVE LASTS

one of the characters. Enrique laughed hysterically while Max pinched his nipple. He responded by grabbing Max's penis, "Why is your penis so large and hard? Is it from watching old movies?"

✿ ✿ ✿ ✿ ✿ ✿ ✿

"Randy, let's go and watch television. There must be a good movie tonight," Stephen pushed the wheelchair to face the television set and turned it on to a movie channel. "Look, Randy. Our favorite movie. We know all the lines. It's a wonderful movie with two of the world's best actors. They don't make movies like this anymore." It was the same movie Max and Enrique were watching.

"Oh, Randy. Do you remember the 'rat' scene? It was brilliant. The look on their faces made this movie so real to me. I wish I could see it again from the beginning." Stephen got up from the couch, walked over to the window, and stared at the garden for several minutes as he heard the dialogue from the movie. He grabbed his empty glass, refilled it with ice, scotch, and a splash of water, and returned to the couch. The movie was still playing on the television screen. He knew the script well and whispered the dialogue while the actors delivered their lines. He eventually fell asleep on the couch. The television and outdoor flood lights were left on.

✿ ✿ ✿ ✿ ✿ ✿ ✿

Close to the end of the movie, Max wrapped his arm around Enrique's shoulders and brought him closer to his chest. Enrique fell asleep on Max's chest.

CHAPTER 21

FAMILY

Stephen was engulfed by the soft daylight that beamed through the windows onto his face as he awoke on the couch in the family room. At the same time, he heard loud battle sounds from an old war movie on television, which was playing on the same channel Stephen turned on last night. The rain had stopped shortly after midnight, and the skies looked like the start of a beautiful late spring, early summer June day in Connecticut. He saw Randy, still in his wheelchair, watching World War II bombs destroying Europe. "You don't want to watch this movie, Randy. The world hasn't learned when to stop destroying itself." He turned the television off and pushed the wheelchair to the outdoor patio. "I'm going to make coffee and bring it to you." He didn't. Instead, he went downstairs to the treadmill and exercised for thirty minutes, followed by a hot shower. It was almost 9:00 AM when he returned to the patio with two cups of coffee.

"You didn't think I was coming out, did you? I had a few things to do, and time flew by. Sorry. I figured you would entertain yourself while I was gone." Stephen searched his mind to make small conversation with Randy. He didn't realize he was repeating himself. "Did I tell you how wonderful Max's graduation ceremony was organized yesterday? You would have been so proud of him if you were able to attend. I was certainly proud." Stephen continued to chat with Randy. "The perennial gardens are in the best shape ever. Enrique is a genius, don't you agree?" Stephen was having difficulties talking to Randy.

He didn't hear Louise's car drive up and park in front of the garage doors. She casually walked into the house and was surprised to see Stephen outside with two cups of coffee and the wheelchair she kept bringing to the storage area in the garage. She noticed Stephen was having a conversation with the wheelchair.

Louise walked out to the patio and heard Stephen talking to himself. "Oh, Randy, I can't wait to tell Alice you are her father. Thank you for letting me break the news to her. I think she will be pleased that she knows her father and her father's husband." Stephen sounded very happy but did not see Louise standing behind him on the patio by the kitchen door, listening to his conversation with Randy.

"Mr. Stephen, Mr. Randy is not with us anymore. It would be best to accept that he died a few months ago. Don't you remember? We were all at the memorial service in Old Saybrook, the Edwards, me, and your friends. This isn't healthy for you, Mr. Stephen. I'm sorry I must be the one to tell you, but you need to let Mr. Randy go."

About two minutes of silence on the patio. Stephen refused to turn around and acknowledge Louise. Suddenly, without warning, he turned quickly to face her, "Louise, I can't let him go. He is here with me every day. I need him here with me. He won't go even if I told him to leave."

Louise approached Stephen and placed her hand on his shoulder. "Yes, Mr. Stephen, he will go if you demonstrate that you are strong and can care for yourself. Show him you are in command. Tell him not to worry about you. You will be fine. You have friends that are here for you if you need them."

"I don't want him to go, Louise." Stephen stood up to go back into the house and began to cry. Louise grabbed him and hugged him.

"Give it time. Someday you will realize he is always in your heart, and you won't need to drag out the wheelchair to talk to him. Let's go inside. I'll make another pot of coffee." Louise held his hand tight, and they both walked into the kitchen. "I've never told you this before, Mr. Stephen, but I once lost someone I loved very much."

"I've known you for years, Louise, and we never discussed your personal life besides your relationship with your mother. Like family, I feel close to you, but now I realize I don't know much about you." Stephen wiped his eyes and blew his nose.

"Many years ago, I was in love with a wonderful person. We didn't live together but had plans soon." She hesitates for a few seconds. She isn't sure she wants to disclose a name. She does. "His name was Jamie."

"Jamie? Oh, what a great Irish name.

"He was the love of my life, Mr. Stephen, I can still see him in my mind. Unfortunately, an ex-girlfriend did not like the idea that he didn't love her anymore. He wanted to be with me and did not want to be associated with her anymore, so he broke off their relationship. About a year later, one night after Jamie walked me home from dinner, his ex was waiting for him. She had a key to his apartment and had never returned it. Jamie must have seen her when he entered the apartment. She shot him with her gun eight times. The neighbors heard the gunshots in the hallway and called the police. When they arrived, she was found sitting on the floor next to him, crying in a pool of blood. I didn't find out he had died until I read it on the front page of the local newspaper the following day. I can still recall the feeling in my stomach when I read the news on my kitchen table. It was a horrible feeling. I could have saved Jamie if I had been there when he walked into his apartment."

"Don't say that, Louise. You don't know what would have happened if you walked in with him. You could have been there next to him, in a pool of your own blood."

"His family knew about our relationship and disapproved. His mother wanted nothing to do with me because she considered me lower class. They blamed me for his death." Louise began to shed tears. Stephen held her hand. "I mourned Jamie in silence. I didn't tell anyone. I didn't want to let him go, either. The more I pretended he was next to me, the more difficult it was for me to start living again. Eventually, I released him slowly, and that's when I began a new life. He is still with me twenty-four hours a day but no longer follows me everywhere I go.

I regret the loss of years we could have had together. I see how you and Mr. Randy loved each other, which has thrilled me over the years. You are my family. I am grateful for the life lessons you and Mr. Randy have given me all these years I have worked for you. It's time to give back some of those lessons to those I love. I might as well start now." Louise served the coffee and sat with him.

"I don't know what to say, Louise. *'I'm sorry for your loss'* doesn't seem enough. I'm sorry I didn't know you back then. I would have comforted you." Stephen realized how grateful he should be to have spent almost his entire lifetime with Randy. "I don't know where I would be today if I had never met Randy in Boston. I felt like I won the lottery when we met for the first time at that gay cocktail party on Beacon Street overlooking the Charles River. He was stunning. I said to myself, 'I must have him,' and I did."

"You and Mr. Randy were very fortunate to have each other for all those years. You know very well, Mr. Stephen, now is the time to let him go. Keep him in your heart, but don't let him run your life now. You have a new chapter to live." Louise was trying to comfort Stephen.

"By the way, not to change the subject, but I couldn't help hearing you talk about Alice next door being Randy's daughter. Are you making things up? Since I told you my special secret, perhaps we can say it's your turn." Louise got up from her chair and placed her lunch bag in the refrigerator.

"Well, I'm sorry you overheard me. It's true. It's a long story. Alice doesn't know it yet, but I have Randy's blessing to tell her." Stephen was reluctant to tell Louise any more details but felt there was no other way to explain. "Sit down, Louise. Perhaps we should garnish this coffee with some Irish Whiskey. You are going to need it when you hear this story."

Louise laughed, quickly walked to the bar in the family room, and grabbed the Irish Whiskey. "I brought the good stuff, the whole bottle. I have a feeling we will both need it." For the next thirty minutes,

Stephen told her everything and asked her to keep it to herself until he met with Joe and Alice.

"If I didn't know you, Mr. Stephen, I would have said you were lying. This is an incredible story! So, technically, Alice is your daughter, Joe is your son-in-law, and Max and Dana are your grandchildren! When are you going to tell her?"

"I am planning to invite them over on Sunday. I hope I'm doing the right thing." Stephen thought about the process of telling Alice and had concerns about losing the Edwards' friendship. "I hope it will not destroy our relationship. They are my only family besides you, Louise."

"Mr. Stephen, I don't think that will happen. Maybe she knows and doesn't want to say anything to you for the same reasons."

"I'm old, Louise. I can't hold back any secrets. I don't have many years left and don't want to die holding this story back.

✧✧✧✧✧✧✧

Maria returned to work at the hospital two weeks after Manuel's private funeral service. Her supervisor, Dr. Marcos Veiga, supported Maria and encouraged her to take more time off. "I can't stay home all day, Marc. I need to busy my mind. If I am home all day, I get depressed thinking about Manuel."

"I just want to be sure you know you can take more time off if needed."

"Thank you, Marc. I will feel better here at work.

"I don't know if you know about my past. When I lived in California five years ago, I lost my wife and only daughter in a car accident. They were coming home in the middle of the afternoon from the grocery store, and a man in a pickup truck, talking on his mobile phone, ran the red light."

"Oh, Marc. I didn't know."

"I moved to Connecticut to escape my memories. But they followed me. I am glad they did. It took me a year to feel in control of my life again. Give it time, Maria. You will be strong again."

"Thank you, Marc. You are very kind. I have my son and mother around for support."

✧ ✧ ✧ ✧ ✧ ✧ ✧

After Stephen's discussions with Randy and Louise, he picked up the phone and called Alice's mobile phone.

"Hi, Alice. This is Stephen."

"Hi, Stephen. What's up?"

"First, thank you for the invitation to Max's graduation and the BBQ. I enjoyed seeing Max, all grown up, deliver a remarkable speech. I am sure you are incredibly proud of Max."

"Yes, we are. Thank you. He is a fantastic son."

"The second reason for my call is an invitation for brunch on Sunday. We didn't get a chance to talk much at the BBQ with the other guests around, so I thought of inviting you and Joe over for a simple brunch, and it will give us time alone to talk and spend together."

"That would be great, Stephen. I don't have any open houses this weekend, so I am available all day."

"Let's make it noon."

"Perfect. Is there anything I can bring?"

"An appetite is all I require."

"OK, I'll still bring something. You know how I am."

"See you on Sunday."

✧ ✧ ✧ ✧ ✧ ✧ ✧

Stephen left the house to do errands while Louise cleaned. His first stop was a small, secluded public beach in Old Lyme near the mouth of the Connecticut River. He sat in his car to enjoy the views through his windshield and recalled the time he spent there with Randy. He began to talk to himself, *"Where the fuck did the time go? It seems like only yesterday that Randy and I would drive here with our thermos filled with our favorite wine. Those were the days.*" Stephen was fixated on the sailboats entering and leaving Old Saybrook Marina across the river. He associated them with people entering and exiting his life. He stepped outside on the sand, removed his shoes and socks, rolled up his jeans, and walked to the shore. "Randy, if you can hear me, please note that we will no longer have anything to hide from anyone on Sunday. You should be happy."

About a half hour later, he returned to his car, slipped on his socks and shoes, and began his errands. The last stop was the Big Y Super Market in Old Lyme to get everything he needed to prepare bacon quiches and a salad for Sunday's brunch. By the time he returned home, Louise was finished cleaning and had left. He emptied his canvas grocery bags and placed all the perishables in the refrigerator. He went to the pantry, grabbed the box Max had brought to him several weeks ago, and placed it on the kitchen table. Inside were Randy's ashes sealed in a solid green porcelain ginger jar. A small, curved brass plate was glued to the jar with Randy's name, birthdate, and death date. Stephen placed the jar on top of the table in the family room near the window. He fixed himself a cocktail, scotch, ice, and a splash of water, sat facing the window and looked out to the garden. *"I hope someone will take good care of the garden when I'm gone."*

✧✧✧✧✧✧✧

The day after Max's graduation, Enrique visited his mother and grandmother for dinner. He usually visits once or twice a week. Maria comes to the garden center on Sundays for a few hours to help in the retail store. After dinner, Maria discussed the possibility of selling the house. "Enrique, I'm considering selling this three-family house and moving into a condominium with Abuelita closer to work. I don't want to deal with the maintenance of this house."

"Mami, don't make any major decisions like selling the house for at least a year after Papi's death. Don't worry about maintaining the house, I can do that, and in a year, we will be in a better position to make that decision. I want to concentrate on finalizing the paperwork for our mortgage on the business and give it time to see if the business continues to do well." Enrique was trying to convince Maria not to make any hasty decisions.

"I suppose you're right, Enrique. I don't want to burden you with the headache of maintaining this place," Maria agreed.

"You realize that the rental income from the other two apartments pays most of our maintenance, taxes, and mortgage. You live here mortgage-free, Mami. Let's wait one year before we decide to sell. We may have a higher market value if we turn the building into three condominiums. That's why we should hang on to it for now and perhaps consider the condo option during the next few months." Enrique considered getting the most significant value from the three-family house.

Maria agreed with Enrique. "You're right. Let's wait. Meanwhile, let's find out what it takes to turn the apartments into condos and the market values as condos instead of selling the building outright."

✧ ✧ ✧ ✧ ✧ ✧

After an early dinner with his mother and Abuelita, Enrique got inside his pickup truck, and before he drove away, he texted Max.

> ENRIQUE: Hey, I think I fell asleep on you last night. Woke up this morning in bed. I assume you carried me to bed before you left. You are so romantic.
> MAX: Didn't have to. You walked to bed by yourself with your eyes closed.
> ENRIQUE: OH NO! I'm a zombie!
> MAX: YES! You grabbed my dick and tried to give me a hickey.

ENRIQUE: Sorry about the hickey. I'm on my way home.
How about going out for a movie tonight?
MAX: Only if we finish the night making love.
ENRIQUE: You don't have to ask me. My pants are
already halfway down. Ha! Ha!
MAX: You will look funny at the movies with your pants
halfway down. Call me when you are ready to leave.

Enrique arrived at the studio a few minutes later and texted Max.

ENRIQUE: It's too late to drive to the movie theatre.
The movie I wanted to see already started. My pants
are down to my knees. Any interest?
MAX: WHORE! I'll be there soon.

CHAPTER 22

BRUNCH

The smell of bacon on Sunday morning was hovering all over Stephen's house. He woke up early and made two bacon quiches and a large salad with chunks of watermelon and mango. Just before Alice and Joe arrived, he got a large pitcher from the pantry, made a batch of Bloody Mary mix, and placed it on the bar with an ice bucket, a small tray of shrimp laying on crushed ice, celery stalks, and Spanish olives stuffed with blue cheese. The vodka was chilling in the freezer.

He knew the two quiches were too much food for three portions, but he had planned to give the second pie to Enrique for lunch. Less than five minutes before noon, Stephen raced to his bedroom to grab all the letters Sandra had received from Alice's mother, Linda, and all the documents the private investigator gave Randy and Stephen. He arranged them face down on the piano. Next to the ginger jar with Randy's ashes he moved from the table in the family room. Before they arrived, he called Enrique to pick up his quiche and salad, but Enrique was already at work and told him he would stop by later tonight.

"Alice and Joe! Welcome! We are going to eat inside today. I can't take too much of this heat. There isn't even a breeze from the river today."

"We brought you a bottle of your favorite wine. We haven't been inside your home in a while. I had forgotten how beautifully you and Randy decorated your home. I wish all my clients had this much taste. It would be a lot easier to sell houses." Alice looked around the house just like a realtor.

"Oh, thank you. I haven't done anything in a while. Some updating is needed. Perhaps next year. Meanwhile, I'll take the vodka out of the freezer, and you can help yourself to a Bloody Mary. I also have wine if you prefer. All the ingredients for your Bloody Mary are at the bar. We are having Bacon Quiche and a spring salad for brunch."

"Perfect! I'll fix everyone's drink. I assume everyone is having a Bloody Mary." Joe walked over to the bar and fixed all the drinks.

They sat at the small round table in the family room near the large picture window facing the garden and discussed everything from politics, neighborhood issues, weather, Harvard, and the 'good old days.' Stephen picked up the plates when everyone finished their meal and the second round of Bloody Marys. "I have some wonderful orange sorbet and a small cookie I want to serve for dessert. Let's move to the living room. There is something important I want to discuss with you." Stephen was now noticeably nervous and began to stutter.

Alice looked at Joe, who was helping Stephen carry the sorbet plates to the living room and wondered what was so important for Stephen to discuss with them.

"I don't know how to begin this story, but be patient with me, and eventually, it will come out of me." Stephen breathed heavily before he began his story. He noticed the trees in the front yard beginning to sway from a sudden summer breeze. "Back in 1990, Randy received an envelope with a letter from a woman named Sandra Brooks. She used to live in Waterbury and attended Croft High School. Alice, I don't think you knew that Randy came from the same town as your mother, attended the same high school, and graduated the same year."

"Stephen, I think I know where you are going with your story. I have my mother's yearbook, and I saw Randy's picture in it. I know Randy was my father. I didn't say anything to you or Randy when I put the puzzle pieces together a few years ago because I wasn't 100% certain. Also, I wanted to respect my mother's wishes never to disclose my father's name, and I was convinced you and Randy didn't know. I found a shoebox filled with letters from Sandra Brooks my mother stored in her closet. That's how I found Randy's name." Alice raised her level of excitement and was now sitting on the edge of the couch. I don't know why my mother didn't want to disclose Randy's name, but that is all in the past. I wish Randy were still alive. I'm proud to be his daughter.

"Well, I have the letters your mother wrote to Sandra. Sandra mailed them to us back in 1990 before she died." Stephen opens the envelope that he had placed on the piano and spreads the letters on the coffee table. "When Randy received the letters, he hired a private investigator to confirm that you were his daughter. He came back with this report. Randy didn't want to reach out to you either.

Years later, in 2002, after we hired AJR to manage the properties we were buying, we asked them for the best residential real estate broker, and they referred us to you. We didn't connect the dots because you were now married and changed your last name. We also didn't realize that AJR represented the three owners of the firm, Alice, Joe, and Ross. We only found out Alice Peterson was Alice Edwards seconds before you came to greet us in the reception area of your office. It was too late to run away! Then, you had to show us the perfect house, and when you told us you lived next door, we almost walked away, but Randy and I loved the house very much and decided to go ahead and make it our weekend getaway."

"Joe, please go home and get my letters from Sandra. They are in my closet. You know where they are hidden. We must do this right now." Alice insisted on reading all the letters. "Stephen, I also didn't connect the dots when I wrote up your contract to purchase this house. I kept looking at the name 'Jensen' and knew it sounded familiar, but it didn't click. Years later, when I opened my box of letters to read again, I saw Randy's name and finally made the connection. I knew Randy lived in Waterbury but didn't realize he went to the same school as my mother until I reread the letters and saw his picture in the yearbook."

Joe returned with Alice's box of letters from Sandra. They read the letters out loud in chronological order. Alice shared her experiences with her mother and great-aunt in Montpelier, Vermont. Stephen discussed how he met Randy and their time together before moving to Lyme. It was almost 6:00 PM, and they were still together in the living room.

"Joe, we should meet with Max and Dana and tell them the story. I'm certain they'll be as thrilled as I am. Stephen, I want to borrow your letters for Max and Dana to read. They can now read them chronologically with the replies." Alice is excited to tell her children.

"Alice, you can keep all the letters. They belong to you and your family."

Joe gets up and corrects him. "Stephen, you are part of our family. These letters belong to you also."

"Thank you, Joe." Stephen tears up.

Just as Joe and Alice leave to meet with Max and Dana, Enrique pulls into the driveway and parks by the studio.

✧✧✧✧✧✧✧

"Hi Stephen, I'm home," Enrique walked into the kitchen from the patio door.

"Hi, Enrique. You are funny. Randy and I used to say the same thing to each other when we got home. You made me bring back some memories I had forgotten." Stephen stopped to think about Randy. "Sorry, your quiche was not ready before you left for work. It's in the fridge with a great salad and dressing in a separate container." Stephen enjoys having Enrique around the property. "I have an idea. Unless you want to be home alone to eat your quiche and salad, why don't you eat here while I have a cocktail? We can chat and update each other on what's happening in our lives. I have a feeling you will enjoy what I must tell you. Enrique, nothing you can tell me will top my story."

"That's a great idea, Stephen. I'm excited to hear your story now. Why don't you start." And he did. Enrique listened carefully to Stephen's story about Randy being Alice's father. It was challenging for Enrique to eat and listen to this story at the same time.

"Joe and Alice just went home as you drove in to tell Max and Dana. They will be shocked," Stephen can't wait to see Max and Dana.

☼☼☼☼☼☼☼

"Max and Dana! Come into the living room. Your father and I have news to share with you." Alice entered the house with a high level of excitement.

"Don't tell me you are getting divorced!" Dana had two school friends whose parents had recently divorced.

"No, silly girl. We are not getting a divorce. Wait until your brother comes in," Alice laughed at Dana but understood why she thought of divorce immediately.

"I heard that. What's going on? Did we win the lottery?" Max entered the living room, anxious to hear the news.

"Well, we did win a lottery, but not the type you are thinking about. Let me see if I can begin the story at the right time. Joe, you can interrupt me and fill in the areas I leave behind. Do you remember when I told you there was a box from my mother I brought to Connecticut from Vermont? I didn't give you much detail as to what was inside the box. In addition to some memorabilia and jewelry, there were letters from a friend of my mother's. Her name was Sandra," The story continued for at least another thirty minutes. In the end, Alice summed it up, "What this means is that Randy and Stephen are your grandfathers."

"That's nothing new!" Dana was disappointed it wasn't a bigger story. "I always treated them like my grandfathers. Now you are telling us that they are our grandfathers, legally. I expected you to say something earth-shattering."

"Mom, Dana is right." Max was relieved it wasn't bad news. "I'm thrilled that Stephen and Randy are legally our grandfathers. I wish Randy were still alive. I always felt they were related to us, so this news doesn't change anything. It only confirms their relationship with us. I am happy and proud to legally classify them as part of our family."

"When you see Stephen, you might want to acknowledge him as your grandfather. I think he is very proud to be part of our family. Your father and I are very proud to include him." Alice was thrilled that this mystery had been exposed and only wished it was out when Randy was still alive.

✡ ✡ ✡ ✡ ✡ ✡ ✡

Enrique finally ate his dinner, "The quiche and salad were delicious, Stephen. Thank you. There is three-quarters of the pie left and another serving of salad. If you don't mind, I will keep this for tomorrow."

"I made the extra pie just for you, Enrique. Take it home and enjoy it." Stephen was thrilled to see Enrique eating his quiche. "Perhaps share it with Max if he comes over tonight to visit you."

"This is too good to share with anyone." Enrique jokingly rejects Stephen's suggestion.

"How is your relationship with Max these days?" Stephen is slowly trying to determine if they are getting serious or experimenting with a sexual relationship.

"Well, it's funny you ask. Max is leaving for Cambridge in mid-August, and I don't know where I stand with him when he leaves. I have tried to hint around and see if he begins the conversation, but he doesn't grab the hint. My father's death has made my life difficult for the past few weeks, and Max was stressed about his graduation speech. I didn't want to force the question on him before graduation, but now he isn't saying much. He comes over to visit, and we talk about everything and anything, but never our relationship. He is very romantic with me, and I am not embarrassed to tell you that he is great in bed. I don't know what to do, Stephen. I don't want to force myself onto him, but I want to know my place when he leaves." Enrique continued to open up his private concerns about his relationship with Max to Stephen. "I hope you don't think I am acting like a silly, domineering high school teenage

ONLY LOVE LASTS

girl. I have been used before, and I was disappointed and deeply hurt. I don't want to repeat it.

"I agree with you, Enrique. You deserve more than just great sex. Don't let him have the upper hand. You bring up the subject. Don't do it after sex. Bring it up as soon as he comes over to visit. Don't let him have the fruit unless he can afford it. Do you know what I mean?" Stephen felt that Enrique and Max were a good match, and he didn't want either to get hurt.

"Yes, I get it." Enrique laughed at Stephen's analogy. "I want to give him a bit more time. He leaves in seven weeks. Perhaps he is thinking about it and not ready to commit. I will give him more time to consider if he wants to take our relationship further. I need to know before he leaves. Otherwise, we must go our separate ways."

"You are very generous, Enrique. Perhaps way too generous. You have to do what is right for you. Seven weeks is not a long time. I would hate to see your hopes rise and then get crushed as he drives away to Cambridge." Stephen felt they would both feel hurt if they decided to call off their relationship.

"It's the risk I'm taking. Love is risky, isn't it?"

"You are in love with him, aren't you?"

"Yes, Stephen. This is the first time I'm admitting that I love Max."

"Then, you make sure you fight for his love and fight hard. Don't be passive. Take control of the situation. Tell him how you feel. He will have to commit if he feels the same love you have for him. If he can't, the world is your oyster, Enrique. You will find love if you are willing to be loved.

✿✿✿✿✿✿

"What's going on tonight? Are you two staying home? I was thinking of grilling some burgers outside." Joe asks Dana and Max before he creates a significant production in the kitchen and on the patio by the grill.

"I'm here and hungry. I can't speak for Max. He is always running out to see Enrique." Dana teases Max.

"I don't have any plans either, Dad. Burgers sound like a great idea."

"Great, I'll fire up the grill before it gets dark outside. Max, why don't you ask Enrique if he wants to join us." Joe wanted Max to know Enrique was always welcome at the house.

"I'll text him now."

> MAX: Hey, are you hungry? My father is grilling burgers outside and asked me to invite you.
> ENRIQUE: That sounds great, but I just finished eating a large portion of Stephen's bacon quiche pie. I'm in his kitchen with him now.
> MAX: Did he tell you the news?
> ENRIQUE: Which news? The Abuelito news.
> MAX: You are lucky I took Spanish in high school. Yes, the Abuelito news.
> ENRIQUE: Yes, it's a great story. Congrats! He is an excellent Abuelito to have. Tell your father I said thank you, but I just finished eating. If you want to stop by after dinner, send me a text.
> MAX: OK

✿ ✿ ✿ ✿ ✿ ✿ ✿

"Joe and Max invited me over for burgers. I thanked them but told Max I was eating here with you." Enrique was happy to spend time with Stephen. Their conversation was very different from the conversations Enrique had with his father. He feels Stephen is the grandfather he had never met.

"So, is Max coming to visit with you after he has dinner?" Stephen was curious and perhaps too inquisitive.

ONLY LOVE LASTS

"Don't know. He didn't commit. He said he would text me."

"Maybe when he does, you will be busy." Stephen looked at Enrique and hoped that Enrique understood what he was trying to suggest.

"I get it, Stephen. Don't give the fruit away.

"Exactly! It's difficult, but it's the right thing to do."

✧ ✧ ✧ ✧ ✧ ✧

Enrique received a text message from Max.

MAX: Are you in the studio?

ENRIQUE: You mean 'home'? No. I am still at Stephen's house. We are just sitting here getting to know each other.
MAX: I was planning to come over.
ENRIQUE: Maybe tomorrow. I am tired from working all day. Going home soon.
MAX: Oh, OK. We'll chat tomorrow.
ENRIQUE: Good night.
MAX: GN

"That didn't hurt, did it?" Stephen looked at Enrique and raised an eyebrow.

"Yes, it did. I had to. Talking to you tonight helped me realize I must protect myself from getting hurt again. I was going in that direction, and frankly, I am not convinced Max wants to have a relationship with me." Enrique confessed to Stephen about his past. "Stephen, I have had several heartbreaks since I came out. I need to learn how to protect myself. I don't want to be alone for the rest of my life, but I don't want to live with someone who doesn't love me as much as I love them. I want to have a normal life with someone. I want to get married, raise a family, and someday be a grandfather like you."

"WOW! Slow down. All is fine, but you are rushing the grandfather part. You need to enjoy life first. When it comes to being a grandfather, you are going to wish you were back here in your early twenties talking to a grandfather, not being one of them," Stephen wanted to be sure Enrique was not upset telling Max not to visit him. "Listen, Enrique, you will find the love you deserve to have. I guarantee it. If you open your heart and protect yourself, you will attract the love of your life. Trust me. It will happen, and I hope I am here and healthy to dance at your wedding and maybe meet my great-grandchildren.

✿ ✿ ✿ ✿ ✿ ✿ ✿

After texting with Enrique, Max cleaned the outdoor grill and said good night to his parents and Dana. When he got to his room, he removed all his clothes and sat naked on his beanbag chair. He faced the window and grabbed a new book he started to read earlier this week. Before opening the book to where he left off, he thought about Enrique and their relationship. He didn't know how they could continue to develop it when he moved to Cambridge. He looked outside and noticed that Stephen turned his flood light on. He saw Stephen's garden beds in the distance. He knew the garden had been nurtured for years, so the plants were healthy and blooming. *"Relationships need the same long-term care as the garden,"* he whispered. *"I just don't know what to do."*

CHAPTER 23

CAMBRIDGE

The week before Max was scheduled to leave for school, he got a text from Enrique.

> ENRIQUE: I'm still at work. Going home soon and stopping at the deli to pick up dinner. Want to join me for dinner at home?
> MAX: Yes. Text me when you arrive. I'll be there.

Enrique planned to approach the relationship issue with Max that night unless Max brought it up first. During the past several weeks, he has hinted enough times for Max to realize he needed to deal with the issue.

> ENRIQUE: I am home. Food is ready
> MAX: On my way.

Enrique left the door unlocked for Max. Max arrived less than sixty seconds after his text message. "I'm here and hungry!"

"I picked up two portions of vegetable lasagna and spinach salad. Hope you like lasagna."

"Love it, thank you."

Enrique set the table and asked Max to open a bottle of wine he was saving to share with him before he left for Cambridge.

They discussed multiple subjects during dinner, but the relationship discussion was not surfacing. The plates were empty at the end of dinner, and a half bottle of wine remained. Enrique poured the rest of the wine into both glasses. "I am going to miss not having you as a neighbor when you leave for Cambridge," Enrique began hinting again about the future of their relationship.

Max got up from the table, took Enrique's hand and brought him to the bed, where they kissed, removed each other's clothing, and engaged in their usual passionate lovemaking. After they both had orgasms simultaneously, they cuddled in bed and continued their conversation.

"I know I've been heartless to you, Enrique. I'm sorry. I know you want answers about our future, but I don't have any. I have thought about our relationship and what it could be like when I'm at Harvard, but it all looks too complicated. The four years I plan to live in Cambridge is a long time. You might find someone you like while I am gone, and if that happens, you should go for it. You shouldn't feel guilty. Perhaps we should keep our relationship open and fluid. We should not put ourselves in a position where we could hurt each other." Max was uncertain about the direction he was taking with the relationship discussion.

"I won't be able to see you every week. I don't know how often I will be able to visit. I may only be here on holidays, and it is unfair for you to wait for me. At the same time, you can't visit me every weekend because you have a great business you need to manage." Enrique didn't say anything. He wanted to let Max continue with his explanation. "Four years into the future is a long time. I'm certain it will pass quickly. A lot can happen in those four years. Anything we plan today may become obsolete in a year." Max realized he must be careful with his comments and not hurt Enrique, who still had no response for Max.

"Sometimes, I'm overly focused on my studies and not in touch with the real world. I recognize that fault in me, so I try to bring reality into my daily life. I'm not sure it's right for us to make a monogamous commitment to each other." Enrique looked at Max and waited to hear what he wanted Max to tell him. "Who knows where we'll be during the next four years? You'll be very busy at work as I'll be busy with my studies. When I come home to visit during the holidays, we can get together and spend time like we do now. Perhaps you can find the time to leave and come to Cambridge for a long weekend. We have to be realistic, Enrique. It will be difficult for us to be in a committed relationship, and I think it's best for us to be open and date others for a while." Enrique knew that Max's comments were not rehearsed. He kept repeating the same points. That was not what Enrique was hoping to hear. "We will still see each other, but I don't think we can have a healthy and steady relationship if we commit ourselves this early in our lives. Don't you agree? Please say something."

Enrique didn't respond immediately. He thought about how to respond to Max. "That's not what I was hoping to hear. Maybe I should have exposed my feelings for you earlier and not have them dragged out of me and thrown out the window while I'm naked in bed." Enrique gets up and slips on his underwear. "The first time I saw you, about a year ago, you were washing your car in the driveway. I immediately fell in love with you. I created a love fantasy of us living together and perhaps raising a family. Sounds crazy? Yes, it was a crazy thought. I didn't know anything about you. I didn't know if you were gay or what type of person you were or how you would respond if I told you I loved you.

As we got to know each other more, I realized that my little silly love fantasy was perhaps turning into reality. I couldn't believe you would even consider making love to me. Whenever I had sex with other men, I felt used and discarded like a dirty tissue." Enrique's frustration level was increasing dramatically. "I never felt that way when we made love together. Maybe I was deceived."

"I've told you about my first sexual encounter with my High School art teacher. I didn't tell you he took advantage of me in bed, but I kept returning, hoping there was more to it than sex. All he wanted to do was fuck me hard and send me home. Now I feel the same. I feel like you used me as a sex toy over the past several weeks, or, worse, you treated me like a condom where you had your orgasm, rolled it off your dick, and threw it in the garbage. Now that you're ready to go away to college, you're trying to tell me nicely to fuck off because you will have plenty of other options at Harvard. Young, handsome, intelligent men studying to be attorneys with parents who come with plenty of money. Not like Enrique, who isn't very smart, not an attorney, and has a widowed mother that doesn't have plenty of money, especially now that the depressed father committed suicide and life insurance policies don't cover suicides."

"Enrique, stop it. None of that is true. That's not how I feel about you. You are very special to me. I also fell in love with you when we first met. I will never forget you. We must be realistic. We are both young, and a lot can happen in four years. We shouldn't place ourselves in a position where we hurt each other if we meet someone else we want to share our lives."

"I get it, Max. You want to leave your options open if you find someone better." Enrique felt his head was about to burst. "I want more from you. I want to be sure our relationship moves forward in the right direction, not backward. I know a monogamous relationship may not be the answer now, but I need assurance that our relationship is worth our investment. I'm not getting that from you right now. It sounds like all you want is a sex buddy, a friend with benefits, so when you come home to visit your family, you are guaranteed to be sexually satisfied by fucking Enrique."

"Don't say that. I'm trying to be realistic." Max was surprised at Enrique's reaction. "Maybe I am looking at this too seriously, but that is how I feel. I don't want to hurt you, Enrique. I also don't want you to hurt me. Keeping our relationship open without commitment is the only way I see it would work for us. Perhaps two, three, or four years from now, we realize we were meant to spend the rest of our lives together. Who knows?"

"Max, I think you need to leave now," Enrique was furious. The more Max tried to explain, the worse it was for Enrique.

"No, I'm not leaving until we understand each other," Max was confused about Enrique's reaction. He became noticeably nervous and unprepared to respond. He was concerned that the more he talked, the more he hurt Enrique. "Come, sit next to me. Let me hold you. We can't go to sleep tonight unless we straighten this mess I created."

"Our relationship is a 'mess you created'? Why did you do it, Max? Was it just so you can fuck me whenever your dick got hard?" Enrique's anger continued to be visible. He refused to sit next to Max in bed. Instead, he sat on the couch by himself.

"Enrique, I am eighteen years old. You're nineteen. We're both very young. Life will bring us many opportunities to experience. I don't want either of us to ignore them. I care for you deeply. I know you care for me also. All I'm suggesting is that we don't restrict ourselves now. We're both entering a new chapter in our lives. We need to concentrate on this new chapter. If we still care for each other in the end, let's have a deeper conversation about our lives together. Not now, Enrique. Not now."

"And what will happen if you find another person that fits you better than Enrique?"

"That can happen to either of us."

"Well, we'll know our relationship was not strong enough, and perhaps it wasn't worth the investment. Max, I don't think we should see each other again. I don't want to take a chance of having an open relationship with you without any parameters, and then you bring home your new boyfriend to introduce to your parents. How do you think I will feel? Please leave."

"Don't do this, Enrique." Max was upset and looked for words that would make Enrique feel better. He couldn't find them. He got up from the bed, naked, walked over to the window, and looked out to the garden as he searched in his mind what to say to Enrique. "I don't want to lose you, Enrique. Please don't throw me out. Let's keep talking. I am sure we can work it out.

"Max, I don't understand your reasoning. I'm not sure you do either. I feel you are trying to end our relationship and start it again whenever you want to fuck me. You want to control it like the light switch Stephen turns on to see his garden at night. I can't agree with that type of arrangement. Six months from now, I can see you coming home for the holidays with your new Harvard love. What am I supposed to do? Look the other way? I refuse to get hurt again. I can't see you anymore. It's best to end our relationship, or whatever it was, now."

"Enrique, I am not leaving you until we resolve our differences."

"I don't think we can." Enrique began to cry, and Max walked over to him and hugged him. "Please, Max, get dressed and leave. The faster you leave, the sooner I can begin my new life."

Max walked over to the bed, dressed, and started leaving the studio. He turned around and faced Enrique. "I'm sorry if I hurt you. I don't want our relationship to end."

"We don't have a relationship, Max. It seems to me now that one of us never did. Please leave."

Enrique closed and locked the door as soon as Max left.

✿ ✿ ✿ ✿ ✿ ✿

Max tried to reach out to Enrique numerous times after their encounter in the studio. Enrique blocked his contact information from his mobile phone. He walked to the studio several times, but Enrique would not answer the door. Two days before leaving for Cambridge, he called Ashley, arranged to pick her up, and spent the afternoon at Hawk's Nest Beach in Old Lyme, about ten miles from his house.

At the beach, all Max wanted to discuss with Ashley was Enrique. "I don't know what to do, Ashley. I don't want to leave Connecticut without talking to Enrique. He won't take my calls and even refuses to answer the door to his apartment."

"What do you plan to tell him if you see him? You're mistaken if you think more of the same talk you had with him will smooth things out. He will not agree to your definition of a relationship, and frankly, Max, I would do the same." Max was surprised by Ashley's comment. "I don't know what to tell you. I don't know Enrique as well as I know you. If you genuinely love him, you should try harder to reach him before you leave. Fight like hell to get him back. If you are unsure you want to be with him for the rest of your life, give him up, and don't hurt him anymore. You may not realize it but every time you knock on his door, and he doesn't answer, you are hurting him. You have to decide, Max. I think you are afraid to commit because you don't want to hurt Enrique, and you don't want to get hurt yourself if he decides to go his own way later. Yes, it can happen. That is life. It would be best if you learned to live with that possibility. Otherwise, you will never commit to Enrique or anyone."

"Thank you, Ashley. I'm fortunate to have you as a friend. I think I know what to do if only he will let me back in his life."

✧ ✧ ✧ ✧ ✧ ✧ ✧

Max drove Ashley home, and instead of going home directly to pack for his trip to Cambridge, he stopped to visit with Stephen.

Stephen was on the back patio reading a raunchy gay novel. "Hey, Grandpa Stephen!"

"Oh, My God. That sounds like I am an ancient old man. Well, I guess I am. Just call me Stephen in the future. I'm proud to be your grandfather, but let's keep the 'grandpa' adjective to ourselves."

"Fair enough, Stephen."

"What's going on? I hope you are packed and ready for your trip." Stephen had already heard Enrique's side of the story.

"No, I haven't even started. I've been busy this past week. Well, actually, that's not true. I've been distressed and unable to get myself organized for school. Did Enrique talk to you about us?" Max wanted to get Stephen's reaction to his disagreement with Enrique.

"Yes, he did. Before you tell me your side of the story, if that was your intention to come here to visit with me, let me tell you that I'm 'Switzerland.' I'm completely independent. No right or wrong answer will come out of my mouth."

"That's fair, Stephen," Max told Stephen that he cared deeply for Enrique and did not want to lose him. He explained why he only wanted a causal, open relationship.

ONLY LOVE LASTS

"Max, you can't have your cake and eat it too. Understand? At the same time, you both need to experience life as gay men without too many restrictions. You need to go out and get picked up by handsome Bostonians. Enrique needs to experience more sex with others. He is working too hard and doesn't have time to have a little fun. You both need to go out on your own and get laid. Consider engaging in group sex or threesomes with others as long as it is protected sex, of course. Stop wondering if you are going to get hurt. Do it and see what happens. If your relationship is strong, it will survive anything you do to each other. If you truly love him and don't want to lose him, then fight your way to his heart. I'm not sure I'm being clear. I'm old and come with lots of experience. Some of it doesn't translate into words. You have to experience it yourself. I am telling you the same thing I told Enrique the other day. I told him I would say the same to you. You both need to figure this out. Perhaps a 'cooling off' period is required. So, if you don't see Enrique before you leave, that's not the end of the world. You'll have another chance to get together if your love is strong. If that second chance doesn't come around, it's not the end of the world. Perhaps it's meant to be. That's all I have to say. Now you have some decisions to make."

"You're right, Stephen. Thank you. I know just what to do. I hope he will take my calls or open the door when I knock."

✧ ✧ ✧ ✧ ✧ ✧ ✧

Max was home packing and getting ready for his move before leaving for Cambridge. He kept a notepad on his desk where he jotted down notes to discuss with Enrique while he gathered his clothes and folded them neatly in his luggage, assuming Enrique would agree to answer the door. It was 9:00 PM, and Enrique was still away. Max went to the driveway every fifteen minutes to look for Enrique's pickup truck. Finally, Enrique arrived at 10:30 PM. He went to his apartment and locked the door behind him.

Max tried to call him, but Enrique still had his number blocked. He walked over to the studio and knocked on the door. Enrique looked through the window blinds and saw Max at the door.

"Enrique, please open the door. I want to see you. Please open up. I'm leaving the day after tomorrow early in the morning and need to spend time with you. We need to talk about this more calmly. Enrique, I know you can hear me. I need you. Please open up." There was no sound coming from inside the apartment. Enrique was on the other side of the door, listening to Max. Tears began to roll off his cheeks. After a few minutes, Max decided to return home. "OK, you win. I'm going home. Please let me have a chance to talk to you before I leave. I can come back tonight and spend the night with you. Call me, or we can meet when you get home from work tomorrow night. Please, Enrique, give me a chance to talk to you."

Max returned home and began to write a letter to Enrique. He knew that if Enrique refused to see him, he would at least read his letter.

Dear Enrique,
I was wrong. I'm embarrassed about how I approached
our relationship discussion the other night. I was not
sensitive to your feelings and proceeded to hurt you in a
way I would never have considered. I have not been able
to sleep well since you asked me to leave your apartment.
I wish I could erase the hurt I caused you.
I wanted to be honest with you, but I should have
listened to your point of view and how you would like
our relationship to continue while I am at Harvard. I
don't want to lose you. You mean a lot to me, and I am
confident we can work together and enjoy a healthy
relationship that is meaningful to both.
Please, Enrique, All I'm asking is for another chance.

Love you,
Max

It was almost midnight when Max finished the letter. He sealed it inside an envelope, wrote Enrique's name on the outside, and pinned it on his door.

✿ ✿ ✿ ✿ ✿ ✿ ✿

At 5:00 AM, the day before Max was scheduled to leave for Cambridge, heavy rains and strong winds approached the southeastern Connecticut coast. The wind swept Max's letter away from the door and landed between two branches on the ornamental cherry tree in the back of the garden beds.

Max waited patiently for a call from Enrique. There were none. Enrique never received Max's letter. Max considered knocking on his door again when he got home but decided against it. *"Perhaps he needs more time to heal."*

✿ ✿ ✿ ✿ ✿ ✿ ✿

It's moving day. Max was up and dressed by 6:00 AM. He loaded his mother's car with his luggage, backpack, and one small box of personal items, including his computer. He looked at his phone again to see if there were any messages from Enrique. There were none.

When it was time to leave, 8:00 AM, he walked outside with Alice and saw Enrique on an extension ladder cleaning the gutters around Stephen's house. "Mom, give me a second. I want to try again with Enrique. Maybe this time he will talk to me."

"Go ahead, Max. I'll wait in the car."

Max walked toward Enrique and stood at the bottom of the ladder, "Enrique, please look at me. I know you can hear me. I am only six feet away from you. Please turn around. Did you get my letter yesterday?"

Enrique continued cleaning the gutters but stopped to wonder what letter Max was referring to.

"I'm sorry. I want to make it up to you if you let me. Please don't ignore me." Max was frustrated that Enrique didn't even acknowledge him being there. "I don't want to leave without us agreeing to talk more about our relationship." There was no sign from Enrique that he would even consider looking at Max.

After a few minutes of trying to get Enrique's attention, Max didn't say another word and walked away through the path and into his mother's car. When the car pulled out of the Edwards' driveway onto Hamburg Road, Enrique turned around and saw Max in the front passenger seat and Alice driving. Max glanced towards Stephen's house and saw Enrique looking back at him. He also saw Stephen looking out at him through the living room window in his house.

PART FOUR

CHAPTER 24

LATER

A week after Max left Lyme, Stephen was walking through the gardens when he found an envelope addressed to Enrique jammed between two branches of an ornamental cherry tree that framed the rear of the perennial garden. The envelope was soaked from all the rain the previous week, and the ink was smudged. He brought the envelope into the house, stuffed it inside a larger envelope, wrote a note to Enrique, and placed it on the kitchen counter. He called Enrique's mobile phone and left a message. "Hi Enrique, it's Stephen. Sorry to bother you at work. I found an envelope in the garden addressed to you. It was soaked, and the ink on the outside was smudged. I didn't open it. Not sure the inside would be legible. It must have been left on your doorway, and the wind blew it away. I'm leaving it on the kitchen table so you can pick it up when you get home."

After closing the store, Enrique went to Stephen's home directly without stopping in the studio. "Hi Stephen, I'm home. Where is the envelope?"

"Hi Enrique, I'm upstairs. The envelope is on the kitchen counter. I'll be right down." Enrique picked it up, carefully opened it not to tear the wet pages, and read the letter to himself. He realized quickly that this was the letter Max told him he had left for him to read. When he was done reading, he placed it back inside the envelope and stuffed it in his back pocket. "Want to join me for dinner? I grilled some chicken breasts earlier and have root vegetables roasting in the oven."

"Yes, that would be great, Stephen. Let me stop in the apartment to clean up and change. I'll be back." Enrique went to his apartment. He placed the wet letter inside a book on the bookshelves, went to the bathroom for a quick shower, slipped on shorts, a T-shirt, and sandals, and returned to Stephen's home.

"Is there anything I can do to help with the cooking?" Enrique sees Stephen sitting outside having his evening cocktail before dinner.

"Nope, everything is ready to eat, but I thought I would start my evening with a cocktail. Why don't you fix yourself a drink and come and sit with me."

"That sounds like a great suggestion," Enrique goes inside, fixes himself a Vodka Martini in one of Stephen's extra-large martini glasses, and returns outside to sit with Stephen.

"WOW! That will certainly relax you," Stephen saw Enrique's drink and realized he likely needed a drink after last week's experiences. "Well, is there anything new with you since we chatted last?"

"Business has been great at the garden center. I keep ordering plants and trees from the distributor, and they sell as quickly as I put them out for sale. I hope it continues. I'm also planning winter merchandise, including bird feeders and bird food so we can stay open all year. I'm coordinating a Halloween shop at the front of the store, which will turn into pumpkins, mums, fall wreaths, and Thanksgiving-related merchandise when Halloween is over. At the other end of the store, we'll do a large Christmas shop and sell live Christmas trees. Customers can decorate inside their homes and plant them outside when the holidays are over.

"That's a great idea, Enrique."

"I plan to purchase plows for our four pickup trucks to plow our customers' driveways after winter storms. That gives most of our landscapers some additional income for the winter and revenues for the business during a generally very slow time for garden centers," Enrique was very proud of the changes he was making in the store. His employees were happy to discover that most would have jobs all year round.

"That's wonderful. Your hard work will be noticed."

"Thank you, Stephen. I have buried myself with work at the garden center and wonder if I'm doing it to keep Max away from my mind. I'm sure you want to hear more about that letter I just got from Max."

"Not at all. That's your business. I didn't know it was from Max. I told you I was 'Switzerland' and neutral. Do you want to talk about it with me? I'm here for you. Do you want to keep it to yourself? I respect that."

"I need time to think about what happened to my relationship with Max. I don't know if I have any answers. Sometimes, I want to forget the past several months and start a new life. Other times, I want to get in my car and drive to Cambridge to be with him," Enrique took a long sip of his Vodka Martini. He showed signs of strain in his voice and facial expression.

"You look very stressed, Enrique. What you're experiencing is not unusual. You were counting on a specific outcome and got the opposite of what you expected. You have every right to be upset. Don't stay upset for too long. Life is short, and only you control it. Remember what I told you last week? If you genuinely love him, fight like hell to get him.

"Yes, I remember our conversation. I am just not certain Max wants the same things I do. Fighting for him may not be my best decision."

"Enrique, I want you to know that I am your friend. I am here if you ever want to chat. I will not ask you about Max and don't expect to find out anything about him from me. Is that a deal?"

"Yes, thank you. I need time, Stephen. In the meantime, if Max finds another boyfriend, so be it. It wasn't meant to be."

Stephen looked at Enrique and knew that if Max found another boyfriend, Enrique would be crushed.

"That's the attitude to have. You would make a great husband to someone out there. In time, you will find what you are looking for, whether it is Max or someone else. Be patient and strong. Now let's go inside for dinner." As they walked into the house, Stephen put his arms around Enrique's shoulder and whispered, "Oh, by the way, don't block Max's phone number from your mobile phone. You don't have to answer his calls if you don't want to, but you might want to hear his messages." Enrique did not follow Stephen's suggestion.

✧✧✧✧✧✧✧

On Wednesday night before Thanksgiving, Max decided to go home for the holidays and took the train from Boston to the Old Saybrook station with Donato, his straight dormmate who would spend the night with Max because his parent's flight from Spain to Kennedy Airport was delayed, and they would not be home before Donato arrived. The family had a waterfront home in Old Saybrook and spent summers and holidays there. Alice picked them up at the station, and when they turned into their driveway on Hamburg Road, Enrique was getting out of his pickup truck next to the studio at the same time after a long day at work.

"Oh, shit! Enrique is just coming home. He is going to think Donato is my new boyfriend." Max said to himself as he and Donato exited the Range Rover with their weekend backpacks. Enrique looked through the trees at the Edwards' driveway and noticed Max, his mother, and another person coming out of the back seat. He pretended he did not look in their direction and entered his apartment.

"First time he is back home, and he brings a fucking boyfriend," Enrique is talking to himself inside his apartment. *"He is doing this to upset me! That's it! I need to move out of here before the summer!"* Enrique pledged to find an apartment closer to the garden center before Max returned for the summer.

✧✧✧✧✧✧✧

Enrique made a few life changes in the first year Max lived in Cambridge. He closed on his first home during the first week of April 2023. The garden center was very successful, and after the holidays, his mother approved a substantial bonus, which he combined with his savings to make a down payment on a small house in Chester. It was located within walking distance of the center of town. He worked hard at the garden center but forced himself to become more social and would visit the gay bars in New Haven or Hartford on Saturday nights now that he was close to turning 21. Bartenders looked the other way and never asked him for identification because he appeared older than 20. It was unusual for him to go home alone on Saturday nights after spending time cruising the bar scene. After all, Enrique was young and handsome, with a muscular, thin body, dark hair, and grey eyes.

Sometimes, he would take the train on a Saturday night to New York City and visit the bars in Hell's Kitchen. He never worried about finding a place to sleep. He always connected with someone who would take him home for sex and let him stay until morning. It was more than one person if he was in the right mood. His experiences in New York City introduced him to group sex parties late at night. He enjoyed the anonymous aspect of finding sex partners at gay bars. Enrique didn't drink at the bars and would not be associated with anyone doing drugs or unprotected sex. Before he agreed to go home with anyone, he questioned the drug and condom usage and quickly walked away if the answers were not what he expected.

The first summer back in Lyme from Cambridge, Max worked for AJR Investment Management and became Ross' assistant. Ross kept him extremely busy during the day, and the experience was very valuable. The second day after returning home, Max visited Stephen and hoped to get more information about Enrique. "Hi, Stephen. I am back for the summer.

"Welcome home, Max. Glad to see you back. I've missed you."

"I was so busy with school, Stephen, that time just flew by very quickly. I didn't get a chance to miss home at all."

"That's better. If you were bored with school, you would yearn to come home. And now that you are home for a few months, what are your plans?" Stephen would not mention anything about Enrique unless Max brought him up and asked.

"I got a job at AJR for the summer, and I think they will keep me busy the entire summer. I may not have much free time."

"Oh, you're young. You'll survive. Make some extra money to have when you return to Cambridge."

"So, I notice that Enrique's pickup truck is not around anymore. Does he still live in the studio?" Max was bashful about asking but felt he needed to know more about Enrique.

"He bought a house and moved last April. I think he is living in Chester, Deep River, or Essex. I don't recall. He still comes twice weekly for a few hours of work around the house." Stephen was careful not to disclose too much detail.

"I tried calling him numerous times from Cambridge, including last week, but he still has my phone number blocked. I want to see him but don't want to hurt him. I think he saw me come home for Thanksgiving with my dormmate, who is straight. He must have thought I was bringing home a new boyfriend. I tried to explain, but he won't take my calls. I gave up."

"Remember what I told you before you left? If you truly love Enrique, fight like hell to get him. Don't give up! You will never know his feelings for you unless you fight for him. You may lose a battle, but you may win the war. And if you also lose the war, you can tell yourself you tried. Don't give up easily."

When Max returned home that evening after he visited with Stephen, he searched the county's real estate records online and found Enrique's new address in Chester. Instead of arriving at his house uninvited, Max wrote a letter inviting him to dinner after work. Max changed his mind and never mailed the invitation.

During the summer of 2023, Max and Enrique never saw each other. He assumed that was Enrique's desire.

✧ ✧ ✧ ✧ ✧ ✧ ✧

Max volunteered several hours a week at Harvard's Office of BGLTQ Student Life, a resource facility for bisexual, gay, lesbian, transgender, queer, and questioning students at Harvard. While he worked there, he met many new friends, including Connor, a gay Harvard student living in a small studio on the other side of the Charles River near the corner of Mass Ave and Boylston Street. Connor was the same age as Max and planned to attend Harvard Law School after graduation. His parents were from the Los Angeles area and were involved in the film industry. Max met Connor during the beginning of his third year at Harvard.

Connor was very handsome and liked spending time with Max, who stayed with Connor in his studio most weekends. Sex with Connor was very good and kinky at times, but never reached the same level of satisfaction as making love to Enrique. They began to experiment with leather and sex toys. Connor bought a sling and placed it in front of his bed so they would use it whenever Max visited. Their relationship was not getting serious, and much to Max's dislike, the sex was getting rougher. Connor was submissive and wanted Max to be dominant and rough with him during sex. After knowing each other for almost two years, they agreed to go their separate ways a few months before graduation. The decision did not hurt either Connor or Max. They expected its outcome for the past year and remained very good friends.

Enrique continued to work hard at the garden center. He also found time to paint in the basement of his new home. The Chester Gallery continued to feature and sell his art. Small maintenance jobs at Stephen's home were now assigned to AJR. Enrique still visited Stephen at least once a week.

Maria began dating Dr. Marcos Veiga, who worked with her at the hospital. Less than a year after their first date, Marcos proposed to Maria, and they were married in Enrique's home in Chester at a private ceremony with just a handful of their friends and family. Maria and Enrique sold their three-family house to the tenants who lived on the second floor.

Josefa needed more personal care, so Maria found a Spanish-speaking assisted living facility near the new home she shared with Marcos.

In the fall of 2025, Max was easily accepted into Yale Law School and planned to start his law studies in late August 2026. He decided to live at home in Lyme during the first year and commute to New Haven. Many classes and lectures were online, so he only had to travel to Yale once or twice weekly.

✿ ✿ ✿ ✿ ✿ ✿ ✿

After the graduation ceremonies at Harvard in May 2026, Max moved back to Lyme and found himself alone. His few high school friends were not around anymore. Ashley fell in love with another student at UCONN, eloped after graduation, and moved to Chicago, where her new husband's family lived. Enrique was not around anymore. Max rarely saw his pickup truck on Stephen's driveway. Dana went to study in London for a year, so the sounds of Dana's favorite music blasting in her room were non-existent. One day, he decided to drive to Enrique's house in Chester. He went on a Saturday and arrived a few minutes after 6:00 PM, assuming the garden center was closed by that time and he would find Enrique at home. He pulled into his driveway behind a relatively new Honda Civic. He walked over to the front door and rang the doorbell. The door opened, and just as Max was expecting to see Enrique, it was someone else on the other side of the door. A young man in his early twenties in a tight pair of gym trunks, a bulging crotch, no shirt, no shoes, and a hickey on his neck.

"Hi, I'm looking for Enrique. Does he live here?" Max was puzzled and not expecting someone else to answer the door.

"Yes, he does, but he's not at home. Do you want to leave a message?"

"Yes, would you tell him I stopped by to see him?"

"Yes, but what's your name?"

"Max. Max Edwards. What's your name?"

"Aaron. I'm his boyfriend."

Max felt Aaron's words shred his chest.

"Oh, you're very fortunate. Just tell him I stopped by and would like to say hello when he has time."

"Sure, I'll tell him."

Aaron never told Enrique. He knew Enrique's version of the love story between him and someone named Max Edwards. He didn't want Enrique to learn that Max was back in town. Max tried calling Enrique again, but his phone was still blocked on Enrique's mobile phone. Max never wanted to contact Enrique at work.

✿ ✿ ✿ ✿ ✿ ✿ ✿

It wasn't until early August that Max finally decided to leave the house on a weekend night and travel to one of New Haven's popular gay bars. When he entered the bar, he ordered a bottle of non-alcoholic beer and saw Enrique at the other end with Aaron. He knows Enrique saw him but turned his face in the other direction to avoid eye contact with Max. He kept staring at Enrique in hopes he would come to see him without Aaron. Enrique tried to avoid looking in Max's direction, which made him feel awkward and look obvious that he was hiding from Max.

Twenty minutes after Max arrived at the bar, Enrique and Aaron decided to leave. On their way out the door, Enrique stopped, told Aaron to meet him in the car, and walked over to Max, who was still leaning against the bar with his shirt halfway open, partially exposing his muscled chest and nipples.

"Hi, I haven't seen you in a long time," They were both visually nervous. "You look great, as always, Enrique." That was Max's first time at the New Haven bar, and most patrons stared at him. His young, handsome, and athletic look was noticeable. "I've missed you. I stopped by your new home over a month ago to invite you for dinner, but you weren't there. Not sure if Aaron gave you the message."

"No, I didn't get the message. Sorry." Enrique was surprised that Max had come to see him. He was not surprised that Aaron didn't give him the message.

"I can't call you because you still have my number blocked. " Max placed his left hand around Enrique's waist. Enrique did not pull away. "How and where can I reach you to talk?"

"It's been a long time, Max. It took me at least a year to get over you. Seeing you tonight brings back some good memories and also memories of being hurt. I had to move out of Stephen's studio. I couldn't heal from the pain by going there every night after work. Especially after you brought your new boyfriend home for Thanksgiving, the first year you were gone."

"I'm sorry I hurt you. He was not my boyfriend. He was my straight dormmate who needed a place to sleep for one night until his parents arrived from Spain." Max continued talking to Enrique in an apologetic tone. "I want to make it up to you, Enrique. I'd like to see you in a location where we can talk. That's why I wanted to invite you to dinner, but obviously, Aaron felt threatened and didn't give you the message." Max was unsuccessful in trying to convince Enrique to meet with him. "Are you in a relationship with Aaron?"

"We're just dating. He stays over the house when he is not working." Enrique doesn't know what to say. He could agree to meet with Max but was afraid to go with high expectations only to get hurt again. He can easily say no and be done with Max forever or, "Let me think about it, Max. I don't want to revisit my feelings after you left for Harvard."

"That's fair, Enrique. I promise I will not hurt you." He grabs Enrique's neck with his right hand and brings him closer to kiss him. Enrique didn't pull back. He recalled the taste of Max's lips and kissed him back before he left the bar. On his way to the car to reconnect with Aaron, he punches the mailbox at the corner of the street after he yells, "FUCK!" loud enough for Aaron to hear him.

Max intended to stay at the bar for an hour or two until a very attractive man in his mid-40s with a slender, muscular body approached him and invited him back to his apartment. Max arrived back home in Lyme at 5:00 AM.

CHAPTER 25

MEETING

The following Friday, after the encounter with Max at the New Haven bar, Enrique decided to pack his briefcase with paperwork and unopened mail early in the afternoon and go home to enjoy his backyard, which was recently planted with new ornamental trees, rhododendrons and azalea bushes. When he arrived, he found Aaron on his bed with a stranger he had picked up at Hammonasset Beach State Park. It was an awkward scene, more for Aaron and the stranger than for Enrique.

After the stranger quickly left the house, confused and half-naked, Enrique instructed Aaron to pack all his personal belongings immediately and return to his apartment in New Haven. Aaron was a waiter at a trendy restaurant in West Haven and had a habit of calling in sick and staying at Enrique's house. That was the end of the Aaron-Enrique relationship.

Enrique stood by the window facing the driveway to watch Aaron leave the property and his life. After he drove away, he decided to do what Stephen would have recommended. He made himself a cocktail, but before he walked over to the patio while maneuvering his ice-cold martini filled to the rim, he took the sheets off the bed and threw them in the washing machine to wash them with bleach in hot water. It was a symbolic act to erase Aaron from his life.

Enrique looked out to his backyard and realized the scene with Aaron and the stranger in his bed did not hurt him. He was relieved the relationship was over. He never really loved Aaron like he had loved Max. *"Maybe I am still in love with Max. I made love with Max. Aaron was just good sex when I needed it,"* He whispered while sitting on the patio with his martini. He grabbed his mobile phone and removed the block on Max's phone number. "Maybe it's time for changes in my life."

✧ ✧ ✧ ✧ ✧ ✧ ✧

Max was heartbroken that same Friday afternoon because he hadn't heard from Enrique all week. When he got home from work, he decided to visit Stephen to explain what happened at the New Haven bar last Saturday night and tell him he was considering ending his fight for Enrique because he had not heard from him about dinner. Max still thought his phone number was blocked on Enrique's mobile phone. He didn't realize Enrique had removed the block.

"Stephen, if he had any interest in me, he would have called me as I asked him to. At the same time, when I kissed him at the bar, he didn't pull back and kissed me back. I don't understand what is going through his mind." Max was frustrated. He was confident Enrique would call but didn't hear from him. "I can't keep chasing him if he doesn't respond." Stephen didn't respond immediately, but Max kept talking. "I need to move on with my life. If Enrique doesn't think we can work out our differences, I need to hear it directly from him, and then I will stop chasing him."

"You have to give it time, Max. His relationship with Aaron will not last very long. Maybe he is waiting for Aaron to leave him so he doesn't have to throw him out the door?"

"I know, you keep saying to give it time, Stephen, but I am losing my patience. I don't know what else to do."

✧ ✧ ✧ ✧ ✧ ✧ ✧

It was the following morning, a Saturday morning, and Enrique woke up alone on his freshly cleaned sheets at 7:00 AM. Unfortunately, he is headed for work but finds a voice message on his phone.

"Hi Enrique, this is Stephen. Listen, I wonder if you can stop over tomorrow after work, say 5:30 PM. I have some things that I need to give you in the studio. When you arrive, come directly to the studio. If I'm not there, wait for me there. I shall expect you there at 5:30 PM sharp unless I hear back from you. Thank you.

At the same time Enrique was listening to his message, Max was listening to his voice message.

"Hi, Max, this is Stephen. I hope you can meet me at the studio at 5:15 PM tomorrow. I have some things that I need to give you. Just come directly to the studio. If I'm not there, wait for me inside. Unless I hear back from you, I expect you there then. Don't forget, 5:15 tomorrow, Sunday afternoon. Thank you.

Stephen was confident Enrique and Max were interested in each other and cared for each other deeply. They both needed to be alone together and settle their differences. Max was to arrive at the studio first, not knowing Stephen didn't have plans to show up. Enrique was scheduled to arrive 15 minutes later, knowing nothing about Stephen's plan to get them together alone.

✿ ✿ ✿ ✿ ✿ ✿ ✿

It was late Sunday morning, about 11:00 AM, and Max decided to go kayaking alone from Hamburg Cove in Lyme to the marina in Essex on the other side of the Connecticut River. It was a great upper body exercise he had not attempted since high school. It was also a time to be alone, in the middle of beautiful natural surroundings, and think about his life, past, and future. He always enjoyed nature watching, especially in early June when the smell of fresh new growth surfaced on land and in the water filtered by the breeze that funneled from the

Connecticut River. He drove to the Lyme marina at the cove, parked his car, and unloaded his kayak by the boat ramp. He paddled slowly, going west across Hamburg Cove.

On his way to Essex, he navigated close to shore to examine the natural beauty and new plant growth by the cove's shoreline. He always used that time to meditate, and today was no exception. Unfortunately, he was still saddened by his inability to connect with Enrique. He couldn't get him out of his mind.

At about 1:30 PM, he reached the entrance to the cove by the Connecticut River. He ferried across the strong and choppy current into Essex Harbor, avoiding speeding boats, where he docked his kayak on the public docks next to the marina and ran over to the local coffee shop for a latte. Back in the kayak, he raced across the turbulent Connecticut River again and reached the peaceful currents of Hamburg Cove in record time for him, one hour. Upon his return from Essex, it was all about getting an upper-body workout. He stopped to rest and stretch his arms and chest muscles every twenty minutes. His upper body swelled after he reached the marina at Hamburg Cove. He got to the car, and with burning muscles, he loaded the kayak on the roof and drove home for a quick steaming hot shower before meeting Stephen in the studio at 5:15 PM.

✧✧✧✧✧✧✧

Sunday was always a busy day at the garden center. Enrique let his staff deal with the customers. At the same time, he spent the afternoon unpacking a massive delivery of small ornamental bushes, perennials, and annuals they received on Saturday afternoon and placed them under the white awnings he purchased to expand his selling floor.

The lifting and bending all afternoon tightened his thigh and buttocks muscles. He can feel a burning sensation on his back and hips. At 3:00 PM, he left the garden center and went home to shower before meeting Stephen in the studio at 5:30 PM.

After he showered, he reached inside his closet and retrieved a white, tight-fitting pair of shorts he only wore when he wanted to show off his butt. He hadn't worn them since he began his relationship with Aaron. Now that Aaron was not in the picture, Enrique slipped them on with his favorite black sleeveless T-shirt equally as tight as the shorts, emphasizing his perfectly shaped bulging biceps. He looked at himself in the mirror and whispered, *"Well, if this outfit doesn't get me a new boyfriend, nothing will!"*

✧ ✧ ✧ ✧ ✧ ✧ ✧

Max arrived at the studio on time. He knocked on the door, but there was no answer. He recalled the message from Stephen, "If I am not there, wait for me inside." The door was unlocked, so he entered. "Hi Stephen, are you in here?" There was no answer. He looked outside the window towards Stephen's patio and the garden. Stephen was not there. He called Stephen on his mobile phone, and there was no answer. He sat on the couch and searched his text, voice, and email messages to ensure Stephen was not trying to reach him while he was in the shower—no messages from Stephen or anyone.

There was a knock on the door approximately fifteen minutes after Max had arrived at the studio. He got up from the couch, opened the door, and there was Enrique dressed in the hottest outfit Max had ever seen him wear.

It took Max a few seconds to gather his thoughts after he opened the door. "Oh, I thought you were Stephen. He sent me a voice message last night to meet him here. You look great, Enrique."

"Thank you, Max. You look great also. It's been a long time since I have seen you in broad daylight. It looks like we have both matured from our late teenage years."

Max stared at Enrique's eyes, "Yes, we have matured. I had forgotten how beautiful your eyes are. I hope you don't mind me saying that. It's just that you caught me by surprise. I wasn't expecting you at the door, and when I opened it, I just stood there and wanted to stare at your eyes."

"Yes, I was a bit surprised to see you also. Let me call Stephen and let him know we're here. I'm not sure I know what he wants to give me." Enrique reached for his phone, but Max stopped him by putting his hands over Enrique's phone.

"Oh, don't bother. I tried calling him, and there was no answer. I guess we can sit and wait for him. He's not on the patio or in the garden either. The Porsche is not in the garage." Max realized that this was a setup by Stephen to get him with Enrique in a private location where they could be alone and talk.

"You look like you got some sun today." Enrique noticed a slightly sunburned nose and cheeks on Max.

"Yes, the sun hit me through the sunblock. I went kayaking at 11:00 AM and didn't return until almost 4:00 PM. When I showered, I felt the burn on my face and shoulders. It wasn't just my skin. My muscles were also burning from paddling. I haven't been out on the kayak since my high school days.

"My workout today was a bit different than yours. I spent the morning and afternoon unpacking merchandise and moving them around in the store and under the awnings. I still got sunburn, but my skin is naturally darker than yours, so I can tolerate it more."

"Yes, I always loved touching your skin. It always felt smooth and silky."

"Thank you, Max. Glad to know you are still a flirt and a charmer."

Max wasn't sure if the comment was sarcastic or if he was serious. "So, how is Aaron?"

"I wouldn't know. I threw him out of the house the other day. I came home early and found him in bed with his legs in the air and a stranger with an ugly ass fucking him. The stranger was mortified to see me enter the room while his dick was inside my alleged boyfriend. I didn't say anything to them, but the guy acted like he saw a rat and ran out of the house wearing only his underwear with his clothes in his hand. He finished getting dressed in his car and drove away quickly. I wondered what the neighbors thought when he ran out of the house in his underwear. I told Aaron to pack the few personal items he kept leaving in my house and return to his apartment in New Haven. I haven't seen him or talked to him since that day." Enrique paused for a few seconds to think about what to say next. "My relationship with Aaron was not the same as..." Enrique stopped before finishing the sentence.

"Same as what?" Max knew what Enrique was going to say but wanted to hear it from him directly.

Enrique didn't respond immediately. He paused again for a few seconds and got up from the couch to walk over to the window. He looked out and said, "Not the same as ours was four years ago."

"Sorry you had to experience that scene."

"It was no big deal for me. Frankly, I was glad I found an excuse to get rid of him. How about you? Are you dating anyone or have a permanent smart and rich lawyer boyfriend in Cambridge?" Enrique felt Max knew too much about his personal life, and he didn't know enough about what Max had been doing during the past four years.

"Don't be sarcastic."

"I'm sorry. I take it back."

"I had a relationship for just over a year with a classmate. He was from Los Angeles. Before graduation, we both knew it was time to go our separate ways. We had many differences. One was his desire to stay in Cambridge and attend Harvard Law. I wanted to go home. I got accepted at Yale Law School and plan to attend in September. I'm still friends with him. My relationship with him was also nothing like what we had together."

"Are you moving to New Haven? You can be roommates with Aaron." Enrique laughed. "Oh, I'm sorry, it was a bad joke."

"I deserved it," Max admitted sadly. "No, I plan to live at home for the first year. My commute to New Haven will only be once or twice a week. The rest of the time, I will be spending it online. As you can imagine, there's a lot of reading and report writing, so I'll be swamped for the next few years."

"You're smart and an excellent student. I'm sure you will do very well at Yale." Enrique was not saying much and wondered if Stephen ever did intend to meet him at the studio.

"I'm working full-time this summer at AJR Investment Management. They manage real estate properties for owners who don't have the time to deal with their real estate investments but still want to invest."

Enrique interrupted Max. "Yes, I know them. They're managing Stephen's properties and the maintenance in this house."

"When I return to school, I hope to give them eight to ten hours weekly. It's a good experience for me and will give me some spending cash I can use while I'm in school."

A noted silence in the room lasted longer than they both expected. They took turns looking out the window to see if Stephen would ever show up. They both realized that Stephen had arranged the meeting so they could have privacy and talk.

"OK, Max. By now, you know as well as I do that Stephen has no intention of showing up. I think he planned this so we would have time alone together. So, if that's his plan, let's talk. If that's not what you want, it's time to go home. What will it be?" Enrique felt he needed to take more control of the situation and direct the process. He was standing by the door with his hand on the doorknob, ready to leave if Max had decided not to talk. "I am anxious to get the conversation started. How about you, Max?"

"I agree. Since you are anxious to get it started, please do." Max sat on the couch again and asked Enrique to sit beside him.

"I'd rather stand for now, thank you." Enrique looked at Max and saw the same person he had fallen in love with four years ago. "I'll tell you what I want from my life, and I will be direct and honest. If it fits your needs for a husband, then let's talk some more. If you think we are at opposite ends of the landscape, I can be out of here quickly."

"It's a deal." Max made himself comfortable on the couch and watched Enrique intensely.

"I don't need much in life. All I want is for someone to love and love me back unconditionally. Someone I can imagine I will call my husband someday. I want to raise a family. Maybe two kids. I want to be successful. I want to sell the garden center someday and use the proceeds for other business investments, perhaps real estate development." Enrique stops for a few seconds to think about what he wants to say. "Sex is important at my age. I wouldn't mind experimenting sexually with my husband and others as long as there were rules and we went into it together and left together. I would find it very hot to see my future husband in bed with someone else as long as it was strictly sex and not love. I am sure there are other requirements, but I'm too nervous right now and just rambling on like an idiot."

"No, Enrique, you're not asking for anything unusual. If you ask me to go and fuck Aaron, I must say no. He's not my type, and the image you presented of his legs up in the air and being pounded by someone with an ugly ass was a huge turnoff for me."

"Ha! I deserved that. We're even. I might have exaggerated the scene slightly," Enrique laughed at Max's comment. "He was a good fuck. That was all. I now feel guilty that I kept him that long so he was around when I was horny. He probably felt the same. Well, I just flattered myself without realizing it."

"Enrique, your needs are the same as mine. I also want to be with someone I feel comfortable asking to be my husband someday. I also want a family, and I am working extremely hard in school to be successful and provide for my future family as my parents have done for Dana and me. I want to do all this with you. I would also find it sexually satisfying to jump in bed with you and one or two other hot men. After the past four years without you, I realize we are soul mates. I know we can have a wonderful and fulfilling life together. I want to grow old with you, just like Stephen and Randy. Please come and sit next to me.

It's uncomfortable watching you pace back and forth in this small room. You're wearing out the carpet!"

"Not now. We're still in discussion mode, and I need to keep moving, or I'll lose my thoughts." Enrique knew they would be naked in bed if he sat beside Max. "What if you get tired of me or meet someone else? Someone as smart as you?

"You are brilliant, Enrique, and you don't give yourself enough credit. Look what you have done with the garden center. You are in your early twenties and have developed the business your father started to become one of Connecticut's most successful garden centers. I'm not a betting man. I don't go to the casino to play cards, roulette wheels, or slot machines. I'm willing to bet on the success of our relationship. We have had four years apart, which helped me realize that you are the person I should live with for the rest of my life. I want to share everything with you, including my body. I don't want to waste any more time. Nothing else is more important to me right now. I'm hopeful that you feel the same as I do. If you don't feel the same, we should not waste more time and go our separate ways as friends and not as lovers."

There was another long silence in the room. Enrique stopped to look out into the garden. "Nothing in life is instant. It takes time. It takes nurturing and care. It takes love and patience. Just like Stephen's garden." Enrique paused to look at the garden again. "We plant the seeds, and all we can do is sit back and learn to manage the growth. Believe it or not, Max, I have learned much about life and myself at the garden center and working in Stephen's garden for the past four years. I created a fairy tale image of our relationship the first time I saw you. It was love at first sight. I tried to erase that fairy tale image for years after you left for Cambridge, but I couldn't. My feelings for you never changed, even when I wanted them to change. I tried to ignore them, but the image would always come back. I learned that only love lasts. Gardens will grow, plants will die, some replaced, some ignored. Landscapes change daily, sometimes hourly, but only love lasts. It lasts past a lifetime. I can see how much Stephen loves Randy by just looking at Stephen's eyes when he talks about Randy. That's how I felt whenever I thought of you."

Enrique was still fixated on the outside view. "The love Stephen and Randy shared will last past their lifetime. That is the love I want in my life. A love that lasts." Enrique turned to look at Max's eyes. "I'm not proud to admit that I could have handled our discussion better four years ago. It was all part of me growing up and being afraid to take over the business my father suddenly left behind. I was not prepared. It was too soon after his death." Enrique stopped briefly and looked out the window again. He recalled when he learned of his father's death and its uncertainties.

"When my father died, I felt alone and wanted you all to myself. I was afraid to lose you." Enrique paused again and thought about what he just told Max. "I'm not sure I knew what I wanted. I wasn't sure either of us was ready. I wanted to change you. I don't know why. I was wrong even to consider it."

"I have to take some responsibility also. I was insensitive to your needs, Enrique. I didn't consider the difficulties you experienced when your father died. I was wrong, too. I should have been more caring towards you. I missed it, and I will always regret how I reacted." Max was sitting on the edge of the couch, hoping Enrique would come and sit with him.

"Maybe our experiences four years ago will help us build a stronger relationship going forward?" Enrique was surprised he made this statement. He answered his own question. "Maybe not. We can say all we want here today, and it all sounds compelling and romantic, but after we leave here, will we believe in what we just admitted?"

"I am willing to bet we will. We are both risking our future. It's not just you. I don't see it as too much of a risk. I think we truly understand each other. Frankly, even though we didn't see each other very much during the past four years, I think we were still learning from each other. I never forgot you, Enrique. You were always with me. I'm sorry

I hurt you. I can't take what I said or didn't say back, but please accept my apologies, and let's get on with our lives together."

"I understand, Max. I share some of the blame. I hope you will forgive me also." Enrique came over and sat next to Max on the couch. He placed his left hand around Max's neck and dragged his head closer to kiss him. Max nibbles on his lips like he used to do four years ago. Enrique placed his right hand around his waist and they both embraced.

After kissing on the couch for a few minutes, they removed each other's clothing. "Wait a second, what if Stephen walks in on us while we are naked?" Max was concerned Stephen would show up in the studio while they enjoyed each other's bodies.

"No problem, let's hang our underwear on the outside doorknob. If that doesn't warn him not to enter, he can come in and watch if he wants!" Enrique laughed as he removed Max's underwear.

"Oh, that's great. I'll have my grandfather watch me make love with my future husband. That's a nice way to start our new relationship," Max laughed as he removed Enrique's underwear and walked outside naked to hang both pairs on the doorknob.

Max and Enrique spent the next two hours in bed together. Before leaving for home, they stopped to see Stephen to thank him for his part in getting them together again.

"Oh, you don't have to thank me. Someone had to get you two together. I would have gone crazy listening to you complain if I didn't try to pull this off. I walked over to the studio earlier with concerns that I did not hear from either of you, and maybe you killed each other. I saw the underwear on the doorknob. That was the only clue I needed. Thank you very much for the warning!

CHAPTER 26

LIFE

Thanksgiving morning, 2026, in southeastern Connecticut—a cold and wet early morning in late November. The heavy evening rain from yesterday had ceased around 3:00 AM. The ground was still cold and soaked. The sun was beginning to rise in the east between the tree trunks in the rear of Stephen's property. All the leaves were down on the ground in the woods, creating a sponge effect when you walked through this time of the year.

You could feel the sun's warmth through the picture window in the family room facing the garden and woods. Stephen took a towel from the linen closet and wiped down a chair to enjoy his coffee outside one last time before winter arrived. He returned inside, grabbed the urn on the piano with Randy's ashes and his coffee mug, and went back to the patio.

"Randy, I know I'm not supposed to fertilize the garden at this time of the year, but I need to do this today. It's time to release you, Randy. You will never leave my heart, but your remains must be spread out to nurture the garden so others can enjoy it as much as we have." Stephen realized he was talking to Randy without the wheelchair next to him. *"Yesterday, I signed my new will. I think you will be happy with the changes I made. Half is going to our local community foundation as an endowment to support the civil rights of the LGBTQ+ community. The other half is split evenly between Dana and Max. There are two exceptions. The deed to this house and its contents would be given to Max and Enrique, and the mortgage on the garden center would be forgiven. They would love to live here in Lyme*

after I am gone. I know they will take excellent care of the garden." Stephen was saddened by what he was saying. After a few minutes of enjoying his coffee, Stephen got up from the chair, walked into the garden beds with the urn, and began to spread Randy's ashes in the soil.

☼ ☼ ☼ ☼ ☼ ☼ ☼

It was barely 9:00 AM, and Max was getting ready to kayak with Enrique on Hamburg Cove. He looked out the window in his room, and in the distance, he saw Stephen spreading something in the garden. He saw him carrying the urn from the piano on his left hand.

Alice was in the kitchen preparing Thanksgiving dinner side dishes while Joe was outside by the smoker with a sixteen-pound turkey ready to smoke. Joe looked over to Stephen's property and saw the same scene Max saw in his room. He knocked on the kitchen window to get Alice's attention towards Stephen.

Besides the family, the 3:00 PM Thanksgiving dinner at the Edwards included Stephen, Louise, Enrique, Maria, and Marcos. Dana flew in from London the day before with her new Belgian boyfriend, Liam. Louise recently sold the laundromat at a healthy profit and moved into the studio to care for Stephen, who recently turned 79 and was beginning to show signs of dementia.

"Good morning, Mom. Did you look outside over to Stephen's property?"

"Yes, what is he doing fertilizing at this time of the year?"

"He is spreading Randy's ashes. He is finally letting go." Max knew what was inside the urn. "I feel like we should all be with him, but I think he prefers to be alone. We should not say anything unless he mentions it when he comes for dinner."

"I agree, Max. You better tell your father, he is outside. Oh, be sure to tell Dana, also. If we don't stop her, she will be the first to say something."

"Enrique should be here soon. We are going kayaking before dinner."

"As long as you are both back and dressed at 3:00 PM when the guests arrive." Alice still enjoys playing the motherly role with Max.

✿ ✿ ✿ ✿ ✿ ✿ ✿

Enrique arrived at the Edwards home just before 10:00 AM. He changed into a backup wetsuit Max had set aside for him, and they both carried two kayaks into the back of Enrique's pickup truck. They arrived at the marina's boat ramp, unloaded the kayaks, and paddled around the perimeter of the cove, examining the wildlife on the shoreline and in the water. The warm rays from the sun and their wet suits protected them from the icy chill of the southern Connecticut breezes and the cove's waters. An hour later, Max signals Enrique to paddle to the center of the cove, where they tie each other's kayak side to side, facing each other so they can talk and enjoy the scenery.

They let the currents slowly carry them downstream towards the Connecticut River as they both reclined on the kayaks, stared at the clouds above them, and talked about their future. A few minutes later, Max grabbed Enrique's hand, looked into his grey eyes, retrieved a ring box from inside the hatch of Enrique's kayak, and asked Enrique to marry him.

"Oh my god, I can't believe you are asking me to marry you here in the middle of Hamburg Cove. How will you get on one knee here on your kayak?"

"Enrique, if you want me to risk falling in the water, I will get on one knee, but you will have to jump in and drag me out if I fall in. Please hurry up and say YES before we reach the Connecticut River. The water is too rough today to kayak in that area."

"YES! YES! YES!"

"Excellent decision." Max passionately kissed Enrique after he placed a beautiful white gold ring with Enrique's birthstone on his finger. They both fell into the water. It took a few minutes to get back on the kayaks. Max reached inside Enrique's hatch and pulled out a bottle of Don Perignon, popped the cork, and they took turns drinking directly from the bottle while taking selfies with their mobile phones they had stored in a waterproof bag. "The Don Perignon will keep us warm," Max assures Enrique.

Twenty minutes later, the kayaks were still tied together with their tow leash, and the bottle of Don Perignon was now empty and back inside the hatch. "Now is when we get our workout for the day. We have to paddle upstream to get back to the boat ramp. Otherwise, we may end up asleep on the kayaks in Long Island!" Max was anxious to return home and break the news to his family.

Enrique was eager to show off his ring, "I'm ready. Let's go. I'll follow you, Max. Always and Forever."

✿ ✿ ✿ ✿ ✿ ✿ ✿

Enrique and Max decided to wait for all the Thanksgiving dinner guests to arrive before they told anyone of their engagement. When they got home, they showered together and made love in Max's shower. They dressed for the occasion and helped with the preparations in the dining room. Enrique set up the bar in the living room. Max set the dining room table for ten.

Enrique made all the cocktails as the guests arrived, and Max passed the delicious hors d'oeuvres Dana and Liam had prepared the night before. When everyone had their cocktail, Enrique asked Joe if he could make an announcement. "The floor is yours, Enrique."

"Since it is Thanksgiving Day, I would like to first thank you, Joe and Alice, for inviting us to your beautiful home for what looks to be a fantastic dinner prepared by the family. I am grateful to have my mother and stepfather here and share their love for each other with us. I am thankful to be with my dear friend Stephen today, who has helped me so much when I needed someone to listen. I always love spending time with Dana. She has the scoop on everyone in town! I am glad she is here from London with Liam, whom I have heard about but never met until this morning. I learned that this is Liam's first Thanksgiving dinner in the United States. I am sure you will take this tradition back to Belgium. Thank you, Louise, for your wit, no-nonsense approach to life, and for always taking excellent care of our Stephen." Enrique looked around the room briefly and realized everyone was part of his new family.

"Last but not least, I want you all to know that I am the luckiest man on earth today." Enrique walked over to Max and grabbed his hand tight. "This morning, Max and I went kayaking on Hamburg Cove. We stopped in the middle of the Cove to admire the world around us. It was a beautiful morning in the cove. The sounds of the rushing streams, the birds, the breeze rustling the landscape, and the paddles breaking the water were hypnotizing to us. We stared at the sky, and as I turned and looked all around us while the kayaks rocked slowly downstream, Max pulled out a small box from the kayak's hatch and asked me to marry him." Enrique raised his finger to show the engagement ring. "And of course, I said YES. We are all officially family." Everyone was caught by surprise. They applauded the couple, congratulated them, and wished them both years of happiness.

"Oh my god! I had no clue you were proposing to Enrique today." Alice walked over to Max and kissed him and Enrique. "How did you keep this secret from Dana?" Maria and Marcos walked over to Enrique and Max and hugged them both.

Dana did not act surprised. "Oh, Mom. I suspected it would happen today while the family was here and together!" Dana always pretends to know what is happening around her.

"Well, this announcement merits a champagne toast. Dana and Liam, would you grab ten champagne flutes from the cabinet and place them on the dining room table? I have three bottles of Don Perignon in the basement refrigerator that I would like to open for a special celebratory toast at the start of our dinner."

Max realized he needed to confess about one of the bottles. "Oh, Dad, wait one second. You have two bottles left. The third bottle is empty and in the kayak's hatch." Enrique and Max looked at each other and smiled.

✿✿✿✿✿✿

It was a late June black-tie wedding attended by approximately one hundred guests. Stephen insisted that the ceremony, followed by a cocktail reception, should be held by the perennial gardens on his property at his cost. He also hired a string quartet to play at the wedding ceremony and cocktail reception. Dinner and dancing were arranged under a vast, beautifully decorated white tent behind the Edwards' home. Jason, the florist in Old Saybrook who flirted with Enrique and Max during their initial meeting, made all the flower arrangements and tent decorations. The three had a consensual and fun threesome experience a few weeks before the wedding.

As soon as all the guests were seated in the garden, the string quartet began to play a processional march, which began with Louise, who became a Justice of the Peace to officiate at the ceremony. After selling the laundromat, Louise retained some house-cleaning clients and moved into the studio. Ashley and Stephen, the two witnesses for the official ceremony, followed Louise. Ashley flew back to Lyme for the wedding with her husband, who worked for an international accounting firm in Chicago. Ashley joined a large publishing company as an editor. Stephen looked like a celebrity in his new black tuxedo with a white bow tie and carried a portrait photograph of Randy.

Dana and Liam flew in from London again for the special occasion. They followed Stephen and Ashley down the aisle. Dana and Liam were married in London the following year and gave birth to a baby boy, Lucas, two years after their marriage. The family attended the nuptials and returned to London when the baby was born. Maria and Marcos followed Dana and Liam. Maria cried as she walked down the aisle holding

Marcos' hand and carrying a photograph of Manuel, their daughter Julia, who died at the Mexican border, and Josefa. Unfortunately, Josefa died at the assisted living facility after a brief battle with lung cancer in February. Alice and Joe were next. They looked like a proud Hollywood couple. Alice continued to run her residential real estate sales business, and Joe continued to expand the Commercial Real Estate development company he inherited from his father. Besides their Connecticut investments, the company was now invested in Rhode Island, New Hampshire, and Massachusetts.

The string quartet stopped playing when Alice and Joe arrived at their assigned seats. There was a short pause, and they began to play a classical string concerto. Enrique and Max came out of Stephen's home dressed in identical black tuxedo tails, holding each other's hands. When they were ready to walk down the aisle to face Louise in front, Max put his arm around Enrique's shoulder, and Enrique put his around Max's waist. They walked down the aisle together as they greeted and shook hands with the guests.

✧✧✧✧✧✧✧

Enrique's garden center became one of the most successful centers in Connecticut. Two years after their wedding, he was offered and accepted a substantial sum of money for the business and real estate. He invested the proceeds in residential rental units throughout southeastern Connecticut. Max graduated from Yale Law School and passed the bar exam. He received the highest grade awarded in Connecticut that year and became a partner at a large law firm in New Haven. After five years at the law firm, he resigned and joined his father's Real Estate Development Company. Soon after Enrique sold the garden center, Max and Enrique became parents of identical twin girls, Ava and Mia. They contracted with a surrogate to deliver the twins.

Stephen had a wonderful time at the wedding. He introduced himself to everyone at the reception and walked around feeling like a proud grandfather-matchmaker. He danced with Louise, Maria, Alice, Enrique, and Max, but towards the end of the night, before guests began to leave, he felt tired and walked down the path to his house without saying goodnight. When he reached home, he fixed himself a scotch on the rocks with a splash of water and sat by the window in the family room facing the garden. The floodlights were turned on, and the ceremony chairs were still in the garden. The ground was covered in white rose petals thrown by the guests when Max and Enrique finished their vows and pronounced husband and husband. Stephen looked out and saw Randy in the garden, sitting on one of the front-row chairs, waving to him. Randy turned around, got up, and began to walk into the woods. The picture window in front of Stephen disappeared, leaving a large open hole on the outside wall from the family room to the garden. Randy turned around, faced the house again, and waved to Stephen. Stephen tried to focus his view but could not see clearly. He dropped his drink on the floor, and his head reclined. He saw himself stepping through the wall's large opening and floated toward Randy. Stephen stopped breathing that night and died peacefully and happily. His last words were, *"I'm ready. Let's go. I'll follow you. Always and forever because only love lasts."*

THE END

Printed in the USA
CPSIA information can be obtained
at www.ICGtesting.com
LVHW021216281023
762417LV00018B/36/J